NEVER REALLY GONE

A CASSIE MCGRAW MYSTERY

DAVID ARCHER

RIGHTHOUSE

ISBN-13: 978-1-63696-375-4

ISBN-10: 1-63696-375-7

Cover design by: Damonza

Printed in the United States of America

www.righthouse.com

www.instagram.com/righthousebooks

www.facebook.com/righthousebooks

twitter.com/righthousebooks

CASSIE MCGRAW MYSTERIES

ONE

I'M ONE OF THOSE PEOPLE WHO BELIEVES THAT when life is going good, it's only because the other shoe hasn't decided to drop yet. Considering the things I've been through in the last several years, I think I have good reason for my cynicism, but I try not to let it get me down. I mean, I don't wake up every morning thinking, *Okay, what's going to go wrong today?*

As a matter of fact, most mornings I wake up thinking something along the lines of, *Dex? Now?*

What can I say? My fiancé, Dex, likes to get frisky in the morning, and let me tell you this, he definitely makes it worthwhile. When you start the day out like that, it's really hard to be completely cynical after all.

"Mmm," I said on one particular morning, after an amazing bout of friskiness. "What's on your agenda for today?"

Dex looked at me with his head propped on one hand as he lay beside me. "Got a custom job coming in," he said.

"Vincent Lambert, the guy who owns Lambert Chevrolet, found a '67 Camaro in a barn the other day, and it turned out to be the very first one the dealership sold, back when his dad was running the place. He bought it and wants it completely rebuilt into Pro-Street. I quoted him a hundred and fifty thousand for the job, and he didn't bat an eye. How about you?"

"It's a Monday," I said. "I have clients. I think a couple of them might be ready to take the plunge."

It's been a while since I wrote one of these memoirs, so maybe I should refresh your memory on who I am and what I do.

My name is Cassie McGraw, and I am an abuse counselor. That means I work with abused women and children, to help them escape the violence they suffer. It's something I kind of always wanted to do, but it became more than just a desire a few years back when I became the victim of abuse, myself. Long story that I won't go into here, but my fiancé was abusive—not this one, the one back then—and then I stumbled across evidence that he was actually a serial killer. Pretty bad, considering he was also a highly decorated police detective. I guess I can see why he didn't want me telling anybody about his crimes, but it led to him kidnapping me and a friend who was trying to help me deal with it all and taking us to an old cabin in the middle of nowhere.

At first, I was convinced he was going to kill us, but he started talking about getting us to keep quiet and how we could just go back to the way things were. I was willing to play along, at least until I could get away from him and report what I knew, but then a friend of his showed up. This particular friend was another cop who was involved in the killings, and he wasn't about to let us walk out of there alive. When Mike, my former fiancé, tried to argue with him about it, he shot Mike and then poured gasoline all over me and my friend.

I survived, though I'm burned all the way up the left side of my body. I lost my left eye and my left ear, all of the hair on that side of my head, and that whole side of my body is nothing but one massive scar. I spent quite a lot of time in the hospital dealing with skin grafts and such, and then laid up at home with my folks for a year while I adapted to my new appearance. I often comment that I could easily be Freddy Krueger's half-sister, because that's what I look like on the left. I call that side of me Freda.

Freda is ugly, I'm afraid, and there's just no other way to say it. I try to take away as much of the shock as I can with decorative eye patches, but the reactions I get tell me that bedazzling an eye patch isn't going to make that much of a difference. For that reason, I tend to keep Freda out of sight as much as I can. I sit with my right profile showing to everyone who enters my office, and I don't turn to look at them until I'm ready to make an impact. As soon as they get a look at Freda, the looks on their faces tell me that they suddenly realize just how dangerous an abuser might be.

Still, as ugly as Freda is, she and I were both fortunate enough to survive.

My friend Abby wasn't as lucky. She died in the fire, and she's another part of the reason why I dedicated myself to helping abused women: she had lost a sister and nephew to an abuser. Sometimes, when I have a problem I'm trying to deal with, I can still hear Abby's voice in my head. She was a lot smarter than me when she was alive, and sometimes she still is. And, while I know that her voice is really nothing more than a manifestation of my own subconscious, it's amazing how many times her advice has gotten me through a terribly difficult situation.

Anyway, after taking that year off, I went back to college and finished getting my degree in psychology, and while I was there, the city of St. Louis found that there were other cops who had known what Mike and his buddy were up to, but kept it quiet. Because of that and the lawsuit my parents had arranged to file on my behalf, I was offered a very large settlement, which I took. When I graduated college, I decided to make a fresh start, so I packed up and moved to Tulsa, Oklahoma. I started volunteering as a counselor at an abuse shelter, bought a house and began building a life for myself.

Then one day, one of my clients came in to tell me that her husband had run off with her young daughter, and I had already suspected the man might be grooming the child for sexual abuse. We found out that he had a gun, so the police were worried about what would happen if they confronted him. I decided to go look for him myself, and happened to find him just as a young deputy sheriff stumbled into the scene. The guy panicked and pulled a gun, killed the deputy and was probably going to kill me and his stepdaughter, but when she got loose and took off running, I was able to grab the deputy's gun and blow him away.

That led to a series of adventures, and now I'm not only an abuse counselor, I'm a licensed private investigator in the state of Oklahoma. Most of the work I do still involves abuse cases, though I have worked a couple of missing persons incidents, and occasionally I help out another PI by doing legwork for him.

So, anyway, that's me. If you want to know more, just look up the stuff I wrote before now.

Dex and I got up and showered, then I made breakfast for us and my cat, Critter. Dex and I had been living together for almost six months, and while it was wonderful, there were times when it made me pretty nervous. Dex had presented me with an engagement ring, custom-made to fit my left hand since my ring and pinky fingers are fused together, and our wedding was scheduled for just over a month away.

Don't get me wrong, I was definitely looking forward to it, but everybody gets cold feet not long before it's time to stand up and say "I do," don't they? I may look—well, half of me, anyway—like a monster, but trust me, I'm still human.

Around the same time as we got engaged, I had invested some of my money into a business for Dex. He was an incredible mechanic, and had always dreamed of having a custom car shop of his own, so I bought a building and footed the bill to get him started. The shop he chose was just around the corner from my own office, which made it convenient for us to ride to work together.

When breakfast was over, we got into his car, a fully restored '65 Mustang, and headed off to work. We always parked at the back of his shop, because then I could just zip through the alley to the back door of my own office. When we got there that morning to park, I kissed him goodbye and headed toward the first of several appointments I had scheduled for the day.

I unlocked the back door and walked inside, remembering to lock it behind me just to be safe, and headed toward the front where my office was. Angie, my receptionist, was already at her desk when I got there, and she looked up at me with a smile. We had once worked together at another counseling center, but it had been destroyed by a mad bomber. The same guy had taken Angie and hurt her very badly, so badly she almost didn't survive, and she ended up with some significant memory loss. Luckily, one of the things she forgot was how badly I had scared her back when we first met.

She had already put on coffee so I grabbed myself a cup as I went to my office, and then she came in to go over today's appointments. The first one scheduled was Julia Rice, one of the women I thought was ready to make the break from her husband. The guy had been beating her for years, and lately he had taken to getting pretty rough with her six-year-old son, Louis.

"Your ten o'clock," Angie said, "called last night and left a voice mail saying she needed to reschedule her appointment. She didn't say why, but she was being pretty cautious so I suspect her husband might have been listening. He'll be at work in a little while, so I'll call and see when she wants to come in."

"Okay, good," I said. "I'm hoping she might be ready to get out of there, but she keeps stalling." I shook my head. "Sometimes I wonder how these women can convince themselves things are going to change, but then I remember that I used to do the same thing. Everyone wants to believe the person they fell in love with is still there, even when the evidence says they've been gone for years."

"Yeah," Angie agreed. "Everyone else is still on schedule, but you've only got two appointments after lunch. One is at two, and the other at three." She looked up at me. "I was wondering if it would be okay if I left a little early today. My mom wants me to go shopping with her this afternoon, so I would need to leave around three thirty."

I grinned at her. "Sure, no problem," I said. "How have you been doing lately?"

"Oh, you know," she said with a sheepish grin. "I'm still figuring out who I am, but now and then another little flash of memory comes back. It gets a little confusing sometimes, like when Mom starts talking about people she thinks I should know, but I don't remember them at all." She shrugged. "She says I'm different than I used to be. Do you think so?"

"If I'm going to be perfectly honest," I said, "I'd have to say that I do see some differences. You're not as outspoken as you used to be, and you seem to have a little more compassion in you than before, but for the most part you're still the Angie I remember." She was sitting right up against my desk, so I reached over and laid a hand on hers. "I'm just glad you're here. I don't know what I would do without you."

Angie smiled, then got up and went back to her desk. A few minutes later I heard the bell on the door jingle as Julia, my first appointment, came in.

Julia Rice was one of the women who tugged at my heartstrings. She had married her high school sweetheart, David, shortly after graduation, and then he had gone off to the Army for basic training. They had a lot of wonderful plans for their life together, all of them built around his planned career in the armed forces.

Unfortunately, all of those plans came crashing down when he failed a simple drug test and put up a fight when he was confronted about it. The result was a dishonorable discharge less than three months after he had joined, and he'd been bitter and angry ever since. Without any kind of education, he was only able to get the most menial of jobs, and it wasn't long before he knew he couldn't afford to support a family on what he could earn. Julia had been forced to go to work as well, and for the first couple of years they managed to get by without any major incidents, but then Louis was born.

With both of them earning barely over minimum wage, paying for daycare was not an option, and neither had family that was willing or able to help out. Julia had been forced to give up her job in order to take care of the baby, and David started taking on all of the overtime he could get. That meant working seventy-hour weeks, and it wasn't long before the strain began taking its toll on him.

He had come home one day to find Julia trying to put the baby's crib back together with duct tape. It was an old one they had picked up at the local thrift store, and had broken while she was putting him down for a nap. David demanded to know why she hadn't just waited for him to get home, and she explained that she didn't want to put more of a burden on him.

He took this as her saying that she didn't have confidence in him to take care of his family, and that was the first time his anger got the better of him. Before he realized what he had done, he had punched her in the face and knocked her to the floor, and he let her lie there crying for several minutes before he got control of himself and told her how sorry he was. He promised it would never happen again, and she quickly forgave him, but it was really just the beginning.

The next time was less than a month later, and Julia didn't even know what had set him off. She knew it was something she had said, but she had ended up unconscious that time. When she awoke, she was lying in her bed and David was wiping her face with a damp cloth. Once more, he promised it would never happen again.

A pattern began. He would go two or three weeks without an outburst, but then something simple, like Julia not having dinner ready when he got home, would set him off. After it happened several times, Julia decided she had had enough and had gone to stay with a friend one day while he was at work. David had tracked her down that night and had very calmly explained to her just what would happen if she did not come home. The coldness in his voice had scared her more than anything else ever had in her life, and she had given in to him.

Since then, the beatings had become even more frequent. Julia was one of those women who kept the makeup counter at Walmart in business. She wore large dark glasses and hooded shirts all the time, refused to look anyone in the eye and always had a ready excuse for whatever bruise might be visible.

Unfortunately, she was also convinced that David would kill her if she left him, and I had been working on her for nearly six months suggesting various ways I could help to protect her.

And then, two months earlier, David had lost his temper with Louis and struck him. The little boy had been standing beside his dad, but suddenly he was across the room on the floor and screaming. Julia hadn't seen what actually happened, but it set her on the path to deciding things were too far out of control at last.

David had begun whipping Louis, but his spankings involved dozens of blows. Whenever Julia tried to intervene and cut it short, she would end up bruised and bloody once again, but she preferred that to seeing her little boy beaten.

She had called me up the previous Friday and said that she felt something had to be done, but she couldn't make it in until today. I'd had Angie shuffle appointments around so she could be the first one in, and I was really hoping today would be the day we would get the two of them out of that situation.

The big sunglasses told me she had taken another beating over the weekend, but this time I noticed a large bruise on Louis's face. I couldn't help staring at it as they came in and sat down, but then I turned my eye to Julia.

"I can make a phone call right now," I said, "and David will be in jail within an hour. The DA will stall his arraignment as long as possible, so by the time he has a chance to make bail, you and Louis can be in another city. I have contacts with shelters all over the country—they'll help you get on your feet. They'll help you get a job and a place to live for the two of you, and help to make sure David can't find you."

Julia looked at me for a moment, and then the tears started to flow. "Are you sure?" she asked. "Cassie, I'm scared to death. If we do this and he ever finds us, I'm terrified of what he might do."

I leaned forward, letting her get the full brunt of my split personality. "Julia, if you stay, it's still going to happen.

Whatever you're afraid of, it's coming, and it'll probably be worse than you could even imagine. Between the bruises you're sporting and the one I can see on Louis's face, my friend Alicia with the police department can charge him with felony domestic abuse. Our DA is extremely tough on domestic cases, and he'll get David's bond set as high as possible. The best your husband can hope for is that he might get a chance to take a plea bargain that will get him less than ten years in prison. I really don't think he's going to be in any position to come looking for you, but we can take steps to make sure you're extremely difficult to find. We can change your name, get you a new Social Security number, everything. You can make a fresh start, you and Louis."

"Mom?" her little boy said. "Does that mean Daddy won't hit us no more?"

Julia lost it at that point, crying and hugging her son. A moment later she looked up at me and, unable to speak, she nodded.

I picked up my desk phone and called Alicia Perkins, who was the domestic abuse detective with the local PD. She was in, and it took me less than three minutes to convince her that it was time to take action on David Rice.

That meant Julia would have to go to the police department and make a complaint, one on her own behalf and one for her son. Too many times, though, women left my office with every intention of going to the police, then gave in to their fears and went home instead. Alicia had learned not to trust them, so she immediately arranged for a patrol officer to come and pick up Julia and Louis.

"An officer is going to come and get you," I told Julia. "They'll take you to Alicia so you can do the paperwork, and

I'll get started on setting everything up for you. Alicia will have David arrested within an hour or so, and then you can go home and pack what you need to take with you. As soon as you're ready to go, I'll have transportation arranged and you can be in a new city and sleep without being afraid by tonight."

"Okay," she sniffled. "And he won't be able to find us?"

I shook my head. "I'll do everything possible to make sure he never can," I said. "But you have to take some precautions, as well. If you decide to stay in touch with your family, you need to get a mail drop service. Never give anyone your new home address, and never tell them where you live. If you want to visit with them, go and meet them somewhere else. Of course, David is likely to be locked up for a long time, so that might not be quite as bad as I'm making it sound, but you just need to be cautious. Okay?"

"Okay. I just—I just want this to be over. Oh, God, it's been such a nightmare."

"I know," I said. "But now it's time for a whole new dream to begin. By the time you get your things packed, I'll have a new name already in the works. Once that process is complete, it will be almost impossible for him to find you."

Angie buzzed me a minute later to tell me that the officer had arrived, and he escorted Julia and her son out the door. I waited until they were in the squad car and gone, then picked up the phone and called Alfie.

Alfie is the other PI I work with sometimes, and for a while I actually worked for him as an unpaid intern. He helped me get my license, and he provides a number of services that I find useful. For one thing, he's an incredibly talented computer hacker, so good that he's often employed by attorneys and government agencies. That's why he got into the PI business, to legitimize the work he did for clients like those.

On the side, though, he's what's known as a "gray hat." That means that while he doesn't use his talents to make himself rich, he's not above breaking a law or three if it happens to be in the way of him finding out what he wants to know. He's also very good at creating new identities, usually by simply appropriating one that somebody else no longer needs.

Yeah, that's exactly what it sounds like. He keeps a healthy database of people who have died without leaving a lot of assets behind. In cases like those, there's rarely any problem in simply reactivating their Social Security numbers and other items of identification, such as a driver's license.

"Gimme some lovin'," he said as he answered the phone. Alfie prided himself on having a different line every time he answered, and I hadn't caught him using the same one twice yet.

"It's Cassie," I said. "I'm sending you some information on a client. I'm going to be relocating her to Dothan, Alabama, and she needs a name and ID."

"Just make sure I have a photo," Alfie said. "I'll need to hack the Alabama Drivers Services and change the photo on whatever license I give her."

"It's in the email," I said. "I scanned a copy of her current license, so that should give you what you need. You should have the email by now."

"Let me check." He was quiet for a few seconds, then came back online. "Okay, got it. Give me an hour, and thank goodness you picked Alabama."

I narrowed my eye. "Why?"

"Because they use the same driver's license printer that I've got," he said. "That means I can print her out a license today that'll stand up if a cop checks it out."

"Awesome," I said. "How soon can you have it all ready?"

"I already told you, an hour. Sheesh, impatient much?"

The line went dead. It always did when Alfie was done. I leaned back in my chair and let myself enjoy a moment of relaxation, basking in the glow of a job well done.

That's another one, Abby, I thought. *We saved another one.*

TWO

I WAS FEELING PRETTY GOOD ABOUT MYSELF, SO I got up and refilled my coffee cup, then settled back at my desk. Angie came in a moment later and took the chair in front of it.

"Carrie Vincent, who was your ten o'clock this morning that rescheduled, says she can come in this Friday at ten. Her daughter got sick over the weekend and she's going to the doctor this morning, but her husband will be off for the next three days so she wants to go for Friday."

"No problem," I said. "Who's next for today?"

"Charlotte Waters at two this afternoon. She's a new one, so I'll get the intake packet set up for her."

"Okay, sounds good. I wonder what her story is..."

The bell on the door jingled, and Angie jumped up instantly and hurried out front. I could hear her speaking softly to someone, then she reappeared at my office door. There was a look of concern on her face, so I gave her my full attention.

"Cassie, there's a lady here, Maggie Logan, who says she needs to talk to you about something urgent. She won't tell me what it is, but said she was told that you're the only one who could help her."

"Okay," I said, curiosity making my eye narrow. "Send her in."

The woman who came into my office wasn't anything like the majority of the clients I get. She was about five foot seven, with professionally styled auburn hair and emerald green eyes, the kind of figure that you don't get without a gym membership, and dressed in the kind of clothing you probably don't buy in Tulsa, Oklahoma because we don't have stores that fancy. A quick glance at her hands showed me that several of her fingers were adorned with diamonds, and the fake stuff doesn't sparkle like that.

I got all of this out of the corner of my right eye, because I was keeping Freda out of sight for the moment. I pointed at the chair in front of the desk.

"Hi, I'm Cassie," I said. "Won't you have a seat?"

"Thank you," she said. She settled herself into the chair, carefully smoothing her skirt. She sat perfectly upright, as if she was almost afraid to lean back. "And thank you for seeing me. I've been told you're the only one who might actually be able to help me, because I've already exhausted other possibilities."

"No problem, I'll certainly try. Your name is Maggie?"

"Yes, Maggie Logan. Sorry, I didn't think to offer my name when I came in."

"No problem," I said again. "How can I help you, Maggie?"

"Ms. McGraw," she began, but I held up a hand.

"Just Cassie, please."

She gave a small smile. "Cassie, I'm hoping you can find my children. They've been gone for almost a year, and I feel like I'm going to go completely insane if I don't see them."

This wasn't something I usually heard, so it caught me off guard. Without thinking, I turned my face and looked directly at her. She didn't even blink when Freda came into view, so I knew someone had already warned her about my appearance.

"A year? I take it your ex has them and won't let you see them?"

Another soft smile appeared on her face. "Yes," she said. "However, this isn't a custody situation." She cleared her throat. "Let me start at the beginning."

"Yes, please," I said. "Would you like coffee, or a soft drink?"

"No, thank you." She took a deep breath. "Cassie, according to both the state of Oklahoma and the United States Government, my children are dead, along with their father. I know it sounds crazy, but—I simply don't believe it. My kids are alive, I can feel it. I just can't find them."

I think my eye was as big as it's ever been. "Can you tell me how they are supposed to have died?" I asked cautiously.

"We were planning a family vacation," Maggie said. "A couple of days before we were scheduled to leave, I was told that I would have to work a little longer on a project than I had expected, and so my husband and the kids would have to go without me, and I would catch up a few days later. They got into our motorhome and drove away, and I was supposed to fly out two days later and meet up with them in Tucson. Things like this had happened before, so I didn't think much of it. They called me that night from a campground in Utah, but that's the last I ever heard from them. The next day, I got a call from the Arizona Highway Patrol near Kingman saying that the motorhome had been found on the side of the road, and that it had apparently caught fire."

She swallowed, really hard. "There were the remains of three people inside. All three had been burned beyond any possibility of recognition, and to the point that even DNA couldn't be used to identify them. The best they could do was analyze the evidence, and they came to the conclusion that it was my husband, my daughter and my son, mostly because of items found with the remains. My daughter had a ring made of titanium that survived the fire, and my husband's watch was identifiable. As for my son, they just went on the fact that the remains they found were just about right for a nine-year-old boy. The coroner ruled that there was sufficient evidence to confirm identification, and death certificates were issued for all three of them. What was left of them was packed up into containers and sent back here for burial."

I had been wrong, because my eye got bigger. "But you believe they're still alive?"

She nodded. "Absolutely," she said. "I—my family has always had this, well, this thing. All the women in my family have dreams, and those dreams come true so often that it's beyond the possibility of just being chance." She reached into her purse and brought out an old book, which she laid on my desk. "That is my mother's diary. She passed away a couple of years ago, but I've kept this close to me ever since.

There are a couple of bookmarks in it. Please take a look at what she wrote on those days."

I slowly reached out and picked up the book, then turned to the first of the bookmarks. The date that had been written on the page was November 19th, 1963.

I had a weird dream last night. There were a lot of cars, and one of them was a big convertible. They were in a line, almost like a parade, and there were policemen on motorcycles with them. I saw them coming around a corner, moving very slowly, and the people in the convertible were waving at crowds who were standing along the street. I recognized the man and woman in the backseat, it was President Kennedy and Jackie. Then suddenly there were some loud noises, like guns going off, and all of a sudden the cars took off fast. It looked like the president was hurt.

I went back and read it a second time. Everyone knows Kennedy was assassinated on November 22nd of that year. If what I was reading was real, Maggie's mother had seen it all happen three days earlier.

"She predicted Kennedy's assassination?" I asked incredulously.

Maggie nodded. "My mother was only thirteen years old when she wrote that. Look at the next one."

I turned to the next bookmark. The date was August 27th, 2001. A chill went down my spine as I began to read.

Tall buildings, a pair of them. I think it was the World Trade Center in New York, but I'm not sure. I was looking at them from a distance and suddenly one of them burst into flame. Something exploded on the side of that building, and there was fire and smoke, thick, black smoke. I felt like something terrible was happening, and then something happened to the other building, the same kind of explosion and fire and smoke. *I don't know how long I was watching, but then the buildings collapsed, one after the other, and they were gone.*

I realized I'd been holding my breath, and I let it out. I looked up at Maggie.

"Is this for real?" I asked.

She nodded again. "Yes," she said. "Now, I'll show you my own diary. When you have dreams like these, it becomes a habit to write them down."

She handed me another book, this one not as old. It also had bookmarks, and I turned to the first one without any prompting. The date was July 30th, 1997.

Another dream. A big car, like a limousine, and it was driving in a tunnel. It was going very fast, and I could see inside the car. Princess Diana was inside with a man, sitting in the back of the car, and there were other cars that looked like they were chasing it. Then I was watching the car and I saw it crash, and then I heard a voice say Princess Diana was dead.

I turned to the next bookmark immediately. The date was August 25th, 2005.

The hurricane is going to hit New Orleans. Everywhere along the coast is going to be destroyed and in my dream I saw houses moving along in flooding waters, cars floating and buildings falling over. There were boats rammed into build-ings, and I heard voices saying thousands of people were hurt or killed.

I closed the book and passed both of them back to her.

"Okay," I said. "I gotta admit this is pretty strange. If those are real, then you could have warned people about Hurricane Katrina. Did you?"

"I actually tried," she said. "I need you to understand

that the last thing in the world I want is to be known as some kind of psychic. I don't have any control over the dreams, I just see things that are going to happen; all the women in my family have done that for as long as anybody can remember. My great-grandmother actually dreamed about the Titanic, or so they say." She shrugged and gave me another of those soft smiles. "People don't listen. They don't want to hear about what's going to happen, because that means the world isn't what they want it to be. I only showed you those so you'll understand that I have reason to believe another dream I keep having."

"A dream involving your children?" I asked.

"Yes. I've had the dream a dozen times or more, and it's always the same. I see my son and my daughter, and they are both healthy and alive. They seem to be in some remote place, and they are frightened. I don't know what is scaring them, but they are in a house and trying to hide from someone. I don't know who they're hiding from, I've never seen that person, but I see my daughter telling my son to be quiet so they won't be found. They both stay very quiet, and I think they're hiding under a bed or something, because they are lying on the floor and there is an open door nearby. In the dream, I can feel just how frightened they are, but then a shadow falls on the door and they both scream." She shook herself. "That's where the dream always ends."

I looked at her for a moment, then cocked my head to the side a bit. "In your diaries, the dreams always come true within a couple of days. But you've had this dream several times?"

"Yes, quite a few. At least a dozen, maybe more. And I should tell you, not all dreams come true that quickly. In

2010, I dreamed about a movie theater, and there was a Batman movie on the screen. I barely knew who Batman was, but all of a sudden a man started shooting people in the theater, and I knew that twelve people would die. That shooting didn't happen until July of 2012, in Aurora, Colorado. Twelve people died and fifty-eight more were wounded." She took out her diary again and slid it across the desk to me. "Take a look, it was October third of 2010."

I shook my head. "I believe you," I said. "So, whatever this thing is that has your children so scared, you think it hasn't happened yet?"

"I'm sure of it," she said. "And that means my kids are alive. I haven't seen their father in a dream, so I don't know for sure about him, but I think that he might have somehow faked their deaths." She grimaced. "He and I were not exactly on the best of terms when this happened. He had been—he had an affair, and this vacation was supposed to be a chance for us to try to reconnect as a family. I can't help wondering if maybe he just decided he was done with me." Another sad smile. "I never found out who he had his affair with. For all I know, she might be with them even now."

I sat there silently for a few moments, just trying to think of some way to approach this situation. I mean, yes, I'm a private investigator, but my specialty was abuse cases. How was I going to find someone who had apparently gone to such fantastic lengths to disappear?

"Maggie, I'll be honest, I don't know how I can help you. I wouldn't know where to start on a case like this."

She nodded understandingly. "I know," she said. "But I also know that you're the only one who can help me."

"You said that before," I said. "Can I ask who told you that?"

She picked up her diary and turned to a page in it, then turned it around and handed it to me. I looked automatically, and the date on the page was the very day when I was burned so badly. My eyebrow shot up, and I read the entry underneath it.

A weird dream. I was looking for my children, and I didn't know where to go. I felt like I had been looking for them for a long time, and then I met a woman. She had been burned on the left side of her body, from her foot to the side of her head. She only had one eye, and was horribly disfigured, but I felt a sense of peace when I saw her. I asked her to find my children, and she smiled at me. She said, "I'm the only one who can," and somehow I knew it was true. Is this a dream that will come true? If it is, then I pray God will let me find this woman.

I looked up at her, shock probably evident on my face. She was nodding again.

"Yes," she said. "You are the one who told me that you alone can help me."

"I don't know what to say," I mumbled. "Maggie, I honestly wouldn't know where to start."

"But you will try? Please, Cassie, please tell me you'll try."

I opened my mouth to say something, but then I closed it again. When I opened it a second time, I was shocked to hear myself say, "Of course I will."

Her smile became genuine, then, and she reached into her purse once again. She took a check out and handed it to me, and I saw that it was made payable to me and was for twenty thousand dollars.

"Maggie, I can't accept this," I said. "I'll be honest, I don't know if am going to be able to do you any good."

"Take it," she said. "That's only a retainer. When you find them, I'll add another hundred thousand dollars to it."

I pushed the check back toward her. "No, really," I said. "To be honest, I don't need your money. If I find them, then you can pay me if you want to, but I can't take this today. Please, just keep it. I promise you that I'll do everything I can to find your kids, but I don't want to get your hopes up. I've never tackled any case like this."

Sabrina, I heard in the back of my head. Abby was reminding me that the very first case I ever took on was a missing person who had basically faked her own death. *You can do this, Cassie. You can find her kids.*

Maggie was thanking me, and I noticed there were tears in her eyes. I suppose, if I were in her shoes, just hearing someone say they would try would at least be some kind of relief. With the coroner insisting her kids were dead, I doubted the police ever bothered to listen to her at all.

She dug in her purse once again and came out with a small notebook. "I took the liberty of writing down everything I could think of about my husband," she said, "as far as things you might need. This is everything, a fairly complete biography, and I added some information about the children. I hope it helps."

I accepted the notebook and glanced at a few pages. Her husband's name was Harold Logan, and he was forty-six years old. There were references to where he had grown up, his family members, jobs he had held and other things. He had been an only child, and both of his parents had passed away in the past few years. The kids were her daughter Jody, who had been fourteen when they supposedly died, and her son Ryan, who had been nine years old at that time. There were photos of all of them paper clipped into the notebook, two or three of each. I thought about what I was agreeing to do, and then another thought struck me. I looked back at Maggie.

"I'm curious," I said. "If you had that dream about me so long ago, why did you wait a whole year to come to me?"

She made a face. "Because I forgot all about it," she said. "When you have dreams like these, you have a tendency to put them out of your mind as quickly as you can. I had forgotten all about that dream, but something was nagging at me to go back through my diary. I found that entry, and then I remembered seeing something about you in the newspaper a while back. You had caught a serial killer and a bomber, and both times you made the paper. One of them had a photograph, and that was how I figured out that it had to be you. That picture looked exactly like the woman in my dream."

I shrugged. "Okay," I said. "Give me your contact information. I'm going to get started on this today, but don't expect a miracle to happen overnight."

She handed me a card that already had her name, phone number, address and other information printed on it. I slipped it into my desk drawer and then got up to walk her out. When we got to the front door, she turned and suddenly threw both arms around me, weeping as she held on to me for dear life.

"Thank you," she said again. "You can't know how good it feels to actually be face-to-face with you."

"I just hope your faith isn't misplaced," I said, hugging her. "I'll be in touch."

She let go and walked out the door, and I turned to look at Angie. Her eyes were wide, because people didn't hug me very often. Folks don't get cozy with a girl who's been toasty.

"So," she said. "What was it only you could help with?"

"Come on in my office, and I'll fill you in," I said. She got up and followed me instantly, and I told her the whole story. While I was talking, I noticed that Maggie had left her diary there, and I showed Angie the entry that described me so perfectly. Her eyes got wide, as she looked up at me after reading it.

"Okay, this is weird," she said. "That's like almost three years ago."

"Yeah," I said. "And the interesting thing is, that's the exact date when I got burned."

Her eyes got even wider. "Okay, that's just spooky."

"Tell me about it," I said. "Now, how in the world do I find these kids?"

Angie went back out front, and I glanced at the time on my computer. It was only a quarter after ten, and I didn't have another appointment until two. I got up and told Angie I would be back in time for my next client, then turned and walked out the back door. This was something I needed to talk to Dex about.

When I stepped into the shop, I had to wait a few minutes before Dex could even hear me. He was using a sander on the side of the big truck he was working on, and it made a loud racket. When he stopped for a moment to look at his work, I called out to him.

"Cassie," he said. He put down the sander and came over to me, but he was so covered in dust that I held out my hands to ward him off. He grinned. "Okay, no hugs right now. Everything going okay?"

"I'm not sure how to answer that," I said. "Let's go to your office, I need to talk."

He blinked, but turned around and called out, "Jimmy, keep going on the wiring, I'll be in the office for a few minutes." Jimmy held up a hand with the thumb sticking up and Dex led the way into his office. He grabbed a rag and wiped his hands off, but dust was falling off him as he walked, so I was careful to stay back a bit. I was wearing a black pantsuit, and the sander made a lot of light pink dust. I didn't want it on me.

It took me twenty minutes to tell him the whole story, and I'd even brought along the diary to show him. He nodded as he read the various entries, and then handed it back.

"So," he said. "Your first real private eye case. This one ought to be a dandy."

"Yeah, no kidding. Now all I have to do is figure out how to do the impossible."

"Well, you know where to start," he said. "Get Alfie on it. I think the first thing you need is all the background you can get on the kids' father. If you can find out who the affair was with, that might give you an actual lead, and you need Alfie for that. Otherwise, he can look for whatever new identity the guy's set up for himself."

"Oh, you can bet I'm going to Alfie for this," I said.

"You really think he might be able to find out who the guy was boinking?"

"In most cases, he can find out what color underwear somebody is wearing. I would just about bet he can get you at least some idea of where to look for these folks."

I nodded. "Okay," I said. "I'm free until two. Care to join me for pizza at Alfie's place?"

"Sounds like a good deal to me," he said. "I'll be ready to go by eleven thirty."

"Good. And be sure to clean up, I don't need all that dust getting all over me."

He chuckled, then leaned over and kissed my cheek. When he pulled back, he narrowed his eyes and then picked up a clean rag from the pile on his desk and handed it to me.

"Then you might want to wipe that off."

I scowled at him, which would've absolutely terrified anyone else who ever saw me do it, but he only chuckled. I took the rag and wiped the dust off my face, then wondered if I should have just left it there. He had kissed my left cheek, the one that was burned. That bit of dust might have actually been an improvement.

It was already getting close to eleven, so I called Angie and told her I was going to be hanging out at the shop until it was time for lunch. She would take her own lunch at noon, her regular time, and I told her I would be back before the two o'clock appointment.

Then I sat on one of the stools in the office and watched Dex and Jimmy work through the big window he had installed. They were building a custom truck for a client, a 1955 Ford COE, which Dex had told me stood for "cab over engine." It was a strange-looking truck, to me, because the hood was only about a foot long. The engine literally was under the cab, right beneath where the driver and passenger would sit.

Originally, it had been some sort of box truck, the kind they deliver furniture in, but the customer wanted it converted into a motorhome. They had already taken off the original box and welded up the framework for the new camper area, then covered that with new sheet metal that was molded right into the back of the cab. Dex was in the process of getting it ready to paint, which was what resulted in the sander being put to work. Every part of the exterior had to be perfectly smooth before the paint went on, or every little flaw would show. They used a special putty made specifically for this kind of work to fill in any little dents or creases, and then the sander made them smooth and perfect.

About twenty minutes later, Dex put down the sander and went into the bathroom he had expanded. He took a quick shower, put on a fresh work uniform and came out at exactly eleven thirty. This time, I accepted the hug and even got a kiss in the process.

He told Jimmy to go ahead and take a break for lunch, then we walked out and got into his Mustang once again. The drive over to Alfie's place only took about fifteen minutes, but we stopped along the way and picked up a pair of large meat eater pizzas, the kind with plenty of sausage, pepperoni, and other semi-identifiable chunks of meat. Alfie was a sucker for pizza, so bringing some along was always a way to get him in the mood for whatever I wanted him to do.

With this case, I wanted him in as good a mood as I could possibly arrange.

THREE

DEX KNOCKED ON ALFIE'S DOOR AND WE HEARD him call out, "It ain't locked, but you'd better have food!" We both laughed as we opened the door and stepped inside, and I was delighted to see my little friend again.

Alfie was a dwarf, just a little over three feet tall. He was also one of the smartest people I have ever met, and as I've mentioned before, he was absolutely incredible with computers. He glanced over from the stool he sat on in the midst of half a dozen different computers that were arranged in a semicircle and grinned at us.

"Good timing," he said. "Your girl's new ID is ready."

"Good," I said. "But that's not the reason we came by. Come on, we brought pizza."

He hopped down off the stool and joined us in the part of his living room that held a couch, a chair, a coffee table and a TV. It was all crammed together, because the computers took up most of the space in the room, but I'd gotten used to it. Dex and I plopped onto the couch and Alfie took the chair.

"The Carnivore Special," he said as I opened the first box. "Based on prior experience, that means you got something big you need my help with. Am I right?"

"Eat first," I said. "Then I'll answer that question."

"You just did," he said as he grabbed a large slice. For as little as he is, that guy can put away pizza faster than anybody I've ever seen. That slice disappeared in about four bites, and he grabbed another.

"Okay," he said, "I'm on my second piece. That means my blood sugar is in no danger of crashing, so start talking. What's the new problem?"

I swallowed the big bite I had just taken and then began telling him about Maggie Logan and her situation. I gave him all the details, including how the husband and kids had supposedly died, her reference to the husband's affair and all the stuff about the dreams that ran in her family. When he looked at me with doubt on his face, I handed him the diary she had left behind, open to the page that seemed to describe me.

"Okay, that's pretty weird," he said. "I admit that sounds a lot like you, but..."

"Did you notice the date?" I asked.

He glanced at the page again. "Yeah. So?"

"That's the very day I got burned," I said. "You tell me how that could be nothing but a coincidence, and I'll drop this case in a heartbeat."

"I don't believe in coincidence," Alfie said. "Okay, so this lady gets to peek at the future from time to time. Has it ever really done her any good?"

"Probably not, before now," I said. "She said she has tried to warn people about things she has seen in her dreams, but nobody wants to listen. Add the fact that she doesn't want to be known for this kind of thing, and I suspect she hasn't tried very hard. This time, though, that prediction about me seems to have struck home with her. She thinks my reference to being the only one who can help her, in the dream, I mean, is because I'm the only one who's going to be able to find her kids."

"I can see why she might think that way, after a dream like that. You said the kids and their dad have been gone for a year? Why hasn't she come to you sooner?"

"I asked the same question and she said she had forgotten about that prediction. She was looking through her diary and found it, and remembered seeing the newspaper articles about me a few months ago. As you undoubtedly remember, they put my picture right on the front page on one of those, a full-on shot that showed Freda in all her glory. She put two and two together and came up with me, so that's why she came in this morning. She even tried to give me a twenty-thousand-dollar retainer."

Alfie looked up at me suddenly. "And you didn't take it?" he asked. "Are you crazy or something?"

"I don't need her money, Alfie," I said. "I told her she can pay me if I actually find them, but I'm not holding my breath about this even being possible."

"Why not?" Dex asked. "You found Sabrina, and she had been gone even longer."

"Yes, but she didn't stage her own death with three convenient bodies burned to ash. If her husband really did fake their deaths, then how could they find the remains of an adult and two kids in that burned-out motorhome? I mean, how hard would it be to get hold of bodies the right size and everything, just to pull the wool over the eyes of the authorities?"

"Considering the fire was hot enough to destroy DNA," Alfie said, "it might not be that difficult. If he had been planning this for any length of time, he probably had those bodies stashed somewhere in a freezer. The same fire that ruined the DNA would make it impossible to tell they'd ever been frozen, so he could get away with that."

I rolled my eye. "But where would he get the bodies in the first place? I mean, they don't exactly have a supermarket for dead bodies, do they?"

He grinned at me. "You are such an innocent," he said. "In the United States alone, there are more than thirty body brokers, places where you can buy anything from an eyeball all the way up to a whole body. You can even specify gender, age, race, all that stuff, and if you're willing to part with five to ten grand, you'll get what you want. If old man Logan was even halfway intelligent, he could make purchases like those with cash and leave little or no trail to follow. He could keep the bodies frozen until it was time to use them, then load them into the motorhome and set it on fire. I'm guessing the motorhome was a diesel, and probably had full tanks when it was set ablaze. That would produce enough heat to destroy the DNA and maybe even crumble the bones. That would be a way to avoid identification by dental records, maybe."

My mouth was open. "You're serious? There are actually places where you can buy a body?"

"In all but four states," Alfie said. "I know Florida and

Virginia don't allow it, and there are a couple more but I can't remember which ones. I can look it up if you want."

I shook my head. "No, that's okay. But what you're telling me is that he could've actually planned this out, gotten the bodies and had them ready for when he got the chance to take the kids and disappear. Right?"

"Bingo," Alfie said. "You got it on the first try."

I shook my head again. Sometimes this world was so screwed up that I had trouble believing I actually lived in it.

"Okay, so where do we start? What you just told me only makes me want to find the bastard even more."

He held out a hand. "Give me everything you got on the guy," he said. "Let me see what I can do while you're here."

I handed over the notebook Maggie had given me, the one with all the details about her husband, Harold, and Alfie flipped through it quickly as he walked back over toward the computers. He reached up and put one hand on the stool and another on the desk, then popped up onto the stool like he was jet propelled.

He laid the notebook beside his keyboard and started typing away. Within less than a minute he had the guy's Facebook account on the screen, and a whole bunch of other things started appearing after that.

"This guy is good," he said after a few minutes. "I've got his cell phone, and it hasn't been used since the fire. His Facebook account has not been touched, same for his LinkedIn, Twitter and Instagram. I've got his picture from his driver's license and I'm running it through every facial recognition database there is, but that's going to take a while. If he's got a driver's license under another name, I should come up with a hit."

"What about this affair he supposedly had?" I asked. "Maggie said she didn't know who it was, but Dex seems to be of the opinion that you could find out. Think you can?"

Alfie grinned. "Already did," he said. "Her name is Donna Kemp, but she hasn't disappeared."

My one good eyebrow lowered. "How could you possibly know that already?" I asked.

"I went through his cell phone records," Alfie said, "and made a note of the numbers he called a lot. Hers was one of them, and there were a number of calls from her phone back to his, as well. Then I just checked their GPS histories and found out that they both were at the same place pretty regularly, about once a week. That place turned out to be the Garden Way Hotel, out on the loop. His name never showed up in their guest registry, but hers did. They were also texting with each other, and made veiled references to the next time they would be together, things like that."

"But she didn't disappear with him?"

"Nope. She's still here in Tulsa, and still working at the same place, Allen's Furniture Rental. Her phone records for the last year don't show a lot of calls to unknown numbers, at least not repetitive ones. I'd say he dumped her at the same time he dumped his wife."

"I still want to talk to her," I said. "She might know something about where he would go if he got away like this."

"That's possible," Alfie said. "Couples do tend to fantasize about the future during pillow talk in situations like that. I'll send you her info now."

My phone gave a ding a second later as the text message came in. "Okay," I said. "Now, what about money? These folks apparently had some, and he would've needed money if he was going to disappear, right?"

"I'm already on it," Alfie said. "I've got a program scanning through their bank accounts and credit cards now, looking for any suspicious transfers. I'm also looking for any accounts he may have set up that his wife might not have known about."

I nodded. "Okay. That'll probably take a while, right? Any suggestions on how I might approach this in the meantime?"

Alfie had been a private investigator for several years, and was basically my mentor when it came to this kind of work. Before I got my own license, I had worked on a provisional license under him as an intern, to learn the business.

He turned his stool so he was looking directly at me. "A couple of ideas come to mind," he said. "The Logans were what you might call moderately wealthy, and most of it came from investments, but they both worked as well. She's an architect, but her husband was a surgical nurse at OSU Medical Center. You might talk to his coworkers, see if any of them might have some idea where he would go." He reached up and took off his glasses, then cleaned them on his T-shirt and put them back on. "My other idea would be to visit the school the kids went to. It's a private school called Clear Skies, one of those places that's run by a bunch of old hippies. You know as well as I do that kids have a habit of trying to contact their friends, even when you tell them not to because it could be dangerous. If those kids are anywhere near cell phones or the Internet, some of their buddies will have heard from them. They may not admit it to you, but if you get the feeling some of them are lying, let me know. I can hack their phones and accounts, see if they had any contact with Jody or Ryan."

I blinked. "That wouldn't exactly be legal, would it?"

"Not without parental consent, but you're not letting a little thing like that stop you, are you?"

"Of course not," I said. "I just like to know which laws I'm breaking, that's all."

"Welcome to the world of the private eye," Alfie said. "I warned you about this, remember? Sometimes you gotta break eggs to make omelettes."

"Okay, so I talk to the other nurses at OSU, and then I only have to figure out a way to get close to the kids who were their classmates. That ought to go well. I'm sure their teachers will be delighted to let me bring Freda into the classroom."

Alfie shrugged. "You're the one who took the case," he said. "You'll figure it out, I have faith in you."

He hopped down and came to grab another slice of pizza, but one of his computers chose that moment to sound off. He shoved a huge bite into his mouth, dropped the slice back into the box and bounced up onto his stool again.

"Oho," he said. "I'd say we can now confirm that Mr. Logan did indeed fake at least his own death."

"How's that?" I asked.

"He set up an account nearly two years ago, a brokerage account that he funded with two hundred thousand dollars. The money to fund it came from a real estate deal, some property he had bought years earlier and then sold at a tidy profit. He bought it a few years before he and his wife were married, and it looks like maybe she didn't know anything about it. That brokerage account grew to well over three hundred thousand, but then it made a transfer of ninety thousand dollars to a real estate investment trust. Looks to me like he bought a place somewhere, but it's going to take some digging to find out where. There are also some smaller payments, less than ten thousand at a time, that are sent out by mail periodically. Hang on a second." He beat on the keyboard for half a minute, then nodded. "The address the payments go to is a mail drop in Los Angeles. That means somebody there receives mail for him, then forwards it on somewhere else. I'll see if I can get into their system and find out where it goes when it leaves their hands."

"What about the checks?" I asked. "Can you find out where the checks get cashed?"

Alfie shook his head. "Nope. There aren't any images of the checks, and that wouldn't necessarily tell you anything, anyway. Somebody being this cautious probably has them forwarded to an attorney or trustee who cashes them, and then sends the money to him some other way. Maybe Western Union, MoneyGram, something like that. You have to know who was sending it in order to find out where it went."

"But a letter sent to that mail drop would eventually find its way to him, right?" I asked. "Isn't that how that works?"

"Usually, but not necessarily. Like I said, the mail is probably going to an agent who acts on his behalf. That agent is probably being paid well not to give up any information about him."

I scrunched up my face as I thought about what he said, then decided to leave that to the expert. I would have to work on finding other leads, and Alfie's suggestion about talking to Harold's coworkers and the kids' classmates seemed reasonable.

The three of us finished off the pizza and then Dex and I headed back. As soon as we got into the car, he looked over at me.

"Don't worry," he said. "You'll find them. It's like I told you back when we first met: you don't do things the way everybody else does. Most people ask the usual questions, but you come up with some that nobody else would think of. That's one of the things I love most about you."

"Thanks for the vote of confidence," I said, "but I'll be honest, Dex. This may be bigger than I can handle."

"Nah, it's not. What makes you say that?"

"Something Alfie said," I said softly. "He said we could be sure that Harold Logan faked 'at least his own death.' Dex, what if the kids are really dead?"

"You're thinking he may have killed them himself, part of his plan to disappear?"

"It wouldn't be the first time I've heard of such a thing," I said. "It used to be unthinkable that a parent might murder his or her own child, but it's hard to get through a week without a news story about that kind of case anymore. It's almost like kids have become just another thing you have to deal with, and some people don't want to bother."

"Then why didn't he just disappear on his own? Leave the kids with their mother?"

"That," I said, "would probably depend on just how much he hated his wife." I shook my head. "Something about this is starting to bug me. It's very difficult to disappear and change your name when you've got kids, because they just don't really understand why they have to be somebody else. If he just wanted out, it would've been a lot easier to do it without taking the kids along. Taking them with him could mean a number of things, including the possibility that he didn't feel they were safe with their mother."

I took out my phone and dialed Alfie's number.

"Smoke it, baby," he said.

"Alfie, something I forgot. I need everything you can get me on Maggie Logan. I want to know as much as possible about this woman, and I mean everything you can possibly find. If there's a skeleton in her closet, I want to hear his bones rattle."

"I'm already working on it," he said. "I figured you'd want that sooner or later. I'll send you an email in a couple hours, with lots of stuff you need to look at."

I grinned. "Thanks, Alfie," I said. The line went dead and I put the phone back into my purse.

"He's already on it, right?" Dex asked.

"Of course," I said. "Thanks for coming with me, Dex."

"Hey, how could I refuse? Not only did I get to spend some time with you, but I got free pizza."

I playfully slapped the back of his head.

He dropped me off in front of my office and I walked through the front door to find Angie at her desk, her face red and bearing the tracks of tears. I hurried over to her and pulled a chair close.

"Angie? Honey, what's the matter?"

Angie sniffled a couple of times before she managed to speak. "Nothing's really wrong," she said. "It's—it's just my memory, it still gives me problems sometimes. I was putting together the hard copy file folder for your case this morning, Mrs. Rice, and all of a sudden I couldn't remember which files I need to print out to go in it. I've been sitting here for the last twenty minutes, trying to remember, looking at all the files on the computer to see if that would help, but I just —just can't remember."

I put an arm around her shoulders. "Well, that's not that big a deal," I said. "Let's see the folder, what have you got in it already?"

She slid the folder over to me and I opened it up. The intake packet requires four forms: basic information, like name, address, phone, etc.; general circumstances, which requires the client to tell me the type of abuse they're dealing with; affected persons, which means their kids and anyone else in the household who might be hurt; and abuse history, which looks into times when police were involved or it was necessary to get medical treatment. Angie had all four of those forms in the folder already, so I turned to her and smiled.

"You got them all," I said. "This is the whole file, right here."

She stared at me for a moment. "But isn't there something else? There was another form, wasn't there? I just can't remember which one it is."

"Nope, this is it. You already had it together, but your sneaky little mind was trying to play tricks on you. Remember, your doctors said this might happen from time to time. What did they call it, phantom memories? When you think you remember something, but you can't quite get it?"

She sniffled again, but managed to grin. "Yeah, phantom memories," she said. "They happen because of damage to my long-term memory, and it feels like I'm forgetting something that I should be able to remember. It's frustrating."

"Yes, I'm sure it is, but you didn't really forget anything. Maybe we should make a list of what files go in each packet, so if this happens again, you can just check the list and see that you already got it done."

She chuckled. "Yeah, that might help," she said. "Do you mind?"

We sat there then and made the lists for each of the packets she would have to put together. There were intake packets, abuse report packets, legal action packets and a few more, all part of the record-keeping I had to do in order to keep the state happy. Angie was normally very efficient, but she had suffered some brain damage from the beatings she took when she was abducted. These were things we simply had to work with, and one of the reasons I was glad she had accepted the job I offered her. Some employers might not have understood what she had been through.

"Okay," I said, "now go fix your face. I'll watch your desk while you get pretty again."

She giggled, then got up and headed toward the ladies' room with her purse. She was back ten minutes later, and there was no sign left that she had been crying. I gave her one more hug for good measure, then went into my own office.

It was only one o'clock, so I had some free time before the next appointment. I thought for a moment about what to do with it, then looked at the text message Alfie had sent me. Donna Kemp worked at a furniture rental place, and would most likely be at work at that moment. I decided to take a chance on calling her at work, to see if she might be willing to talk to me. I googled the number for the store and dialed it from my office phone.

"Allen's Rentals," said a male voice. "How can we help you today?"

"Hi," I said. "I was wondering if Donna Kemp might be available."

"Donna? Yeah, sure, just hold on a moment." He put me on hold and I listened to—and no, I'm not kidding—Barry Manilow singing about trying to get the feeling again. Now, I personally think Manilow had a beautiful voice and I love his music, but it had been years since I heard any of it. Listening to it while I was on hold was almost a surreal experience.

He was just starting the second chorus when it suddenly ended and Donna was on the line. "This is Donna," she said. "How can I help you today?"

"Donna, my name is Cassie McGraw and I'm a private investigator. I was wondering if you might be willing to sit down with me and discuss Harold Logan."

There were two seconds of hesitation on the other end of the line, and then she came back with a smile in her voice. "Harold Logan? I'm not sure I know who you mean."

"Oh, sure, you remember Harold," I said. "I mean, you should, considering how much time you spent with him at the Garden Way Hotel. Now, only you and I know about that at the moment, and I suspect you'd like to keep it that way, so how about we get together after you get off work and talk about it?"

Four seconds of hesitation. "Well, I don't get off until six," she said. "I suppose we could meet somewhere."

I grinned. "That sounds great," I said. "How about meeting me at Grizzly's, say around six thirty? You know where it is?"

"Yeah, I know the place," she said. "How will I know you?"

"Oh, that's easy," I said. "Just look for the woman who looks like Freddy Krueger's half-sister. Any barmaid there will bring you right to me."

"Freddy Krueger?" she asked incredulously. "Like, the guy from the nightmare movies?"

"Yep. I got burned sometime back, all over the left side of my body. Just look for the girl who doesn't have any hair on the left side of her head, that'll be me."

"Um, well, okay," she said. "I guess I'll see you then."

FOUR

I HUNG UP THE PHONE FEELING PRETTY COCKY that I had gotten her to agree to a meeting. She had been smart enough to realize that, if I knew about the hotel, there might be other things I knew that she would be concerned about anyone finding out.

I still had plenty of time, so I decided to look into making some contacts with Harold's coworkers. I looked up the number for OSU Medical and called the personnel department.

"OSU Human Resources," answered a woman. "How may I direct your call?"

"I'm not exactly sure," I said. "My name is Cassie McGraw, and I'm a private investigator. I'd be interested in speaking with people who worked with Harold Logan while he was there. Can you tell me how I might go about finding out who they are?"

The woman hesitated for a couple of seconds. "Harold

who?" she asked. "I don't think we have anyone here by that name."

"Not anymore—he was reported to have been killed about a year ago, a freak fire in a motorhome. I'm looking into some things about it, and thought some of his former coworkers might be able to give me some insights. Can you help me get in touch with some of them?"

She hesitated again. "I don't believe I can give out that kind of information. You might try talking to the head of the nursing staff, I see that he was in that department when he was here. To be honest, though, they probably can't tell you anything either."

"Well, it's worth a try. Who should I ask for?"

"That would be Mrs. McKinney," the woman said. "Just a moment and I'll transfer you."

I heard ringing again for a couple of seconds, and then another woman came on the line. "Daphne McKinney," she said as she answered.

"Mrs. McKinney, my name is Cassie McGraw. I'm a private investigator looking into Harold Logan, and I'm hoping you might be able to connect me with some of his coworkers."

"Harold Logan? I haven't heard that name in a while. What's this about? As far as I know, Harold is dead."

I put a smile on, so she could hear it in my voice. "Yes, ma'am, that's the official story," I said, "but I've come across evidence that he may actually have faked his death. I'm hoping some of his coworkers might have some insight into where I should look for him and his children."

"Oh, God, that's right, he had his kids with him, didn't he? And you think they're really still alive?"

"I've found some evidence that definitely suggests that possibility," I said. "Naturally, his wife is very concerned and she also has reason to believe they are alive, so she's hired me to try to find them."

"Hmmm," she said. "I've gotta think about this. I'm not sure that I can really help you. What is it you're trying to do again? You want to talk to his coworkers?"

"Yes, ma'am, if at all possible. In particular, I'd love to know about anybody he was particularly close to. Do you know if he had any close friends that he worked with?"

"I honestly wouldn't know," Mrs. McKinney said. "I don't actually work on the floor or in the surgery, I'm more of a manager for the department. Although," she said, and then paused for a couple of seconds. "I probably shouldn't do this, but—well, if he faked his death and took those kids away from their mother, then he deserves whatever he gets. I would suggest you talk to Rick Lancaster. I seem to remember that he and Harold were pretty close, and Rick is still with us. Can you avoid telling him how you got his number if I give it to you?"

"Sure, no problem," I said. "I can always say it turned up on Harold's cell phone records."

"I'm sure it's there," Mrs. McKinney said. "Okay, here it is." She read off the number to me and I scribbled it down on my desk pad. "He's here at work right now, but he gets off at four PM. Other than that, I wouldn't know what I could do for you, but I do wish you luck."

"No problem, and thank you." I hung up the phone and sat back, feeling smug once again. I had two concrete leads, which I felt was a pretty good day's work. I would call Rick Lancaster at a little after four, and then meet with Donna

Kemp at half past six. With any luck, one of them had heard something that could give me a direction to start looking in.

There were still nearly forty minutes before my new client would come in, so I got myself a fresh cup of coffee and started preparing for her visit. The only thing I knew about Charlotte Waters was that she had called the previous Friday and asked for an appointment, and said she was in an abusive relationship and wanted to explore ways to get out.

Well, that was my specialty. I took a mirror out of my drawer to make sure my "pretty side" was presentable, then adjusted my eye patch because it was slipping just a bit. The last thing anyone needed to see, especially when they met me for the first time, was the gaping hole where my eye used to be. My eyelid had actually burned away, so when I wore the glass eye and prosthetic mask I kept in a dresser drawer at home, people sometimes noticed that my left eye never blinked. In fact, a few men had actually thought that I was winking at them.

I didn't wear the mask very often, because I'm just not ashamed of Freda. And ironically, the publicity I had gotten a few months earlier had actually resulted in a lot of people in the area becoming more accepting of burn victims. I can't count the number of times I've been greeted by perfect strangers who knew me because of that photo in the newspaper, and I've met children whose parents had begun teaching them that scars don't affect who the person is on the inside. If my looking like this can make a positive difference in even a few lives, then I'm willing to put it out there for the whole world to see.

Of course, when I do put on the prosthetic half-mask, people don't ever recognize me. That's because the burn scars are what stick in the mind, not the unburned part of my face. I've run into people that I knew fairly well while wearing the mask, and they didn't recognize me at all.

Even I can only daydream for a few minutes before I get bored, so I finally turned to the Internet to entertain myself until my next appointment. My Facebook account said I had a couple dozen new messages and an equal number of friend requests, but I have a policy of not accepting requests from anyone I don't actually know. Some of the messages were from clients, but I discourage them from using Facebook as a way to contact me. Their platform has been hacked enough times that I worry about who might be able to see the messages, and there's always the risk that the abuser can get into their accounts.

That day, I had a message from Sabrina Moss, the girl I had tracked down for Dex back when I first met him. She had been through a bad situation, a stalker who had actually threatened to kill her if she refused to marry him, and she had ended up killing him in self-defense. After that, however, she panicked and decided to hide his body and run away, changing her name and disappearing. She had started a new life working in a homeless shelter when I found her, and I was able to convince her to come back and face the consequences of her actions. Dex arranged an attorney for her, and things weren't nearly as bad as she had been afraid they might be once the entire story came out. She had spent some time on probation, but had been allowed to return to Oklahoma City and her job at the shelter. We had become friends during her ordeal, and kept in touch this way.

Hey, girl, she had written. *I just wanted to reach out and say hi. Okay, that's only partially true. The real reason I'm messaging you is because we are starting to see women and kids come into the shelter who are trying to get away from abusive situations, and we just aren't set up to handle those things. I talked with the bishop and he said he would be willing to consider starting a shelter for families like that, but he's looking for information on how they have to be run. Any chance you could help me out with that?*

How's Critter doing? I miss that cat sometimes. And how are you and Dex, now that you are engaged? Everything still good? I know he can be a handful but I think he might be worth it in the long run. I should have realized it back then, but he turned out to be more like a big brother in my case.

Give both of them a hug for me.

I read through it twice, grinning at the second paragraph, then I picked up the phone and called Mitch Reynolds over at New Beginnings. NB is the biggest and probably best battered women's shelter in the area, and I had placed a number of women there.

"Cassie," he said when he found out it was me on the line. "What can I do for you?"

"I just got a message from a friend in Oklahoma City," I said. "She works at a homeless shelter for families, but she's seeing a lot of abused women with children, lately. Her bishop is willing to fund an abuse shelter, but he needs information on how they work. You got anything written up that I could send to her?"

"I can do better than that," Mitch said. "We've been talking about expanding to OKC. How about you give me your friend's phone number and I'll go speak to the bishop myself. We might be able to do a joint venture so that it doesn't cost them or us as much as it would to do it individually."

"That would be great, Mitch," I said. I gave him Sabrina's work number and he said he would call right away.

Yep. Cassie was getting stuff done today!

There weren't any other important messages, so I started browsing through the posts. I'm a sucker for cat videos, of course, and I've followed so many of them that they take up half the page most days. I laughed out loud at a few of them, and then—it seemed like only seconds later—I heard the bell on the door jingle.

I quickly closed out Facebook and brought up my professional screen, then made sure I was positioned just right for the first meeting. I had my desk set up so the door into my office was to my right, and I always kept my face turned toward my computer monitor, which was on the left side of my desk. When people first came in, all they saw was my "pretty side," and I kept Freda hidden away until she was going to have the most positive impact.

A couple of minutes later, Angie escorted Charlotte Waters into my office. I pretended to be doing something on the computer and pointed at the chair in front of my desk, and Angie ushered her into it, then put the intake she had done on my desk and went back to her own.

"Hi, I'm Cassie," I said. "You're Charlotte?"

"Yes, ma'am," she said politely. "I don't know if I really need to be here or not, but I just thought it couldn't hurt to come in and ask a few questions. Right?"

"Of course not," I said. "So, tell me about your situation. Are things getting pretty bad?"

From the corner of my eye, I could see that she nodded.

"Yeah, sometimes," she said. "Chuck and I have been married for almost eight years, and he's always been a little rough around the edges. I used to say that was one of the things I loved about him, but in the last year or two, he's gotten—I don't know, maybe worse isn't the exact right word, but he seems to get mad a lot more lately. And it's usually over little things, you know, like if I forget to put the salt and pepper on the table, or the toilet paper roll gets too small, silly stuff like that."

"I see," I said. "What form does his anger usually take?"

"I'm sorry, what form? I don't know what you mean."

"I mean, does he give you dirty looks, does he yell at you, does he hit you?"

She grimaced. "All of that, sometimes. I mean, he doesn't hit me all the time, but he has a few times. Usually, he just yells and sometimes he throws things around the house." She bit her bottom lip for a second. "He broke the TV last week, from throwing an ashtray at it. Put a big crack in the screen, and then he got mad about that, said it was my fault because I made him mad in the first place." She licked her lips. "He did hit me that time. I still have to put makeup on my eye."

I had noticed the thick makeup, but I wanted her to tell me what was going on. "How often does he resort to violence, Charlotte? Does it happen once a week, once a month?"

She hesitated for a couple of seconds. "It used to be just once in a while, once every couple months or so, but now it's once, sometimes twice in a week."

"Have you ever needed medical care after one of those

episodes?" I asked. "Ever had to go to the emergency room or make a doctor's appointment because he hit you?"

"Well, I went to the emergency room once. He hit me pretty hard, that day, and they said I had a concussion."

"But you didn't tell them that your husband had hit you, did you?"

She lowered her eyes to the floor and shook her head. "No. I said I tripped over a shoe on the floor and bashed my face on the coffee table."

"And did the nurse believe you?"

She shook her head again, still keeping her eyes down. "No, she kept asking if somebody had hurt me. I just smiled and said no, I'm just a klutz, that's all."

"Okay," I said. "What you're telling me is that there has always been some form of anger or violence in your marriage, but that it is accelerating lately. He's gone from just yelling at you to hitting you, from hitting you once every couple of months to hitting you once or twice a week, and those are common patterns. What they mean is that the process is going to continue, and it will accelerate even further. Pretty soon, he'll be hitting you every other day, maybe even every day. When that becomes commonplace, then he might start actually beating you, hitting you over and over. If you let it go that far, then sooner or later you're going to end up in the hospital or the cemetery."

She looked up at me suddenly. "Oh, I don't think he'd ever..."

"Neither did I," I said, and then I turned and looked straight at her. Her mouth fell open when she got her first look at Freda. "I had a fiancé who seemed like the greatest guy in the world at first, but then he started getting rough.

He had a stressful job, and he started coming home and taking that stress out on me. Things continued until I reached the point where I knew I had to leave, and he wasn't happy about it. He tracked me down and took me and a friend who was trying to help me out to an old cabin, and then a friend of his poured gasoline on us and struck a match. I survived; my friend didn't. My fiancé was actually a cop, so nobody would've believed he would ever do something like this. If I had died, he would have gotten away with it."

Yeah, yeah, I know I altered the story a bit. Trust me, I felt guilty when I started doing it, but most women can't relate to my finding out Mike was a murderer. When I just say that the abuse accelerated until I decided to leave and this was the result, it strikes home with most of them pretty quickly. Call me a fibber if you want, but if it saves one woman's life, or one child's, then I'll take whatever punishment the good Lord decides to give me for it.

"Oh, my God," Charlotte said. "And this is normal, this pattern you're talking about? Men like this just keep getting worse?"

"In far too many cases, they do," I said. "Why do you think there are so many headlines about women being murdered by their husbands and boyfriends, even after they get restraining orders against them? Violence is addictive, Charlotte, and like any other addictive substance, the more you use it, the more you need. Do you have children?"

She nodded slowly. "Yeah, two boys."

"And does he hit them, as well?"

A tear suddenly appeared on her cheek. "Sometimes," she said. "He whips them, you know, with the belt. Sometimes—sometimes I make him stop, but then he just gets mad at me."

She lowered her eyes again and I got a funny feeling. "Charlotte? Does he hit you with that belt?"

She nodded, and took a shuddering breath. "Yes, sometimes," she said. "If I get in the way when he's whipping one of the boys, then he uses it on me. He hits my legs, and sometimes my back with it."

"Charlotte, when you came in here, you said you weren't sure if you needed to be here at all. Let me tell you that you definitely do. Tell me this, what time does Chuck get off work today?"

"Oh, he gets off at seven, tonight. This is his day to work late, he's a car salesman."

"Okay, I just wondered. You see, this situation is only going to get worse, and it honestly could end up with you or one of your children seriously injured or dead. Now, we need to fill out some paperwork so that we can start talking about the best way to get you out of it. Are you ready?"

She wiped away her tears and looked at me again, then started to say something. She opened her mouth to speak, but nothing came out, and suddenly the tears were flowing again and she just nodded her head.

I turned to my computer and started asking her all the questions that were on the intake forms I had to complete, typing in her responses as she gave them to me. When we got to the abuse history form, I was shocked to find out that she had been making things sound less terrible than they really were. By the time she was finished, I knew that action had to be taken immediately.

One of the things I learned while we were completing

the forms was that her husband, Chuck, had just the night before decided that both of the boys needed punishment. He had made them drop their jeans, kneel in front of their sofa and bend over it in just their underwear, then stood behind them and swung the belt like a whip, and the boys screamed as the belt lashed them over and over. Charlotte said she counted more than forty times, and then overcame her own fear to get in the way. This time, miraculously, Chuck simply threw the belt down and walked away, but she spent an hour cleaning the boys up and treating their bottoms, where welts were actually seeping blood.

"Okay, Charlotte, here's the thing," I said immediately after she signed the statement. "I have no choice but to notify the police about these incidents, and I can guarantee you that Chuck is about to be arrested for child abuse. He will also be charged with abusing you, but the child abuse is the more serious offense in the eyes of the law. Our DA is very good, and she doesn't put up with this type of stuff. The best he can hope for might be a plea bargain that will get him less than fifteen years. Now, I would advise you to go home and get your children and let me put you somewhere safe for tonight. By tomorrow, you should be able to go home again. He won't be able to make bail for at least a few days, so that will give us time to decide on the next move."

"He's going to go to jail?" she asked. "But, is that really necessary? I mean, when he gets out, he's going to be so mad..."

"If he gets out on bail, I'll have you hidden away some-where safe," I said. "However, he's going to do time, and the judge may set the bail high enough he can't reach it. I can assure you that we're going to ask for that, because there's no doubt he presents a danger to you and your children. Now, like I said, I don't have any choice but to report it right now. If you do anything to warn him, they'll be coming after you, as well, and your children will end up in foster care."

She shook her head vigorously. "I'm not going to warn him," she said. "I just don't want him to be able to find me if he gets out of jail. You can really hide me away somewhere, me and the boys?"

"I can, and I will. Now, hold on, I've got to call the police right now."

I picked up my desk phone and hit the speed dial button for Detective Alicia Perkins. She wasn't in her office, so I dialed her cell number.

"Perkins," she said as she answered, and I quickly filled her in on Chuck Waters and the situation. She asked me to email her the abuse history and said she would get back to her office within ten minutes. She would need another half hour to get a warrant for Chuck's arrest, but he should be arrested before he could even get off work. I told her that I was going to put Charlotte and her kids out at NB for the night, just in case they had any trouble finding him, and she promised to let me know as soon as he was in custody.

I explained all of this to Charlotte, and she alternated between crying and thanking me for a couple of minutes.

"Charlotte," I said, "you need to go get your kids and come right back here. I'm going to make arrangements for a place for you to stay tonight, a place where he won't be able to get to you no matter what. Can you go get the boys by yourself, or would you like me to come with you?"

She stared at me for a couple of seconds, then finally asked me to come along. I gave her my best smile and said I would be glad to, then got up out of my chair. I let her lead me out to her car, then climbed into the passenger seat while she got behind the wheel.

It was a thirty-minute drive to her place, and the boys were sitting in the living room playing video games on the TV. She walked in and told them that they were going to stay somewhere else for the night, and that their father was probably going to jail because of the way he beat them. The two boys looked at one another for a few seconds, then turned back to their mother and began cheering.

As much as I'm proud whenever I get a family out of a situation like that, it still breaks my heart to see children who fear or hate their parents. I think back to my own childhood and the very rare spankings I got, spankings that I definitely deserved at the time, and I thank God above that I have the parents that He gave me.

FIVE

I CALLED MITCH FROM MY CELL PHONE AND TOLD him about Charlotte and her two sons, and he told me to bring them on out. There were those who thought I got preferential treatment at New Beginnings, but I didn't really think so. Other abuse centers placed people there as well, but if I got any kind of special consideration, it was probably because I had caught the bomber who had blown up their building sometime back.

Okay, the twenty thousand dollars I had donated toward the reconstruction probably didn't hurt, either.

I rode out with Charlotte to get them settled in, and then Mitch had their shuttle driver give me a ride back to my office. I got back right at four o'clock, and was surprised to find the door locked. It took a second to remember that Angie had asked to leave work early that day, so I fished out my key and opened the door. I went into my office and found Rick Lancaster's phone number, waited a few more minutes and then dialed it.

"Go for Rick," he said as he answered.

"Mr. Lancaster, my name is Cassie McGraw and I'm a private investigator. I was wondering if I might meet up with you to talk about an old friend of yours, Harold Logan."

"Harold? Harold Logan? Hell, he's dead."

"Yes, I've heard that," I said. "How would you feel if I told you I've come across evidence that he's actually alive, and has taken his children and hidden somewhere to keep them away from their mother?"

Lancaster laughed. "Are you serious? Geez, that bastard. I can't say I'd put anything past him, but that does sound a bit far-fetched, you know. Way I heard it, he and the kids burned to death."

"Yes, I do know," I said. "However, it turns out that staging their deaths wouldn't really be all that difficult to accomplish, and I know that he had a special account set up with money that is sending checks out every month. They go through some pretty serious rigmarole to hide where the checks go, but there's not much doubt in my mind that he's collecting the cash. Now, everything I know about the kids suggests that they were happy and wouldn't necessarily want to get away from their mom, so I have to think he didn't give them much choice in the matter. Does that still sound like the guy you know?"

"Hell, yeah," Lancaster said. "Hank hated his wife, but you probably already know that. I know he had a girlfriend, but I'm not sure who she was. If he faked all that and disappeared, you might want to try tracking her down. Two birds with one stone, right?"

"Already did, but he didn't take her along. Looks like he may have dumped her at the same time he dumped the wife.

Would you have any idea where he might want to go, if he was going to start over?"

"Me? No, not anyplace in particular. Well, let me think, now... You know, Hank was always one of those survivalist types. He liked taking the kids out into the forest on camping trips, but he liked doing it the hard way; no tents or sleeping bags, and whatever they ate had to come from the woods or the water. He used to say everything we need can be had from the earth, all we have to do is learn where to look. If he disappeared, he's probably living in a cabin in Wyoming or Montana, someplace like that, with no electricity or phones. He said modern technology was going to end up killing off the human race, sooner or later, and the only hope we had was if we went back to the way things were done a hundred years ago."

I mentally groaned. If this guy was that far off the grid, he could prove impossible to locate.

But Rick wasn't done. "Something else," he said. "Hank worked here as a nurse, but he's also a naturopath, a doctor who uses natural remedies rather than chemical medications. He was always trying to get the hospital board to accept some naturopathic treatments for some of the patients here. Wherever he's at, I would just about bet he'll be working in that line."

"Thank you," I said. "Can you think of anything else that might help me find him?"

"Not off the top of my head," he said, "but I'll save your number in case I do. You said your name was Kathy?"

That's a pretty common mistake. "No, it's Cassie, Cassie McGraw."

"Oh, sorry. Wait a minute, Cassie McGraw? You're the one who caught the bomber a while back, right?"

Gee, thanks, newspapers. "Yeah, that's me," I said with a groan. "And yes, that was my picture they put on the front page."

He was quiet for a moment, and I thought maybe I had gone a little too far with the snarkiness, but then he chuckled. "Then you're pretty awesome," he said. "I worked a burn unit for a couple of years, and I've seen way too many people give up on life after a bad burn. You obviously didn't, so good for you."

I smiled. "Thank you," I said. "Listen, I really appreciate your help. If you do think of anything else, please call."

"I'll be sure to," he said. "Good luck, Cassie McGraw."

He hung up, so I put the phone back in its cradle. What he had said about not giving up on life had been simple, but it felt like high praise. I knew what he meant about people giving up, because I had seen it. When I was in the burn unit in St. Louis, there were several others there with me. Most of them weren't burned nearly as badly as I was, but they acted like their lives were over. Some of them didn't even have facial scars, and I just couldn't see why they would be so willing to give up and hide themselves away.

Oh, well. I'm only responsible for my own life, right?

Hey! What about me? I heard Abby's voice ask. It wasn't really her, of course, just that part of my subconscious mind that still thought I was responsible for what happened to her. I mentally assured her that I would never, ever forget her, and then closed up the office and walked over to the shop.

Dex and Jimmy were in the process of closing up when

I got there. I told Dex about my appointment with Donna Kemp, and he suggested we head on down to Grizzly's and have dinner before she got there. Grizzly's has a full kitchen and some of the best food you can get in Tulsa. My personal favorite was either the prime rib sandwich or the Western-style pot roast; I never could make up my mind.

Jimmy was going to Nicole's for dinner, so he volunteered to finish locking up. Dex and I thanked him and headed out the door, but instead of going to the Mustang, Dex led me toward his roll-off truck, the one he used for hauling cars.

"We gotta take the truck tonight," he said. "Remember me telling you about Vince Lambert's Camaro this morning?"

"Yeah," I said. "Did he bring it in?"

Dex chuckled. "He tried," he said. "He called me about an hour ago and said he made it less than a mile after leaving his place before the engine threw a rod. I told him to leave it where it was and I'd come pick it up tonight."

My jaw dropped. "He blew the engine?" I asked. "Oh, I bet he was furious."

"Not really. That engine was going on the scrap pile, anyway—it's just an old six-cylinder. We're putting in a new crate motor with about five hundred horsepower. I'm just saving him the cost of the tow bill by picking it up for him."

I rolled my eye. "Still, it had to be a pain to have the engine blow up when he just got the car."

"Probably more an embarrassment than a pain," Dex said. "Heaven only knows how many people saw him stranded on the side of the road in a beat-up old car. Considering he's got the biggest Chevy dealership in the state, an awful lot of people would recognize him."

I grinned. "Yeah? But wait till they see what you do with that Camaro. It won't be embarrassing then."

We got to Grizzly's a few minutes later and Dex found a place to park the truck near the back of the lot. It meant we had to walk a little further, but that didn't bother me any.

The hostess, a girl named Bethany, smiled as we came in and asked if we were alone.

"We are at the moment," I said, "but somebody should be joining us in an hour or so, just for a drink. We came ahead so we could grab a bite to eat."

"Okay, follow me," she said. She led us to a table in a corner behind the salad bar, probably about as private as it's possible to get in there. We each ordered a beer and I went for the prime rib sandwich with steak fries while Dex ordered hot wings.

On weekends, Grizzly's is one of the hottest clubs in town, but weeknights are primarily about quieter socializing. There were no live bands during the week, but the place sported an honest-to-goodness antique Wurlitzer jukebox, the kind with forty-five rpm records in it, and I was rather notorious for dropping quarters into that machine. It was filled with older country music for the most part, the kind of stuff I grew up on. While we waited for the food to arrive, I dropped a couple of bucks on Garth Brooks, Alan Jackson, Randy Travis and Dolly Parton.

A few people headed toward the dance floor once the music started to play, and Dex gave me a look that asked if I wanted to join them, but I shook my head.

"I'm good," I said. I told him what I had learned from

Rick Lancaster, and he went into deep thought. I always know when he's in deep thought, because he tends to chew on the inside of his cheek. "What?" I asked. "You're thinking something, what is it?"

"You said the guy mentioned Wyoming or Montana," he said. "I was just thinking that there are a lot of places in both those states where you can go miles and miles without ever seeing a house, and that's just on the main highways. This guy could be out in the middle of nowhere."

"Yes, I thought of that," I said. "On the other hand, if he's working as a natural doctor, then he has to have a way to get patients. I'm thinking he might be in some small town or something."

"That would make sense," Dex said. "You know, there are a lot of people who have gone into that part of the country looking for a way to get out from under what they consider government oppression. There are parts of either of those states that probably don't see a police car once every five years, and whole communities of freedom-lovers have sprung up in some places. I'm thinking there might be a way to get a line on some of them, maybe find out if they have a naturopath in the area."

I narrowed my eye. "Intriguing thought," I said. "And how would one go about getting a line on such communities? Any ideas?"

"There are lots of survivalist forums on the Internet. Not everybody who wants to shun government is willing to give up email, and it's a great way to share information. We could post on some of those forums about how we're looking for someplace to settle, someplace where we don't have to worry about Big Brother watching every move we make, but we want a place that has a naturopathic doctor or clinic." He shrugged. "There might be lots of them, so I don't know if this is really helpful or not."

"It can't hurt. Maybe we'll stumble across one of those doctors who has a couple of kids and just moved to town a year ago."

A waitress brought our food and we settled in to eat. One of the things I love about the prime rib sandwich is that it's got a half-inch-thick slab of prime rib tucked between two huge slices of freshly baked bread, and I'm sure I've mentioned before that burn victims need to consume a lot of calories. That's because we've lost a lot of fat and have a hard time keeping our core temperature up. We burn up the calories pretty fast just regulating the thermostat. I keep some high-calorie granola bars in my purse all the time, just for backup.

Of course, we also get in the habit of eating quickly, because we're usually pretty hungry by the time we sit down to eat. Dex went through eighteen wings in the time it took me to consume the sandwich and a couple of dozen really big fries.

By the time we finished eating and the plates had been cleared away, it was just six o'clock. Somebody put more quarters in the jukebox and Dex grabbed my hand. I rolled my eyes and pretended to resist, but then I let him pull me up out of my chair and onto the dance floor.

Three songs later I protested that I was worn out and we went back to our table. Dex and I were both grinning, and I already had a few frisky ideas of my own in mind for later that night. We each sat and nursed another beer while we waited for Donna, and it was only ten minutes later when I saw Bethany pointing us out to a woman who looked like she was probably in her late thirties.

She approached us slowly and Dex rose to his feet. "Donna?" he asked. "This is Cassie, and my name is Dex. Please have a seat."

Donna looked nervous, so I tried to keep Freda under control as I gave her a smile. "Thanks for coming, Donna," I said. "I really do appreciate it."

She bit her bottom lip, but then sat down in the chair beside mine. The hostess must have taken her drink order, because a waitress brought it over just then. "Okay," she said. "Well, I'm here. What do you want to talk about?"

"Look, first I want you to know that I don't judge," I said. "I don't feel like I have the right to judge anybody else, because I know just how messed up I can be at times. The thing is, I'm looking for Harold Logan, and you likely know him pretty well. I'm pretty sure he's still alive in spite of the death certificate that was issued for him, and it looks like he took his kids and disappeared. No matter how you feel about Harold, I'm sure you can understand that his wife wants to see her children again."

I'll give her credit, she was looking me straight in the eye the whole time I was talking. That's hard for anybody to do, but especially when the circumstances could be stressful.

"I won't say I can't understand that," she said slowly. "On the other hand, one of the reasons Harold wouldn't leave his wife for me is because he didn't think she could actually take care of the kids properly. He said he couldn't run out on them, because their mother drank a lot and had a really bad temper."

I considered what she was saying, but it was the first I'd

heard about any kind of drinking problem or anger issues. "Did you ever see any evidence of those problems?" I asked.

She bit her lip again. "Well, not directly, I suppose. She did call him occasionally when we were together, and he always said she was drinking or really angry. A lot of times, he would say he had to go after one of those calls, even if we hadn't..."

She made a facial shrug and I let it slide. It was pretty obvious what she meant, anyway.

"I understand Harold was a fan of nature," I said. "Do you know anything about that?"

"Oh, yeah," he said. "He used to talk about what we would do if he ever got away from his wife, and one of the things he wanted was a log cabin in the middle of nowhere. He wanted to make his own electricity and live off the grid, away from cities and anyplace that was crowded."

"He wanted to make his own electricity? I was under the impression that he would prefer to live without it."

"Oh, no," she said. "His big hang-up was cell phones and computers, not electricity. He was convinced that cell phone and Wi-Fi signals were causing brain tumors and other kinds of cancer, and he wanted to live somewhere out of reach of such things, but he didn't want to give up electric lights, TV, stuff like that. He said he had been trying to talk his wife into it for years, but she wouldn't hear of it, and that's what caused a lot of the problems between them."

I nodded as if I understood. "Okay. Do you have any idea where he might've wanted to go if he decided to live out this dream?"

She shrugged. "He talked about a lot of places," she said. "He talked about places in Tennessee, Kentucky, Montana,

Idaho—lots of places, I can't really remember them all. Any place where he could be at least forty miles from the nearest cell tower."

That certainly didn't narrow things down for me. "Donna, did he ever talk to you about any plan to disappear? We know he had to have been planning for at least a couple of years, because he had set up an account that his wife didn't know about, and that account makes payments every month to someone. We figure it's most likely to him, but they go through a process that makes it hard to find out where they end up."

She bit her lip again, and glanced around as if making sure no one was paying attention to us. "He—he did mention it a couple of times, but mostly just like it was some kind of daydream. He talked about how if he could find a way to take the kids and disappear, his wife would never be able to find him and we could eventually be together."

I stared into her eyes for a moment. "Donna, has he been in contact with you?"

"No," she said. "Until you called me today, I firmly believed he was really dead. Now—now I wonder why I haven't heard from him. I guess maybe I wasn't as important to him as I thought I was, right?"

"I know that's gotta be hard," I said sympathetically. "I was told earlier today that Harold is actually a doctor? A natural doctor of some kind?"

"A naturopath," she said. "Herbal remedies, that kind of stuff. That's something he always wanted to do, open his own practice, but he said his wife threw a fit every time he brought it up. She said they needed his paycheck from the hospital, but I don't know why. She made five times as much as he did."

I thought about what other questions I should ask, and something suddenly struck me. Maggie Logan was about five foot ten, tall and willowy with long dark hair and brown eyes. Donna Kemp was a dishwater blonde with blue eyes, but she was only about five foot three and just a bit on the chunky side. Appearance-wise, the two women couldn't be much more different.

"You and Mrs. Logan are exact opposites in appearance," I said. "Did Harold ever mention what his preference might be, when it comes to women? I apologize for the question, but I'm curious."

She grinned. "Don't worry about it," she said. "He always told me he liked me just the way I was, but I noticed he was often looking at other women even when we were together. If he had a preference, it was probably for small women with short blonde hair. That's who I always caught him looking at, anyway. Whenever I asked him about it, he always said whoever it was reminded him of somebody." She sounded cynical with that last bit.

"Okay, just one more question," I said. "Did you ever, at any time, get the feeling Harold might have presented a danger to his children, or anyone else?"

She blinked. "His kids? No way, he adored them. His wife, now, that's another matter. He used to tell me that he wished he had the courage to get rid of her, but he just didn't have it in him. He even joked once about trying to find a hit man, but I told him I didn't ever want to hear anything like that again. If you asked me if I thought he might be a danger to her, I'd have to say it was possible, but not his kids. They were his life."

"I was told earlier that he actually hated his wife," I said. "Does that sound right to you?"

"Absolutely," she replied. "As a matter of fact, he came right out and said so quite often. 'I hate her guts,' he would say, or 'God, I hate that woman.' That one was usually after she called him."

"Did he ever say why he hated her so much? Ever give a reason?"

She shrugged one shoulder. "What do men always say? She didn't understand him, she was always angry at him, she had to have everything her way, he was always having to kiss her ass... One time, when she called and he said he had to go, I asked him why he was always trying to placate her. I mean, whenever she called, all I would hear out of him was 'yes, honey,' or 'I'm sorry, honey.' I asked him point-blank why he didn't just tell her he was busy or something, but—well, he said it was because he was trying to avoid conflict in front of the kids, but I actually got the impression he was scared of her."

I blinked. "He was scared of her? As in, physically?"

She shook her head. "I don't know for sure, but I don't think so. Maybe he was afraid she'd kick him out, or something. I mean, let's face it, with the money she made they were living pretty high on the hog. Harold drove a Beemer, one of those little convertibles. He couldn't afford anything close to that lifestyle on his hospital salary."

"Donna, did you ever meet his kids?" I asked.

She gave a half smile. "A couple of times," he said. "He took them over to Frontier City in Oklahoma City one time, and had me meet them there. He told the kids I was just a friend, and we hung out together for the whole day. That happened twice, the summer before he disappeared."

"How would you say he got along with the kids? Did they act happy, or did they seem distant from him?"

"They seemed pretty happy, to me," she said. "His daughter, Jody, I think she was about eleven at the time, she got me to go on some rides with her and actually asked me if I liked her dad. I laughed it off and said we were just friends, but I got the feeling she was suspicious. Harold said not to worry about it when I asked, and I guess she never said anything to her mother about me being with them. But if you asked me if they were happy with their dad, I would have to say they were."

I tried to think of anything else I should ask her, but I was coming up blank. "Okay," I said. I took one of my cards out of my purse and gave it to her. "Donna, thank you so much for coming, and if you think of anything else that might help me find them, please call and let me know. I would really appreciate it."

She took the card and finished her drink, then got to her feet and looked at me once again. "If you do find him," she said, "please let me know. I'd just like to know for sure that he's alive, you know?"

"I will," I told her. "Thanks again for coming."

Donna turned and walked away, and I looked at Dex. "Well? Impressions?"

"I think she was being honest with you," he said. "On the other hand, you've got to consider the fact that she's just found out that her lover ran off without her. There could be a little bit of 'woman scorned' in the things she said to you."

"Yeah, maybe," I said. "What I'm thinking about is the fact that both she and Rick Lancaster said Harold hated his wife, and Donna thinks he was somehow afraid of her. Is it possible we could be looking at a case where the guy was simply trying to get away from another kind of abusive situation?"

Dex bit the inside of his cheek again. "Maybe," he said. "On the other hand, this is a guy who would go into the forest and live off the land. Most guys like that aren't too terribly afraid of anybody, in my experience. Could be she's right, and he was afraid of losing a meal ticket. That might even explain him setting up a hidden account, in order to have plenty of money for when he decided to split."

"Yeah. That could be it." I sat there for a few seconds, just thinking. "Maybe I should look into Mrs. Logan a little deeper. If there was some kind of abuse going on, I want to know about it."

SIX

I PAID THE CHECK AND WE HEADED OUT TO THE truck. We still had to go pick up that blown-up Camaro, so Dex headed toward where it had been left on the side of the road and I sat there on the passenger seat, just thinking over everything I had learned.

Suddenly, I remembered that I had asked Alfie to do some background digging on Maggie Logan, as well. He was going to send me an email, he said, but I had been so busy with Charlotte that I had forgotten to check. I took out my phone and opened my email, scrolled through the list for a minute and found it.

He'd been thorough. There were two attachments to the email, and I began reading through the first one, which was on Harold. He'd grown up an only child, which I'd already known, in a little Oklahoma town called Stillwell, but the family moved to Tulsa when he was thirteen. Harold graduated from high school just after turning eighteen and had then joined the Army, where he received training as a combat medic. He spent four years on active duty, including two tours in Afghanistan, then had come home and gone on to college in Dallas. The guy actually pulled a double major, spending six years to earn doctorates in both Nursing Practice and Naturopathy.

After graduation, he had gone to work first at a hospital in Little Rock, Arkansas, spending three years there before getting hired at OSU. He had come back to Oklahoma because his father had died of a heart attack, only weeks after his mother had been diagnosed with stage IV colon cancer. He met Maggie, who was five years younger than him, shortly after arriving in Tulsa. They dated for six months, and then were married only three weeks after his mother passed away. Their first child, Jody, was born a year and a half later, and Ryan came along when Jody was almost five.

Harold had started at OSU as an ER nurse, but had transferred to the surgery department a year later. He had been there ever since, and was considered one of their top employees all the way up to the day he supposedly died. He had no criminal record of any kind, and had never even been in trouble as a teenager as far as Alfie had been able to determine.

I opened the other attachment, on Maggie.

Maggie Easton had been born in Germany while her father was deployed there in the Army. She was almost a year old by the time they returned to the United States, settling in her father's hometown of Columbus, Ohio. A brother and sister were born over the next three years, making her the eldest of three children. She had grown up in Columbus, attending high school and earning several awards for art, then had gone to the Massachusetts Institute of Technology for the architectural program. It was during her first year in college that her parents and both siblings were killed in a tragic auto accident. Maggie had thrown herself into her studies and had graduated at the top of her class.

She had been hired by the architectural firm of Benson-Dawes and Associates immediately after graduation, and started as an architectural assistant in their Baltimore office. Two years later, she was transferred to their Tulsa office as a lead architect on commercial developments. Company records indicated she was the youngest lead architect they had ever had.

Her transfer to Tulsa happened about a month before Harold accepted the job at OSU. It almost looked like divine intervention had brought them together, and her bio on the company website mentioned Harold and her children, expressing how proud she was of them.

Unlike Harold, however, Maggie Logan did have a minor criminal record. While she was in Baltimore, she had been charged with misdemeanor assault against another woman in a fight over a man. During an argument, she had apparently pushed the other woman, resulting in the arrest. She had hired an attorney and the charges were reduced to creating a public nuisance. She paid a small fine and the matter was settled. Then, just before being transferred to Tulsa, she had been arrested a second time over a road rage incident. Someone had sideswiped her car and Maggie had chased the person down and tried to force them out of the car while making numerous threats. Once again, she hired an attorney and got the charges reduced to simple assault. She was ordered to anger management training and the charge was dismissed once the class was completed.

Alfie had gone through her social media accounts, however, and had found quite a few instances of anger and verbal threats that she sent to other people. The woman still seemed to have something of an anger management problem, though she apparently had learned to keep it below the point that would result in police involvement.

Because of these things, Alfie had dug just a bit deeper and found that she had been reprimanded without citation by police officers twice here in Tulsa, during arguments in public places with her husband. She had apparently raised her voice and caused a disturbance each time, but the officers involved decided not to charge her with anything. She was warned verbally and released.

Alfie, seeing the anger issues, had then checked into any complaints with Family Services, to see if anyone had ever reported any type of abuse or neglect about her children. There was one report with her name on it, filed by a teacher at the private school the kids attended. The report alleged that Jody had come to school with a mark on her face that the teacher thought came from being slapped. A social worker had spoken with Jody and Maggie, but the final determination was that the report was unfounded. There was no explanation for where the mark actually came from.

I closed the file and told Dex about the things I had learned.

"I can't help wondering," I said, "if it's possible that Mr. Logan actually did what was necessary, or what he felt was necessary, not only for himself but to protect his children. If his wife actually is abusive, I'd be the first one to advise him to get away from her and take the kids with him."

"Yes," Dex said, "but you wouldn't advise him to burn

up some bodies in the process. I'm pretty sure that's a crime, no matter why he did it."

"Yeah, there's that. Probably falls under insurance fraud, at the least. Speaking of that, I wonder if Mrs. Logan collected insurance money when they were reported dead."

Dex nodded. "You know who to call," he said.

I chuckled, then took out my phone and called Alfie.

"Sing me a song," he said. "What's up, princess?"

"Something I forgot to ask you about earlier," I said. "Can you check and see if there was a life insurance payout on Harold Logan and the kids?"

"Nope," he said.

My eye went wide. "You can't?" I asked. "Why not?"

"I mean, nope, there wasn't. I thought of it myself after I sent you off those files earlier, so I checked it out. Life insurance policies on the whole family lapsed a month before the alleged deaths. Seems that somebody forgot to pay the premium, and the company canceled the policies."

"That's interesting," I said. "I was thinking that faking his death would at least constitute insurance fraud, but if there was no claim filed or paid, I guess it wouldn't."

"Nope, sure wouldn't."

"Alfie, what laws did he actually break if he did fake his own death this way? Do you know?"

"Well, I suppose the state of Oklahoma could prosecute him for fraud, because he let people believe he was dead when he wasn't, but they probably wouldn't bother. It might actually be embarrassing. Other than that, the only other thing I could think of might be abuse of a corpse, but if he bought them legally, then they were his property. Theoretically, he could do anything with them that he wanted."

"So, you're telling me that he might not have broken any actual laws?"

"Well, the fire happened in Arizona. You'd have to check out their laws to see if burning the bodies would be an infraction, and I suppose it's possible that deliberately burning his motorhome might be some kind of offense. I know his automotive insurance paid off for the fire department call and all the expenses of cleaning it up and recovering the remains, so there might be an insurance fraud charge there. They might be pretty pissed, but it's possible that would only be a civil case they could bring against him." He yawned in my ear. "I'm not sure there's really any consequences he'd be facing, other than a really ticked off future ex-wife."

"What about parental kidnapping? He took the kids without his wife knowing what was going on."

"Again, depends on the reason. That lady has some issues, and if he honestly believed he was doing what was in the best interest of the children, he might very well have a defense that would convince the DA not to bother prosecuting."

"Wow," I said. "This is a strange case, isn't it?"

"I've seen stranger," Alfie said, "but I'll admit it's been a while. Anything else?"

"No, that's it for now. I'm sure I'll think of something else later."

"Then save it for tomorrow," he said. "I'm thinking about hitting the bed early tonight." The line went dead.

"Turns out Mr. Logan may not be in any real trouble at all," I said. "If he really felt his wife was a danger to the kids, it's possible that nobody would do anything to him."

Dex shook his head. "Seems to me you need to find out more about Mrs. Logan before you take this too far. Cassie, if she was abusing her kids, you don't want to put them back into that situation."

"No, of course not," I said. "But how do I find out for sure if she was?"

"You know who kids confide in?" he asked. "Other kids. You need to find some way to make contact with their friends."

I nodded, but didn't say anything. We had gotten to the Camaro, and Dex was backing the truck up in front of it. He stopped and set the parking brake, got out and worked at the controls to slide the flatbed back and tilt it down, then took a cable and hooked it onto the car. He made sure it was out of gear, then came back to the controls on the side of the truck and pulled the Camaro up onto the bed. It tilted back up and slid forward, and then he hooked the safety chains to make sure it wouldn't fall off.

Forty minutes later, he backed the truck into the parking lot of the shop and locked it up. We closed the gate and got into the Mustang, then headed for home.

Critter was thrilled when we walked in, stropping our legs and weaving in and out between them, meowing the whole time. That was her way of telling me I was late getting home and putting food in her dish, so I went straight to the kitchen and let the can opener sing its song. When I dumped the can into the dish and set it on the floor, Critter decided to forgive me.

It wasn't even eight o'clock yet, so we settled in the living room and binge-watched a few episodes of one of our current favorite shows. It was a slightly goofy police procedural about a guy who could read people so well that everyone thought he was a psychic. I enjoyed the program immensely, but I often wished I was able to read people the way he could. Man, what a difference that ability would make!

Unfortunately, I'm just a farm girl who is pretending to enjoy life in the city. Well, not really pretending; I do like Tulsa, and I've been here long enough now that I'm used to it. I guess I'm just trying to say that I'm nobody special. I don't have any special insights into what makes people tick, other than personal experience. When it comes to cases like the one I was tangled up in now, I was starting to wish for a program so I could tell who the players were.

After the third episode, I remembered the frisky ideas I'd had while we were dancing. It only took me a few minutes to distract Dex from the TV, and then we headed for the bedroom.

The next morning, after a quick repeat of the night before and a shower that almost led to an encore, we opted for breakfast on the way to work. I took care of Critter before we left the house, and then Dex and I each drove our own cars. His classic Mustang always looked great parked beside my new one, and they both got a lot of attention in the parking lot at McDonald's that morning. Three sausage and egg biscuits later, I was ready to face whatever the day was going to bring. I followed Dex until we got to the alley, then pulled in behind my own office while he went on to the shop.

Angie was at her desk and fresh coffee was in the pot. Everything was right with the world as far as I was concerned, so I got a cup and sat down across from Angie.

"So, how was your afternoon?" I asked. "You have a good time with your mom?"

She smiled. "I had a great time," she said. "I actually started remembering some things from when I was younger, stuff I had lost. Mom got excited when I was able to tell her about the last time she took me to see my grandmother before she passed away. I hadn't been able to remember her before yesterday, so it was nice."

"I'm glad," I said. "I think you needed a break. You're feeling better today?"

"I am," she said. "I feel—I feel a little bit more together. Oh, and there were a couple of voice mails when I got here this morning. I'm afraid both of your appointments for today have canceled. They both want to reschedule, so I'll give them a call in a little while."

I sighed. "That's okay," I said. "This case I took yesterday is turning out to be a headache, so I can use the time." I told Angie the basics of what I had learned the day before, and she was appropriately sympathetic.

"My only problem at the moment is how to make contact with the Logan kids' friends," I went on. "I need to know whether those kids were actually afraid of their mom or not. I'm just not sure how to go about finding out who their friends were, let alone how to approach them without setting off alarms in people's heads."

"Didn't they go to a private school?" Angie asked.

I nodded. "Yeah, Clear Skies. I understand it's one of those progressive schools, the kind that let kids learn at their own pace."

Angie's face screwed up in concentration. "I know some-body there," she said. "I'm trying to remember." She sat there for another minute or so and I kept quiet to let her think.

Suddenly her eyes opened and she broke into a smile. "Oh, it's Eric," she said. "Eric Hamilton."

My eyebrow rose slightly. "And who is Eric Hamilton?"

"Eric is their phys ed teacher. I went on a few dates with him, and he came to see me in the hospital. He's a real nice guy, and I bet I could get him to help you out."

She turned to her computer and looked up the number of the school, then started dialing on the office phone. When she got an answer, she asked for Eric, then smiled and gave me a thumbs-up. A moment later, he came on the line.

"Eric? This is Angie, remember me? Okay, great. Listen, I wanted to know if I could ask a favor?" She gave him a brief outline of the case I was working on, stressing the fact that it appeared the deaths of the kids and their father had been staged. "Anyway, Cassie needs to talk to any of the kids who were friends of those two. Do you think there's any way you could help?"

She listened for a second, then told him to hold on. She put the phone on speaker, and asked him to start over.

"I was saying that, officially, I can't give out any kind of information about our students. What I can do, though, is invite Ms. McGraw out to the school to talk to the kids about abuse. I mean, I'm pretty sure all the staff here know who she is, so I should be able to sell it easily. While she's here, I could sort of introduce her to a few of the kids who knew the Logans. Would that help?"

"It sure would," I said. "Eric, this is Cassie McGraw. How soon could you set that up?"

"Hold on a minute," he said. He put the phone on hold,

and we got to listen to some kind of Eastern sitar music. We sat there for about three minutes, and then he came back. "Ms. McGraw? I talked to Doctor Ely, the headmistress, and she says she can put together an assembly at about one o'clock this afternoon. Could you make it then?"

"Sure," I said. "That would be awesome. Do I need to bring anything?"

"Well, the official reason for your visit is to talk to the kids about abusive relationships," he said. "If you've got any literature that might be appropriate, you might bring some along. Other than that, I can't think of anything else."

"I'll be there with bells on," I said. "And thank you. This means a lot."

"No problem. I think the kids could actually benefit from hearing you speak, anyway. A few of them might be in some bad situations at home, but they don't seem to want to talk about it."

"I think you'll find that in every school," I said. "Maybe some of them will open up after I talk to them."

"That's exactly what I'm hoping, and maybe we can help you out with this other case at the same time. I let Doctor Ely know about that, and she told me to just handle it quietly."

We said goodbye and I leaned over and gave Angie a hug. "Angie, that was awesome. Thank you so much."

She blushed. "Just trying to help," she said. "Now, what about literature? We do have some brochures that are directed at kids. Want me to pack some up for you?"

"Yes, please," I said. "I'm going to my office to try to prepare a little speech."

A few hours later, I took a bundle of brochures and got

into my car. Clear Skies was situated well outside the city, and it was going to take me close to an hour to get there. I wanted to make sure I was there on time, so I left a few minutes earlier than I needed to. I called Dex as I was leaving and told him what was going on, adding that I was going to get lunch after my appointment at the school, and he wished me luck.

As I'd said, I left a few minutes early, so I stopped at a coffee shop and hit the drive through, grabbing a large French vanilla cappuccino to drink on the way. I crunched down on a couple of granola bars as well, just to make sure I wouldn't run out of energy halfway through my speech. This was an opportunity to accomplish a couple of things at once, and I wanted to do both of them right.

Kids are the most vulnerable victims of abusive situations, and most of them don't even understand what's happening. In a lot of cases, they assume that whatever is going on is their own fault, and that the abuse is some sort of punishment they deserve. While the same can also be said for a lot of women in bad situations, it's even more devastating for children. As I drove toward Clear Skies, I started thinking about approaching the other schools in the area about doing some sort of program for all of them. I could tailor it for different grade levels, speaking to the kids in ways they would be able to understand.

Abby thought it was a great idea. *You know our mantra,* she said in my head. *If we save one life, it's worth it.*

I had to agree with her. This was an idea I needed to work on, one I needed to bring to reality. Maybe it would make a difference in the lives of some of these kids, if not now, then maybe later when they were adults and found themselves in bad situations.

I arrived at the school with ten minutes to spare, so I took a few extra sips of the cappuccino and then went to find the office. I walked in and introduced myself, and a tall, regal-looking woman came out of another office to meet me.

"Ms. McGraw," she said. "I'm Janine Ely, the headmistress. I can't tell you how much we appreciate you doing this for us."

"I'm delighted to have the opportunity," I said. "It's making me think about offering a program to all the schools around here."

"I think that would be an excellent program," she said. "If there's anything I can do to help you accomplish it, please let me know."

"Well, if this one goes okay," I said, "I could probably use a referral."

She smiled and patted my hand. "And you'll get it," she said. "I think this is something that every school in every community actually needs."

I thanked her, and then she led me toward their auditorium. It wasn't huge, because the school only had about a hundred students. It was set up like a small theater, and there was a chair on the stage that she told me to sit in while I waited.

A few minutes later, the students began filing in. They took their seats as a young man came down toward the stage and motioned for me to approach him.

"Ms. McGraw, I'm Eric Hamilton," he said. "When you finish your presentation, I'll introduce you to some of the kids I think might be able to help."

"I appreciate it," I said.

"No problem, glad to help. Did you bring some literature along? I can pass it out for you, if you like."

I gave him the brochures and he went to sit down. I had suggested he pass them out as I finished up, rather than at the beginning. I wanted them to listen to what I was saying and not be distracted by trying to read the brochures while I spoke.

A minute later, Doctor Ely stepped onto the stage and introduced me. I got up out of the chair and walked to the edge of the stage, where she handed me a microphone.

The kids were staring, and I turned from side to side so they could all get a good view. I wanted them to see not only Cassie McGraw, but Freda Krueger as well. There was some muffled whispering and I even saw a few fingers pointed my way, but I let it go on for a moment before I said anything.

"Hey, kids," I said finally. "My name is Cassie McGraw, and I'm here to talk to you about something that some people find to be an uncomfortable topic. What I want to talk to you about is what we call abusive relationships.

"Now, an abusive relationship is what you have when someone close to you is being mean. If they talk mean to you, or do things that hurt you, that's abusive. It's not a good thing, and it's not something anybody should ever do. There are different kinds of abuse, and I'm going to talk about a few of them.

"But first, I want to ask a question. Do any of you know what I mean when I say verbal abuse?"

Clear Skies was open to students from the first grade to the twelfth, so I was dealing with kids as young as six and as old as eighteen. A number of the older kids raised their hands, probably from about sixth grade up.

"Very good," I said. "Verbal abuse, for those of you who don't know what it means, is when someone is talking really mean. If they are insulting you, if they are calling you names, if they're telling you you can't do something right, if they say you aren't very smart, things like that, that's verbal abuse. People should never talk to you that way. Do any of you have people who treat you that way now?"

A few hands went hesitantly into the air, and I saw some of the teachers making notes.

"When somebody is being verbally abusive, when they are talking mean to you just to be mean, you need to tell someone about it. You need to go to your mom and dad, or your teacher, or somebody who will listen to you. Can y'all do that for me? Can you go to somebody if you're in that kind of situation?"

A lot of voices answered in the affirmative, and I gave them my best smile.

"Okay, that's good. That's real good. Now, let's talk about physical abuse. Physical abuse is when somebody hurts you. One good example of that is me. Can you all see the way I look?"

That time I got more voices, all saying yes. I chuckled at them.

"That's good. The reason I look this way is because I was in an abusive situation once. I was living with my boyfriend, well, my fiancé at the time, and he used to hurt me sometimes. Well, one day I found out he was doing something really, really bad, and I was going to tell on him, tell the police. He got mad at me and he took me somewhere and put gasoline on me and lit it on fire. That's how I got this way. Because of that, I decided I want to try to help people who are in abusive relationships, help them get out of them.

"Now, I hope that most people never end up like me, but sometimes abusive relationships can be even worse, because sometimes people get killed. If someone is hurting you physically, especially if they do it without any reason at all or just because they're mad or having a bad day, that is abuse. I'm not necessarily talking about things like when your mom slaps your hand or pops you on the bottom; sometimes parents do that for discipline, to teach you something. I'm talking about when people hurt you just because they want to, because they're mad or because they feel bad and want to take it out on somebody. Are any of you in a situation like that now?"

Three hands slowly raised into the air, and I saw teachers making notes again.

"If you are in a situation like that, you need to tell someone. You need to tell your mom or dad, or your teacher, somebody who is going to listen. This is very important, so please pay attention to what I'm saying. If somebody is hurting you, you need to tell someone. That's the only way to make it stop. If you don't let anyone know it's happening, nobody can do anything about it. Do you understand?"

They all said they did.

I took a deep breath. "Now, I'm going to talk about something that may embarrass some of you. I'm going to talk about sexual abuse. How many of you know what that is?"

Most of the bigger kids raised their hands, and I saw some of them snickering. A few of the younger kids put their hands up, as well, and I quickly hoped that it was because their parents were smart enough to tell them what to watch out for.

"Okay, very good," I said. "Now, some of you are thinking that sexual abuse is just when people do — well, naughty things. The thing is, that's not all it is. Any time somebody touches you in any way that makes you uncomfortable, you should tell someone. Other than your parents, nobody should ever touch you without your permission. Nobody should ever touch certain parts of you at all, of course," I said, getting a number of snickers out of the crowd, "but even if it's just a matter of touching you on the back, or on your arm or your leg, if it makes you uncomfortable, they should not do it. You have the right to say you don't want to be touched that way, each of you has that right. If someone touches you in any way that makes you uncomfortable, any way that makes you feel bad or scared or nervous or whatever, then what do you need to do?"

I put my hand up to my good ear, and I was rewarded with a hundred kids shouting, "TELL SOMEONE!"

"That's right," I said. "You need to tell someone. You need to tell your mom and dad, or your teacher or any other grown-up who will listen to you. Now, Mr. Hamilton is going to give you some brochures that I brought along. These were written for younger kids, so you older kids will just have to put up with it, but they explain a little more about the different kinds of abuse. And if nobody else will listen to you, then there's a phone number on there that goes to my office. If you feel like you are in an abusive situation and no one will listen, or you're afraid to go to anybody else for any reason, you can call me. This is my job—this is what I do."

SEVEN

ERIC GOT UP AND STARTED PASSING OUT brochures, and a couple of teachers took some to help. Doctor Ely came back on the stage and took the microphone from me.

"Okay, kids," she said, "what do we say to Ms. McGraw?"

"THANK YOU MS. MCGRAW!"

Oh, it was all I could do not to burst into tears. While it was likely that a few of the hands that came up were simply kids who didn't like the way they were being disciplined at home, there was a strong possibility that some of them really were in abusive situations, and they had just taken the first step to dealing with them.

I smiled and waved at all the kids, and then Doctor Ely told them all to stay in their seats for a few minutes. I noticed Eric calling a few of the kids out of their seats, and when he had five of them standing near him, the rest were allowed to go back to their classrooms.

I came down off the stage and walked over toward Eric, and he motioned for me to follow him and the children into a smaller room. There was a table there with several chairs around it, and we all sat down.

"Ms. McGraw, these are Lisa Taylor, Belinda Story, Jeannie Packer, Billy Roberts and Steve Herford. They all knew the Logan kids pretty well. I told them that you wanted to find out a bit more about those kids, and they said they'd be willing to talk to you."

I smiled at the kids. The two boys were younger than the girls, so I suspected that the girls had been friends of Jody and the boys had been buddies with Ryan.

"I really appreciate it," I said. I turned to the girls, first. "You girls knew Jody?"

"Yeah," they all said. Lisa went on, "It was really sad what happened to her."

"Yes, it was," I said. "Can you tell me what she was like? I mean, was she happy, did she ever talk about how things were at home, stuff like that?"

All three of the girls looked at one another, and then Lisa seemed to be silently elected as their spokesperson.

"She was happy most of the time," she said. "She never talked about things at home very much, but she always seemed okay when she did. I think the only thing that really bothered her was that she wanted to go out with Johnny Summers, and her folks said she was too young for that."

"Did she ever talk about her mom?"

"Not a lot," Lisa said. "She talked about her dad sometimes."

"Oh? What did she say about him?"

Lisa giggled. "She used to say he was a butthead," she

said. "She said he was always taking her and her brother out to the woods and making them eat wild plants and fish and rabbits. She said he made her learn how to set traps for rabbits and skin them and everything."

"Eww," I said, because that was the look on the girls' faces. "Really? Did that upset her?"

"I don't think she was upset about it, except maybe the skinning part," Lisa said. "I kinda think she liked it. She just talked about it like it was something weird about her dad." She twisted her mouth like she was thinking for a couple of seconds. "I think the only thing she ever really said about her mom was that her mom and dad argued a lot. Oh, and that her mom would let her go out with Johnny if her dad would agree to it, but he wouldn't."

"Yeah," Jeannie said. "She told me her mom was cool like that."

I turned to Jeannie. "Did she say anything else about her mom?"

Jeannie glanced at Lisa, then shrugged as she turned back to me. "She told me once that her mom let her go to a party while her dad was at work, and I guess they had some pot and some beer. She smoked some and then she got drunk, and somebody called her mom to come get her. She said her mom was real cool about it, didn't get mad or anything, but just told her she shouldn't ever do it again." She grinned. "Jody got so sick that she threw up in her mom's car. She said she didn't ever want to drink beer again."

"Wow," I said, "her mom does sound pretty cool. Did she ever talk about anything else? I mean, was there anything, you know, bad going on in her life?"

All three girls looked at one another again, and then the third girl, Belinda, leaned toward me. "She told me once that she was scared," she said.

"Scared of what? Did she say?"

She shrugged. "It was one time when her mom was working out of town, and we were waiting for our folks to come pick us up after school. She said she was scared to go home. I asked her why she was scared to go home, and she said she just was, and didn't want to talk about it."

I looked into her eyes. "She didn't want to talk about it," I said, "but I get the feeling you might have had some suspicion as to what it was about?"

She shrugged again, then slowly nodded her head. "Jody —sometimes she had these dreams, and they would come true. Like, this one time, she came to school and told me that she dreamed that I fell down while I was running and broke my arm, and a couple days later during gym class, I tripped while we were running around the track and my arm broke when I fell."

The other girls were nodding, and each of them commented that they were aware of Jody's prophetic dreams.

"So, are you saying she had some kind of dream that was making her scared to go home?" I asked.

Belinda nodded. "She told me that morning that she had a dream about a fire, and that in her dream, she and her dad and Ryan were all dead. I think she was afraid that it might come true, because her mom wasn't at home."

"I see," I said. "Was there anything else any of you can tell me about her?"

All three of them shook their heads, so I turned to the two boys.

"What about Ryan? Did he talk much about how things were at home?"

Steve nodded. "All the time," he said. "He talked about the camping trips, and how much he loved going on them. One day, he showed us how he makes rabbit traps. They're like sticks to hold open a string, and the rabbit runs through the string and gets it caught around its neck. It can't get away, so then Ryan would cut its head off and skin it, so they could roast it over a fire."

"He didn't like his mom, though," Billy said. "He said his mom was always yelling at his dad, and he didn't like it."

"Did she yell at him, too?" I asked.

The boys looked at one another. "I don't think so," Billy said. "He just didn't like the way she yelled at his dad all the time."

I looked at the kids for a moment, then asked, "Did either of them ever act strange? Like, acting in a way you wouldn't expect them to act?"

Billy nodded, and Lisa spoke up and said, "Yes, sometimes."

I looked at Billy first. "What did Ryan do that you thought was strange?" I asked.

"Well, it's kind of weird," he said. "He used to say that him and his dad were going to go live in the woods forever, but they never did. Then he changed it and said they were going to build a log cabin somewhere and live in it."

I grinned at him. "Really? That almost sounds like fun."

He shrugged. "Yeah, maybe," he said, but he didn't appear convinced.

I turned to Lisa. "What were you going to say?"

"Well," she began, "Jody told me that she wasn't going to have to finish school, because she was going to be a nurse and work with her dad. I told her that being a nurse meant she had to go to school for a long time, like to college, but she said she wouldn't have to because her dad was already teaching her everything she needed to know. I mean, she said she was going to quit school like any time, and be a nurse. I thought that was kind of weird."

"Yes, it does sound strange. Listen, I want to ask a weird question. Have any of you gotten any kind of weird messages that seem to be from Jody or Ryan?"

All five of the kids looked at one another, then they turned their eyes to me and I got the impression they thought I was a little bit crazy. All of them shook their heads in the negative, but something about the way Jeannie did it caught my attention. I didn't want to call her out in front of the others, so I turned to Eric.

"Okay, I think I'm done," I said.

Eric nodded and told the kids they could head back to their classrooms. I waited until they were almost to the door, then I called Jeannie back. The rest of them stopped and looked back at us, but I told them they could go on. I just had one more question for Jeannie.

Jeannie walked back toward me slowly as the rest left the room. She stopped beside the table, but didn't sit down. "Yes, ma'am?"

"Jeannie," I said softly, "when I asked if any of you have heard from Ryan or Jody, you didn't shake your head as quickly as the other kids did. You've heard something, haven't you?"

She looked at the floor and shook her head again. "No, ma'am," she said quietly.

I reached out with my right hand and put a finger under her chin, tilting her face up to look at me. "Jeannie, this could be very important. Have you heard something that makes you wonder if they might still be alive?"

She looked me in the eye for a couple of seconds, then a single tear appeared on her cheek. "I didn't hear anything," she said. "But—I got a message on Facebook, and it was supposed to be from Jody. All it said was, 'I miss you,' and I answered it but no other message ever came."

"And when was that? When did you get that message?"

"It was—I guess it was around Christmas."

I didn't want to tell her that I had reason to believe Jody was still alive, because I didn't want rumors to start that way. "You think somebody got into her Facebook account and was playing games?" I asked.

Her eyes got a little bit bigger as that possibility suddenly seemed feasible to her. "Yes, ma'am," she said. "I think so."

"Well, thanks for telling me about it anyway," I said. "I think you're probably right. You can go now, and thanks again."

She smiled at me, and I could tell that my suggestion had given her some peace. "Yes, ma'am," she said, then turned and walked away.

Eric watched her go, then turned to me. "You think you learned something here today?" he asked.

"Oh, yes," I said. "I found out that Jody, at least, is still alive, and probably Ryan, as well. If their dad was letting them in on his plan to disappear, even just by daydreaming about it out loud, then it's a safe bet that he really did take them with him. He's a naturopath, so if he's running his own little clinic or practice somewhere, his daughter probably is working with him. Knowing that could prove to be the break I need."

"Well, you definitely made an impression on the kids," he said. "All of us have asked before if any of the kids felt like they were in bad situations, and we never got the kind of response you got today."

I grinned. "People have a hard time being dishonest with someone they find frightening," I said. "I've learned to use that to my advantage."

Eric grinned back. "Well, it seems to have worked today. Each of the kids who raised their hands when you asked will be talking to our counselor. If they really seem to be in abusive situations, we will take steps to do something about it."

"Then this has been a good day for all of us," I said. "Listen, you heard what the girls said about Jody having dreams that come true, right?"

"Oh, yes," he said. "Jody's dreams were a topic of conversation among the teachers from time to time. I know it may sound a little hard to believe, but she told Mrs. Riley, her English teacher, that she was going to have to take a trip somewhere all of a sudden and would be gone for a week. Mrs. Riley didn't have any plans to go anywhere, but that evening she got a call that her mother had been in a car accident and was in the hospital. She called Doctor Ely and said she was flying out to California that night, and she came back a week later. There were other incidents like that, but that's the one I remember most."

"Interesting," I said. "Her mother also has dreams like

that, and one of them is what prompted her to hire me. She dreamed the kids were hiding from somebody or something, and that's what convinced her they were still alive."

Eric walked me back to the office, where I thanked Doctor Ely for letting me speak to the kids, and then I headed back out to my car. As soon as I got into it, I called Alfie.

"Hit me with your best shot," he sang.

I couldn't help it, I laughed. "You crack me up," I said. "If you ever just say 'hello,' I'm going to come rushing over there with a gun in my hand because it will mean you're in some kind of trouble."

"Hey, that's a good thought," he said. "If I ever have some crazy idiot holding a gun on me when you call, that's what I'll do. What do you need, princess?"

"A little bit of your time," I said. "I just got to talk to some kids who knew Jody and Ryan, and I picked up on a couple things. I'm starving at the moment, so I'm going to grab some lunch and bring it with me. You want anything?"

"Where are you going?"

"Heck, I don't know, I'm in the middle of nowhere. Probably the first place I see with a drive-up window."

"Then call me when you get there," he said. "I'll figure out what I want then."

He hung up, so I dropped my phone back into my purse and started the car. It was a bit of a drive back into town, but I was on some pretty decent and curvy back roads, so I pressed down on the gas pedal and enjoyed the ride.

Twenty minutes later, I spotted a cluster of fast-food restaurants, so I grabbed my phone and hit redial.

"Talk fast, I'm trying to hide a body," Alfie said.

When I stopped laughing, I told him which restaurants I could see. There were two burger joints, a taco place and some fried chicken outfit I'd never heard of.

"Chicken? Yeah, just grab a bucket of chicken, and maybe some biscuits or something, or French fries. We can munch on that."

"Okay, that sounds good," I said. "I'll be there in a bit."

The chicken place didn't have biscuits or French fries, but they did have something called roasted potato wedges. I bought a twelve-piece box of chicken with a dozen of the potato wedges, and tried. one as soon as they gave me my order. Those potato wedges were delicious, they were sort of baked in the same coating they put on the chicken. Really good. I ate three of them before I got to Alfie's place.

We sat down in his living room and ate at the coffee table, like usual. While we ate, I told him about visiting the school and my conversation with the five kids who had known the Logan children.

"So, let me get this straight," Alfie said. "The girl, Jody, thinks her mom is cool and her dad is too strict, but she seems to be closer to her dad, and the boy thinks his mom is mostly just an angry witch and idolizes his dad. Sound about right?"

"Yes, and both of those are pretty normal. Girls tend to be fans of their mothers while almost getting into some kind of hero worship with their fathers, and boys usually see Mom as a limiting factor on the things that the guys want to do."

"Listen, I may not have your psychology degrees, but I know a lot about human nature. None of this is surprising to me. Now, about the girl who got the Facebook message. You think it was real?"

"I think it probably was. Most likely what happened was that Jody somehow got access to the Internet, maybe a smartphone or something, and sent a message to the girl she felt closest to. It was probably a one-time fluke and she never got a chance to see if there was a response. If I could find out where it came from..."

"Say no more," Alfie said. "Gimme another drumstick. When we finish eating, I'll get into the girl's account and see where the message originated. There's a location tag on every message."

We spent a few more minutes eating, then he hopped up on his stool in his computer wonderland. His fingers flew over the keyboards and then he turned to me with a grin.

"Well, it looks like Jody got into her Facebook account on the twenty-first of December. That was almost six months to the day after they disappeared a year ago, and it was done on a public access computer in Cheyenne, Wyoming."

My eye shot open. "Cheyenne? Can you find out if there are any naturopaths around the area?"

"Another minute," he said. "As a matter of fact, there are more than a dozen naturopathy clinics in Cheyenne itself, which is surprising considering there's only sixty-three thousand people in the whole city. Now, if we expand out fifty miles, that number grows to more than a hundred. Some of them are probably no longer in business, but they still get listed."

I frowned. "Six months after they'd disappeared, they were in Cheyenne. Sounds to me like they're probably living somewhere around there, but I doubt if it's in the city itself. Everything I know about Harold Logan says he would be out in the boonies, somewhere. Maybe they went into town for groceries or something, and Jody got a chance to get on a computer."

"Sounds about right. The computer she used was at a motel, the Cheyenne Wagon Wheel. It's listed as public access, so it's probably the one in their lobby that they set up for guests to check email and such."

"That makes me wonder if Daddy knew she was doing it," I said. "Somehow, I think she was probably sneaking the chance while he wasn't looking."

Alfie nodded. "I'd bet you're right. He's not going to want either of the kids doing anything that could lead back to them, not now. Maybe he sent her to the lobby for something and she grabbed the chance while she was alone."

"Okay," I said. "So there's a good possibility they're somewhere near Cheyenne, close enough to make it the logical place to go for supplies. How far is it from here to Cheyenne?"

He tapped on the keyboard. "Almost eight hundred miles," he said. "With stops for gas and food, you're talking twelve, maybe thirteen hours of driving time."

I made a face while I thought about everything I'd learned. It would be a long day's drive, but I was thinking it might be worthwhile to pay a visit to Cheyenne. "Natur-opaths would probably get a lot of their supplies out of health stores, right?" I asked.

"Yes, and there are several of them in Cheyenne. Some of them specialize in foods, but a few of them carry naturopathic medicines. If he's running a practice of his own, they probably know him."

"Yes, but if I go in there showing his picture, it would be a toss-up whether they would tell me where to find him or swear they didn't know and then call him as soon as I left. I get the impression Mr. Logan is quite a charmer, and he probably would make friends with these people. I don't need him being tipped off that I'm looking for him, you know?"

Alfie thought about it for a moment, then held up one finger. "Give me a few minutes," he said.

He went to work on his computer, looking at different monitors as his fingers almost became a blur. I didn't have a clue what he was doing, so I picked up and ate the last potato log. I was stuffed, but I knew that my metabolism would burn it all off pretty quickly.

My phone rang at that moment, and I saw that it was Dex calling. I answered and brought him up to speed on my afternoon.

"You're spending an awful lot of time hanging out with Alfie lately," he said. "Do I need to feel jealous?"

I snickered. "Not even a little bit," I said. I lowered my voice and added, "I like a man I can look up to."

"I heard that," Alfie said. "No short jokes, okay?"

"Sorry," I called out, then went back to speaking softly into the phone. "At least I got a lead out of this," I said. "We have a pretty good indication that Logan and the kids are somewhere near Cheyenne, Wyoming. Now all I have to do is figure out how to narrow it down."

"I got that solved," Alfie said. The printer began whirring as he hopped down off the stool, and a moment later he handed me the photo he had just created.

My eye went wide. I was looking at a photograph that looked like a selfie I had taken while hugging Harold Logan. I stared at it for a few seconds, then looked up at Alfie. "How did you do this?" I asked.

"I got you out of a selfie you took with Dex," he said, "and I got him out of an old picture with his wife. Ain't it just amazing what Photoshop can do?"

I nodded. "Yeah, but why? What's this supposed to do for me?"

"You don't want to go asking about him and just showing a picture," Alfie said, "without a reason that's going to make sense. You show this one and say that you met him back around Christmastime when you were visiting Cheyenne, and he gave you some medicine that really worked, but you can't remember what it is. You want to visit his clinic, but you've lost his business card and can't even remember his name. If they know him, they'll probably be glad to tell you where to find him."

I rolled the possibility around my head and had to admit that it was a good idea. There was still some chance that the store operator might want to give him a call, but I'd cross that bridge when I came to it.

I described the picture to Dex. "So," I said then, "it looks like I might be taking a trip to Cheyenne. Feel like going along?"

"Do you honestly think you're going out there without me?" Dex shot back. "Why don't we leave early tomorrow morning? Jimmy can run things here for a couple of days, and you can have Angie reschedule any appointments for next week, right?"

"That sounds like a plan," I said. "I'm going to head

back to the office and then I'll probably go home. I'll see you there when you close up."

"Okay, babe," Dex said. "I might just have to knock off early, myself."

I grinned. "You wouldn't get any objections out of me," I said seductively.

Alfie was printing out more pictures when I got off the phone, and I was amazed at what he had put together. He had another picture of Logan and his kids that he had inserted me into, and then there were a couple pictures of Logan and the kids by themselves.

"Give me your phone," he said, "and I'll put these into your photo gallery and date them for back in December. That way, you can show them on your phone and that will make your story more believable. I added the other pictures because they just help to build its credibility. I mean, who takes just one picture anymore?"

"Good point," I said. "This makes it look like I might have hung out with them for a little while."

"Yep, that's what I was going for. Little details are what make a story believable."

I handed over my phone and it took him a few minutes to get everything set up the way he wanted. When he gave it back, I asked for my bill.

"Call this one a freebie," he said. "Maybe those kids are happy, but something is itching in my guts about them. I think the sooner you find them, the better off they're going to be."

"I hope so," I said. "The jury is still out on their mother —I'm not completely convinced she's the innocent victim she claims to be. Even that bit about how she's extremely lenient and permissive with Jody; that almost makes it sound like she was trying to win the girl over, like capturing a pawn in a chess game. I see that all the time with couples I deal with, and it's never good for the kids. It's possible this whole thing will simply boil down to which parent is best for the kids to be with."

"Yeah, I get it," he said. "But if I know you, you'll figure it out. It's just what you do."

EIGHT

It was nearly three thirty by the time I got back to my office, and Angie was sitting there bored to tears. I thought she was going to jump up and hug me when I walked in through the front door.

"There you are," she said. "I was beginning to worry."

"Nothing to worry about," I said. "I got a little information from the kids that I got to speak to, and that made me stop by Alfie's place. I was able to get a lead on where Logan and the kids might be hiding, and I'm actually going to be taking a trip tomorrow morning. I need you to reschedule all my appointments for the rest of the week, just tell everyone I had to go out of town for a few days so I need them to come next week, instead."

"I can do that," she said. "And by the way, you had some calls while you were gone. Two new potential clients, and luckily I already scheduled them for next week. The other call was from Mrs. Logan. She wants you to call her back when you get a chance and let her know if there's any new developments."

I frowned. I wasn't ready to tell her that I thought her husband and kids might be in the Cheyenne area.

"Okay, I'll do that now," I said. I went to my office, stopping at the break room for a fresh cup of coffee, and settled down behind my desk. I sat there and composed myself for a moment or two before picking up the phone and dialing Maggie's number.

"Cassie?" she asked as she answered the phone.

"Yes," I said. "I got a message to call you, but I'm afraid I don't have anything earth shattering to report just yet. I have learned a few things about your husband that might help, though."

"I didn't really think you would have much this soon," she said. "I guess I was just hoping for reassurance that you're working on it."

"Well, I am," I said, smiling so she could hear it in my voice. "But while I've got you on the phone, I wanted to ask you a couple of things. Can you tell me how you got along with your kids? Were there any problems between you and them? Forgive me, but I'm trying to wrap my head around why they would go along with their father's plan."

She hesitated, just for a few seconds. "Jody and I got along very well," she said. "Ryan—well, Ryan idolizes his father, and as I told you, we had been fighting quite a bit not long before the—before they disappeared. Anytime Harold and I got into it, Ryan would get upset and try to take his father's side. I'm afraid he was pretty angry with me quite a bit of the time. Not constantly, thank God, but enough that it made it a little difficult to deal with him some days."

"That's fairly normal," I said. "How did Jody and her dad get along?"

"Quite well, actually," Maggie said. "She was extremely interested in naturopathy, and she's incredibly intelligent. She started studying his textbooks when she was eleven, and he would drill her on different ailments and what the proper natural remedy might be. By the time they disappeared, she almost never got an answer wrong." She chuckled. "She said she was going to be his nurse, one day."

The story I had heard from the girls at the school, about Jody saying she was going to quit school to be her dad's nurse, suddenly felt a lot more real. If the girl had honestly been studying that hard, she was probably a capable assistant to him.

"I can imagine," I said. "I used to daydream about when I would be big enough to drive the combine, but I grew up on a farm. Now, Jody was just into her teens. How was that going?"

"Probably about the way you would expect," Maggie replied. "Like any teenage girl, and I know because I used to be one many years ago, she thought she was considerably more mature than she really was. As far as she was concerned, at thirteen, she was ready to start dating. Her dad put his foot down and wouldn't hear of it, though I tried to work out a compromise where she could see the boy she liked with my supervision. Harold still wouldn't go for it, though. I think that caused an occasional rift between the two of them, but it never lasted long."

I stayed silent for a few seconds, and she went on.

"She—she was starting to show a bit of a wild side. Like, one night when she was supposed to be staying over at a friend's house, I got a call that she was sick and needed me to come get her, but it was at an entirely different place. When I got there, I found out she was drunk. She'd been drinking beer and smoking marijuana, and she was terrified that I was going to tell her father. I promised her I wouldn't, as long as she would promise me she wasn't going to be doing that anymore, and she agreed." Another chuckle. "And then she threw up all over my car. I had to clean it up before her dad got up the next morning, so I didn't get a lot of sleep that night."

"Most kids want to spread their wings when they get into their teens," I said. "And of course, they have to learn from the mistakes they make. It sounds to me like you handled it pretty well, to be honest. What other kinds of issues did you run into with her?"

"More of the usual. She began asking a lot of questions about sex, but she promised me she was only curious and not seriously considering becoming sexually active. I answered her questions honestly, and that seemed to help. We went through a phase where she wanted clothing that I didn't feel was appropriate, and that caused a few minor fights between us. My way of dealing with things like that is to compromise, so I allowed her to have certain limited control over what she wore, but I kept a veto power over her outfits. I remember one time when she came down supposedly ready for school, and it dawned on me that she had cut off a new pair of jeans to the point that part of her butt was showing, and she threw a fit when I told her she had to go change her pants. No way on earth was I going to let her go to school like that. Oh, and then there was the time she came home from school with a permission slip for a trip to San

Diego. Now, she was only in the seventh grade, so I called the school to find out more about the trip. It turned out that the trip was for the high school-age kids, juniors and seniors, and she was trying to convince her teachers that I would let her go along. Because her grades were so good and she was actually taking advanced courses, they almost fell for it."

I laughed softly. "Yep, she sounds like your average teenage girl. Back to Ryan for a moment, other than taking his dad's side in arguments, were there any other particular problems you had with him?"

She was quiet for a few seconds, and I got the impression she was deciding just what she wanted to tell me. "Well, yes," she said. "And before you say it, I know it's not necessarily atypical behavior for a boy, but—well, his bedroom and Jody's were right next to each other. That little stinker had drilled a hole in the wall between their rooms, and I caught him watching her change clothes. There were also other signs that he was entering puberty a little early, if you know what I mean."

"I can guess," I said. "How active were they on the Internet?"

"Well, we have a computer in the living room that the kids were allowed to use, mostly for homework and such. I had let Jody set up a Facebook account a year or so earlier, and she was always talking to her friends on it. Of course, I monitored her account to make sure there was nothing to worry about, and she always behaved herself. I kept tabs on the computer's browser history, as well, which was one of the things that tipped me off about Ryan. He was sneaking onto some porn sites when he thought no one was home, but he didn't know how to remove them from the history, so

I confronted him about it. At first he tried to deny it, even tried to blame his sister, but finally he owned up. I took away his computer privileges for a month, and never saw any sign of it again after that."

"Sounds like you handled it right. Did the kids have cell phones? Of their own, I mean?"

"Jody did, but not Ryan. Well, I should rephrase that. He had what he called a 'kiddie phone,' one that can only call three numbers or make an emergency call to 911. He could call me, his dad or his sister, but nobody else. That was just for safety's sake."

"Then I'm sure it wasn't a smartphone," I said. "What kind of phone did Jody have?"

"Hers was an iPhone, just like mine. Why do you ask?"

"Because everything I've learned about your husband suggests that he'd want to be far away from that kind of technology," I said. "Not only because he doesn't approve of it, but I'm sure he'd also be aware that it would be a major risk to keeping his identity and location a secret. I'm just curious whether either of the kids would know how to use a smartphone if they managed to get hold of one."

"Oh, either of them probably could," she said. "Even Ryan, I used to let him do things on my phone as long as I was sitting there with him. He had his own email account, which I monitored, of course, and he knew how to send emails and check his email on my phone. I suspect that if they got hold of a phone, I would probably hear from one of them."

I suddenly wondered why Jody had sent a message to her friend, but not her mother. A chill went down my spine as the realization led me to believe that while she might miss her old life, she was somehow in agreement with her father about leaving their mother behind.

"You're probably right," I said, even though I didn't really think so. "Well, listen, I appreciate you taking the time to answer my questions. As soon as I learn something, I will be sure to let you know."

"All right," she said. "And, Cassie? Thank you for calling me back so quickly."

I hung up, feeling just a bit hypocritical. The way she answered my questions had been open and honest, so I had to consider that some of my reservations had less substance than I had been giving them—and yet, Jody had not bothered to try to contact her mother when she had the chance. I did know something, namely that they were possibly somewhere in the Cheyenne area, but I still felt it best not to reveal that just yet.

I shook my head to chase away the slight guilty feeling. Maggie had hired me to do a job; now she was just going to have to let me do it my way.

I turned to the computer and googled Cheyenne, Wyoming, just to get a feel for the area I was going to visit. It was the capital of the state, and the county seat of Laramie County. Urban sprawl had caused smaller towns to be engulfed, so the metropolitan area pretty well covered the whole county.

I read quite a bit about the history of the area, and how the railroad had brought prosperity to the region. It turned out there were a few historical tourist attractions I might want to take a peek at, if we had time. I made a couple of notes and slipped the paper into my purse, then shut down the computer and started to get up from my desk.

I sat back down again. Considering the situation I was dealing with, I thought it might be a good idea to find out just what the legalities were that could be involved. I picked up the phone and dialed the number for Alicia Perkins's office.

"Perkins," she said.

"Alicia, it's Cassie. Listen, have you got a couple of minutes to talk?"

"Sure, Cassie. What's up?"

I told her quickly about the case and asked her opinion about it. When I was finished, she let out a low whistle.

"Well, this is a doozy. First off, while he may have bought those corpses legally, there are still some limitations on what you can do with human remains. I'm not sure about Arizona law, but I suspect he would be dealing with some sort of criminal charges over that issue. Even worse than that, though, is the fact that he took the children without his wife's consent. I'm quite certain that would fall under parental kidnapping, especially since he went to great lengths to convince her that they were dead. I know we would charge him with parental kidnapping here, and it's likely that the feds would pick it up because he crossed state lines. He might have a legitimate defense or mitigating circum-stance if he can prove his wife is dangerous or unfit, but he'd have to prove that in court. He could be looking at life in prison, Cassie, and he probably knows that. If I were you, I'd go into this knowing that the man is likely to be dangerous if he feels like he's going to be caught."

"Dangerous? There's nothing violent in his history," I said.

"There's nothing violent in the history of most rats,

either, but check out what happens when you corner one. If he feels that he's about to be caught and could lose his freedom forever, I'd just about bet this guy will put up a fight. If you find him, don't let your guard down. Call the local authorities for backup before you try to take him."

I was suddenly glad I had called to ask her advice. "Okay," I said. "You make sense. Listen, thanks. I really appreciate it."

"Any time. Just be careful, Cassie. You're a valuable asset to this city, and we don't want to lose you."

I hung up and sat there for a few minutes, just thinking over what she'd said. I probably should have thought of it myself, but I still had an innocent side that wanted to see the good in people. Well, at least sometimes; I did have a tendency to think that most husbands were dirty pieces of crap. In my defense, I was right more often than wrong about that, at least with the clients I had to deal with.

I got up and grabbed my purse, then walked out front.

"Angie, I think we might as well call it a day," I said. "I'll probably be gone the rest of the week, but you'll need to come in tomorrow and Friday, at least. Nicole will be here and she has several appointments of her own scheduled." Nicole used my office two days a week to work with children, a symbiotic relationship we both benefited from.

"Okay," she said. "I'll call Mom and let her know we can spend Thursday together. She'll like that."

We turned out the lights and locked up, then went our separate ways. I headed for home and was greeted by Critter, who was delighted to see me get back earlier than usual. I gave her fresh food and water, warning her that she was going to get fat if she kept eating so much, and then went to start packing for the trip.

That's when I ran into my first problem. I had a couple of suitcases, the ones I had brought with me when I moved to Tulsa in the first place, but I didn't have extra ones for Dex. I thought about running out to buy some, then decided to take a look in the garage. Since Dex had moved in, it was really nothing but a storage unit, so I stepped into it and turned on the light.

Déjà vu. Suddenly, without warning, I was reminded of when I had gone into the garage at the house in St. Louis, looking for the videos Mike had hidden away. The piles of boxes and furniture suddenly looked sinister to me, and it was all I could do not to bolt back into the house.

I stood there just inside the garage for several minutes, breathing deeply and forcing myself to relax. I was only looking to see if Dex had some luggage, not hunting for hidden evidence of wrongdoing, but some evil little voice in the back of my mind kept asking me just how well I knew Dex, after all.

Okay, I'm weak and I'm human. So sue me.

I spent the next hour peeking into boxes. I saw a lot of papers, some of them from the Army when Dex had been discharged; I saw a lot of books, most of which were Westerns; I saw a lot of magazines, almost all of which were automotive ones; and I saw an incredible amount of what I can only call pure junk, the kind of stuff that should have been thrown away years ago but was still languishing in boxes, probably "just in case" he ever found a use for it.

I did not find anything that looked like my current fiancé had an evil streak. By then, I was laughing at myself for my earlier apprehension. I stopped what I was doing and then looked around again, spotting a pair of heavy leather suitcases that looked like they might have come over on the Mayflower. They were old, but they were definitely serviceable, so I carried them into the house, dusted them off thoroughly and set them on the bed.

Dex came in while I was packing his clothes and just stood there and watched.

"Hey," I said. "You want to help?"

"Looks like you've got it covered," he said. "Don't forget to pack me some extra socks."

"I already did," I groused. "I figure we'll probably be there until the weekend, so I'm packing enough to get us through till then. Can you think of anything I'm missing?"

Critter chose that moment to wrap herself around his legs. He glanced down at her, then looked up at me. "What are you doing with the cat?"

I opened my eye wide. "What do you mean, what am I doing with the cat? She'll stay here. I'll put down a big bowl of her favorite dry food and a big bowl of water, and she'll be fine."

Dex looked at me. Now, perhaps this is the point where I should mention that Critter doesn't use a litter box; she goes in the toilet. That way, all I have to do is flush now and then and it's all taken care of.

"We're going to be gone for four or five days," he said. "Don't you think the toilet might be a little backed up by the time we get home?"

I stared at him. "Dex, she's a cat. She's not even a big one. How much poop do you really think she puts out in five days?"

He grimaced, but then he shrugged. "Okay," he said. "All I'm saying is, if it backs up the toilet, you're calling a plumber."

I threw a shirt at him.

We were all packed up a half hour later, and the bags were sitting in the living room. Critter was meowing a lot, and seemed to have some idea that there was something going on she wasn't going to be happy about. I decided to try to win her over by making us salmon steaks for dinner, which she knew by now would mean she was going to get some leftovers. As soon as the aroma of salmon started wafting through the kitchen, she got into a better mood.

After dinner, we sat down in the living room to watch some TV, but we decided to head for bed early. By nine thirty, we were both showered and wrapped up in the blankets, ready to get some serious rest.

"Dex. Now?"

He mumbled something in the affirmative and I yielded to the inevitable. The inevitable was quite enjoyable, and afterwards I slept like a big baby.

We woke when the alarms went off at five thirty and got another shower, then I went to the kitchen and got out two of my biggest bowls. I filled one with water, then opened the box of Frisky Kitty or whatever it's called and dumped it into the other one. Critter watched, her face nothing if not accusing. Yep, she knew we were leaving, and for more than just the day.

Then it was time for our breakfast. Dex is much better at cooking breakfast I am, so I happily sat back and watched as he fried half a dozen eggs and a whole package of bacon. He had introduced me to grits, something you don't get very often in southern Illinois, and I'll admit it took me a few tries before I actually began to like the stuff, but it made a great side dish with those two staples. A little bit later, he set a plate in front of me that looked and smelled so good I was ready to ask him to marry me all over again.

We ate, then rinsed the dishes and stuck them in the dishwasher before we headed out the door. Dex insisted on carrying our bags out, and suddenly I got a surprise.

Back when we first decided to open his custom shop, we had bought a couple of old cars for him to start with. One of them was a 1970 Cuda, a sports car that had been built by Chrysler Plymouth. We found one that was fairly solid, and I had mentioned that I happened to like the way it looked. Dex made some comment about rebuilding it for me, which I took as just so much BS, but apparently he had been serious. The Cuda, looking like a brand-new car, was sitting in the driveway where he normally parked.

"When did you do this?" I asked.

"We've been working on it since we got it," he said, "me and Jimmy. I kept it in the paint booth most of the time, and if we had to take it out we covered it with a tarp. I couldn't have you seeing it before it was ready, now could I?"

I walked around the car as he put the bags into the trunk. It was absolutely gorgeous, painted in my favorite candy-apple red and with a black vinyl top. He had gone for restoration, rather than full custom, and I was pleased.

He came around front and raised the hood, pointing at the mountain of chrome that was the engine.

"I kept this baby original," he said. "That's the same 340 engine that came in the car. We sent it out to Colorado to be completely balanced and blueprinted, then rebuilt with some minor modifications. It's turning out about four hundred horsepower, now, compared to the two hundred and ten horsepower it had when it was new."

I looked up at him. "And it's really for me?" I said, coquettishly. Okay, as coquettishly as Freda and I could manage.

"She's all yours," he said. "I figured this would be a good trip to break it in."

"Fine by me," I said. "Can I drive?"

He tossed me the keys, and I got behind the wheel as he climbed in on the passenger side. I started the engine and smiled as it purred, then grabbed the pistol-grip shifter and found reverse. When I eased out the clutch, it backed out smoothly into the street.

I put the shifter in first gear and we were off. Cheyenne, Wyoming, here we come!

NINE

THIRTEEN HOURS LATER, AT JUST BEFORE SEVEN IN the evening local time, we rolled into Cheyenne. Dex was driving by then, though we had only switched a couple of hours before. The car was an absolute joy to drive, and I intended to enjoy it a lot in the future.

Because it made sense, we checked in at the Cheyenne Wagon Wheel motel, the same one Jody had sent her Facebook message from. I saw the computer in their lobby as we entered, and had a brief mental image of the girl sitting there.

"Hello, and welcome to the Wagon Wheel," the clerk said. He was of some indeterminate Middle Eastern descent, but his English sounded like that of a native.

"Hello," I said. "We need a room for a couple of days, please."

Getting registered and checked in took only a few minutes, and then we drove down the length of the building to the room we were assigned. Dex parked the car right in front of our door and we got the bags out of the trunk and carried them inside.

The room was decent, although this was not a five-star hotel by any stretch of the imagination. There were two queen-size beds and a dresser, a small table with four chairs and the typical TV, microwave and mini fridge. Dex opened the fridge and looked inside, then looked up at me with a grin.

"Somebody left a jar of pickles in here," he said.

"Oh, you're kidding," I said. I leaned over and looked, and sure enough, there was a large jar of hamburger pickle chips sitting there. "Well, don't eat them. You never know what kind of crazy person might've put something in there."

"Don't worry, I wasn't planning to." He reached inside and picked up the pickles, carried the jar into the bathroom and flushed them down the toilet. The jar went into the trash. "On the other hand," he said, "I'm a little hungry. You ready for dinner?"

"I've been ready for the last two hours. There's a pizza place across the street, want to go grab us a large supreme?"

He shot me a thumbs-up sign and walked out the door. I took the opportunity to shimmy out of my jeans and slip into something more comfortable.

Wait a minute, I don't want to give you the wrong kind of mental image, here. I don't do sexy lingerie, so don't be thinking that's what I mean. When I want to get into something more comfortable, it's a pair of light cotton shorts and a simple T-shirt. It's really hard to look sexy when half of you resembles an overcooked steak, but Dex says the simple look is sexy, anyway.

He came back fifteen minutes later with a large super-supreme-carnivore-special pizza and a couple bottles of orange soda pop. We climbed onto a bed with the pizza between us and turned on the television.

"I can't help wondering," I said after a minute, "if this was the very room the Logans stayed in. I know it probably isn't, but I can just about see those kids sprawled on one of these beds."

"This case is really getting to you, isn't it?" Dex asked me.

"Yeah, it is," I admitted. "Maggie seems genuine, but at the same time, I have to wonder what kind of motive a man could have for faking the deaths of his children, along with his own. Donna—the mistress—told me that he didn't believe his wife could take care of the kids without him, but I'm not sure I actually find that credible. She seems perfectly capable to me, but I barely know her. If Harold Logan had a valid reason for taking his kids and disappearing, then I may end up feeling like a real piece of crap if I get him busted."

Dex looked at me, and the look on his face said he was reading me again. "You're planning to try to talk to him, aren't you?"

I nodded. "I have to, Dex," I said. "I have to know why he decided to go to such extremes. I mean, the guy is looking at the possibility of life in prison if he gets caught, and being that he's an intelligent man, he probably knows that. That means he took one hell of a risk to take his kids along with him. I need to know whether that risk was justified."

Dex nodded. "I get it," he said. "I just don't want you putting yourself in danger. This is one time when I'm going to insist on being with you through the whole thing, okay?"

"I'm okay with that," I said. "To be honest, you read people better than I do, so I want your opinion on this guy. I sympathize with Maggie, but if bringing these kids back to her is going to ruin their lives, I'm just not sure I want to do that."

"And that's why you're the best," he said, and then he leaned over and kissed me on the cheek. I had taken the right side of the bed, so he was able to kiss the cheek that wasn't burned. "You always go for the best possible solution, no matter what that might be."

Dex always makes me smile.

The long drive had taken it out of us, so it wasn't long after we finished the pizza that we shut off the TV and curled up in the bed. This was one time even Dex was too tired for any friskiness, and I was glad; I can't sleep in a car while it's moving, so I was pretty bushed.

The next morning, we got up and showered—together, of course, and after some incredible friskiness—and then went looking for breakfast. There was a diner just a couple blocks down the street from the motel, and we pulled in. We hadn't even made it to the front door before the car was surrounded by a group of young men who were obviously trying to decide whether to take a photo of it or make love to it.

"Should we go back and talk to them?" I asked, but Dex shook his head.

"Nope. Just let 'em drool." He opened the door for me and I stepped inside.

There was no hostess, so we chose a booth and settled into it. I took the side that let me keep Freda pointed toward the wall, and Dex slid into the one facing it. The place didn't look very busy, but we sat there for almost a minute before a waitress who looked like she was ready to run screaming out the door came over with water glasses and menus.

"Having a rough day?" Dex asked.

"Honey, you know it," she said. "We just had a busload of people here, they pulled out about five minutes ago. Sixty-five people and I'm the only waitress on the floor." She brushed a loose strand of hair back behind her ear. "You guys want coffee? Tea?"

"Coffee," we said in unison. The waitress, who had a name tag that said Marlene, nodded and disappeared. She was back a minute later with two cups and a coffee pot.

We had glanced at the menus during that minute, and both of us had decided on the steak and eggs. Dex ordered for both of us, telling Marlene to add two extra eggs to each order. She wrote it down, then leaned over to pick up the menus—and that's when she spotted my ugly sister.

She jumped back a foot, staring at what little bit of my burnt side she could see. I sighed, then turned my face so she could see it all. I've found that people stop staring sooner if I do that.

"Good Lord, honey, what the hell happened to you?" she asked.

"Ex-boyfriend got pissed and set me on fire," I said matter-of-factly. She looked at me as if I were crazy, so I nodded. "Seriously, that's what happened. It's a long story, but it's true."

She shook herself and managed to look into my good eye. "Is he in jail?"

I shook my head. "Nope. Dead."

She gave one curt nod and said, "Good. Be back in a bit with your breakfast."

This time she held out a hand and Dex picked up the menus and passed them to her. She turned and walked away, and I could see her shaking her head as she went.

"You love to shock people with that, don't you?" Dex asked me.

"Hey, if they're going to stare, they can deal with it. Besides, it really is kinda the truth, remember?"

"I know, I know. I think it's about the only time when you show any sign of a sadistic streak, when people ask what happened."

"You want me to be sadistic?" I asked. "I'm sure I can think of a way to accomplish that for you."

Dex laughed. "No, that's okay," he said. "I happen to love you just the way you are."

Marlene brought breakfast a few minutes later and made a point of engaging us in a moment of small talk. I think she was feeling bad about her earlier reaction and just wanted to try to make me feel normal again. I kept Freda turned away from her the best I could and did my best to show my appreciation.

Tip for those of you who might travel to Cheyenne, someday. When those folks mention steak and eggs, be sure to bring your appetite. We were expecting something along the lines of a small New York strip; what we got, each of us, was a porterhouse. We both managed to finish the entire meal, but I was not going to need any kind of snacks before lunchtime.

We paid the check, adding a slightly generous tip for Marlene, then walked out the door to find some of those young men still standing around the car. They completely ignored me as I got in, but cornered Dex before he could get his door open.

"That's a beautiful car, buddy," one of them said. "You build her yourself?"

"I did the bodywork and put it all together," he said. "It had the original engine, so I sent it out to be properly rebuilt. All the numbers match the build sheet."

"Awesome," said another one. "Three sixty?"

"No, it's got the three forty, but it's been built. Four hundred horsepower, now, bit of an upgrade from when it was new."

He talked with them for a couple more minutes, then finally managed to get in and start the car up. A lot of them stood there and watched as we backed out and drove away, and I wondered if we might need to worry about the car being stolen from the motel later that night.

I expressed that concern to Dex, but he laughed.

"They won't bother it," he said. "Those boys are just wishing they could build something like it, but it's the kind of thing you have to do for yourself. Stealing it from somebody else just wouldn't be as satisfying."

I rolled my eye. "Okay, if you say so," I said. "Just bear in mind that if the car gets stolen, I am not walking home."

Dex chuckled. "Okay, so where do we start?"

I reached into my purse and took out the list of health food stores that I had printed out for the area. I had also printed out the map that showed me where each of them was located, so that let me pick the one closest to where we were at.

"J & J Health and Nutrition," I said. "Straight ahead four blocks, then make a left. It'll be down two more blocks, on the right."

We got to the place about ten minutes later, and Dex followed me inside. I went directly to the checkout counter and waited while the clerk finished up with the customer. After a couple of minutes, she turned and looked at me, and I gave her a moment to acclimate herself to what she was seeing.

"Er—can I help you?" she asked.

I held up my phone with the picture Alfie had created on the display. "I do hope so," I said. "I was here a few months ago, visiting Cheyenne, and I met this doctor. He's a naturopath, and he was in town to pick up supplies, he said. He gave me his card but I've lost it, and—well, he gave me some salve that has just done wonders for my skin." I held up my left hand and waved it toward my face. "The stuff is great, it takes away the pain and makes my skin so much softer, but I can't remember what it was. Do you happen to know him? I really want to see him again."

The young woman looked at my phone and stared at the photo for a moment, then looked up at me and shook her head. "Sorry, no," she said. "But hang on a minute, Jerry might know him." She picked up a microphone from under the counter and spoke into it. "Jerry? Can you come to the front counter, please?"

Dex and I stood there and waited for about a minute, and then a short, chubby fellow appeared. He actually came to a screeching halt when he got a look at me, but then he shook himself and came on toward us.

"I'm the manager," he said. "How can I help you?"

I went through the spiel again and showed him the picture. He looked at it the whole time I was talking, but then he also shook his head. "I'm sorry, I don't think I've ever seen this man before. You said he's a naturopath?"

"Yes, he's got a practice somewhere around here. I'm hoping to find him so I can make an appointment to see him again."

"Well, I would suggest you try Great Life Nutrition or Nature's Own. Most of the professionals do their shopping there, because the company gives them a discount. We're a small operation and we just can't match the discount they offer."

I smiled and thanked him, and we went back out to the car. Great Life Nutrition was actually next on my list, just a few more blocks away. I gave Dex directions and we headed out.

Unfortunately, the entire staff of the store had recently been changed. The manager had been transferred elsewhere and a new manager brought in to run the store, because all three of the lower employees had been involved in a scheme to steal merchandise out the back door. They had all been fired and prosecuted, so there was no one in the store who had been there six months earlier.

"Well, that sucks," I said as we got back into the car. "You know my luck, that'll be the store he uses."

"Possibly," Dex said, "but it's a safe bet he doesn't get everything in one place. Let's go check the other one."

I looked up Nature's Own on my map and told him how

to get there. It was actually all the way across town, which took up nearly thirty minutes. When we pulled up in front of it, though, I suddenly had a very good feeling. The place had a rustic look to it, and it hit me that it would appeal to someone like Harold Logan.

I hit paydirt. The checkout clerk didn't freak out when she saw me, and she recognized Logan as soon as I held up my phone.

"Oh, that's Doctor Jackson," she said. "He's just the nicest man." She looked back up at me. "Are you one of his patients?"

"Well, kind of," I said. I gave her my cover story and she nodded sagely.

"I've heard from several people that he's really good," she said. "Hang on a minute, and I'll get you his address."

She turned and walked away and I looked at Dex, my face reflecting the amazement I was feeling at how well this had gone. I couldn't quite believe that we had located him so easily. Something about it just seemed unreal.

She was back a few minutes later with a piece of paper in her hand. "Here you go," she said. "He lives up near Horse Creek, it's about thirty miles or so. That's his address and phone number."

"I don't how to thank you," I said. "I can't wait to see him again."

"Oh, don't worry about it," she said. "People come in looking for several of our customers, so we get used to it. I hope you find him soon and have a great day."

We hurried out to the car and got in, while I punched the address into the navigation app on my phone. It took a moment for the app to process the route, then it told me that we were fifty-eight minutes away.

"According to the map," I said, "it looks like he lives about ten miles away from the actual town, to the west. It looks like it's down a dirt road."

"Hope it's not too rough," Dex said. "This car is not exactly built for off-road use."

I nodded. "Yeah," I said. "Times like this, I miss my little Kia."

"So, how do you plan to approach him when we get there?" Dex asked me. I nibbled on my bottom lip as I turned to look at him.

"Well, I want to get inside his clinic if possible," I said. "I'll start out by saying the girl at Nature's Own suggested I see him, and hopefully he'll be willing to see me without an appointment. The idea is simply to confirm that he really is Harold Logan, and then we can bring in the Wyoming authorities. I think that's the best way, don't you?"

"Probably the safest," Dex said. "On the other hand, I think you really just want to get a look at the kids. I don't think you've actually decided yet whether to bust him or not."

I gave a slight shrug. "There might be some truth to that," I said. "Dex, I still don't know for sure whether he did the right thing by taking the kids and disappearing. If those kids look happy, then I'm going to probably have to admit why I'm there, that his wife hired me to find them. He's going to have to explain to me why he did all this. Why the kids' deaths had to be faked along with his own."

"At which point," Dex said, "he will suddenly decide you are a threat to his family's safety and security, pull out a gun and shoot us both dead." He leaned toward me and gave me a meaningful look. "I'm not sure I like that plan."

"Well, how do you expect me to find out, then? I need to know whether or not he had a valid reason for doing what he did, Dex. Can you come up with another way to figure that out, without tipping him off?"

He bobbed his head from side to side, something I call a "Dex Wimble." "Maybe," he said. "If you can get him to treat you like a patient, I'll try to visit with the kids. I should be able to figure out from the way they talk to me whether they're happy, or if they're scared. If they seem scared, I'll find out why."

I sat there in my seat, turned so I could look at him with my good eye, and nodded. Dex has a talent for reading people, and this wouldn't be the first time I had taken advantage of it. "If they are, and it has anything to do with him taking them away like this, then we definitely go for the authorities. I'm just not sure what to do if it turns out the kids are happy in their new life."

"Well, realistically," Dex said, "the guy has broken a lot of laws. Hell, we don't know for sure where he got the corpses that were burned in that motorhome; it's actually possible that he's a murderer on top of everything else. From a strictly legal standpoint, you do have something of an obligation to report him to the police, right?"

"Actually, a private investigator has some discretion on that. We're not official law enforcement officers, so the only time we have a duty to report anything is when it might prevent a crime that hasn't happened yet. On the other hand, being aware of a crime that did happen and not reporting it could conceivably be construed as concealing evidence, and that could blow up in my face."

"Well, your face is a lot more important to me than his," Dex replied. "If you decide to leave them alone, then I'll back you, but I would hate to have it blow up on us."

"Yeah," I said. "So would I."

We made it into Horse Creek on the two-lane blacktop, then the GPS took us a little north of town and directed us to turn left. I had guessed correctly; this was a dirt road, which meant a pair of ruts with an endless strip of grass between them. There were high spots and low spots that caused Dex to slow the car to a crawl, and a couple places actually made him start cussing. He was particularly not fond of the spots where we had to cross shallow creeks, occasionally deep enough that we could hear the exhaust bubbling up through the water. He kept the transmission in low and the engine revved up high during those spots, just to make sure water wasn't backfilling the exhaust pipes. That could kill the engine, and we'd be stuck in all that water.

The GPS had said we were fifty-eight minutes from Logan's place when we left Cheyenne; it was wrong, because getting there down this road took almost an hour by itself. By the time we actually heard the GPS say, "You have arrived," it was nearly eleven o'clock.

This place looked like something out of *Little House on the Prairie,* a log cabin that looked like it had probably been here for fifty years or more. It had a cedar shake roof, which I only know because Dex told me, and the lumber that made the porch looked like it was probably cut by hand with one of those long, two-handled saws. There was a well with a bucket on a rope beside the place, and an old barn stood just a couple hundred feet away. Inside the open door of the barn I could see a big four-wheel-drive pickup truck, the kind with four doors, and I quickly made a note of the license number. The finishing touches on this throwback into history were the chickens and goats that were wandering around loose.

Dex tapped my arm and pointed off to the left, and the whole thing suddenly became less nostalgic. There, in a clearing about fifty yards from the cabin, were a number of solar panels collecting light and converting it to electricity. There was a small concrete block building beside them, and heavy wire ran from that little building to the cabin.

"Donna was right," I said. "He might shun some technology, but he wasn't willing to give up electricity."

"Under better circumstances, this might be a great place to live," Dex said. "Look, here comes the man himself."

The door opened and a man stepped out. He was wearing blue jeans and a flannel shirt, and sported fairly long hair and a full beard. He stood on the porch and looked at us, and I got the impression he was actually admiring the Cuda. I took a deep breath and opened my door, stepping out and standing so he could see me over the front end of the car.

I was looking directly at Harold Logan.

"Doctor Jackson?" I asked.

"Yes," he said cautiously. "And you are?"

"I'm Debbie Crawford," I said, "and this is my boyfriend, Jim. One of the health food stores in town suggested that I try to see you about my burn scars. They're only a couple of years old and still give me some pain from time to time, and my mom told me I should look into natural remedies. We were visiting in Cheyenne and stopped at one of the stores to ask about something, and the guy told me I should come see you."

He looked at me for a long moment, then stepped down off the porch and walked toward me. He was looking at me studiously, basically doing a visual examination of the scars on my face and head. I held up my hand for him to see as well. He glanced at it, and his eyebrows rose.

"You were burned rather extensively," he said. "How bad?"

"The whole left side of my body," I said. "It was a car accident, and gasoline spilled out under the car. Something ignited it, and it was a few minutes before the fire department could put it out and get me out of the car."

He nodded. "I'm so sorry," he said. "But I'm not sure why they would tell you to come to me. I don't really do much with burns."

I raised my eyebrow. "You don't? Oh, I'm sorry, I was given the impression that you were experienced with burns like mine."

"Well, I do have some experience," he said, "but it's not exactly a specialty or anything. May I?" He lifted his right hand and was reaching for my left. I nodded and held it out to him again, and he took hold of it and began feeling the scar tissue. He noticed that my ring finger and pinky had grown together and actually smiled when he saw the custom engagement ring Dex had gotten me.

"You're still getting a little bit of contraction," he said. "That should be just about over, but I'm sure it can be uncomfortable. Does it itch a lot?"

"Everywhere," I said. "Not constantly, but enough to be

annoying. The biggest problem is the pain; it's intermittent, not constant, but sometimes it can be absolutely debilitating."

He nodded. "All right," he said after a couple of seconds. "Why don't you come on in, and we'll see if we can do you some good." He turned toward the cabin, and that's when I noticed what I first took for a young woman standing in the doorway. "Jenna, this is Ms. Crawford. Let's get her into the exam room, shall we?"

TEN

"Jenna" smiled and motioned for me to follow her, so I did. My brain was racing, trying to find Jody Logan in this young woman, but there were a number of striking differences. First off, Jody had dark hair and "Jenna" was a blonde. Jody stood five foot one when she disappeared, but this girl was nearly three inches taller. I glanced at her feet to see if she was wearing heels or lifts, but she was wearing simple white sneakers, the kind any nurse would be wearing.

Of course, I'd known girls back in school who had sudden growth spurts in their early teens. If I concentrated on her face, then I could see enough of Jody to know that must have been what happened in this case.

She led me into a room on the side of the cabin and handed me a typical hospital gown. "Change into this," she said. "The doctor will be here in a few minutes."

"Okay," I said as I began undressing. "You get a lot of patients here?"

She shrugged. "We have a pretty steady following," she said. "I think we have about two hundred regular patients, and we seem to be getting new ones all the time lately."

I grinned. "Doctor Jackson seems to have a pretty good reputation."

The girl turned and smiled at me, and I caught a glimpse of some dark roots in her hair. "He's very good," she said. "Probably one of the best there is."

I looked her over carefully. Besides the blonde hair, she was wearing very sophisticated makeup, and the way she carried herself was more mature than I would expect of a girl Jody's age, but I was sure that's who I was actually looking at.

"Are you Mrs. Jackson?" I asked innocently.

Her eyes got wide. "Oh, no," she said. "He's my dad, but you aren't the first one to ask that question. I guess because we live out here in the boondocks, people think we're one of those couples."

"One of 'those' couples?" I asked. "What do you mean?"

She grinned. "Well, let's just say there are a lot of couples around here where the husband is a whole lot older than his wife. I mean, there's a few of them where the guy is in his sixties and the girl is maybe nineteen or twenty. Whenever I get married, I want somebody closer to my own age."

I ignored the fact that she was seeing all of my scars, telling myself this was just like any other medical appointment even though I knew it wasn't. I slipped into the gown and tied it in the back, then sat down on the examination table.

"So, it's just you and your dad and your mom here?" I asked.

Her face clouded over. "No, my mom—my mom passed away about a year ago. It's just me, my dad and my brother."

"Oh, I'm so sorry," I said. "You must miss her terribly."

She nodded. "I do, but you learn to live with it. It was something that happened unexpectedly."

"I see," I said. Strangely enough, I was almost getting the feeling she believed the story she was telling. "May I ask what happened to her?"

She pursed her lips and thought for a moment, then looked into my eye. "It's going to sound kind of crazy," she said, "but my mom was actually murdered. I didn't know it at the time, but Mom was involved in something that she wasn't supposed to be, and somebody broke into our house and killed her over it. We lived somewhere else, back then, and the FBI came and told us we needed to move away, someplace where those people couldn't find us. That's how we ended up here." She bit her lip. "Maybe I shouldn't have told you. Please don't tell my dad I did, okay?"

"I won't say anything," I said. "It'll be our secret."

"Sometimes I miss having a mom," she said sadly. I made a sympathetic noise and she looked up at me. "You got any kids? I bet you're a good mom, aren't you?"

My eye shot wide open, and I chuckled. "Well, I hope I will be someday," I said, "if I ever had kids, that is. No, I don't have any right now, unless you count my cat."

"Oh, I'm sorry," she said. "I didn't mean to imply..."

I shook my head, grinning. "It's okay, honest. I mean, I don't know if I'm ever going to have kids or not, but I hope that if I do I'll be a good mother to them. My own mother was very good, and I learned everything I might know about it from her."

She stood there and looked at me for a moment, and then narrowed her eyes. "I'm not meaning to stare," she said. "It's not your burns, there's just something about you that seems familiar. Have you been around here before?"

I shook my head. "Nope, first time," I said flippantly. "It's awfully beautiful around here, isn't it?"

"It's nice," she said. "Sometimes I miss things back home, though." She reached out and touched my arm, the one that had been burned. "Does that hurt?"

I shook my head again. "Not at the moment," I said. "Touching it doesn't really hurt, but sometimes there's pain that just flares up. That's why I came to see your dad."

She leaned her head to one side. "Sometimes I wonder how God can let things like this happen. I mean, you seem like a really nice person, it just doesn't feel fair that you went through something like this."

There was something in her face and voice that reached out and took hold of me, and it dawned on me that this girl was lonely. Considering the situation she was in, she probably didn't have any friends to speak of. I had a feeling her father wouldn't want her to get too close to anyone, because he'd be afraid she might open up and tell them too much. Something inside me wanted to reach out and pull her into a hug, tell her that things were going to be okay, but I knew I couldn't.

Instead, I said, "Oh, things happen. We don't always know why, but even something like this can be just a step on the road to whatever your destiny is." I leaned close and lowered my voice. "You saw my boyfriend out there? If I hadn't had my accident, I never would've met him. Believe me, the things that have happened in my life since then have been worth everything I went through."

You're talking about the good we've done, right? Abby asked inside my head, and I silently answered her in the affirmative.

"Wow," Jody said. "You must be an amazing woman."

"Me?" I asked, making my eye go wide again. "No way, I'm about as screwed up as they get." I turned my head to the left so she could tell I was winking, rather than blinking. "I just happen to be extremely lucky, that's all."

Her eyes became big and round and she looked at me strangely for a moment, and then suddenly I noticed tears brimming over onto her cheeks. "I can't imagine what you've been through," she said. "I've had—I've had some small burns, and I know how bad they hurt. I can't imagine how you must have felt. God, I couldn't even imagine wanting to live after that, but you just seem so positive, so upbeat."

I gave her my best moderately sarcastic grin. "Well, I wasn't always this way," I said. "That first six months or so, I did a lot of screaming and begging God to let me die. Of course, so did almost everybody else in the burn unit; I can't even say it was pain, it was so far beyond pain that I've never been able to describe it to anybody."

"I can believe that. Even the little burns I used to get, they hurt so bad it was unbelievable."

That phrase she used, "the little burns I used to get," sounded odd to me. I started to ask what she meant by that, but she cut me off. "Anyway, that's all over with now, and if you can smile, I guess I can, too."

She grinned again, and then a couple seconds later there

was a tap on the door. She called out that I was ready and "Doctor Jackson" stepped into the room.

The examination he gave me was definitely professional, I can say that. Jody/Jenna remained in the room, as her father ran his fingers over almost my entire left side. Where I was burned close to the nether regions, he took a quick, careful glance but didn't touch, and the same was true for what remained of my left breast. My bra is specially designed to make them both look the same under clothing, but my left breast is actually half the size of the right. A lot of tissue was burned away, and I even lost the nipple.

When he was finished, he asked a few questions about my chronic pain, which I was able to answer honestly; I really do have pain, I just don't like to talk about it very much. Not sure I ever mentioned it in any of these memoirs before, but I try not to ever let it stop me from doing what I need to do.

"Most of your skin is fairly well healed, and the coloration is probably as light as it's going to get. From what I can tell, the pain you are experiencing is probably from where scar tissue has replaced other underlying tissue. That's known as regeneration pain; there isn't actually any kind of permanent cure for it, and the bad news is that you're likely to develop more of it over time. What have you been using for pain so far?"

"Acetaminophen, mostly," I said. "I try not to use it unless I have to. I know that all NSAIDs have some unwelcome side effects."

"More than you want to be dealing with," he said. He took a couple of bottles off the shelf and set them next to me, where I was sitting up again on the exam table. "These are burdock root capsules," he said. "Burdock root is a natural anti-inflammatory and pain reliever, and it's very effective on this type of pain." He reached up and picked up a small jar and handed it to me. "This is a beeswax cream with jojoba oil. Beeswax is an anti-inflammatory and antibacterial, and the jojoba oil has some amazing pain-relieving qualities. It will also reduce the itching that you've been feeling. You can apply it as often as you need to, you really can't overdo it."

He opened the jar and began applying the cream to my left arm, and I felt an instant relief from the itching that I had actually been experiencing at that moment. He also rubbed some into my left leg, which always seems to hurt just a bit, and the pain subsided within a matter of seconds. I was genuinely impressed.

"Wow," I said. "That stuff is working already."

He grinned. "It wouldn't do a lot of good if it didn't work, right? I noticed your license plates were from Oklahoma. Can I ask where you live?"

Dex and I had talked about what to say if he noticed our tags, so I had it on the tip of my tongue. "Cherokee," I said. "If you're familiar with Oklahoma, it's down in the southeast corner, right by the Arkansas line."

He nodded. "Well, I don't know if there are a lot of naturopathic suppliers around there, but you can order these online when you run low. The place to get them is listed on the bottles."

"Thank you," I said. "Are we finished?"

He grinned again. "We're done," he said. "I'll step out and let you get dressed again." He turned and walked out of the room, and I began putting my clothes back on.

"See?" his daughter said. "He's the best."

I smiled back and agreed, but inside I was torn. Part of the problem was that she had seemed so sincere when she was telling me what happened to her mother, even though I happened to know that her mother was alive and well. Was it possible that Harold had actually pulled the wool over his children's eyes, as well as everyone else's?

"I can believe it," I said. "Now, if only you guys would move closer to me. I'd be a regular patient, I think."

She laughed. "That would be great," she said, "but Dad loves it here. Me, I miss living in the city." She shot me a mischievous grin. "Hey, I got an idea," she said. "Why don't you and your boyfriend move out here? You can be one of Dad's patients, and maybe we could hang out together sometimes."

It dawned on me that she was more than a little bit serious, and that confirmed my thought that she must not have any friends. I let myself chuckle, and told her that I would talk to "Jim" about it. She knew I was just being polite, but I could see a tiny spark of hope in her eyes, and once again I felt the urge to wrap my arms around her and just hold her. Sometimes, that's the best medicine you can give anybody.

I still hadn't decided whether I was going to bring the authorities in on the case, and the indecision was eating at me. This girl needed something, someone in her life that she could relate to and reach out to. Before I even realized what I was doing, I had picked up a pen and notepad that was lying on the desk in the room and scribbled down my cell number. I wrote "Debbie" on it and handed it to her.

"Keep this," I said. "If you ever just need someone to talk to, call me. You can call collect if you have to, I'll accept it."

She looked at the number, then looked up at my face and I saw that her eyes were moist. "Thank you," she said softly. "You know, it's really kind of weird that you gave me this," she said. "A few days ago, I had a dream about a lady with blonde hair who gave me her phone number and told me to call her if I needed to talk. She said someday I would need her, and she'd be there for me."

I smiled. "Well, I don't know if that was me in your dream, but you can definitely call me anytime. I'll do anything I can for you, I promise you that."

She looked at me for a couple of seconds, then tucked the number into her pocket and told me to go ahead and get into my clothes.

When I was dressed, she led me back out and into their living room, where I found Dex sitting with a boy I was absolutely certain was Ryan Logan. He still looked almost exactly the way he had in his photos, and there was no possibility that it was anyone else. Dex looked up at me and grinned, then got to his feet.

"You all set?" he asked. I realized that he wanted to get away from there as quickly as possible, which told me he probably had something to say that he didn't want anyone else to hear.

"Yep," I said. "All done, and the stuff he gave me is awesome."

Dex looked back at Ryan and held out a hand. "Good talking to you, Rex," he said. "When you get ready to start building your dream car, you come find me, okay?"

The boy looked up with a huge smile on his face. "That'd be great," he said. "We could work on it together, right?"

"You know it," Dex said. "There's nothing like taking an old car and turning it into something beautiful. I'd love to show you how it's done." He and the boy shook hands, and then he turned back to me.

I looked around for the doctor, but didn't see him so I turned to his daughter. "How much do I owe?" I asked.

She stepped over to a desk and picked up a file folder, then ran her fingers over a calculator. "With the visit and exam, plus the medications, it comes to a hundred and thirty-five dollars."

I started to reach into my purse, but Dex pulled out his wallet. He handed over the cash and thanked the girl, and then we walked out the door.

"Doctor Jackson" was standing in the yard, just looking at the Cuda. He smiled and thanked me as we walked by, then waved as we started the car and turned it around. I waited until we were completely out of his line of sight before I turned to Dex.

"Okay," I said. "What did you find out?"

"That's definitely Ryan," he said, "although he goes by the name Rex. I got him to talk to me just fine, because of the car, and he opened right up about his family. The trouble is, that kid thinks his mother is dead. He told me that she had been murdered because she was doing something that wasn't legal, and that his dad moved them out here so the killers wouldn't be able to find them. Even implied that the federal government was involved, can you believe that?"

"I sure can," I said. "I got the exact same story out of Jody, and I also got the feeling she believed it. Dex, what in the world is going on?"

"I'm not sure," he said. "I can tell you this, though. Doctor Jackson, there, was rather suspicious of us. I saw him walk around the car three different times. And by the way, he definitely did notice the tags. Did he ask you about Oklahoma?"

"Yes," I said. "I told him what we agreed on, that we were from Cherokee."

"Good, because I said the same thing."

"What about Ryan," I asked. "I mean, did you get the feeling he was unhappy or scared?"

Dex shook his head. "Not a bit," he said. "Considering he believes his mother was murdered by criminals, and that she was actually some kind of criminal herself, I would say the boy's pretty well-adjusted. He did tell me that he really misses his mom, and that she was just about ready for sainthood, in his opinion. Didn't sound to me like a kid who hated his mother."

I turned and looked out the windshield at the road for a few minutes, just thinking over the entire experience. Something about the story the kids told was really eating at me, because I couldn't imagine their father feeding them a line like that just so he could get away from the wife he was tired of. Okay, yeah, men and women can both be cruel at times, but this was just over the top.

I turned back to Dex. "They had a phone and a TV," I said. "Did you see anything that might look like a computer? Internet?"

"Nope. I even asked the boy about whether he had any way I could check my emails, and he almost busted up laughing. He said they can't get Internet out where they live, but who needs it, anyway? I guess he thinks the Internet is one of the big problems in the world today."

"That makes sense," I said. "Logan wouldn't want them able to go online and check his story. Of course, we know that Jody got online at least once since they disappeared, but it may not have occurred to her to try to verify what she was told."

"There's a phone sitting there," Dex said. "Don't you think they might try calling somebody back home at some point?"

"That's nothing but a landline," I said. "Odds are it doesn't have long-distance capability, and they probably don't have cell phones at all."

"Wouldn't do them any good if they did," Dex said. "There's no signal out here, not anywhere. Nearest cell tower's probably the other side of Horse Creek, too far away to pick up any kind of signal in these hills."

I took out my own phone and looked at it. He was right, there was no signal at all. Logan had chosen the ideal spot to keep his kids completely off the grid.

"Wait a minute," I said. "How did my GPS work to guide us out here?"

"That's a different system," Dex said. "It actually receives signals directly from the GPS satellites. The strength of the signals tells the phone where it is, and that's how it can calculate the directions."

"Oh," I said. I was a little disappointed, because I was about to come off with some crazy theory about Logan having a machine that would jam cellular signals. "Well, then, we have to wait until we get somewhere with a signal, because I think we need to go ahead and bring him in. I don't know about Ryan, but Jody is definitely not happy in this situation. The girl practically begged me to move out here so that she could have a friend, can you imagine that? I'm a perfect stranger to her, but she is lonely enough to try to reach out to me."

He turned and looked at me. "I'm not all that surprised," he said. "I've noticed that just about everyone who meets you tends to want to know you better."

I rolled my eye. "Oh, really? I take it you don't remember all the people who have hurried to get away from me over the last few months?"

"I remember them," he said. "I'm talking about people who actually get a chance to talk to you. They all seem to want to know more. Maybe it's because they're amazed at how positive you sound after all you've been through."

I shrugged. "Yeah, maybe," I said. "In any case, I think we need to get those kids out of whatever situation their father has dragged them into."

Dex nodded. "I think that's a good idea," he said. "It'll be a shock to them, but I think finding out their mother is alive will help them get through it."

Getting back to Horse Creek took just as long as getting out to the cabin had taken, because the dirt road was still just as rough. When we finally got onto the blacktop again, I held up my phone and found that I had two tiny bars. I googled the number for the local sheriff's office and dialed it immediately.

Horse Creek is an unincorporated community, with a population that is officially set at only thirty-nine, but that doesn't include a few hundred people who live in the surrounding hills. It has a small school building, a single gas station/convenience store and a satellite of the sheriff's office. When I explained where I was and what I was calling about, I was transferred to that satellite.

"Deputy Begay," said a feminine voice, "Horse Creek Sheriff's Office."

"Deputy, my name is Cassie McGraw and I'm a private investigator from Tulsa, Oklahoma. I'm calling because I have just located someone in your area who has gone to great lengths to disappear, including the commission of several crimes."

"Really?" she asked. "Can you tell me more?"

"Yes," I said. "Listen, we are just about to come into Horse Creek now. Would it be better if I stop by?"

"Yeah, sure," she said. "We're in that little concrete block building, right next to the gas station. How soon will you be here?"

"Probably about two or three minutes," I said. The wide spot in the road known as Horse Creek was right in front of us, and getting bigger. "I'll see you then."

We pulled in about three minutes later, just as I had thought, and walked into the building. It turned out that Deputy Pauline Begay was the only one there, and she was leaning back in her chair with her feet on the desk, reading a book when we walked in. It took a couple of seconds for her to tear her eyes away from the page, and after doing the inevitable double take at my appearance, she invited us to sit down in chairs in front of her desk.

I handed her my file on the Logans and gave her the whole story, which took almost half an hour. She made a couple of notes, looking up at me incredulously from time to time. When I was finished, she looked at her notes for several seconds, then turned to look up at me.

"So, you think Doctor Jackson is this Harold Logan, right?" she asked.

"I'm certain of it," I said. "He and the kids have changed their names, but it's them."

She looked down at her notes again and doodled something on the pad, then leaned over and looked out the window at the Cuda before turning back to us again. "You know, it's kind of strange that you're coming to me with this," she said. "You see, about an hour before you called me, I got a call from Doctor Jackson. He says that a couple driving a car like yours, and he described your scars perfectly, had come to him using phony names and asked a lot of questions that were none of their business. Are you sure you couldn't be mistaken? Doctor Jackson is a very valuable member of the community around here."

I think my eye almost popped out of its socket. "No, I couldn't be mistaken," I said. "If you like, I can give you the name of the Tulsa police detective you can check with on this. She can verify that the mother of these kids is alive and well, and not the victim of some criminal murder scheme."

The deputy looked up at me again, biting her bottom lip like she wasn't sure what to do. "Look," she said, "I can't go accusing Doctor Jackson of something like this without some pretty solid evidence. I mean, I can't just go on your say-so, you know?"

"Then let me suggest you look at that file I just gave you," I said. "If you've ever met 'Doctor Jackson,' you'll know it's the same guy." I had made finger quotes when I mentioned the name. This woman was actually starting to piss me off.

She bit her lip again. "Okay, Miss McGraw, here's the thing. I'm not sure what the whole story is about his wife, whether she was really murdered or not, but I do know this. Doctor Jackson and his children were brought here by an FBI agent. I get the impression they're in some kind of witness protection, and it's quite possible that by poking around at them, you could be putting them in danger." She looked from me to Dex and back to me again. "Here's what I'm going to suggest," she said. "You need to get back in your fancy car and go home. Whoever you're really working for, you need to just tell them you couldn't find anybody. Because, believe me, you don't want the FBI getting upset because you were poking around out here."

I stared at her in shock. "Deputy Begay, this man faked his and his children's deaths by burning his motorhome with three bodies in it. His wife is not dead, she's the one who hired me to find them. If it isn't obvious to you that there's something fishy going on here..."

"The only thing fishy about this, to me," she said, raising her voice, "is that you are even here. Now, I have explicit instructions to contact that FBI agent if anyone asks questions about Doctor Jackson, so that's what I'm going to have to do. I offered you the chance to bow out gracefully, and you don't seem to want to do that. Please just stay where you are for the moment, while I make a phone call."

She picked up the phone, then pulled a card out from under the plexiglass sheet that was lying on the desk. She looked at the card and dialed a number, then waited while it rang several times on the other end.

"May I speak with Special Agent Rogers, please?" she said, and then she smiled. "Agent Rogers, this is Deputy Pauline Begay with the Laramie County Sheriff's Office, Horse Creek satellite. If you remember, sir, you told me to contact you if anyone came around asking questions about Doctor Jackson. I'm sitting here with a couple of private investigators who claim they were hired by his wife, who they also claim is still alive." She listened for several seconds, glancing up at me once, and suddenly her eyes got wide. "Yes, sir," she said. "I'll be waiting to hear from you."

She hung up the phone and then sat there looking down at her desk for a few seconds, before looking up at me again. I thought she was going to say something, but then her hand came over the desk and it was holding a pistol.

"Put your hands on the desk," she said, "both of you, right now. Agent Rogers just gave me a clear description of you, Ms. McGraw, except he says your private investigator license is really just a cover for the fact that you're a professional killer. You make the slightest wrong move and I'm going to blow you away."

Dex and I looked at one another, then slowly put our hands on the desk in plain sight. She got up and came around the desk, then put the gun right against the back of my head as she frisked me. Luckily, my gun was locked up in the glove box of the car. I think if she had found it, she would've shot me just for good measure.

"Deputy," I said, "would you stop and think for a second? If I was a professional killer, why would I be sitting here? Wouldn't I have just killed them while I was out at the clinic?"

"Just shut up," she said. "I'm just a small-town deputy, I

don't know much about how all this organized crime stuff works. That's why I leave that to the FBI. Agent Rogers can figure out what you're really up to; all I gotta do is follow orders."

When she was done frisking me, she gave Dex the same treatment. He was also unarmed, so then she stepped back and I saw that she was holding both of our cell phones.

She waggled the gun and told us both to get to our feet. As we did, I noticed the little Andy Griffith-style jail cell in the back of the building.

"Okay," she said. "Very slowly, walk over to the cell and step inside. We only got one so I have to put both of you in there together, but if you try anything funny…"

Shocked, we did as we were told and she slammed the door behind us. I heard the latch click loudly, and knew that we were definitely locked in.

"Deputy, if you would call the detective in Tulsa…"

"Just be quiet," she said. "Agent Rogers will be coming to deal with you, so I need you to just sit down and be quiet."

"Well, would you at least call your sheriff? I'd like very much to talk to him."

"Don't worry, I have every intention of it," she said. She walked back over to her desk, and a moment later I could hear her telling the sheriff that she had arrested us on the orders of the FBI. From the way she was preening, I got the impression he was telling her what a good job she had done.

"Hey!" I shouted. "Tell the sheriff I need to talk to him!"

It didn't do any good, because she hung up the phone. She turned around in her chair and looked at us, her face smug.

"Like I said," she said. "All you need to do is sit there and be quiet until Agent Rogers gets here."

I turned and looked at Dex, but he was just as shocked and confused as I was. We sat down on the single bunk and spoke quietly between us.

"What the hell is going on?" I asked. "Can you believe they really are in witness protection? I mean, for what?"

"No idea," Dex replied. "I guess we'll find that out when we meet this agent. I'll tell you this, though: something about this doesn't feel right."

"No kidding," I said, rolling my eye. "The last thing I expected was to get arrested for trying to do the right thing, you know?"

"No, I mean the whole situation. Cassie, the FBI does not run witness protection; that's run by the US Marshals Service. You wouldn't call the FBI, and I'm pretty sure local law enforcement is never informed when a protected witness is put into their community. There's no way they could do a complete background check on every cop and deputy; that would be like locking up the bank but leaving the windows and vault standing wide open. Anybody looking for that witness, if they had an idea where to look, could probably bribe or blackmail any of a dozen cops into giving up their location."

I stared at him. "You're right," I said. "They'd never trust all these local yokels. Dex, I get the feeling we're in some pretty serious trouble right now."

He put an arm around me and pulled me close to him. "We'll just play it by ear," he said. "But I'll tell you this: whoever this Agent Rogers is, I don't think he's really with the FBI. Something about this just smells, and it smells like horse shit."

I agreed with him, but there wasn't anything more to say. I sat there and let him hold me, rocking gently as we tried to figure out just how serious our problems had become.

A few minutes later, Dex stood up and went to the bars. "Hey," he said. "We do get a phone call, remember?"

Deputy Begay turned her chair and looked at him. "You will," she said. "After Agent Rogers gets here."

"Agent Rogers is going to want to question us," Dex said. "The Miranda Decision says we have the right to have an attorney present during questioning. We need to make a phone call in order to arrange for attorneys. If you want to keep that badge you're wearing, you might want to think about what a charge of violating our civil rights would do to your career."

She looked at him for another moment, then picked up one of our cell phones from the desk and walked over to the cell. "Make it quick," she said. "And stay right here, so I can hear everything."

Dex looked her in the eye as he handed the phone to me. It was my phone, so I hit the speed dial icon for Alicia Perkins, praying she would be in her office.

The good Lord heard my prayers, because she answered. "Perkins."

"Alicia, it's Cassie," I said. "I'm going to need an attorney in Horse Creek, Wyoming." I quickly gave her a short synopsis of what was happening, including the fact that the deputy had arrested us and contacted someone who was allegedly an FBI agent supervising the Logans in witness protection.

"FBI doesn't handle witness protection," she said. "Something isn't right, Cassie. Do you really want me to get you an attorney? Or is this a genuine call for help?"

"Who else would I call for help?" I asked, sure she would realize what I was saying.

"All right, sit tight," she said. "Let me make a couple of phone calls. Are you going to be able to call me back?"

"I sincerely doubt it. Madam Gestapo, here, doesn't seem too keen on dealing with facts."

Deputy Begay glared at me. "All right, that's enough," she said. "You asked for an attorney, now hand over the phone."

"Gotta go," I said. I ended the call and handed the phone to the deputy. She continued glaring for a few more seconds, then turned and walked away, dropping the phone back onto her desk as she sat down, and picked up her book and started reading again.

"Well?" Dex asked.

"She's going to make some calls," I said softly, "see what she can find out. She said we should just sit tight."

Dex rolled his eyes around the cell. "Yeah, that's good advice."

ELEVEN

ONE THING I CAN SAY ABOUT ALICIA PERKINS IS that she doesn't waste any time. I found out later that she had contacted Jim Pennington, the detective I had worked with on the bomber case sometime back. When she told him what was going on, Jim had picked up the phone and called a friend of his at the FBI and they went through the story again.

That agent made a couple of calls, finally connecting with an agent in the Cheyenne resident agency. Once again the story was told, and Special Agent Ben McIver got into his car and headed for Horse Creek.

Dex and I had been sitting in the cell for slightly less than an hour by the time McIver arrived. He walked in and looked at Deputy Begay, smiled and held out his ID.

"I'm Special Agent Ben McIver with the FBI," he said. "I understand you are holding some suspects for another agent?"

The deputy looked at his ID suspiciously. "Yeah, that's

right," she said. "Special Agent Rogers. He should be here in a couple of hours, so I think I'll hold on to them and turn them over to him."

McIver smiled. "I think you might want to reconsider," he said. "You see, Deputy, there is no Special Agent Rogers anywhere in the Denver FBI district. I don't know who you've been talking to, but he's not with the FBI."

I'll give Begay credit for guts. She looked him dead in the eye and said, "Really? And how do I know you didn't get your ID out of a Cracker Jack box? You're more than welcome to wait for Agent Rogers, then you two can sort it out. How about that?"

The smile disappeared. "Deputy, look up the number for the Cheyenne resident agency of the FBI, then call them and ask about me."

She sat there and just looked at him, without moving. Slowly, very slowly, he leaned forward and put his hands on her desk.

"Do it now," he said, "or I will charge you as a co-conspirator with whoever this fake FBI agent is, and since your arrest of these people is probably based on criminal activity between you and your co-conspirator, that could add kidnapping to any other charges we decide to file. Would you like to be looking at life in federal prison, Deputy?"

Her eyes had gone wide. "No, sir," she said.

"Then you have about thirty seconds left to make that phone call. I suggest you start looking up the number now."

Nervously, she picked up the same card she had used earlier when she called Rogers. She started to dial the number that was listed on it, but McIver snatched it out of her hand and looked at it.

"This is the number you've been calling for the FBI?" he asked.

She nodded. "Yes, sir," she said. "He said that was the number to reach him on."

"Special Agent William Rogers," McIver read from the card. "This number isn't even a Cheyenne number. In fact, it's not any number at all connected to the FBI. Now, use that computer in front of you or grab a phone book, I really don't care which, but look up the real number for the office in Cheyenne. I want you to look it up so you can't say that I gave it to you."

The deputy turned to her computer and googled the number, then called it. She identified herself and asked if they had an agent by the name of Ben McIver. A moment later, her eyes wider than before, she hung up the phone and looked up at him.

"Okay, they said you're real," she said. "Sir, I really don't understand what's going on here. Special Agent Rogers came to us because he works with witness protection and they put a family in our county. He said we were to let him know if anyone came around asking about them."

"First off," McIver said, "there is no Special Agent Rogers. Secondly, the FBI does not participate in the witness protection program. And third, you people should damn well know that." He looked at the card in his hand again, then took out a cell phone. He dialed a number and put it to his ear. "This is McIver. I need you to run a phone number for me." He rattled off the number from the card, then waited a few seconds. "Really? Isn't that interesting? No, that's all right, I think I've got it under control."

He ended the call and put the phone into its holster on his belt. "The number on this card goes to a cell phone, a burner that gets very little use. Obviously, it's nothing more than a way for you to make contact with this Rogers character." He glanced up at me and Dex, still sitting on the bunk in the cell. "Let those folks out of there."

It seemed like she couldn't comply fast enough. She was so nervous that she had trouble getting the key into the lock to let us out. We walked with her back over to the desk and Agent McIver watched me carefully, probably trying to figure out if he was really seeing what he thought he was.

"Ms. McGraw," he said, holding out a hand. "I was given a description of you. I take it you're okay, other than the inconvenience?"

"We're fine," I said. "You were told what's going on? About the Logans, I mean?"

"I was told something," he said. "You mind filling me in a little more completely?"

The three of us sat down in the chairs in front of the deputy's desk and I explained the whole story, reclaiming my file from the deputy and handing it over to McIver. That took about half an hour, and when I was finished he turned to the deputy.

"Get your sheriff on the phone," he said, and she grabbed the phone even before he finished speaking. When she got the sheriff on the line, she simply held the receiver out to him. "Sheriff Wilder? This is Special Agent Ben McIver from the Cheyenne FBI office. I don't know what kind of office you think you're running, but apparently you're not aware that the FBI does not conduct affairs for the witness protection program?"

He listened for a moment, then began explaining the situation even more concisely than I had. When he was finished, he strongly suggested the sheriff send a couple of deputies out to pick up the Logan family and bring them in. Apparently the sheriff agreed, because McIver handed the phone back to the deputy.

"Yes, sir? Yes, sir. Yes, sir." She hung up the phone and sat there looking down at her desk. "He's calling in a couple of deputies who are in the area and telling them to go pick these people up. When Agent Rogers arrives, I'm supposed to follow your orders."

"Now, that's the first smart thing that's gone on here," McIver said. He turned back to us. "Rogers isn't due for a while. What do you say we ride out there and see if those deputies need any assistance?"

"Sure," I said. The three of us got up and walked out the door, and Dex got into the back seat of McIver's SUV. I climbed into the front and gave him directions.

The FBI vehicle didn't have to worry about scraping bottom, and we made it back out to the cabin in less than twenty minutes. By the time we arrived, there were a pair of sheriff's department SUVs sitting in the front yard, but the deputies were standing beside them. McIver pulled in and held out his ID as he stepped out of the vehicle, introducing us at the same time.

"What's the situation?" he asked.

One of the deputies, a tall black man, looked at him and shrugged. "Nobody here," he said. "When we got here, the door was standing wide open and it looks like somebody gathered up their things in a hurry. Dresser drawers are scattered all over the bedrooms and it looks like somebody ransacked the whole place. Whoever was here, they left in a rush."

Instinctively, I turned and looked at the barn. The pickup truck I'd seen earlier was still sitting there, so it wasn't going to help me locate them. I shook my head, figuring that they'd had another vehicle I hadn't seen, either stashed further back in the barn or maybe even behind the cabin while we were there. The best I could hope for was that they might have left a clue inside about where they would be going.

McIver motioned for us to follow and we stepped inside the cabin. The deputy had been correct, because it looked like a tornado had hit the place. Things were scattered all over, and it was obvious that somebody had rather quickly packed up whatever they just couldn't bear to leave behind.

I smacked the wall. "They ran," I said. "Dammit! It'll be even harder to find them, now."

"You found them once," Dex said, "you can do it again. I guess they figured out that we weren't who we said we were."

"I'd say that's a pretty good supposition," McIver said. "I've told the deputies to secure this place as a crime scene, and I'm going to have our forensic technicians come and look it over. In the meantime, I think we'd better get back to the deputy and wait for Mr. Rogers to show up."

"Yeah," I said. "Maybe he'll have some idea where they've gone."

We climbed back into the SUV and McIver pushed it even harder going back. It didn't really save a lot of time, but it was satisfying to feel the big vehicle bouncing along.

We pulled in at the satellite office and climbed out of the vehicle, and suddenly Dex held out a hand to both me and McIver. "Something's wrong," he said. "Lights are out."

I looked toward the windows in the little building and saw what he was saying. The deputy had every light on when we had gotten there earlier, but they were off, now. McIver whispered for us to stay back out of sight, drew his weapon and tried the front door. It opened easily and he stepped inside.

A moment later he came back out.

"Apparently, Rogers didn't take kindly to the idea of being arrested. Deputy Begay is dead. She's been shot once through the head." He took out his cell phone and dialed a number. "This is Special Agent Ben McIver with the FBI, and I am at your Horse Creek satellite. Your deputy here has been murdered. Please put me through to your sheriff."

I sat down on the hood of the Cuda in shock while McIver explained to the sheriff what he had found. He described the scene inside as being somewhat of a bloodbath, and I heard him say that the deputy had her service weapon in her hand when she was shot. It did not appear to have been fired, however, so whoever Rogers was had managed to get the drop on her.

He ended that call and immediately dialed again, calling his own office. He asked for his supervisor and quickly recounted everything that had taken place since he arrived, then asked for a warrant to trace the cell phone from the number on Rogers' card. The conversation continued for several minutes, then finally he ended the call and turned to us.

"The fact that the people you found have gone into the

wind indicates that you are correct about who they were," he said. "Add to that the fact of the deputy being murdered, and we now have a major mess on our hands. Not only do we need to find Mr. Logan and his children, but we need to track down a killer before he can strike again. I want to tell you how much we appreciate the work you've done so far, but I think it's time to let the professionals take over. Because Logan's crimes are in multiple jurisdictions and there is very little doubt that the deputy was killed in relation to him and his crimes, the FBI will be assuming jurisdiction. Go home, Ms. McGraw. This is out of your hands, now."

I stared at him, my one eye open wide. "You can't be serious," I said. "The girl is dead because I came here asking questions—you can't expect me to back off now."

"That's exactly what I expect you to do," he said. "This is no longer a matter of a simple missing persons case, this is federal fraud, possibly kidnapping and the murder of a law enforcement officer. The case is beyond the purview of a private investigator." He cocked his head slightly and looked at me. "I can't actually order you to stand down," he said, "because you are not officially a law enforcement officer. However, I hope you will take my advice very seriously. Continuing to pursue this case would probably put you and others in grave danger. Let it go, and let us handle it."

I looked at him for another couple of seconds, then slowly lowered my face and nodded. Sirens that had been building in the distance suddenly became a scream and roared in beside us, as the deputies from Logan's cabin arrived. They briefly conferred with McIver, then both of them went into the satellite office. They both came out a moment later, and the younger deputy was retching.

"Do you need us for anything?" I asked McIver.

He looked at me and then nodded once. "I need an official statement from you," he said. "Are you staying in Cheyenne?"

"Yes, at the Wagon Wheel," I said. "If you just tell us when and where, we'll be there."

"I've got your numbers," he said. "We'll deal with this today, and I'll call you tomorrow morning. My office is in Cheyenne, so we can meet there."

He turned and walked away, and I looked at Dex. He glanced at McIver and shrugged. "I know a dismissal when I see one," he said. "Let's go."

Even though I was seething on the inside, I forced myself to get calmly into the car and let Dex drive us away from the satellite. As soon as we were out of sight, I took out my phone.

"Who are you calling?" Dex asked.

"Maggie Logan," I said. "She has a right to know that she was correct, and her kids are alive." I hit the contact and put the phone to my ear. It rang three times before she answered.

"Cassie?"

"Yes, ma'am," I said. "I want to let you know that we have confirmed that your husband and the children are alive. I located them outside of Cheyenne, Wyoming, where your husband was running a naturopathy clinic. I saw both kids, and they seem to be doing well except for the fact that they seem to think you have been murdered. Both of them claim they are in witness protection because you were murdered over something criminal you were supposedly doing."

"Oh, my God," she said. "Harold told them that?"

"Apparently," I said. "However, the story gets worse. It appears that your husband has an accomplice who poses as an FBI agent. The kids think the FBI is protecting them, that it was the FBI who put them into witness protection." I gave her a quick but complete summary of what had happened after we found them, including the murder of the deputy and the phony FBI agent who seemed to be an accomplice of her husband.

Maggie sobbed. "Oh, my dear God," she said. "I can't believe any of this. If you had asked me before today, I would've told you that Harold could never hurt anyone, but I don't know what to think. How could he be involved in something that would end up in murder? Do you think my kids know what he's doing?"

"I don't think so," I said. "I think they swallowed the line about witness protection completely. They seemed genuinely convinced that you are dead, and I was not able to tell them differently at the time. I had gone in under a phony name, pretending to be a patient so I could check out the situation, but I guess he was suspicious. He called the sheriff's office before we even got there. I would imagine he also called the phony agent, and then he must've told the kids to grab whatever they had to have and they left."

"Then there's still hope for them," she said. "If they've been deceived, then they aren't really part of whatever is going on. Do you think you'll be able to find them again?"

I had a grim smile on my face. "I'll find them," I said. "Your dreams said so, remember? And now, the FBI is looking for them as well. That's only going to help bring your kids home."

She was quiet for a moment. "Thank you," she said

finally. "I can't believe how much it helps to know that they really are alive. I felt sure they were, but hearing it—I guess maybe I was having a few doubts, after all. I'm not, not anymore. Is there anything you need from me right now?"

"No," I said. "If I were you, though, I would prepare for a visit from the FBI. They're going to want to hear it all from you, firsthand."

"That's fine," she said. "I'll be more than happy to talk to them. Oh, Cassie, as terrible as it is that someone has died, to me this is all good news. Now we just have to get the kids out of there before they get hurt."

"I intend to," I said. "I'll be in touch as soon as I know more."

I ended the call and sat there looking through the windshield as we drove back toward Cheyenne. After a moment, I dialed Alfie's number and put it on speaker so Dex could hear.

"Alfie is going for pizza. Please leave your message at the beep. *Beeeep!*"

"Beep yourself," I said. "That was a lousy impression of an answering machine."

I heard a yawn. "So, sue me. I'm tired. What do you need, princess?"

"I need you to put your amazing skills to work," I said. "There's a number I need you to track down, a burner phone. I need you to find out everything you possibly can about it."

"No problem," he said. "What's the number?"

I froze. It suddenly dawned on me that I didn't know what the number was. "Um, well—you'll probably need to hack into the phone records of the Horse Creek satellite of the Laramie County Sheriff's Office to get it. There was a call placed to it about three hours ago, and..."

"Three oh seven," Dex said, "five five zero, nine nine four six." He glanced at me and shrugged. "I peeked over McIver's shoulder at the card. I had a feeling you were going to end up wanting that number, so I memorized it."

I rolled my eye. "Did you get that, Alfie?"

"All but the last four, gimme those again."

"Nine nine four six," Dex said.

"Okay. Give me a little time, princess, and I'll call you back."

"Thanks, Alfie," I said. "I'll order you a pizza and have it delivered. What do you want on it?"

"How about making it a Mexican pizza? Something spicy."

"You got it," I said. I ended the call, then looked through my contacts for the number of the Pizza Shack. That was a local place in Tulsa that claims to make international pizzas. According to their advertising, they can make a pizza the way it would be made in any country around the world, so I figured a Mexican pizza wouldn't be too hard for them. I put in the order, gave them my credit card and told them to deliver it to Alfie's address, then put my phone back in my pocket.

"Good job on getting the number," I said. "I hope your memory is accurate."

"You doubt me?" Dex asked with a grin. "If I hear a phone number twice or read it once, I'll never forget it. It's one of those weird little talents I have."

"Not all your talents are weird," I said. "I find some of them quite exciting."

We were just coming back into Cheyenne, and it suddenly hit me that I was starving. "You know, we didn't have lunch. We should remedy that situation."

"I agree," Dex said. "Find us a steak."

I googled. "We got a Texas Roadhouse, Outback Steakhouse or a local place called Charlie's Chuckwagon. Which one do you want? I'll get directions."

"Let's go local," he said. "I like trying the local flavor when we travel."

I pulled up the GPS directions for the Chuckwagon and Dex followed them through town. We pulled in a few minutes later and got out of the car, then walked inside.

The hostess stared at me for a full thirty seconds before she got control of herself and led us to a table. We sat there for several minutes before the waitress approached us, and she looked almost terrified as she handed us menus and asked what we wanted to drink. We both ordered coffee even though it was midafternoon, and she scurried away.

Another several minutes passed, and then I glanced up to see a man approaching us. He was wearing a name tag and I knew instantly that he was the manager.

"Hello, folks," he said, nervously. "Listen, I'm really sorry about this, but—well, I'm afraid you're upsetting some of our other customers. I'm afraid I'm going to have to ask you to leave."

I had been through this before; some people are so terrified of my burn scars that they simply can't be in my presence, and I had been asked to leave restaurants a couple of times in the past. I gave him a sympathetic smile and reached for my purse, but Dex put a hand on my arm.

"Are you freaking serious?" he asked the manager.

"You're honestly going to refuse to serve this lady because she was unfortunate enough to be injured in a fire?"

The poor man look like he was about to have a seizure. "Sir, I really, really am sorry," he said. "I, personally, no, I wouldn't do that, but some of the other customers are complaining to their waitresses. They say—they say they can't eat with her in the room, and I can't afford to have them all walk out."

"You think you can afford the lawsuit we're going to file?" Dex asked, but I'd had enough.

"Dex," I said, "let it go. It's certainly not this gentleman's fault that some people are frightened of my appearance. We're not going to sue anybody, sir," I said, turning to the manager. "Believe me, I really do understand." I picked up my purse and started getting to my feet, but then a man a couple of tables over stood up.

"I hope you folks will forgive me," he said. "I couldn't help but overhear, and, miss, I'm afraid I agree with the gentleman with you. You shouldn't have to leave. You have as much right to be here as anybody else, and your scars don't give anyone the right to ask you to leave." He was speaking loudly, as if he wanted to make sure that everyone in the place could hear him. "I'm just here on vacation, but I happen to run a restaurant back home in Galveston. To be perfectly honest, if I had customers demanding that I make one customer leave because they didn't like the way she looked, I would instead invite them to depart and suggest they not bother to return." He looked the manager dead in the eye. "If I had to compromise my morals to succeed in business, then I'd much rather be a pauper on the street."

The poor manager looked like he was ready to run out the door.

"Listen, really..." I said, but that was as far as I got. Two other men had stood up and were echoing the first man's comments, and then suddenly it looked like almost everyone in the place was on their feet. In fact, I saw one couple look around with expressions of disgust, and then they got up and walked out the door. A lady near the door called out, "Bye, Felicia," after them and the whole place erupted in laughter and applause.

Dex looked around. "Sir," he said lightly, "it appears you were merely mistaken. I don't see anyone complaining about my fiancée's appearance now, do you?"

The man was looking at all the people on their feet and then he turned back to Dex and swallowed, hard. "No, sir," he said. "And your meal is on the house."

That got him a round of applause, and I protested that we would pay for our lunch, but he refused to hear it.

"No, ma'am," he said. "I'm afraid this gentleman was correct." He indicated the first man who had spoken up for me. "That couple is somewhat powerful in this town, and I was merely giving in because I was afraid of them, but he's right. If I have to treat people badly to satisfy one or two customers, then I don't need those customers no matter who they are. Please, please accept my sincerest apologies."

They say all's well that ends well, and I think that this particular incident was an object lesson. We ended up with several of the other patrons insisting on joining us for lunch, and the waitresses hurriedly put together several tables so we could all sit in a single group. Dex and I made several new friends that day, and they were all interested in the fact that I was a private investigator.

We finally got the order and had our lunch, and it was absolutely delicious. I tried again to pay for it as we were getting ready to leave, but I was told in no uncertain terms that it was not going to be allowed, so I compensated by tipping all of the waitresses. When we had ended up in the group, it took all of them to wait on us, so I didn't mind a bit.

TWELVE

AFTER THE DAY WE'D HAD, AND THEN PUTTING down a big meal that started out with a very large T-bone steak, I was ready to rest. We went back to the Wagon Wheel and to our room, and I had just stretched out on the bed when my phone rang.

It was Alfie, so I put it on speaker as I answered. "Hey, Alfie," I said. "Did you find anything?"

"Did I ever," he said. "You are aware that the FBI has taken over the investigation into Harold Logan, right?"

I sighed. "Yes, we know," I said. "Now, what did you find out?"

"I was just asking. I mean, technically, if I find anything that actually could lead to discovering his whereabouts, I really should be turning it over to the FBI. I probably shouldn't tell you about it at all, you know that, right?"

"Is the FBI going to pay you for the information?" I asked.

"Which is why I could give a flying fig what the FBI thinks," he said. "Okay, princess, here's what we got. That number definitely goes to a burner phone, but it seems to belong to an idiot. Most people, if they use a burner to try to keep anyone from knowing who they really are, they turn off the GPS features of the phone, but not this guy. As a result, I was able to go through its location history. That didn't take very long, because it's only been in a very few locations, and one of them is where it's been for the last several months, without moving."

"Really?" I asked excitedly. "Could you nail down where that is?"

"Geez, princess, you're talking to me, remember? For more than seven months, that phone was completely stationary in the office of one David Garibaldi, Attorney at Law in Casper, Wyoming. Want the address?"

"Hell, yes," I said. "What is it?"

"Check your text messages, I sent it to you a couple of minutes ago. And before you ask, I've been doing some deep background on Garibaldi, and guess what I found out."

"A connection between him and Logan?"

"And the lady wins the banana! They happen to be old Army buddies, served in the same unit. When I went back through some of Logan's communications, I found out that he had been calling Garibaldi regularly for more than a year, right up to the time he disappeared."

"I'm just wondering, but why didn't you notice that before?" I asked. "You went through his phone calls the first time we talked about him."

"At the time, I was looking for a local mistress, remember? Not a lawyer that he might have discussed a plan to disappear with. Give me a break, I deserve one."

"So what did you find out about Garibaldi, himself? Is this a man who might be dangerous?"

"He's a sleazeball lawyer," Alfie said, "and I'm not saying that the way I talk about most lawyers. This guy is a shyster, the lowest of the low. He doesn't handle many cases personally, but he gets called in by other attorneys from all over the state to come up with dirt on people or sometimes even create it. He's the kind of guy that will do anything, and I do mean anything, to get what he wants. He's been considered a viable suspect in two different murders over the last ten years, but he definitely knows how to cover his tracks. Cops and feds have never found a single shred of evidence to back up their suspicions."

Dex nodded. "Sounds like he could be our guy," he said. "Alfie, any idea where that phone is right now?"

"Nonexistent," Alfie said. "The GPS signal was lost about two and a half hours ago. Now, considering that the person who answered that phone when the recently deceased deputy called the number is the number-one suspect in her murder, I'm going to go out on a limb and suggest that it's probably been smashed or tossed into a river. Either way, it's never going to do you any good, now."

I winked at Dex. "Okay," I said. "But since you know that it belonged to Garibaldi, I figure you've already tracked down his usual cell phone. Where is that one?"

"Ding, ding, ding," he said. "You get another banana. Unfortunately, that's not going to help you much, either, because that phone is now sitting back at his office. I guess he was smart enough not to carry it along today."

My eyebrows came down a bit. "Did Logan contact him today?"

"On the burner, yes," Alfie said. "Twice. Once about the time you left him, and then again about forty minutes later. Actually, that second call was from Garibaldi to Logan, not the other way around. My guess is that's when Garibaldi told him to pack it up and split."

"Which means Garibaldi knows where he's going," I said. "They are undoubtedly planning to meet up somewhere, so they can set up a new hideaway. The question is how we find them."

"You'll be glad to know that I'm tracking Garibaldi's credit cards," Alfie went on. "As I said, this guy is an idiot. One of them was used twenty minutes ago in Fort Collins, Colorado to secure a pair of motel rooms. Foothills Motel, just off I-25, rooms one one three and one one four. Not exactly five-star accommodations, but I suppose it's any port in a storm."

Dex was looking up the distance to Fort Collins. "About forty-five minutes away," he said.

"Alfie, you're the man," I said. "Send me a picture of Garibaldi, will you? I want to know what he looks like before we get there."

"Sending it now. Don't you think you ought to let the FBI know about this?"

"Not yet," I said. "Not until I nail this bastard. That deputy he murdered was really nothing more than a clerk, and he only killed her because she tried to stop him. When she found out he was a fake, she was only trying to do her job the right way, and he shot her for it. You better believe I want to be the one to bring his ass in."

"Dex? Can you talk any sense into her?"

"Do I look that crazy?" Dex asked him. "I'm looking into her eye right now, and there's no way in the world I'm going to try to argue with this woman. I like living too much."

"Then, just try to be careful, okay? And if he goes for a gun, be sure you shoot first. You can ask questions later, if he survives."

The line went dead and I looked at Dex. "So much for a nap," I said. "Give me ten minutes in the bathroom, and then we can head out."

"No problem," he said. "Where's your gun?"

"In the console of the car," I said, and then I pulled the bathroom door shut behind me. I took care of necessities, then freshened up and ran a brush through my hair before stepping out again. Dex was standing there, holding out a box to me. I glanced at it and realized it was the box with my prosthetic mask and glass eye.

"What?" I asked.

"You want to get close to these people? They'll spot Freda a mile away, but they won't recognize Cassie. You put this on, and I'll see to my own disguise."

I glared at him for a couple of seconds, but he was making sense. People who have seen me up close only remember the burnt side, not the "pretty side." The mask made my face look completely normal, and even filled in my missing ear and hair. I grumbled as I took it and stepped back into the bathroom.

First things first: I washed my face again, to make sure I got any dirt or airborne pollutants off of my scars. They could interfere with the glue that held the mask in place, and having it suddenly come off could be traumatic for anyone who happened to see it. Once that was done, I picked up one of the two blue bottles that came with the mask. It was a special cleanser that would remove anything that soap and water left behind. That way, the adhesive would be in direct and unfettered contact with my scars.

I put some onto a soft cloth and wiped it over that side of my face, the side of my head, my neck, shoulder and even down the front of my chest. All of that had to be clean, because the mask extended down that far. Once it was in place, I could wear a dress with a fairly revealing neckline if I so chose, and even my cleavage would look normal.

That cleanser has to dry for five minutes, so I opened the compartment where my glass eye was stored and took it out. I really, really hate that thing, because it makes this horrible popping sound when I put it in. The scar tissue around my eye is really tight, and while it doesn't really hurt, it's very uncomfortable to have to press it in so hard. I rinsed it off and told myself to just get it over with. I put it up to the socket and shoved, and then I shivered as it popped into place.

It made that sound I hate so much, which is actually a result of pushing air out of the eye socket as it goes in. I can even feel some of the scar tissue fluttering as the air is forced out, and it always reminds me of a tiny little fart. Can you imagine having to deal with a fart coming from your eye socket? I have to, and I hate it.

The other blue bottle held the adhesive, and when I was sure the cleanser had dried completely I poured a small amount onto the applicator sponge and spread it evenly across the inside of the mask. The trick is to make sure that it goes everywhere, because you can't risk leaving an air bubble. Body heat alone is enough to make that air bubble expand, and that starts the process of breaking down the adhesive. Sooner or later, that would lead to the mask starting to come loose, and that would be a great way to ruin a date.

Once the adhesive was in place, I had fifteen minutes to get the mask on and make sure it was lined up properly with the unburned skin. That took almost ten minutes by itself, but finally the girl looking back at me in the mirror showed no sign of her ugly half-twin. I gave it five more minutes to set completely, then brushed my hair so that it all came together without leaving a visible seam.

Then I picked up another bottle, the makeup that blended the artificial skin with the real skin. The mask had been made in the exact shade of my normal skin tone, and this makeup was a kind of thick paint that I brushed on and then smoothed. It was flexible, so it would move with my face as it needed to without breaking, and I really couldn't even feel it as I applied it. It dried rather quickly, so as soon as I finished, I was able to start putting everything away.

I stepped out of the bathroom and Dex gave me an approving nod. "Looks good," he said. "Now, change your clothes before we go. You were wearing those this morning when you met him, so we don't want them to give you away."

I sighed, but he was right. I changed into a different outfit, a red pantsuit that would be considerably different than the jeans and T-shirt I had been wearing all day. The slacks were a little long, so I passed up my sneakers and put on a pair of low heels.

When I stood up and turned around, it was my turn to

offer approval. Dex had put on a blond wig and added a mustache of the same color. He was also wearing a pair of round glasses, but I knew they were a costume pair we had bought for the purpose of disguise. They didn't actually offer any vision correction, because his vision was perfect. He had just finished putting on a very nice shirt, and was slipping on his leather vest over it.

That vest was something I had bought him, a black leather vest that was designed for concealed carry. Dex had gotten his own CCW permit, and carried an Army Colt .45 in the hidden pocket inside the vest. My own gun was a Kimber Ultra .45, a small-framed pistol that was designed for my smaller hand. It was also rather pretty, a beautiful red gun that was known as the "Crimson Carry."

"My, my," I said. "You look very handsome in that outfit. How come you never wear those kind of clothes when we go out?"

"Because you never asked me to," he said. "I will if you want."

I stuck my tongue out at him. "Maybe once in a while," I said, "but I kind of like the rough and tumble side of you. Are you ready to go?"

"Yep," he said, picking up his jacket and slipping it on. "Let's go get these guys."

We walked out of the room and went to the car, but Dex stopped me from getting in. "Just grab your gun and holster," he said. "We went to a lot of trouble not to be recognized, it would be a shame to have the car give us away." He pointed at a shiny Cadillac that was sitting a few feet away. "I rented that. It was delivered while you were putting on your face."

"Nice," I said. I reached into the console and pulled out my Kimber .45, then slipped it into the holster that clipped inside my waistband at the back. The jacket of the pantsuit hung down over it and made it invisible. We locked up the Cuda and climbed into the Cadillac.

"This is very nice," I said. "Maybe I should buy one of these."

"Where would you put it? You've already got the Mustang, and now the Cuda is yours. I'm going to have to start parking on the street so that both of your cars can be in the driveway."

"Okay, good point," I said with a grin. "But, realistically, shouldn't we keep the Cuda up at your shop? I mean, it's worth a lot of money, right?"

"Yes, but the shop doesn't have the extra room, and I wouldn't want to leave it sitting outside." He put the Cadillac in gear and we headed out of the parking lot to the street. "I've actually been thinking about building onto the shop, making a storage area to use for finished cars. Maybe it's time to go ahead and do it."

"I think you should," I said. "Besides, that would make it a little harder for anyone to steal one of them, right?"

He grinned. "A little bit harder."

It only took us a few minutes to get to I-25, and then we were headed south. The Logans and a killer named Garibaldi were waiting for us in Fort Collins, and I didn't want to disappoint them.

It was just after six p.m. when we arrived at the Foothills Motel, and we found the rooms we were looking for rather quickly. Unfortunately, the lights were off and no one seemed to be present in either of them. We also noticed that there were no vehicles parked outside the rooms, and Dex expressed the opinion that they must've gone for dinner. With no idea what they might be driving, it didn't make any sense to go looking for them, so we parked the Cadillac toward the back of the parking lot and settled in to watch.

An hour passed and several vehicles pulled in, but none of them stopped at either of those rooms and no one entered them. I was developing the need for a bathroom, and I turned and looked at Dex.

"I wonder if Garibaldi only got these rooms to throw us off?" I asked. "He probably figures somebody knows who he is by now, so using his credit card would be a good way to decoy us off his trail."

"I've had the same thought," he said. "On the other hand, this guy is supposedly really good at covering his tracks when it comes to murder and other crimes, but he was dumb enough to leave the GPS function turned on in the cell phone he was using. What does that tell you?"

I narrowed my eyes and looked at him. Dex had a way of seeing things about people that no one else would notice, and I was trying my best to learn from him. "Well, let me think," I said. "Alfie said he's a suspect in at least two murders before this one, but he's never left evidence behind. That makes him sound extremely smart, and so does the fact that other attorneys hire him to help build cases for them, but maybe he's just ruthless. It could be that he manages to cover his tracks because he's got a fair idea of what the police look for, but technology might be beyond him. Turning off the GPS tracking on that phone might not have occurred to him at all, but—I'm sorry, I still can't believe he would use his own credit cards right after committing a murder."

"You missed it," Dex said. "The key to this man is the fact that he's extremely arrogant. He's so confident in his ability to cover his tracks that he doesn't even consider the possibility that he can be tied to any particular crime. Since there's no way to prove at the moment that he was anywhere near Horse Creek today, he wouldn't expect to be a suspect yet. He probably hadn't planned ahead enough to get some cash together, so he's taking the Logans and putting some distance between them and Horse Creek before he worries about it. Now, in that scenario, I don't have any problem imagining him being so cocky that he would use his own credit card here at this motel. In fact, we probably should've called Alfie when we got here; he might have been able to tell us where they were eating."

I grinned. "Probably not," I said. "Most restaurants, you don't pay until after the meal is finished. By the time he spotted a credit card charge at a restaurant, we wouldn't get there before they were gone. Okay, I buy your logic on him using his credit cards here, so I guess we're doing the right thing. Right now, though, I gotta go pee. You stay here and keep watch while I walk over to the gas station across the street."

I got out of the car and cut through the trees behind where we were parked to get into the parking lot of another business. From there, I walked toward the street and waited until the traffic was clear and I could cut across. There was a gas station and convenience store on the corner, directly across from the motel, and I hurried inside and found the ladies' room.

A few minutes later, feeling considerably relieved, I stopped at the coffee counter and got two large cups. There was no telling how much longer we would be waiting, and we both needed to stay alert. When I walked up to the counter, the young man behind it looked up at me with a smile, and that's when I remembered that I was wearing the mask. I smiled back and set the coffee on the counter.

"Is that going to be all?" he asked.

"That'll do it," I said. "No, wait..." I reached down into the candy rack on the front of the checkout counter and grabbed a couple of the big chocolate bars and added them to my purchase. "Okay, now I'm done."

He smiled even wider. "No problem." He rang up the purchase and gave me the total, and I handed him a twenty-dollar bill. As he made change, he looked into my face and said, "I don't think I've seen you around here before."

"No, just passing through," I said. "I'm staying at the motel across the way."

"Oh. All alone?" he asked.

Now, I've mentioned many times that I don't get flirted with very often. I mean, let's face it, most guys won't flirt with a girl who's been burnt, right? It was such an unusual experience for me that I felt my face turning pink, and the smile I gave back was quite genuine.

"All alone," I said, "except for my fiancé. Two coffees, remember?"

He chuckled and shrugged. "Hey, we don't see too many beautiful girls around here," he said. "You can't blame me for trying, right?"

I grinned. "Actually, I'm flattered," I said. "Have a great evening, I gotta go."

I walked out of the store and headed back the way I had

come, cutting through the other parking lot again so that anyone pulling in at the motel wouldn't pay any attention to me. A couple of minutes later I climbed into the Cadillac and handed Dex a coffee and a candy bar.

"You're smiling," he said. "How come?"

"Cute guy at the store decided to flirt with me," I said. "Of course, he's a little young for me, but it was nice to get hit on for once."

Dex blinked. "I hit on you all the time," he said. "I even get quite enthusiastic about it."

"Yes, but you're not a stranger. Believe me, the cute guy didn't mean anything, it was just the fact that he was flirting that felt good. It's not something that happens to me much anymore."

He sat there and looked at me for a few seconds, then shook his head and grinned. "Okay, I guess I get it. However, I would invite you to remember that I started flirting with you the first time I met you, and you weren't wearing that mask that day."

"Which only goes to prove that you are an extremely unusual man," I said. "And that is something for which I will be eternally grateful."

He grinned and winked at me, and we went back to watching the motel rooms. We sat there another twenty minutes with nothing happening, and then a big black Chevy SUV pulled in and parked right in front of room one thirteen.

All four doors opened and I saw Jody Logan, first. She climbed out of the back seat on the driver's side, and I noticed that she was keeping her face pointed down toward the ground. I saw Ryan a second later, and then their dad. Harold grabbed hold of Ryan's arm and pulled him toward the door of room one fourteen while Jody followed along.

The man who stepped out of the driver's seat was David Garibaldi. When Alfie had sent me his photo, I noticed that Garibaldi was a tall, chubby fellow with a receding hairline. He sort of reminded me of an older version of John Candy, but there was nothing comedic or jovial about the man I was looking at now. He looked around the parking lot as if he was expecting some kind of trouble, then followed the Logans into their room.

"That's them," I said. "And that is definitely Garibaldi."

"Yep," Dex said. "How do you want to handle this?"

I thought about it for a moment. "I don't want to go barging in on them," I said. "Everyone says Harold is not dangerous, but we have to remember that he's probably desperate not to get caught. That makes him a cornered rat, and Alicia reminded me what they can do. I wonder if there's any way to get Garibaldi to come out alone, take him first. If we could subdue him, then I could just knock on the door and confront Harold. I don't think the kids are going to present any problem."

"That might work," Dex said. "The only question is how to get him out by himself? I could go knock on the door and ask him to step outside, but my disguise isn't nearly as good as yours. It's possible Logan would recognize me, or Ryan might."

"No, I don't want you to try that. Let's just think about this for a few minutes. It looks like maybe the Logans are in one fourteen, which probably means Garibaldi is one thirteen. I'd say there's a good chance he's going to come out of their room sometime soon to go to his own. Maybe we can take him then."

Dex bit his bottom lip. "Not from way back here," he said. "We'd have to be able to move fast, and it would take us longer to get close to him than for him to get inside the room and slam the door. If that happens, we'll have no choice but to contact police and turn it over to the feds."

"True," I said, "and I really don't want to do that just yet. Okay, you want to move us up closer?"

Dex started the Cadillac and put it in gear, then let it idle up toward the motel. He turned into a parking space in front of room one eleven, which put my side of the car facing the Chevy. If Garibaldi came out, I was in a perfect position to get the drop on him.

"Okay, here's how we handle it," I said. "When he comes out, I'll open the door and point my gun at him, order him to get down on the ground and freeze. I'll keep him covered while you take my handcuffs and put them on him, then we'll take him into his room and let you watch him while I knock on the other door."

Dex looked at me for a moment, then bit his bottom lip again. "I don't like that plan," he said. "No offense, but with that mask on, you don't look even a little bit scary. Somehow, I'm afraid he might decide you won't pull the trigger, and go for his gun. While it might be satisfying to blow him away, I think the idea should be to take all of them alive and unhurt, shouldn't it?"

"That's why I want you to cuff him as soon as I get him covered," I said. "Trust me, he makes a move, he'll know just how serious I am."

He mumbled something under his breath.

"What? What did you say?"

"I said I hate it when you're in charge. I know, I know, I promised to let you call the shots, but that doesn't mean I like it."

I smiled sweetly at him. "That's okay, baby," I said. "Just as long as you remember who's boss."

THIRTEEN

THE WINDOWS ON THE CADILLAC WERE TINTED, and were very dark. With the sun going down, it was probably just about impossible to see that there was anyone sitting in the car, and that made me feel a little better. At least, if Garibaldi came out alone, he wouldn't know I was there until it was too late.

Another half hour went by. The lights were on in the room the Logans had entered, and there was a flickering that told me the kids were probably watching television. I wished I could see what Logan and Garibaldi were doing, but it didn't look like there was any gap in the curtain.

Suddenly, a light came on in the other room, and I smacked myself in the forehead.

"Adjoining rooms," I said. "Why didn't it occur to us that they had adjoining rooms?"

Dex shook his head. "We should've thought of it," he said. "So much for Garibaldi coming out alone. Now what do we do?"

I sat there for a moment and considered his question, then turned to look at him. "I'm going to go knock on his door," I said. "I'm going to see if I can get him to come out, follow me away from the room the Logans are in. I want you to come up behind us if he does, and when he turns to look at you, that's when I'll draw my gun and we'll take him down."

"Are you serious?" Dex asked me. "If you want to knock on his door, you should already have your gun in your hand. When he opens it, you shove it in his face and make him move back, and then I'll rush him and take him down. As soon as I get him down and make sure he's disarmed, we can cuff him and then go after the Logans."

"No, I want to try it my way," I said. "If we try to take him in his room, it's going to make a lot of noise and they could come running in to see what's happening. I don't want to take any chance on those kids getting hurt." He started to say something else, but I cut him off. "Come on, Dex," I said. "With the mask on, I look like a helpless little blonde, right? I'll tell him that my car won't start and ask him to come look at it. I mean, the parking lot is almost empty, so all I gotta do is say I've been knocking on any room that had a vehicle. If he doesn't follow me out, then we'll try it your way next."

He huffed, but finally gave in. "Okay," he said. "We'll try it."

I turned and got out of the car, leaving Dex sitting there behind the wheel. I watched the curtain on Garibaldi's room closely as I eased the door shut, but nobody peeked out. I walked quietly up to his door and stood there for a moment before knocking.

"Who is it?" Garibaldi asked from behind the closed door. There was a peephole in it, so I was pretty sure he was looking out at my face.

"Oh, I'm sorry to bother you," I said. I was using my Illinois country girl voice, which was a little different from the one I used normally nowadays. "I've been knocking on all the doors, trying to find some help. My car won't start, I think maybe the battery is dead. Could you help me?" I put as innocent an expression on my face as I possibly could and smiled into the peephole.

He was quiet for a moment, but then I heard the dead-bolt unlock and the door swung open a few inches. His chubby face looked out at me, and there was a lecherous grin on it.

"Do you have jumper cables?" he asked.

"No," I said, "but I've got one of those things that you use to jump-start a car. My daddy bought it for me, but I don't how to use it. Would you mind helping me?" The "confused little kitten" expression I was wearing seemed to appeal to him.

He shut the door for a second and took off the safety chain, then opened it again and leaned out. He looked right and left, I suppose to make sure there wasn't somebody hiding out there ready to hit him over the head or something. He turned back to look at me again, then held up a finger as if telling me to wait a moment.

He stepped back into the room for a second, then came out again. He had almost shut the door, so I wasn't sure what he had gone back for, but I figured it was probably the key to the room. He pulled the door shut behind him and waved a hand to indicate that I should lead the way.

"I really appreciate this," I said as I turned toward the back end of the building. "I'm right around the corner, but I just don't know how to use that jumper box thingie. I mean, Daddy tried to show me, but I guess I didn't really pay attention." I kept rambling, trying to give the impression that I was just a scared little girl in need of help.

I heard the car door close behind us, and I glanced back just in time to see Garibaldi turn quickly and look back toward the Cadillac. While his back was to me, I reached up under my jacket and snatched out my gun, raising it and aiming it toward his head before he turned back around.

He watched Dex for a second, then turned back to face me and his eyes went wide when he saw the barrel of my forty-five. He opened his mouth to say something, but then he moved so fast I didn't even see it coming. He slapped my hands, throwing my aim off to the right and then back-handed my face, knocking me to the ground.

"Freeze!" Dex shouted, and Garibaldi spun to face him. By this time, the big man had his own pistol in his hand, and he squeezed off a shot toward Dex as soon as he turned and saw another gun pointing at him. Dex returned fire, one shot that caught Garibaldi in the shoulder. He dropped his weapon and fell against the wall of the motel, but he didn't go down. Instead, he turned and stepped right over me as he began to run.

Dex was also running, and he stopped to look down at me as he got close. "Go, go," I shouted. "Get the bastard!" I was scrambling for my gun and my feet at the same time, and a moment later I was up and running right behind him.

Garibaldi was about six foot three and probably weighed in at close to three hundred and fifty pounds, but the man could run. He made it into the next parking lot, the one I had taken toward the gas station earlier, and was halfway across it by the time Dex got close enough to grab the back of his jacket. He took hold, then slammed on the brakes and yanked backwards, dropping Garibaldi onto the pavement and knocking the breath out of him. He stood over him with his forty-five aimed at his face, and Garibaldi uttered a string of curses as he held on to his wounded shoulder.

I caught up a second later and kept him covered while Dex applied the handcuffs. It took both of us to lift the man to his feet, and we marched him back toward the motel room where the Logans were waiting.

And now I have to correct myself, because the very first thing we noticed as we came around the corner of the building again was that the big Chevy SUV was gone. The door to room one fourteen was standing open and there was no one there.

We took Garibaldi inside the room and made him sit on the bed, and then I called 911. I identified myself as a private investigator who had just apprehended a potential murder suspect, gave my location and requested both police and paramedics.

Then I reached into my jacket pocket and took out the card I had stuck there before we left our own motel. "Supervisory Special Agent Ben McIver," it said, and I dialed the number he had written on the back.

"This is SSA McIver," he said as he answered.

"Agent McIver, this is Cassie McGraw. I was able to identify a suspect in the killing of Deputy Begay, and I just apprehended him in Fort Collins, Colorado. He was with the Logans when we first arrived, but they have escaped and vanished while I was dealing with him." I gave him the address of the motel, but also explained that I had police and paramedics on the way. "I'll give your number to the arresting officer, and I'm sure he'll be waiting for you in the local jail."

"Now, you just hold on a moment," he said. "How did you identify a suspect in the deputy's murder?"

"I was able to ascertain that the burner phone had been located at a specific place in Casper, Wyoming, for several months. That place turned out to be the office of an attorney named David Garibaldi, so then I was able to track his credit card activity. When I found that he had paid for two hotel rooms in Fort Collins, I figured he probably brought the Logans down here to start setting them up in a new location. I wanted to try to verify that before I told you, and it turned out I was right. Unfortunately, when I tried to apprehend Mr. Garibaldi, he knocked me down and drew a gun. My fiancé, Mr. Tate, was able to wound him and that enabled us to capture him. The police are on the way to take him into custody now."

"Ms. McGraw, did I not tell you that the FBI was to take jurisdiction on this case? What the hell do you think you're doing interfering in an FBI investigation?"

Can you believe that? Ungrateful, wasn't he?

I bit my tongue to keep from telling him what I really thought, and simply said, "I was doing my job, Agent McIver. I was hired to find the Logans, and that's what I intend to do. If I am able to hand you a killer on a silver platter in the process, I would think you would regard that as a bonus."

"Assuming I decide not to press charges…" he began, but I cut him off.

My temper flared. "Agent McIver, I'm sure you are aware that a licensed private investigator can pursue an investigation unhindered by law enforcement. The last I checked, law enforcement included the FBI. Now, you can take the win on the deputy's murder, and I'll keep my mouth shut about how he came to be in custody, or I can take credit for it and share with the newspaper how a simple little private eye was able to track him down when you couldn't. Which of those options seems most appealing to you at the moment?"

McIver was quiet for a moment, but then he burst out laughing. "I checked you out, McGraw," he said. "I read your whole file, so I know that you turned out to be one hell of an investigator. Of course, I also learned that you have a reputation back in Tulsa of being a real spitfire, and I guess you earned it. Okay, you win this time. I'm in Cheyenne, so I'll get the sheriff's helicopter to get me down there in the next half hour or so. We'll talk then, okay?"

"That sounds fine," I said. "I'm sure I'll still be with the police when you arrive."

A siren had been sounding in the distance, and it suddenly got louder as it turned into the motel parking lot. Dex was standing outside the room and waved to get the attention of the officers, so they pulled right up to him and jumped out of the car with their hands on their weapons.

"Everything's under control," Dex said, keeping his hands in plain sight anyway. "Ms. McGraw has the suspect inside this room, waiting for paramedics to come and check his wound."

An ambulance roared in only a moment later, and the

police stood around and watched as the paramedics checked the bullet wound and dressed it. As it happened, Dex's slug had gone all the way through, and while it had missed any major blood vessels, there was a good chance Garibaldi was going to lose the use of his right arm. They loaded him into the ambulance for the ride to the hospital, and one of the half dozen police officers who had arrived climbed in with them while three different squad cars followed. That left me with a Fort Collins detective who had been sent to find out what was going on. His name was Valentine, but this guy was anything but a Cupid.

"Tell me again," he said. "After you became certain that you had found the people you're looking for, why did you not call us in to help with the arrests? As it stands now, you've got your murder suspect in custody, but the family you were supposed to find has disappeared despite the fact that the FBI is also looking for them. Wouldn't it have been better to bring us in before it got to that point?"

The bad part was that he was right—I should have contacted the police to help with the arrests. The problem was that my ego had gotten in the way; I felt some irrational responsibility for Deputy Begay's death, so I wanted to be responsible for bringing in her killer. My heart was in the right place, but my head went off in the wrong direction.

"I'm partly to blame for the murder of a deputy," I said. "Had I not tracked down this family in the first place, she wouldn't have been in the position of trying to arrest a phony FBI agent, and she'd probably still be alive." I shrugged. "I wanted to catch the son of a bitch myself. I messed up, and I know it, but that's what happened."

Valentine nodded. "You messed up, all right," he said.

"You said the Logan family took off in this guy's vehicle? I don't suppose you got the tag number, did you?"

I bit my lip. "No, I'm afraid not," I said. "I thought I had him, so I didn't think about it. It was a black Chevy SUV, I think it was a Tahoe. Fairly new, not more than a couple of years old, I'm sure."

"Okay, so they're driving the same kind of vehicle that every state and federal official uses. I suppose we can just pull over everyone we see, but that might make an awful lot of people mad. You got any idea where they might be headed next?"

I shook my head. "No, I'm afraid not," I said. "But I'm going to find them. You can bet on that."

"Yeah?" he asked. "And how many more people do you think might be dead by the time you do?"

He turned and stomped away from me, then said something to a police officer that was standing there. That officer was talking to Dex, and he motioned for me to approach them. When I got close, he told me that Dex and I were going to have to go downtown to give our statements.

We got into the Cadillac and followed the officer to the Fort Collins Police Department, then into the building where we were each put into a separate room. I started to think they were trying to make it look like we had broken some kind of law, and I was getting pretty anxious after sitting there for nearly two hours with no one coming in to talk to me. When the door finally opened, I looked up with a sense of relief, ready to deal with whoever stepped inside.

It was McIver. He stuck his head in and then turned to somebody outside in the hallway. "Wrong woman," he said.

"The one I'm looking for looks like she took a nap on a barbecue grill. Ugly as sin, at least on one side."

"It's me, McIver," I said grumpily. "I'm wearing a prosthetic mask, it's designed to make me look normal. Whenever I wear it, nobody who ever saw me without it recognizes me."

McIver looked at me again, then slowly stepped inside and shut the door. He walked over and sat down across the table from me and just stared at me for a moment. "Holy cow," he said. "If I didn't know your voice, I'd never believe it was you."

"So I heard," I said, glaring at him. "I'm not ugly enough at the moment, right?"

He chuckled. "Sorry about that comment," he said. He laid a file on the table and looked me in the eye.

I gave him a frown. "Don't worry, I noticed how ugly I am," I said. "What the hell is taking so long? Why am I just sitting here?"

McIver looked at me for a moment, then spoke. "How you holding up?" he asked. "They got you scared yet?"

"Maybe a little apprehensive," I admitted. "Is there something I should be worried about?"

"Not really," he said. "I know Valentine, I've had occasional dealings with him. He likes to think he's in charge around here, even though he's actually pretty low on the totem pole. He used to be one of their top detectives, but then he started drinking." He shrugged. "That's a good way to waste a lot of talent, and ruin a good career."

He opened the file and took a sheet of paper out of it, turning it so that I could see it. It was a summary of several crimes for which Garibaldi was or had been a primary suspect. My eye got wider as I read through the list, because it contained everything from shoplifting to capital murder. He had been named as a person of interest in blackmailing, kidnappings, assaults that left people crippled, threats that forced witnesses to change their testimony and dozens of other things. Alfie had found him named as a suspect in two murders, but this sheet listed seven.

"Mr. Garibaldi is a pretty bad boy," I said. "Do you think you'll be able to hold him this time?"

"Pretty sure of it," he said. "The gun he was using was recovered back at the motel, and it matches the caliber of the bullet that killed the deputy. We'll get a ballistics match on it, I think, and that'll pretty well lock this case down." He yawned, putting a hand over his mouth as he did so. "We may not have to worry about it, though," he said. "Garibaldi has figured it out for himself, and knows he's finished. Of course, he also knows he's looking at the needle, so he's already trying to make a deal. In return for a guarantee that he won't face the death penalty, he's offering to give up an awful lot of information. The US Attorney will have to make the call, but I suspect they'll take him up on it."

"Either way," I said with a shrug, "he's off the street. I get the feeling a lot of people might sleep better knowing that."

"Damn right. I get to interview him in just a bit, now that he's back from the hospital. Turns out he wasn't seriously injured, though I understand his right arm is going to be a lot weaker from now on. Your boyfriend blew away a big chunk of muscle and nerves."

He took the sheet of paper from me and put it back in the file, then handed me another one. I looked it over and this time my eye got narrower.

"Holy crap," I said. "Is this for real?" What I was looking at was a list of more than forty people who had disappeared in the last five years. It seemed Garibaldi had made a lot of money by helping people to change their identities and vanish, so Harold Logan had simply taken advantage of the service his old Army buddy was already offering.

"It is," McIver said. "You'll notice Mr. Logan on the list; I figure, if you want to join me for the interrogation of Garibaldi, we might persuade him to give us some idea of where Logan would be going."

I looked up at him. "You think he'd already arranged a new place for them?"

"I think it's definitely possible, don't you? I mean, they were probably talking about where they would be going next all the way down here from Cheyenne. If anyone is going to have an idea where that might be, it's Garibaldi."

I looked at him for a moment, wondering if he was being sincere, or if I was somehow being set up. "Where's my fiancé?" I asked.

McIver grinned. "He's in the next room," he said. "It seems the local police were trying to find a way to charge him with discharging a firearm inside city limits, because he's not licensed as a private eye, like you." I think the look on my face told him I was about to explode, because he quickly waved a hand. "Don't worry, I handled it. The charge wouldn't have stuck in any event, since he actually fired only in self-defense and his actions resulted in the arrest of a murder suspect. I convinced Valentine that it's better to have a hero to parade in front of the press than to try to prosecute a man who took a criminal off the streets. I might have even implied that I was aware that the two of you came here looking for them, and that you had my blessing."

I looked at him in a new light. He had stuck his neck out for us a bit, and that sort of surprised me. "Dex reads people better than anyone I know," I said. "If we go in to interrogate Garibaldi, I want him there with us."

"Not a problem," McIver said. "As far as my superiors and local police are concerned, you are assisting the FBI with this investigation because you have intimate knowledge of some of the subjects involved. That gives me a little leeway in terms of letting you in on what we know, and things like interrogations. You ready?"

"I'm ready to get out of this room," I said. "And incidentally, where's the bathroom? I gotta go."

He chuckled and got to his feet, then led me down the hall to the ladies' room. I took care of what was necessary, then stepped over to the sink to wash my hands and caught a glimpse of myself in the mirror.

If we were going in to interrogate Garibaldi, I wanted Freda to be with us. I could take off my mask, and I could even stuff it into the pocket of my jacket, but I didn't have an eye patch with me.

Oh, well. The glass eye is even more disconcerting when it's surrounded by scar tissue, so I just left it in.

When I came out a couple of minutes later, Dex was standing beside McIver, who did a double take. Dex only grinned; he knew exactly what I was doing.

I think McIver figured it out, as well. "Shall we?" he asked, and I just nodded.

Garibaldi had been taken directly to the hospital, but the wound was through-and-through and non-life-threatening, even though it was going to restrict the use of his arm in the future. Surgery had not been required, and doctors had simply cleaned and packed the wound, then wrapped it securely. He had been released back to the custody of the arresting officers and was now in another interrogation room.

The police officer standing guard on him opened the door and let us enter. Garibaldi was sitting there at the table, his left wrist handcuffed to it, but his eyes indicated that he wasn't feeling a lot of pain. He looked at me curiously, but I didn't see any sign of the usual revulsion. I guess whatever drugs they gave him at the hospital were pretty good.

There were only two chairs on the opposite side of the table, so Dex chose to stand. McIver and I sat down and I let him start the conversation.

"Mr. Garibaldi," he said. "This is Ms. McGraw, the private investigator who figured out who you were and tracked you down. She's actually looking for the Logan family, so she's got a few questions for you."

Garibaldi was grinning at him, and he turned his grin to me. "Damn, girl," he said slowly. "Somebody hit you with the ugly stick."

"That's true," I said, "but I got the better end of the deal." I let Freda grin back at him. "You were helping Harold Logan hide his family. Where is he going now?"

"Hell if I know," he said, shrugging his left shoulder. "I was planning to send him to Oregon, but I never got the chance to give him the details. I was just getting ready to when you showed up at my door and ruined everything." He continued grinning.

"Oh, come on," I said. "You guys are old friends, you

must have some idea where he'd go. I mean, you're the one who set all this up for him, right? You're the one who makes sure his money gets to him every month, things like that?"

"Well, not anymore," he said, and then he chuckled. "He's got people of his own that handle the money situation for him, and he's got enough cash to last quite a while in any case." He screwed up his face as if he were trying to concentrate. "You want my guess, he's probably going to head for Montana. There's a thousand places a guy like him can get lost in Montana, and there's always a demand for doctors of any kind."

"Montana is a pretty big state," I said. "Where would he go in Montana?"

"Hell if I know," he said again. "He just used to talk about Montana a lot."

McIver leaned forward a bit. "Garibaldi, let me jump in here for a moment. Logan is not really important to me, but he's definitely a person of interest in some outlying cases, and his kids could be in danger as long as they're with him. You say you want to make a deal to keep you out of the execution chamber, right? Helping Ms. McGraw find Logan and the kids would be a good step in the right direction."

I stifled the urge to look at McIver and grin appreciatively, keeping my eye on Garibaldi's face. The painkillers he was on were apparently pretty potent, because the guy was absolutely in a good mood even though he was facing life in prison at the very least.

"And if I could, I would," he said. He turned back to me. "Quick Draw McGraw," he said, and I heard Dex snicker. "I used to love that cartoon when I was a kid. Look, Quick Draw, I don't remember Hank ever talking about a specific place in

Montana, but he always seemed to be a little fascinated with the state. If he's looking for a new place on his own, that's where he's gonna go. Other than that, I don't know what to tell you."

I glanced around at Dex, who was watching Garibaldi intently. He noticed me turning to him and subtly shook his head.

I turned back to Garibaldi. "Hey, man," I said. "You see this guy standing over here? They used to call him the human lie detector, and he says you're not telling the truth. I think you do have an idea of where Hank might go, and Agent McIver's already told you that helping me out will help your case as far as getting a deal. You want to try again?"

Garibaldi threw back his head and laughed. When he finished, he looked at me again and winked. "Can't blame me for giving it a shot, right? There are three places in Montana he used to talk about. Rosebud, Marion and Drummond. Three little towns, all of them popular with survivalists, right? I don't know if he'll actually go to one of them, but that's all I know."

I looked at Dex, and he nodded. For whatever it might turn out to be worth, Garibaldi was telling the truth.

But Garibaldi wasn't finished. He leaned forward as far as he could and looked closely at my face. "I thought so," he said. "You're the girl who came to my door asking for help. What the hell happened to your face?"

"A bastard like you decided to set me on fire one day," I said. "Remember how I said I got the better end of the deal? He's sitting on death row for other crimes he committed."

"Yeah, but you didn't look like this when I first saw you. Some kind of makeup or something?"

I decided it couldn't hurt to answer. I pulled the mask out of my pocket and shook it out. He stared at it for a moment, then began laughing.

"If I was you," he said, "I'd wear that all the time. You are seriously ugly without it."

"Okay," McIver said. "Enough of that. Let's talk about Logan a bit more. I know you've known him quite a while, since the Army; when did he contact you about setting this up?"

"Couple of years ago," Garibaldi said. "We were at a unit reunion in Miami and I had told him and some of the other guys that I had gotten into the relocation business." He chuckled at that. "Hank waited until he could get me alone and said he wanted to find out more about it, so we took the bottle back to my hotel room. He said his wife was a nagging bitch and he wanted to get away from her, but he didn't want to leave the kids behind. I told him, oh, hell, no, you don't want to take kids when you disappear because they always get homesick and try to go back, so it all blows up in your face. He wouldn't listen, he said no, his kids would be more than willing to go with him and do whatever it took." He forced his eyes to focus on McIver for a second. "I guess he was right."

"Did he ever say why?" I asked. "Why the kids would want to go with him, I mean?"

"Not anything in particular. I gather they just weren't all that fond of the mama. According to Hank, the only good thing she ever contributed to their family was money, but he had some of his own stashed away."

McIver had leaned back in his chair and was watching

me, so I pressed on. "Tell me about the bodies in the motorhome," I said. "Where did they come from?"

Garibaldi grinned again. "That was kind of slick, wasn't it? You'd be absolutely amazed what you can get for a few hundred dollars at a lot of crematoriums. Most of them have a pretty fair supply of ashes lying around that they can hand off to the grieving family, so sneaking a body out the back door in the middle of the night is pretty easy and all you gotta do is promise it won't come back on them. Five hundred smackers each, and you've got bodies you can leave behind. By the time the fire was done there was no way to prove it wasn't him and the kids."

"And you were waiting to pick them up when the fire started, I suppose?"

"Aww, get real. I met up with them in Utah and paid another guy to drive the motorhome down into Arizona and light it up. Hank and the kids got into a truck I brought him and were probably already in Wyoming by the time the fire started." He winked at me. "Hardest part of the whole job was convincing that little girl she had to give up the ring she was wearing. I knew that was a little detail that would cinch the identification, but she was really pissed about it."

"Hmph," I said. "Too bad she didn't give you a swift kick in the nuts while she was at it."

FOURTEEN

DEX AND I SAT IN WHILE MCIVER TALKED TO Garibaldi about some of his other crimes, and the man actually seemed to be cooperative. He didn't confess to any murders, including the murder of Deputy Begay, although he didn't quite deny that one, either; he did admit to helping a number of people hide from authorities, and even offered to give up those whose whereabouts he knew. He claimed not to know where most of them ended up, and Dex was of the opinion that he was telling the truth.

When we finally left the interrogation room, McIver took us down the hall and that's when things went crazy. A couple of dozen reporters were sitting in the lobby of the station, and they all jumped to their feet when we came through the door.

McIver took the lead with Detective Valentine standing beside him. He told the reporters how I, a private investigator, had been looking for missing persons and stumbled across a lawyer named Garibaldi who was a person of interest to the FBI in many different crimes. Thanks to my quick thinking and that of my "assistant," Mr. Tate, Garibaldi had been captured with enough evidence to convict him of at least one murder and several other crimes.

Valentine wanted to stress that private investigators are not law enforcement officers, and that it was he who actually made the arrest of Garibaldi. He suggested that people should come directly to the police rather than hiring a private eye, but the reporters wanted him to shut up so they could start talking to me.

I answered a few questions, stated "no comment" to others and declined to say who the missing persons I was looking for might be. It took nearly half an hour to get away from them, and then McIver led us to an office that he was using temporarily. He still had to get our statements about what happened that morning, and the fact that it was getting late didn't deter him in the slightest. We worked together, Dex and I, to make sure we gave him the accurate details, and then he printed the statement out and had us both sign it.

"All right," he said. "I think that's all I need. Since the Logans were not actively involved in the deputy's murder, I'm not going to waste a lot of time on them. If you do find them, however, I want to be notified. They would still be useful as witnesses against Garibaldi if we need them." He held out a hand to Dex, who shook it, and then held it out to me. "Ms. McGraw, you are free to go. I wish you luck in your efforts to find those kids, because their father seems to be a bit of a crackpot. Hopefully, their mother will be better for them."

I shook his hand, thanked him for everything and then

got to my feet. Dex and I walked out of the police station at a quarter after eleven, and both of us were tired and hungry.

"Food first, or sleep?" Dex asked.

"Food," I said. "I'm starving."

There was a twenty-four-hour restaurant just a couple of blocks down the street and we pulled in. I followed Dex inside and we took a booth in a back corner, with me keeping my "pretty side" pointed toward the rest of the room. A waitress came over and brought us coffee without even asking, then gave us a couple of minutes to look over the menu. They didn't have steaks, but they did have something called the "All-American Feast," which included two pork chops, a chicken breast and a catfish fillet. Dex and I each ordered one, with a double order of American fries.

"So," Dex said after the food arrived. "What's next?"

"Next we go home," I said. "I figure there's no chance we're going to find Mr. Logan in the next few days, because he's going to be bouncing around and trying to stay off the radar. Garibaldi says he has a lot of cash with him, so there's no credit cards to track, and he's smart enough to get rid of that SUV as soon as possible. McIver has an APB out for it, but I'd bet that when it's found, it'll be abandoned. We'll go home and give him a couple weeks to find a place to settle, then start looking again."

He nodded. "That sounds pretty smart," he said. "Frustrating, though. If there's anything I hate, it's waiting."

"Me, too," I said. "Unfortunately, I think our best bet is to let him choose a spot to settle. He'll almost certainly open a new clinic, and that's likely to be our best bet for a lead."

We wolfed down the food and a couple of cups of coffee each, then settled up and left. We drove back to the Wagon

Wheel and stumbled into our room, fell onto the bed and slept in our clothes.

The next morning, Dex was in the shower when I woke up. I managed to sit up and realized that I was still wearing the clothes I had put on before we went to Fort Collins, and started stripping out of them. When I took off my jacket, the weight of the mask in the pocket caught my attention, and I took it out and laid it on the bed to get the wrinkles out. That thing cost a small fortune, and I was hoping it didn't get damaged while it was stuffed in that pocket.

When Dex came out, I was naked as a jaybird and holding a towel. He leaned over and kissed me, then I walked into the bathroom and took care of morning necessities first, then stepped into the shower, turning it up as hot as I could stand. I scrubbed myself clean and washed my hair, then climbed out and toweled off. I caught a glimpse of myself in the mirror and saw that blasted glass eye staring back at me, so I popped it out, rinsed it off and put it back into its compartment in the mask box.

I walked out of the bathroom and picked up the mask, took it back into the bathroom and cleaned it thoroughly, then put it away. I had no intention of wearing it again anytime soon, so closing the box on it was satisfying.

Back in the main part of the room, I climbed into some comfy sweatpants and a T-shirt for the long drive home. We stuffed everything back into our bags and carried them out to the car, then went to the breakfast room and pigged out on waffles.

Forty-five minutes later, we checked out and I drove the Cadillac to the rental agency while Dex led the way in the

Cuda. We turned it in and settled up, then I took the first turn driving on the way back to Tulsa.

As soon as we hit the interstate, Dex took out his phone and called Alfie, setting the phone to speaker so I could hear.

"Don't tell my heart, my achy-breaky heart," Alfie sang. "What's up, Dex?"

Between the two of us, we told him everything that had happened the day before, including the fact that the Logans had gotten away while we were dealing with Garibaldi. I figured they heard the gunshots and Harold probably looked outside, saw us running after Garibaldi and decided to make a break for it. Garibaldi must've left his keys where Harold could get to them, so he threw the kids in the vehicle and took off. We knew that the only thing left behind in their motel room was a bottle of shampoo, probably Jody's. I couldn't imagine Harold and Ryan using lilac-scented shampoo, anyway.

"Wow," Alfie said, "that sucks. I'll see what I can find out about those towns in Montana, maybe I can figure out who he would approach to see about getting a place in any of them. Without his buddy the lawyer, he might not be able to get a new identity set up anytime soon. I'll check his own identity and the Doctor Jackson one. If I get anything, I'll let you know."

"I don't think you'll find anything for the next few days," I said. "Most likely, he's going to be staying at dumpy motels and driving the most nondescript car he can get his hands on. I figure to give him a couple of weeks to get settled somewhere, and then maybe he'll make a mistake that will send up a flare for us."

"He'll make mistakes," Alfie said, "but the trick is going

to be spotting them when he does. The problem with a flare is that you have to be looking in the right direction in order to see it."

"Well, we'll just try to look in every direction at once, I guess," I said. "In the meantime, Dex and I both have day jobs. If we stay out here, we'll just be wasting time. I have clients and he has cars to build, so we might as well go back to work."

"I gotcha," Alfie said. "I'll still dig, but you're probably right that I won't find anything yet. I'll let you know if I happen to get lucky."

The line went dead and Dex laid his phone on the console. A moment later, he reclined his seat and was snoring within seconds.

I decided it was time to do what I was dreading. I took out my phone and called Maggie Logan.

"Cassie?" She obviously had me in her contacts, because she knew it was me calling.

"Yes, it's me," I said. "I need to give you an update, Maggie, but before you get excited, I'm afraid I don't have any good news."

"Cassie, any news at all is better than nothing," she said. "Okay, I'm ready. What is it?"

I took a deep breath. "We found out that the phony FBI agent was an old Army buddy of Harold's, and he's the one who killed the deputy yesterday. Late last night, we tracked them down to Fort Collins, Colorado, but while we were dealing with that guy, Harold and the kids got away. I'm afraid we don't know at the moment where they are, but we have reason to believe they might be headed to Montana. It'll probably be a week or two before they settle somewhere, and that's going to be our best chance of finding them again."

She let out a sigh. "But now we know they're alive, and that they're healthy. Cassie, that's more than I knew three days ago, and it proves my dream was right about getting you to find them. I'm just worried about the other dream, the one where my kids are so scared. I just wish I knew what it was they were so frightened of."

"I understand," I said. "I can tell you that I didn't see any sign they were afraid of their dad, but that doesn't really help anything. All I can tell you is that I'm not going to give up until they come home to you."

As soon as I said the words, I wished I had been able to bite them off. There was some part of me that still wasn't sure those kids would be better off with their mother, but I knew it was a decision I was going to have to make at some point. Garibaldi's comments about Logan saying his wife was a bitch didn't really help, because what else would a man say when he was enlisting help to escape his wife?

What I needed was to know what the kids thought, but the only way I was going to learn that was by asking them point-blank. With them believing their mother was dead, it wasn't going to be easy to do.

Maggie thanked me and we said goodbye. I laid my phone in the console beside Dex's and concentrated on the highway.

It was late that night when we got back home, and Critter was in rare form. She made it perfectly clear that I was on her list, the one that probably belonged in the litter box, and even a fresh can of cat food wasn't enough to earn her forgiveness. For that, I had to sit down and let her jump into my lap, where she proceeded to explain to me in kitty-speak just what she thought of being left alone in the house. That took another half hour, and when she finally settled down, I picked her up and carried her into the bedroom.

Luckily, I had been right about just how much damage Critter could do to the toilet. Dex had grunted when he stepped into the bathroom and took care of his own business before he flushed. When he came out, he grinned at me. "Okay," he said. "Teaching the cat to use the toilet was a good thing."

I grinned back, then set Critter down on the bed as Dex and I hit the hay, with the cat curled up around my feet.

The next morning was Friday, and I had already given Angie that day off, so there was no point in going to the office. Instead, I told Dex I wanted to go to the shop with him. He grinned and said that was fine by him, but I think I actually managed to hide the fact that I had a surprise in mind. I waited till he went into the shower, then grabbed my phone and called David LaBarre on his cell phone.

David is my personal banker. Whenever I have any kind of business to take care of that's going to involve money, I call him and let him handle it.

"Cassie," he said. "To what do I owe such an early morning call?"

"Remember the shop building I bought?" I asked. "I need to have a garage built on the same property, something to store vehicles in. It needs to be secure and big enough to hold several cars. Can you arrange that for me?"

"Well, of course," he said. "I can arrange a contractor to meet you at the property whenever you like, so you can discuss the details. When would be good for you?"

"I'm actually going to be at the shop all day today," I said. "Any time other than lunch would be good."

"All right, then," he said. "I'll get on it as soon as I get to the office. And don't worry, I'll get you a good deal."

I grinned. "I know you will, you always do. Thanks, David."

"No problem, I'm always glad to help."

When Dex got out of the shower, I grabbed a quick one of my own. By the time I came out, he had breakfast cooking on the stove and the coffee was hot and ready. I poured a cup and sat down at the table, and a moment later he set a plate full of scrambled eggs and sausage in front of me.

"So, who did you call so early this morning?"

His question caught me off guard. I couldn't figure out how in the world he had heard me over the shower. "How did you know I made a phone call?" I asked, looking at him with my narrowed eye.

"When I went into the shower, your phone was in your purse. When I came out, it was lying on the bed beside where you were sitting. Ergo, you made a phone call. Anything I need to know about?"

"Not unless you want to ruin a surprise," I said. "And you know how thoroughly pissed off I get when you ruin a surprise."

He stared at me for about three seconds. "So, I noticed the weather is really nice today," he said.

We finished breakfast quickly and I rinsed the dishes and put them in the dishwasher, then we walked out the door and climbed into the Cuda. I let Dex drive that morning, just because I wanted to relax and act mysterious about the upcoming surprise, but he's very good at simply tuning out anything he doesn't want to think about. He chatted with me about superficial things all the way to the shop.

Jimmy had been busy. The truck they had been working on when Dex and I left had been painted and the new engine was in place. Dex looked it over and nodded with satisfaction, then climbed inside the camper area they had built on the back. I followed him, just to see what was happening inside, and I was definitely surprised.

The walls had been thoroughly insulated and some of them had paneling installed. It appeared that this was what Jimmy was working on currently, and Dex said it was something Jimmy was exceptionally good at. When they had worked together at the Ford dealership, Jimmy was the "trim man." That meant he was a specialist in dealing with the interiors, and he was skilled at general building trades, as well. Building a motorhome required all of his talents.

There was a beautiful smooth panel that went around the area where the camper section connected to the cab of the truck, and I was quite amazed by it. "Is this something you guys were able to buy ready-made?" I asked. "This is like a plastic."

Dex grinned. "That's another one of Jimmy's specialties," he said. "That's actually nothing but a fleece blanket that has had a mixture of body filler and fiberglass resin applied to it. Jimmy built a form out of Styrofoam and covered that with aluminum foil, then sprayed it with adhesive and stretched the fleece onto it. Once that was done, all he had to do was paint on the mixture with a paintbrush, and then sand it smooth after it dried. Shoot a few coats of shiny paint on it, and it looks like something turned out by a factory. We use it for all kinds of things, and he'll probably even make the table and shelves out of it. It's lightweight and strong, so it will last a long time."

"That's amazing," I said. "I can think of a few things you guys could make for me out of that stuff."

He chuckled. "Make a list, and I'll tell Jimmy. He loves working with it."

Jimmy arrived a few minutes later and was surprised to see that we were back. I let the two of them discuss what he had accomplished while I went to the office and sat down at the desk. I was there less than five minutes when a pickup truck pulled up out front, and the sign on the side read, "Harrison Commercial Construction."

"Dex?" I called out. "Somebody's here."

He stepped into the office a second later, as the driver and another man climbed out of the pickup truck. He looked out the window and saw them, read the sign on the truck and then turned to look at me.

"What are you up to?" he asked.

"I told you there was a surprise, right?" I asked. "Well, surprise! You said you need a garage, so let's get one built."

Dex opened the door and let the contractors in, and they turned out to be a father and son. Richard and Daniel Harrison introduced themselves and managed not to stare for more than a couple of seconds when Dex presented me.

The four of us went outside, and I told Dex to show them where he wanted the garage and let them know how big it needed to be. He started out by describing an area that might hold three cars, but I interrupted.

"You can do better than that," I said. "You've got more than three quarters of an acre that's nothing but a paved parking lot. I think you want to use at least half of that for the garage, don't you?"

"Do you have any idea what that would cost?" he asked me.

"Do I look like I'm worried about it? Dex, you were right. You need a place to store finished vehicles that will keep them safe from the weather or vandalism. There's no point in building a garage if it isn't going to be big enough or you're going to outgrow it in a short time. Go ahead, get what you need."

The rest of the morning was spent discussing the whole project and shooting spray paint at different spots on the asphalt. By the time they were done, they had laid out a plan for a building that would be one hundred feet wide and sixty feet deep. It would have fourteen-foot ceilings, to accommodate the twelve-foot-high doors. That way, trucks could be backed right into it when cars needed to be loaded, and there was even going to be a very nice showroom where cars could be featured.

By lunchtime, the whole thing was laid out and priced. I told the Harrisons to go back and see David so that he could arrange the financing to get them started, and they said they would be back Monday morning to begin. The first phase was going to be ripping up the asphalt and leveling the ground, then pouring the concrete floor for the whole building.

Dex and Jimmy were both delighted, and it felt good to see them smile so much. When it was time for lunch, I insisted that we all go to Grizzly's to celebrate. Jimmy called Nicole, who had been working at New Beginnings that morning and was free for the afternoon, and she joined us there. The four of us spent the rest of the afternoon at the shop together after lunch and ended up back together at Grizzly's that evening.

It felt good to let my hair down and dance, have a few drinks and just celebrate being alive and in love and happy. Later that night, Dex took me home and showed me once again how wonderful it was to have a man who loves me the way he does.

We took it easy for the weekend, lounging around the house and catching up on some of our favorite TV shows. Critter seemed quite delighted to have us taking some time off, and most of the weekend found her sitting in one lap or the other. We were so contented that we didn't even bother cooking all weekend, which was unusual for us.

Okay, it was unusual for Dex. He's a far better cook than I am, and seemed to enjoy creating moderately elaborate meals for the two of us, but that weekend we simply ordered in everything except breakfast. I think Dex would rise from the grave to fry eggs and bacon and sausage.

The only thing that unsettled me that weekend came on Sunday afternoon. We were kicked back on the sofa, me leaning against Dex with Critter in my lap as we watched some movie on the TV, and then my phone rang. The caller ID said "Restricted," so I narrowed my eye and answered it.

"Hello?"

"This is a collect call from," said the recording, and then I heard a voice say, "Jenna Jackson." The recording continued, telling me to press five to accept the call, and I did so.

"Jenna?" I said. "Where..."

"Why did you do this?" she asked, and there was a vehemence in her voice that surprised me. "We were doing just fine, we were happy there. Why did you have to mess it all up?"

"Jenna," I said, carefully using the name she had been going by, "sometimes things aren't exactly the way they seem. My real name is Cassie, and I'm a private investigator. I was hired to find you and your family because..."

"You should've just left us alone," she said. "Everything was going so good, and now it's all screwed up. Now we have to start all over, and my brother and my dad are so upset I can hardly deal with them. Why couldn't you have just left us alone?"

The line went dead, and I turned to Dex. He was looking at me sympathetically. "Jody?" he asked.

"Yeah," I said. "I guess she just wanted to tell me how pissed off she is."

I called Alfie, but he was unable to track where the call had come from. I was nearly in tears by then, worried sick about this poor young girl who was taking on so much adult responsibility.

"Maybe she's right," I said. "Maybe I should've just left them alone. I mean, at least until I could be certain there was a problem, you know?"

"And how did you plan to accomplish that?" he asked. "It wasn't like we could hang around there for a couple of months."

"No, but maybe if I could have..."

"You're doing it again," he said. "You're second-guessing yourself. Cassie, you did what needed to be done. It's not your fault her father is some kind of lunatic, and you can't put that blame on yourself. You just keep working the case, find them again, and then maybe you'll have a better idea of what to do."

I let out a sigh. "Yeah, I guess," I said. I settled back against him again and tried to watch the movie, but I can't even tell you what it was about. No matter what my eye was looking at, all I could see was the tears that I heard in Jody's voice, and my heart was breaking for her. I didn't even know the girl, but there was some part of me that wanted to hold her close and protect her from all the pain and suffering that was a part of life.

Monday morning came, and both of us needed to go back to work just to recover from loafing all weekend. I walked into my office ten minutes earlier than usual, and found Angie in the break room making coffee.

"Oh, you're back," she said with a big smile.

"I told you I would be," I said, returning the smile. "I still have to take care of clients, you know."

"And you've got plenty of them," she said. "Five new ones, all since you left last week. When I came in the other day with Nicole, there were messages on the machine and I called them all back. I actually have a couple new messages this morning, but I haven't had a chance to reach out to them yet."

"Wow," I said. "How many appointments today?"

"Six," she replied. "Four of the new ones, and the two ladies who rescheduled from last week. Your first appointment is due at nine thirty, and I've already got her file on your desk. I have intake sheets for the new ones all ready for you." She smiled again, obviously proud of herself.

"Good work," I said excitedly. "Angie, I don't know what I would do without you."

She made a funny face and stuck her tongue out. "You'd have to make your own coffee, for one thing," she said. "But I'm only kidding, I don't mind. I'm just grateful for the job. With the way my memory messes up, you're probably the only one who can put up with me."

I chuckled and brushed that one off, then we stood there and chatted about our respective weekends until the coffee was done. I poured myself a cup and headed for my office, where I found Mary Barton's file lying on my desk.

Mary was a particularly critical case to me, because she had six children and all of them were under ten years old. I was fairly sure her husband was abusing those kids, but Mary wouldn't come right out and say so, and she wouldn't bring the kids to my office so I could get a look at them. I had considered making a child welfare report, which is sufficient to get welfare workers out to check on their safety, but it could also result in the kids being removed from her care if any evidence of abuse was found. My goal was to get them all out of there together if at all possible, and I had decided that it was time to be blunt with Mary.

I read through her file again, even though I almost knew it verbatim. Mary was twenty-nine years old and had been married to Chester for ten of those years. His abusive nature had shown itself in the very first year of their marriage, but she was one of those girls whose mother had suffered silently with abuse, so she thought it was just part of married life. It wasn't until she saw a few movies about abused women who went to extremes to escape their abusers that she began to realize there might be a way out.

She had originally come to the Outreach, back when I worked there. I had only met with her once back then, shortly before the bomb that destroyed the place. Afterward, when I was setting up my office, she was one of the ones I contacted to offer services to. She hadn't bothered to come in for the first few months, but then she'd called about a month ago for an appointment and had been back twice since then.

Chester's abuse was mostly verbal and emotional, but he could become violent on occasion. She told me that he was constantly calling her names, telling her how stupid she was and that she would never manage to be a decent wife, and how it made her feel helpless and hopeless. When I asked her point-blank about whether he was abusing the children, she only said that he would spank them when they needed it, but I had noticed that she always looked away when she said it. It was like she couldn't look me in the eye and lie to me at the same time, which was another effect that Freda had on people.

She had been scheduled to come in the previous Tuesday, but was one of the ones who had called to reschedule. I was glad she was coming in on this particular day, because I had intended to put my foot down with her the week before. I was going to give her a choice; either tell me the truth about Chester and the kids, or I was going to send Family Services out to find out for sure.

I heard the bell over the door at a couple of minutes before she was due, and Angie brought her to my office a moment later. I looked up in surprise when I realized she had all of her children with her, because she'd never brought them in before.

"Well, hello, there," I said. I could tell that she had warned them about my appearance, because they were all staring without looking like they wanted to run screaming out the door. "Come on in."

"I'm sorry to have to bring them with me today," Mary said. "I usually leave them with my mom or Chester, but neither of them was available today. I hope it's all right."

"It's fine, Mary," I said. "Who do we have here?" The kids' names were in the file, of course, but I was doing my best to put them at ease. I pointed to the biggest one, a boy. "What's your name?"

"I'm Charlie," he said shyly.

"Well, hello, Charlie. I'm pleased to meet you." I looked to the next child.

"I'm Susie," she said.

"I'm Lindsay," said the next girl without prompting.

The other three were acting shy, so I leaned forward and winked at the next one. "Come on, you can tell me your name, can't you?"

"Billy," he said. Then, he surprised me by pointing at the two youngest kids. "That's Bobby and Darla. They don't like to talk too much."

"Oh? Why is that?"

Billy started to say something, but Mary cut him off. "Because their daddy yells at them for talking too much," she said. "That's why they all act so shy and bashful."

I turned back to look at Mary. "Is that all he does?" I asked bluntly. "Just yell?"

She sucked on her bottom lip for a couple of seconds, then slowly shook her head. "He whips them, and sometimes he whips them pretty hard. I try to stop it, but then he just gets mad at me." She shrugged. "Better he hits me than them, though, right?"

FIFTEEN

"No," I said. "Better he doesn't hit anyone. Mary, with what you just told me, I have no choice but to make a report of child abuse. I'm required to by law, do you understand that?"

She nodded. "Yeah, I guess I do," she said. "What's going to happen then, though?"

"If I make the report, he's going to be arrested. He will be taken to jail and will spend a few days there, while he's waiting to go to arraignment. At that point, the judge will set his bail, and if he can pay it, he'll be released. Are you afraid of what he might do if he gets out?"

"I'm not really afraid, I don't guess," she said. "I just know he's going to be mad, so I don't guess anything will really change."

"Then it's up to you to change it," I said. "I'll help you get an order of protection against him, so that he can't come close to you until everything goes to court. At that point, the judge will decide whether he will be allowed to see the children or not, and under what conditions. He may have to only visit the kids with supervision, or he may be required to go to counseling for some time before he can see them. In the meantime, I can place you in a shelter with the kids so that he can't get close to you even if he wants to violate the order. If he tries, he'll simply be arrested again, and that time he's likely to go to prison."

Mary sat there for a moment and just looked at me, then turned to her oldest boy, Charlie. "You understand what Ms. Cassie is saying?" she asked.

Charlie nodded. "She says Daddy could go to jail for being so mean," he said.

"That's right," Mary said. "And she's also saying that we can go live somewhere else, so he can't be hitting on us no more. You think that would be a good idea?"

Charlie looked at her for a moment, then looked down at his brothers and sisters. Susie and Lindsay both nodded to him, but the other kids just looked at him. He looked back at his mother for a moment, then he turned to me.

"Mom is scared," he said. "Daddy whips on her a lot. I ain't afraid of him, and he knows it, but he can still whip me in a fight. Can you make the cops keep him in jail, so he can't whip on us no more?"

I sighed. "They'll take him to jail, but when he goes to court to see the judge, he'll get a chance to bail out. That's why I want to put all of you in a place where he can't get to you."

Charlie, who couldn't have been more than nine years old, looked at me with eyes that were far older than his true age. "Yeah, I think we'd better do it," he said, and I saw a relief hit Mary's face. Unable to make a decision on her own, she had put the responsibility for the choice on her oldest child, and I was amazed that the nine-year-old boy accepted it without hesitation.

I called Angie to take the younger kids back out to the lobby and let them play with the toys I kept there, while Mary, Charlie and I stayed in my office. As soon as they were gone, I picked up the phone and called Alicia. As always, she immediately put things in motion to have Chester Barton arrested and charged with spousal and child abuse.

Then, I took the official statements from both Mary and Charlie, detailing instances of abuse that were far worse in some cases than I had even suspected. Charlie, for example, had once gotten his left arm broken from a belt whipping his dad had delivered, although the hospital was only told that he fell out of a tree. Lindsay, who was seven, had been forced to stay home from school for three days because she was literally unable to sit. She had laid on her belly the whole time, because sitting on her bruised bottom was simply too painful. Those were only two of the stories I heard, and I had to work at keeping the rage out of my voice.

When it was finished, I scanned the signed statement and emailed it to Alicia. It was all she needed to finish getting a warrant for Chester's arrest, and she called me minutes later to tell me that officers were on the way to his place of employment to pick him up. Another officer was on the way to my office, and would accompany Mary and the kids to their home to pack clothing and essentials so that I could send them out to New Beginnings.

By ten o'clock, Chester was in jail and Mary and the kids were gone. Alicia had sent a police officer to take her back to the house to pack clothing and such, and I had given her directions out to New Beginnings. They would be given rooms there as soon as they arrived.

The rest of the day was spent doing intakes on some of the new clients, but then I had Carrie Vincent, the other reschedule from the week before. She came in at three thirty, my last appointment for the day.

Carrie was a different kind of case. She wasn't being physically abused; instead, her husband was essentially apathetic toward her. She came to see me primarily just to have someone to talk to, and I was trying to get her to understand that being ignored is another form of emotional abuse. She was miserable, but she was unwilling to leave him because her little girl, who was only three, idolized her dad.

Her husband, Donnie, didn't seem to care that much for the child, either, but at least he put up with her attention. He would let her sit in his recliner with him, always on the side so she could snuggle under his shoulder, but as soon as she would fall asleep he would snap his fingers for Carrie to come and take the child to bed. The majority of his communication with his wife was similar to that, finger snaps or grunts to get her attention, then pointing to indicate what he wanted.

Personally, I thought Donnie might have some serious mental issues, but I couldn't point to anything that made him a danger to his wife or child. The best I could do for Carrie was be a sympathetic ear, and she took advantage of it from time to time.

I spent her hour listening, letting her pour out her heart while knowing that she wasn't going to take any action to improve her situation. To me, those are some of the saddest cases. Donnie wouldn't stop her if she tried to leave; he might not even notice she was gone until it was time to eat. It was Carrie who kept herself trapped, but there was little hope she was ever going to do what it took to improve her lot in life.

When she left, I walked out to the lobby and sat with Angie for a bit. There wasn't much to say, but at least we had made a difference in Mary's life that day. I told her to go ahead and close up, and I would see her the next morning.

I walked over to the shop where Dex was getting cleaned up to go home, and took the opportunity to look inside that custom motorhome again. They had gotten the rest of the walls covered with paneling, and were in the process of laying carpet. The interior was really starting to take shape, and it occurred to me that I might like for us to have something along that line, one day.

"Like what you see?" Dex asked, slipping in behind me and catching me off guard.

I smiled at him. "I do," I said. "How much does a machine like this cost, anyway?"

"By the time we get finished," he said, "the customer will have about two hundred thousand invested. Parts and components cost about eighty thousand, and the rest is our labor. Lot of hours go into building something like this."

"Wow," I said. "I wouldn't mind having one, but that's a lot of money."

"Oh, it wouldn't cost us that much. I could build us something along this line for no more than about fifty, sixty thousand. In this case, the customer wanted top-of-the-line components. The engine we put in this thing cost twenty-five thousand, and we're using some pretty expensive interior materials. We could do just as good a job with stuff that didn't cost nearly as much, if you decide you want one."

"It would be nice. What would you want to start with? What kind of truck, I mean?"

He got a twinkle in his eye. "There is an old International cabover I've had my eye on for a little while. It's something out of the early forties, not sure what year, but if you're game I'll see what I can get it for."

"Go for it," I said, grinning. "But I want to help build it."

Dex burst out laughing. "Okay," he said. "Just be careful what you ask for."

And that was the exact moment when my phone rang. I took it out of my pocket and saw that it was Alfie calling.

"Hey, Alfie," I said. "What's up?"

"My fees," he said. "Because I, princess, am the man who can do the *impossible!*"

My eyebrows shot upward and Dex looked at me, curious. "What is that supposed to mean?" I asked.

"It means, my little darling, that I have found a seriously solid lead on the Logan family. How soon can you get over here?"

I blinked. "We'll be there in half an hour."

The phone went dead and I told Dex what he had said. Dex called out to Jimmy that we were leaving and he would have to lock up, then we hurried out to the Cuda and were gone.

We swung through the pizza shop and picked up a pepperoni, then hurried on to Alfie's place. When he let us into his apartment, I simply opened the box and let him grab a slice as he hustled back to his stool.

"Okay, spill it," I said. "There's more pizza, but you don't get any unless you really have something for me."

"I got something, all right," he said. "And you're not going to believe it, but it's true. I thought about what I would do if I was Logan, got nowhere to go but with a good supply of cash, and wanting to stay completely incognito. I'd probably be looking for something that would provide me a place to live that wouldn't be in my own name, right?"

"Okay, I can see that," I said.

"Good. So I wrote a program to search all the survivalist boards, the property boards and all the job boards looking for something that might be down his alley, and I got a couple of hits. One of them was an ad for a natural healer for an intentional community in Montana, and it specifically said that it came with a fully furnished cabin. I sent an email to inquire about it, but all I really wanted was the headers from the email they sent me in response. That gave me what I needed to hack into their account and read all the emails they got, and one of them jumped out at me. It was a Doctor Albright with two kids, and he was looking for a chance to settle in Montana because he said it would be better for his children there. He said he was a widower, trying to put his life back together after his wife was murdered, and made it such a beautiful sob story that almost nobody could have passed it up. He was asked to show up for an interview, and he must've gotten the job because everyone else was told it was filled later that day. I figure, with a story so close to the one he was using before, it's got to be our guy."

"You're kidding," I said. "Alfie, that's incredible. Where is he?"

"The place is called Harmony Valley, and it's about fifty

miles east of Helena, near White Sulphur Springs. The people who put it together bought twelve hundred acres and have started their own little town. They use wind and solar for electricity, and they actually dammed a small river to make a reservoir, so they have plenty of fresh water. I mean, this place is so out there that they don't even use septic tanks, everything is composted. That's why they need a naturopath, because they don't allow any chemicals of any kind, not even antibiotics. If it ain't natural, it ain't coming in."

I stood behind him and looked at the image on his monitor, which was apparently taken by a satellite. It showed about a hundred little buildings, and I felt a shiver go down my spine as I realized that the Logans were living in one of them.

I turned to Dex. "If we leave in the morning," I said, "how long would it take us to get there?"

"You'd be looking at almost twenty-four hours of driving," Alfie said. "Or, you could fly into Bozeman and rent a car, and be there in about eight hours. I already checked all the flights."

Dex grinned at me and nodded. I turned back to Alfie.

"Okay, go ahead and book us on a flight in the morning," I said. "And this time, I'm going to turn Freda loose completely. They're not getting away again." I handed him my credit card so he could book the flight, and then he printed out everything we would need the following morning. We'd be flying out at six thirty, arriving in Bozeman at just a bit before noon their time. We also went ahead and arranged a car, a Jeep that could handle the rough roads we expected to encounter.

I wasn't really in the mood for pizza, so we left it with Alfie and headed for home, stopping at KFC on the way for a bucket of chicken and all the trimmings. Critter was particularly happy when we came in, because she knew she was going to end up getting a few pieces of chicken out of me; let's face it, I spoil that cat.

Then we packed, and Critter figured out instantly what was going on. Her mood went from "life is good" to "I'm going to kill you in your sleep" in five seconds flat.

Dex called Jimmy, and I called Angie to let them know that we were going to be gone again for a few days. Hopefully it wouldn't be long, but it depended on what happened. I was not about to let Logan slip away again, even if it meant I had to arrange for someone to come take care of you-know-who. I was staying on his trail until I got him, this time.

Then I took a deep breath and called Maggie.

"Maggie, it's Cassie. I'm pretty sure we found them, but I won't know for certain until tomorrow afternoon. I'm flying up to Montana in the morning to make sure, and I'll call you when I have something more to tell you."

"Oh my God," she said, "are you serious? You really think you found them again?"

"Yes," I said. "A friend of mine who's good with computers has been looking for them, and he stumbled across a job that seemed like it was tailor-made for your husband. He did a little snooping and found out there's a good chance that Harold contacted them, and it looks like he was hired. It's in an intentional community that's not too far from Bozeman. My fiancé and I are flying up there in the morning and will rent a car to drive out to the place. If he's there, I intend to nail him, this time."

"And if you do, what happens with the kids? Will they be all right?"

"Since they were told you were killed, and that's not true, there's no reason not to release them to your care. I'll probably need you to send me some kind of written authorization so that I can pick them up and bring them back to you, but it shouldn't be any kind of problem. With any luck, they should be back with you within the next few days."

Maggie was in tears, but they were tears of happiness. I tried to caution her that we weren't one hundred percent certain that it was them, just yet, but she was sure it was. All I could do after that was pray that I was right. I promised to call her as soon as I knew for sure, and we said good night.

I started to put my phone away, but then remembered Special Agent McIver. I had to rummage in my purse to find his card, and then I dialed his cell phone once again.

"McIver," he said. "Ms. McGraw?"

"Yes, sir," I said. "I thought you'd like to know that we got a lead on the Logans. Dex and I are flying up to Montana in the morning to confirm whether it's them or not."

"Where?" he asked.

I didn't want to give up their actual location just yet, because that ego of mine still wanted to be the one to nail Harold for what he had done to his wife and his kids. "In the middle of nowhere," I said. "We are flying to Bozeman, and then we have to follow a bunch of directions to get to where they are supposed to be. If it's them, I will call you immediately and let you know." *Immediately after you put them under citizen's arrest, right?* Abby's voice said in my head.

"Be sure you do," McIver said. "We don't want to take a chance on them slipping away again, now do we?"

"No, sir," I said. "I have absolutely no intention of it."

"Very good, Ms. McGraw. I'll talk to you when you know more."

Dex and I got showers and then I took out that dreaded mask. I was pretty sure Logan never got a look at my face there in Fort Collins, and I didn't want him to recognize me as soon as we showed up, so it just made sense to put it back on. I cleaned it thoroughly and then washed off the glass eye, popped it into place and applied the mask. I made sure the glue was covering every part of the inner surface, because I was probably going to be wearing it for a couple of days. When I got it, the instructions said I could wear it for up to a week, but three days was the longest I'd ever kept it on without at least taking it off for a little while. Burned skin tends to dry out and has to be moisturized periodically. More than three days, and it would really start to hurt.

Finally, when that was finished, we went to bed early. We had to be up by four in order to get to the airport by five, because we had to check in ninety minutes early. We put our guns in our bags, making sure they were unloaded and the ammunition safely stored, and made sure we had our paperwork ready, because we had to declare them as we got on the flight.

Four o'clock in the morning comes way too early, I don't care how early you go to bed. Dex had to drag me out from under the covers, but then I managed to focus and get myself ready to go. We left the house with just enough time to make it to the airport and start the check-in process.

Luckily, there was no line ahead of us. We used the automated check-in kiosks and then waltzed through security without being flagged. Even declaring the guns didn't cause any problems as far as I could tell, and we had breakfast in one of those little restaurants that are inside the security area. That and some coffee helped me come to life a bit more, and then all we had to do was wait for our flight to be called.

One thing I've never figured out is why, when you're flying out of Tulsa, Oklahoma and headed for somewhere north like Montana, you have to make a stop in Dallas. That just doesn't make any sense to me. I mean, why do I have to go south in order to go north? I'm sure there's a good reason, but I really didn't feel like expending the brain-power to try to make sense of it that early in the morning. When they finally called the flight, I was happy to get into my window seat—Dex was gracious enough to let me have it—and drift off to sleep before the plane even left the ground.

I woke up again as we were descending, and Dex told me would be landing within fifteen minutes.

"Great," I said. "Oh, I needed that nap. Did you get any sleep?"

"No, not really," he said. "I had somebody snoring in my ear, made it hard to drift off."

Silly me, I looked around for a moment before I realized he was talking about me. I gave him a sheepish smile, and he started chuckling.

"I'm kidding," he said. "I was asleep just a few minutes after you, and I only woke up when the bell went off to tell us to fasten our seat belts again. If you snored, I didn't know it."

I got him in the side with my elbow and he laughed

again. "I'll get you back," I said. "You just wait and see if I don't."

I grudgingly got up and followed him off the plane, and then we found that we only had twenty minutes to make it across the Dallas airport to where our next flight would be boarding. Whispering a prayer that our bags would get transferred properly, we hurried along and got there just in time. Once again, Dex let me have the window, but this time I stayed awake while he leaned back and snoozed like a content little baby.

I nudged him when we began descent, and he woke instantly. The plane landed a few minutes later and we made our way off, then found the Enterprise counter. They had our Jeep ready to go, and I signed all the paperwork quickly so we could get on the road.

Harmony Valley, here we come. I let Dex drive, and sat back to enjoy the scenery as it rolled by. It was beautiful, I can tell you that. That part of Montana has gentle rolling hills in some places and steep ones in others, but there's one thing that's common no matter where you look, and that's the trees. There were probably hundreds of different varieties, and I was fascinated by all the many colors and shapes that I saw. Add in the big, beautiful sky and the fleecy clouds, and this was a place I could easily imagine living someday.

"I know what you're thinking," Dex said.

I turned to him. "Yeah? And what's that?" I'd grown accustomed to him seemingly reading my mind, but occasionally he caught me by surprise.

"You're thinking this would be a great place to retire to someday."

I grinned. "Close enough," I said. "Don't you agree?"

"I take it you've never been up here in the wintertime," he said. "If you had, you'd know that you get snowdrifts deeper than you are, and stretches of winter that can last for weeks at well below zero. I don't know about you, but my scars don't like cold weather very much."

I stared at him. "It gets that cold up here?"

"Cassie, we are almost five hundred miles further north than we are in Tulsa. That's five hundred miles closer to the North Pole, just so you know."

"Okay, Tulsa gets cold enough," I said. "Forget about retiring in Montana. How about Hawaii? It doesn't get cold there, does it?"

"Nope. Of course, there's the volcanoes and the mosquitoes to deal with. I understand some of them are big enough that you have to swat them three or four times before it kills them."

I cocked my head in disbelief. "Okay, now you're just pulling my leg," I said. "There aren't any mosquitoes that big."

He shrugged. I waited a moment to see if he was going to say anything else, then I leaned closer.

"There aren't, are there?"

He turned and looked at me with a solemn expression, then he couldn't hold it any longer. He burst out laughing and shook his head. "Not that I know of," he said. "But you should've seen the look on your face for a minute there—it was priceless."

I glared. "And speaking of priceless," I said, "guess what it's gonna take for you to ever get into my pants again!"

He roared, laughing, and I held out as long as I could before I joined in.

SIXTEEN

THE DRIVE TO HARMONY VALLEY TOOK ALMOST two hours, mostly because of the curves, but the scenery made it pass like a matter of minutes. We saw mountains and valleys and waterfalls and just about every beautiful scene you could imagine in the wilderness, all from the comfort of the Jeep. It wasn't until the GPS told us we were getting close that we began paying more attention to our immediate surroundings.

The community was down a dirt road, and I was really glad we were driving a Jeep. There were potholes almost big enough to fall into, Jeep and all, and we splashed through creeks that cut right through the road. A couple of them were deep enough that water actually came in under the doors, but Dex just plowed on through.

The road was supposed to be about five miles long, but it seemed like ten. We came around the bend that was at the base of the hill, and suddenly there was the little town right in front of us. Dex pulled over to the side of the road, then reached into the small bag he had in the backseat and took out a wig and a pair of horn-rimmed glasses. He was a redhead, this time, and looked considerably different than he had in Fort Collins. He was also not wearing the leather vest, but had his forty-five tucked into the back of his jeans.

Once he was satisfied with his appearance, he started the Jeep again and we drove on into the little community. There were several houses along a number of dirt trails, but it was easy to see where the downtown area— I'll call it that, for lack of a better expression—was. There were four large wooden buildings there, and one of them bore a sign that declared it to be the Harmony Valley General Store. It was about the size of an average church building, but there were gas pumps out front. Dex pulled up to them and we got out.

Our plan was to let the locals believe we were thinking about settling there, being part of their off-grid world, so we were supposedly visiting the community to ask about options and possibilities. In the course of that, we hoped to slip in an innocent question about whether there might be a doctor in the community. If we were asked why we wanted to know, I was going to smile proudly and say that I was pregnant.

The pumps were an old style that I had never seen, but Dex said there had still been a few like those when he was a kid. There was nowhere to put your credit card, you just had to turn a handle, and that made the dials listing the price and amount of money you spent spin back to zero. Then you pumped the gas, and whatever the total came to, you paid inside. I watched, sort of fascinated, while he filled up the tank on the Jeep and then we walked into the store.

"Hey," said a lady behind the counter. "How y'all doing?"

I was taken aback for a second, because her accent didn't sound like anything I'd heard this far north of the Mason-Dixon line. When I was a kid, we had relatives from Tennessee who used to come and visit, and this lady sounded for all the world like my aunt Judy.

"Doing pretty good," Dex said, using a countrified accent similar to my own, "assuming we're in the right place. This is Harmony Valley, right?"

The lady's eyes went wide. "Well, that's what it says on my sign out front," she said. "So if it ain't, there's something seriously wrong. You folks aren't from around here?"

"No," Dex said. "We are actually from Illinois, but we've been reading about this place in some magazines lately and wanted to come and check it out."

Fortunately, Harmony Valley had been written up in several prepper, survivalist and back-to-nature publications over the last few months. I had found some of the stories and we had both looked through them the day before at home.

"Really?" she asked. "Y'all thinking about settling up here, maybe?"

"It sounds interesting," Dex said, trying not to sound like he was already committed. "We had a little vacation time coming and decided to come look things over, see if maybe it would be a good place to raise a family."

The lady, who was wearing a name tag that said Bernice, glanced at me and her eyes went directly to my belly. She broke out into a big smile. "Well, glory be," she said. "Got a little one on the way, don't we? Well, I'll tell you this, you can't find a better place to raise young'ns then around here. The best air and healthiest environment in the whole damn country, you ask me."

"Ask you what?" said a voice from the back of the building, and we turned to see a gray-haired man coming toward us. He was carrying a box, and he set it on the counter as he got close.

"This young couple is thinking about moving up here from Illinois," Bernice said. "They got a baby on the way, and they're looking for a place to raise a family. I told 'em this is about the best place in the world for that, ain't it?"

The man chuckled and held out a hand to Dex, who shook it. "John Bonfield," he said. "That's my wife Bernice who's trying to sell you on the place."

Dex smiled at him. "She's doing a mighty fine job of it," he said. "I'm Vince Daughtry, and this is my wife Amanda. We read a couple of articles about how you folks have put this community together, and thought we'd come check it out. I mean, if we're going to have children, we want to do it in the best place possible."

"Well, this might be it, but we want everybody to decide that for themselves. The whole point of Harmony Valley is that people can be free to do and live as they wish. We got a pretty good relationship with the county sheriff, and he's promised not to bother us as long as we don't start any kind of serious trouble. It's worked out for the last four years, and I don't see any reason it needs to change. We've got all kinds of folks here, and we don't discriminate against nobody, so that's something you might want to bear in mind. Don't matter if you're black, white, red or green, don't matter if you're straight or gay, don't matter if you're Christian or Muslim or atheist or whatever, as long as you ain't bothering nobody else, we figure how you live is your business. That sound like something you can handle?"

Dex put a mock serious expression on his face, as if he was really thinking it over. "Well, let's see," he said. "I've got one cousin who's black, a brother who's gay and one of my best friends back home is Hindu. This place don't sound a whole lot different than where I grew up."

John laughed, and his wife joined in. "I think you'll do fine around here," he said. "You thinking about buying a place, or would you prefer to build?"

I hadn't expected that question, but Dex took it in stride. "Build, probably," he said. "We've been looking at those log home kits, you know, and some of them are absolutely beautiful."

"Yeah, they are," John said. "They ain't cheap, though. Can I ask what kind of work you do?"

Dex grinned and tried to look modest. "Well, I'm a writer," he said. "I write for a number of magazines, but I'm also turning out the occasional novel nowadays. Doesn't make me rich, but we live pretty comfortably."

"Okay, that's nice," John said. "We got a couple of writers here now, maybe you would know some of them."

"I doubt that," Dex said. "Most of the ones I know are magazine staff writers back in New York, and that's one place I never want to go again."

John chuckled. "Been there, so I can understand exactly what you mean. Well, if you're looking for a place to build one of those cabins, there's quite a bit of land available here. We sell it in plots of two acres, five acres or ten acres, take your pick. If you decide you want to get things started, I'd be the guy you come to about that. We've got some beautiful parcels around here, and I'd love to show you some of them."

"I'll probably take you up on that," Dex said, "but we want to learn a little bit more about the community, first. From what I read, the kids are homeschooled up here, is that right?"

Bernice cut in. "We all believe that public education is a disaster," she said. "A lot of the families here like to stick to homeschooling, but we've got kind of a cooperative thing going on. Ellie Dunhill, she teaches most of the kids their numbers around here, and Marcy Gladstone teaches them about music, because she can play just about every instrument ever made. Bonnie Benning, she's a history buff so she teaches them a lot of history. It's not really a school, but we have a building where all the kids and the parents who help teach get together a couple days a week for special lessons like that. Everything else, the parents kinda teach at home. It all seems to work out pretty good for us."

I smiled. "That sounds great," I said. "I agree about public schools, they suck."

John burst out laughing at my comment, and I realized that saying "they suck" might have been something they didn't hear very often. Bernice pretended to frown at me for it, but I could tell she was holding back a giggle.

"What about hunting around here?" Dex asked. "Is it allowed?"

"Oh, yes," John said. "Of course, you got to do your hunting in season, like everybody else, but there's more elk, deer and moose on our land than you'll ever see anywhere else in the state. That's one of the reasons we bought it, because of the hunting and fishing. We've got five rivers crossing through the property, and all of them are chock-full of fish. We hunt deer, moose, elk, bear and pretty much all the game fowl. There's a lake on the southern border of our property, and we got rights to it in the deal when we bought the place. It's a great place for fishing and duck hunting, I can tell you that."

"You're making me not want to go home at all," Dex said. "What about medical care? Is there a doctor around here anywhere?"

Bernice broke into a big smile. "Oh, yes," she said. "We just got one, just a few days ago. Doctor Albright is a naturopath, because we don't allow any pharmaceutical medicines."

"That's because of the composting," John said. "We compost all waste, even our own, and we don't want to put chemicals on the garden."

Dex nodded. "I can understand that," he said. "Mandy and I both prefer natural remedies, but the stupid laws back in Illinois require vaccinations and things that we just don't really believe in. That's one of the reasons we're looking at getting out of there."

I nodded enthusiastically, even though I was actually kind of amazed at how well Dex was dissembling. It hadn't occurred to me that we might need to be fans of naturopathy, but it made sense as I heard him saying it.

"How about groceries?" Dex asked. "You folks seem to

have quite a selection, but we're partial to organic foods. I'm sure that's what you have here, mostly?"

"It's all we got," John said. "You won't find anything GMO in our store, that I can guarantee. A lot of the stuff we carry is grown right here, and the rest comes from places we've checked out thoroughly. All the meat is local, grass-fed beef, free-range chicken, goat and mutton, and we even buy some of the game meat in season. I've got a pretty good supply of venison and elk, if you have a taste for that stuff."

"I do indeed," Dex said. "I need to pay for my gas, then is it okay if we just drive around a bit, look things over?"

"Sure, you're more than welcome," John said. "Couple things you might want to know about, there is a red building down the end of this road out in front of our store, that's the restaurant. Chuck and Betty Islington run that, and all the meat and produce is local. If you feel the need to have a bite to eat while you're here, I can guarantee you're gonna fall in love with that place. Then, if you go about two miles further, you'll see a white brick building, that's the clinic. That's where you'll find Doctor Albright, and he lives in the cabin right behind it. Super nice fella, and those kids of his are great. His wife died a while back, I understand, but his kids are really well behaved, great kids."

"He sounds wonderful," Dex said. "You think he'd mind if we stopped in to meet him?"

"Oh, no," John said. "Like I said, super nice fella. You just tell them we sent you down, won't be any problem at all." He eyed me for a moment. "You might want to talk to him about his ideas on childbirth, stuff like that. Those are good things to know when you're thinking about moving into an area, you know?"

"I'll be sure to do that," I said. "I've been reading up on natural childbirth, and I'm pretty sure that's how I want to go."

Abby jumped up in the back of my head. *Seriously? Natural childbirth? Girl, are you crazy?*

I ignored her for the moment, but what I had said was strictly for show. I had heard horror stories about what childbirth was like, and if I ever had to go through it, it was going to be with drugs. Good drugs. None of that wide awake, feel every pain and contraction, scream and yell and carry on like an idiot stuff for me. Give me something so I don't feel what's going on, then get that kid out. That would be my approach to childbirth.

"Well, in that case," Bernice said, "we ought to get you in touch with Charlene Loring. She's our local midwife, so you'd want to get her involved."

"Oh, yes," I said, pretending enthusiasm. "I wasn't sure if midwives were allowed up here."

"Oh, sure," John said. "We do a lot of things the old-fashioned way around here."

As Dex paid for the gas, I was looking at some of the items they had on display near the register, and something caught my eye. It was a small book filled with quotations, and all of them were about pursuing your dreams. That was a sort of personal theme for me and Dex, so I decided to get one. I laid it on the counter and pulled some bills out of my pocket. Bernice told me how much it was and I paid for it, then turned around and handed it to Dex.

"I got you something," I said. "I think it's something you'll want to keep with you."

He grinned as he glanced through the book, then shoved

it into his shirt pocket. "I'll read it later," he said. "Let's go look around a bit, okay?"

"You bet," I said with a smile. I waved to Bernice and John, and we thanked them as we left, then got back into the Jeep and headed down the road. As soon as we pulled away from the gas pumps, Dex looked over at me. "I don't know about you, but I'm starving," he said. "It might look good if we put in an appearance at the restaurant before we go looking for the doctor."

"I'm thinking along the same line," I said. "Let's just make sure we keep our stories straight, so we don't end up tripping ourselves."

"That's easy," he said. "I'm Vince, you're Mandy. I thought it was interesting that Bernice jumped to her own conclusion about you being pregnant."

I chuckled. "Yeah, especially since I'm not. We were going to say I was, anyway, so I'm glad you just went along with it."

The big red building came into view and we pulled up into its parking lot. There were a couple of other cars there, and we walked in looking like typical tourists, I'm sure. I kept my left hand tucked into my pocket, just in case we happened to run into the Logans inside, but they weren't there.

A lady wearing an apron waved at us and said to sit wherever we liked, so we took a table near the front windows. There were menus on the table and everything looked absolutely delicious. The special of the day was listed as the steak sandwich, with home fries and baked beans. Both of us decided to go for that, and we were ready to order by the time the waitress came over.

She was an older lady with hair that had recently started to go gray and a beautiful smile. "Hello, there," she said. "I'm Betty, and it's my pleasure to serve you today. Can I ask what you folks would like to drink?"

The beverages listed on the menu were mostly juices, and I asked for apple juice. Dex went for grape juice, and told Betty that we both wanted the special. She beamed at us as if we were a couple of her long-lost children, then hurried away to put in the order. She was back only a minute later with our juice, and I can tell you that I've never tasted better apple juice in my life.

"Mmm, that's good," I said. Dex nodded as he sipped his own grape juice, then told me that he'd never had better, himself.

There were a few other patrons in the restaurant, so we sat there and talked about how beautiful the area was and how we were both leaning toward trying to settle there. I offered a couple of very minor objections, just so that people could hear him overcoming them for me, and a couple of people even spoke up to tell us how much they loved living there. One couple said they had only been there for three months, and couldn't imagine ever wanting to live anywhere else.

If it wasn't for that whole thing about the cold, they might've actually sold us on it. The place was definitely beautiful, and there was an atmosphere of peace and harmony all around it.

When our plates came, Dex and I were both thrilled. I've seen steak sandwiches, but I've never seen one as big as this one. It was about a twelve-ounce round steak between two slices of bread so big that I figure they sliced the loaf lengthwise, rather than vertically. I had to take my hand out of my pocket to pick it up, but I was careful to keep it out of sight as much as I could.

Then I bit into the sandwich, and nothing else seemed to matter. I moaned in pure delight, and so did Dex. The other patrons chuckled, and I realized they had probably seen this happen before.

We took our time eating, not wanting to look like we were up to anything other than just checking out the community. If the doctor here was the one we thought it was, he'd still be there when we finished this magnificent feast. And if he wasn't, well—it might almost be worth it. We found him once; we could find him again if we had to.

Eventually, though, all good things do come to an end. When we had both sopped up the last of the meat juices with the home fries, when we had licked the spoon from the baked beans, we decided it was time to get back to business. Dex happily paid our check and left a very generous tip, and then we headed out and got into the Jeep once again.

"Okay, you ready for this?" he asked.

I opened my mouth to say that I was, but then I was interrupted by a tap on the window beside me. I turned, startled, and found myself looking in the face of Special Agent McIver. I rolled down the window with my eye wide, and the arrogant jerk grinned at me.

"You didn't think I was going to trust you to call me in on this, did you?" he asked. "I've seen you work, remember? You like to be Brenda Badass."

"How did you find us?" I asked.

"I'm FBI, remember? I checked to see what flight you were on, then looked to see where you were getting a rental car. I flew in an hour behind you, got a car of my own and used the rental car's loss locator to find out where you'd gone."

"Loss locator?" I asked. "What's that?"

"Most rental car companies, and Enterprise is one of them, put a GPS locator chip in every car. It checks in with every cell tower it comes in range of, and reports its exact position. Yours reported in about twenty minutes ago while you were sitting here, so I just pulled up here and waited until you came out."

"Jerk," I said. "Are you all by yourself?"

"Of course," he said. "You'll back me up, won't you?" He opened the back door on the Jeep and climbed inside, then put on a seat belt. "Let's go get them, shall we?"

I turned around and looked at him over the back of my seat, then turned to face forward again. "I guess so," I said. Dex chuckled, then started the Jeep and backed out of the parking lot. We drove off sedately, as if we were just looking everything over, and then I turned to look at McIver again.

"I really was going to call you," I said. "I just want to try to take Logan without any problems."

"Then we have the same agenda," McIver said. "Don't worry, I'm not here to steal your glory. I want him to answer some questions, but my report will state that you brought me to him. Voluntarily, incidentally. I'm not going to say I had to track you down to get you to do it."

I finally gave in and grinned. Maybe this guy was okay, after all.

We spotted the white brick building a few minutes later, about five miles outside of the actual community. Dex pulled up to it and we sat there for a moment, the three of us talking about how to approach the situation.

"There's no way he's going to recognize me," I said. "The last time he saw me, I was doing my Freda Krueger impersonation. Let me go to the door and knock, and then you guys can get out and follow me inside."

"I just want to point out," McIver said, "he doesn't know me, either. It's possible he'll recognize your voice, but I've never met the guy at all."

I huffed. "Okay, fine, you can go first," I said. "Let's just get this over with, shall we? I'm really looking forward to letting those kids know their mother is not dead."

"Yes, ma'am," McIver said. He opened the door and got out of the Jeep, then walked up to the door of the clinic. He raised his hand to knock, but then the door opened before he could and Jody Logan stood there with a smile on her face.

"Hello," she said. "How can we help you today?"

"Hi," McIver said. I had the window down so I could hear what was happening, and it sounded like everything was going okay. "I was just down at the little restaurant, and I'm not really feeling too good. They told me I should come down and see if the doctor had time to see me."

"Sure," Jody said. "Come on in." She opened the screen door and held it for him as he stepped inside, and Dex and I waited for the door to close again before we got out of the Jeep ourselves.

We walked up to the door and stood there for a few seconds, then I pulled open the screen door while Dex grabbed the knob and shoved the main door open. We hurried inside, and I remember hearing a car outside as we did so. I heard the sound of tires crunching on gravel, but I was focused on finding Harold Logan and didn't pay any more attention than that.

McIver was standing to one side of the room with Logan right there in front of him. Both men turned to look in our direction, and Logan looked annoyed.

"I beg your pardon? Most people knock."

"They're with me," McIver said. He pulled his hand out of his pocket and showed his badge, and Logan stared at it for a moment as if he couldn't comprehend what he was seeing. When it dawned on him, his face turned white and his eyes grew round.

"Daddy?" Jody said. "Daddy, what's going on?"

"What's going on, Jody," I said, catching her attention by using her real name, "is that this gentleman is an FBI agent, a real one. I'm afraid your father has been lying to you about some things, and the FBI wants to ask him some questions."

She turned and looked at me, her eyes wide. "It's you," she said, shock evident in her expression. "What happened to your burned-up face?"

I was surprised, because no one else has ever recognized me with the mask on. This girl was quite observant, and probably very smart, but then, she also knew my voice.

"Yes, I'm Cassie McGraw," I said, "and I'm a private investigator from Tulsa. Your mother hired me to find you, because she's not really dead."

"My *mother?*" she asked, her face suddenly twisted. "Oh, my God, you didn't tell her where we are, did you?"

It suddenly dawned on me that what I was hearing in her voice was pure panic, and that shocked me. "Wait a minute,"

I said. "The last time I saw you, you told me how your mother was murdered, that she was involved in some criminal plot and..."

"That was the story Mr. Garibaldi told us to use," she said, tears starting to run down her face. "If she knows we are alive... Oh, my God!"

I was staring at her, my own eye just about to pop out of my face. "But, Jody..."

That was as far as I got. The door behind us slammed open, and McIver suddenly went for his gun. For a second I thought he was aiming it at me, but then a shot rang out just behind me and he fell. Dex and I both spun, and there stood Maggie Logan with a pistol in her hand.

"Maggie? What the hell..."

"Thank you, Cassie," she said with a broad smile. "I knew you'd find them for me, and you did. I can handle things from here on out. Why don't you go get in your car and leave, and you can come back to check on your friend later."

The gun in her hand was pointed directly at her husband, and I suddenly remembered the rumors we'd heard about how domineering and cruel she could be. "Maggie, I don't know what you're doing, but this is not the way to handle this situation. The man you just shot is an FBI agent, and if he's dead you're looking at more trouble than you can imagine."

She looked at McIver, then shook the gun as if trying to point at him. "Check him, Harold," she commanded, and Logan squatted down to take a good look at McIver.

He looked up a moment later. "He's alive, but he's in

bad shape," he said. "He's probably going to need surgery, Maggie. Let me call an ambulance, please?"

"No, no, not yet," she said. "Just do whatever you have to do to make sure he doesn't die, then you and I have some things to settle." She looked at me again. "Seriously, Cassie, you need to leave. I appreciate what you've done, and I don't want to have to hurt you."

I stared at her, wondering how in the world I could've missed signs that she was mentally unstable. When she had been in my office, she had appeared rational, even if the stories of her dreams seemed a little spooky. When I spoke to her on the phone, she had also seemed perfectly normal, a mother worried about her children.

And yet, the woman I was looking at now was literally smiling while she held a gun on her husband, right after having shot an FBI agent who might conceivably die from his wound. There had to have been some sign that I missed; there simply had to have been.

"Maggie," I said, "you've got to believe me, this is not the way to handle things. We have to get help for Agent McIver, and we need to do it quickly. He's bleeding, and if he bleeds to death..."

"He's not my concern," Maggie said. "All I want is my kids. They come with me, and the rest of you can do whatever, I don't care." She motioned with the gun for Harold to get up and move away from McIver, then looked at Jody. "Jody? Sweetheart, where is your brother?"

Jody licked her lips, sheer terror evident on her face. "He's—he's upstairs."

"Go and get him, please," Maggie said, her voice sounding completely calm and rational. "I want to have a talk with your father, anyway, and it's not something you kids need to hear."

"Maggie, I..." That was as far as Harold got. Maggie's face changed from calm composure to rage in a split second, and Harold's voice caught in his throat.

"Maggie," I said, "you've got to listen to reason..."

"Cassie, I told you to leave," she said angrily, "but you didn't. Now, both of you, go over there and sit down on the floor." She looked at me and Dex, and waggled the gun again. "Now," she said.

Neither of us could get to a gun without alerting her, so we slowly walked across the room and sat down against the wall as she had told us to do. I was waiting for the chance to reach for my gun, and all I needed was for her to look away for a couple of seconds. If I could bring it to bear on her before she could aim hers back at me, I thought there was a chance I could take control of the situation.

"Now, Harold," Maggie said, her voice collected again. "I want to know exactly what was going through your mind when you took my children and ran away. I mean, what kind of man does that? And you told them I was dead? That I had been murdered? What kind of sickness is going on inside that head of yours?"

Harold stood there without a word, and I got the impression that he had been through similar scenes in the past, though they might not have included a gun. I tried to send him thoughts, telling him to stay calm and try to distract her, but mental telepathy has never been one of my talents.

"Answer me, Harold," she said again. "Tell me how you could do that to me."

She was staring intently at him, and I thought that maybe this was my chance. I tensed myself, ready to reach for my gun and try to get the drop on her, but Dex beat me to it. He rolled slightly to his left, pulled out his gun and raised it to aim at Maggie, but then she spun and fired. Dex slammed back against the wall, and his gun dropped out of his hand as blood began running down his chest.

SEVENTEEN

I screamed, and Harold suddenly took off running. Maggie fired off a shot at him but missed, and he rushed out through a side door. Maggie let out a scream of her own, then looked at me and I thought she was going to shoot me, as well. I was leaning over by Dex, trying to stem the bleeding, but it wasn't working. Blood was spreading, soaking through his shirt.

Suddenly Maggie looked up. "Jody?" she shouted. "Jody! Get your brother and get down here!"

As if she had completely forgotten Harold, me and Dex, let alone McIver lying there on the floor, she stomped past me and started up the stairs. I didn't even try to stop her—I was too busy worrying about Dex and trying to stop the bleeding—but then he suddenly opened his eyes and looked at me.

"I'll live," he said hoarsely. "Get her, before she hurts those kids." His eyes closed again, but he was still breathing. I took my hand away from the bleeding hole in his shirt and watched it for a second, but it wasn't spurting. Something in my head said that if the bullet had struck his heart, the blood would be spurting out, but this was just a slow and steady stream.

"I've got him," I heard, and I turned to see McIver crawling toward me. He had been shot in the shoulder, almost exactly the same as Garibaldi a few days earlier, but he was alive. "Go, get her." He forced himself to crawl, grimacing, until he could get his good hand up on Dex and apply pressure to the bleeding wound.

I looked at both of them, amazed that either was still alive, and I felt a rage start to build inside me. I rose to my feet and pulled out my gun, then made my way to the base of the stairs and peeked around. There was no sign of Maggie on the stairway, so I started up, my sneakers quiet on the carpeted steps.

"Come out, come out, wherever you are," Maggie sang, and I suddenly remembered the dream she had told me about. She was searching for her children, and they were hiding. They were hiding from something that terrified them, but she didn't know what it was.

How ironic that the thing they were hiding from was Maggie, herself. The voice was coming from somewhere left of the top of the stairwell, and I stayed low until I got my eyeball level with the second floor. I could see through the railing, but there was no one in sight so I moved on up the stairs and stepped out onto the second floor, keeping my gun out in front of me but low.

"Jody! Ryan! You kids get out here now, or I swear, I'm going to make you wish you'd never been born!"

This time, the voice was coming from inside one of the

rooms ahead, and I hurried toward the door leading into it. I leaned against the wall outside and went down low, peeking around the base of the doorway.

Maggie was standing in the middle of the room, just in front of a twin-size bed. From the colors, I figured this must be Ryan's room, because there was nothing feminine about it at all. While I watched, Maggie snatched open the closet and looked inside, and it dawned on me that her children had reason to be afraid. Maggie was hunting them, keeping her own gun out and aimed forward. I didn't know if she was actually planning to shoot them, but if one of them were to startle her...

I didn't even want to finish the thought. The trouble was, I also didn't want to have to shoot their mother, but I knew it was coming down to that big a choice. I couldn't let her get the children and leave with them in any case, and I wasn't going to let her get away with shooting Dex. McIver, either, but at that moment my thoughts were about the man I loved.

If he died, I told myself, I would not only shoot her, but I would skin her alive before she was able to die.

I pulled back away from the doorway and leaned against the wall, still squatting down. "Maggie," I called out. "Maggie, this has to end, now."

"Cassie?" she asked, her voice low and normal. "I thought I told you to leave? You really should learn to do what you're told, you know. I mean, after all, you're working for me, remember?"

My anger flared. "You crazy bitch," I shouted, "you shot my fiancé! You really think I'm going anywhere? I'm taking your ass down, and locking you up where you belong!"

A shot rang out and I was suddenly showered in plaster. The bullet had come through the wall not four inches over my head, and I instinctively rolled to the side. The next bullet came through right where I had been sitting, and would have probably split my spine. I rolled once more for good measure, then scrambled to my feet and ducked into another room.

I heard a gasp behind me, and I knew it had to be one of the kids. I glanced around but didn't see them, so I whispered that they should stay wherever they were. If Maggie tried to come into this room, I wasn't going to have any choice but to shoot her before she could shoot me.

I took a couple of steps back into the room, and that's when I heard a sniffle. The sound was coming from down low, and I realized that at least one of them was under the bed. It was a full-size bed, so this was probably their father's room. I didn't know which kid was there, but there was no way I was going to let Maggie get to whoever it was.

"All right," Maggie shouted, "I've had about enough of this. You kids come out right now, or I'm going to—you know what I'll do, I shouldn't have to tell you. Do you really want to make me this angry?"

"Maggie," I heard, as Harold came up the stairs. I moved toward the doorway again, trying to see him and warn him to stay back, but he was walking up the stairs as if there was nothing to fear. I think he saw me, but he didn't give any indication as he stepped out onto the second floor. "Maggie, let's talk about this," he said. "Maybe you're right, maybe I shouldn't have run away. If you'll let me, I'll make it up to you. Let's all just go home, and we can work it out."

"It's a little late for that, Harold," Maggie said, and I

swear I could hear a smile in her voice. "I have to give you credit, though: you really did a good job of disappearing. I understand you had help with that, so I guess that explains it. God knows you were never that smart."

"I don't need to be smart," Harold said. "I have you for that, remember? Come on, Maggie, put that gun away and let's just get the kids and go home. Okay? Go back to the way things used to be."

She was quiet for just a moment, and I thought for a second that he might be accomplishing something, but then I heard her laugh.

"The way things used to be? Do you honestly think I could ever trust you again? Harold, you betrayed me in the worst way any man can betray his wife: you took my children away. My God, you even tried to make me think they were dead. How could I ever forget that? How could I ever forgive you?"

I could see Harold, standing there beside the stairway, and I saw him smile. "Maggie," he said, but then there was a gunshot and a red blossom appeared in the center of his chest. Harold looked down at himself, then his legs gave out and he collapsed, leaning against the railing. For just a second, his eyes met mine, and I nodded once to tell him I would do my best to protect the kids.

A rattle came from him, and his head dropped forward. I didn't have to be a doctor to know that he was dead.

I heard Maggie's footsteps approaching him, and I held my gun out in the classic two-handed stance. She would step out in front of the door in just a second, and I didn't plan to give her the chance to fire at me. This woman was insane, but she was a killer, and sometimes the only thing you can do with a killer is put them down.

I readied myself to squeeze the trigger, but then she stopped. She was just outside my line of sight, around the corner in the hallway. If she had taken another step, she would've been right in front of me, but she must've sensed that I was there.

"Cassie? You're surely not going to try to stand between me and my children, are you?"

That rage flared once more. "You bet your ass I am," I said. "If you want them, you have to go through me."

"Cassie, don't you understand? This is my dream, this is my dream coming true. My children are scared, and they need me to rescue them. You can't get in my way, I won't allow it."

"You're right," I said. "You're right, Maggie, this is your dream. Your children are terrified, and they are hiding, just the way you dreamed it, but what you don't understand is that what they are hiding from is you. *You* are the monster they're terrified of, Maggie. You are the monster they're hiding from right now, and I am not going to let that monster get to them. You can either put down your gun and surrender, or you can come and try to get past me, but either way, this is going to end right here, right now."

There was complete silence from the hallway for several seconds, and then I heard what sounded like a sob. "Jody? Jody, is she right? Are you afraid of me?"

There was no answer, though I suddenly heard more sniffles from down by my feet under the bed. It dawned on me that both of the kids were there, and Jody was probably trying to keep Ryan quiet.

"Ryan? Can you hear me?" Maggie called. "You'll tell me, won't you? Are you really afraid of me?"

There was a scuffle under the bed, and suddenly Ryan's voice called out clearly. "Yes!" he screamed, and I could hear the tears he was fighting. "Yes, Mommy, I'm scared of you!"

Maggie fell silent again, and it lasted almost a minute. I could hear her crying, but I had no sympathy for this crazy woman. I wasn't sure what she was feeling, but all of the misery in this case, all of the pain and heartache and death, boiled down to whatever she had done that made Harold take the children and flee. There was no way I could feel any sympathy for her, when Deputy Begay had been killed as a result of her actions, when Dex and McIver might be lying dead on the floor downstairs, when even the children's own father, who had loved them enough to face what had to be his greatest fear, was lying dead only a few feet away from where I stood at that moment.

"Cassie," she said softly, "you're right. It has to end, and it has to end now. I know you have my children in there with you. I know you're trying to protect them, because that's just who you are, isn't it?"

"You're not going to get to them, Maggie," I said. "Just put down the gun, and we can handle this without anyone else getting hurt. Come on, Maggie, put down the gun."

Ten seconds passed before she answered me. "I can't do that," she said softly, and then she stepped out in front of me, turned in my direction and raised the gun.

I fired. At that moment, there was nothing else I could've done, but as soon as my gun went off and she went backward over the railing, I realized that she had forced my hand. Somehow, when I told her that she was the monster her children were afraid of, I guess it got through to her. All she had to do was surrender, and it was even possible she could have gotten help and eventually been with her kids again, or at least gotten to know them.

Maggie couldn't accept that, for whatever reason. She was willing to let them go, she was willing to bring an end to whatever torment she had inflicted on their young lives, but she couldn't do it without getting the last word. By sacrificing herself, I think she was hoping they would eventually come to believe that she really did love them.

Both of the children screamed when I squeezed the trigger, and then I told them to stay where they were for a moment. I went and looked down over the railing, and saw Maggie lying there with the gaping hole I had blown in her chest. I was confident that my shot had been fatal, but it seemed like fate had decided to make certain. Her head was twisted at an angle that could only mean that her neck was broken, as well. This was one monster who was not going to get up and stalk her victims again.

I quickly checked Harold, but there was no pulse. I went back into the bedroom and got down on the floor, and I found myself looking directly into the faces of Jody and Ryan.

"It's over," I said. "You're safe, but I need you to stay here for a little bit. I'm going to shut the door, and you can come out from under the bed but I don't want you to leave this room, okay?"

Both of them had tears streaming down their faces, but Jody nodded. "Okay," she said, the word coming between sobs. I got up and went back out of the room, pulling the door shut behind me, and then I hurried down the stairs, stepping over Maggie's body.

McIver had managed to sit up against the wall beside Dex, and both of them looked at me as I came back into the room. I dropped to my knees beside Dex and looked at him, and my own tears began again as he managed a smile.

"She's dead," I said. "She didn't give me a choice, she forced me to do it."

"Self-defense," McIver said. "I'm a witness, it was self-defense. What about her husband?"

"He's dead," I said. "She shot him, but the kids are safe. I told them to them stay in a bedroom upstairs for right now, but I'm sure they won't stay there very long."

A car pulled up outside the building, and my instinctive reaction was to pick up my gun again and aim at the door. McIver grabbed my arm and told me to put it down. A moment later, three people came through the door, and one of them was John from the general store.

"Geez Almighty," he said. "What the hell went on out here? Somebody called and said they heard gunshots going off at the clinic, so we came out to see what's going on."

McIver fumbled around and found his ID, then held it up. "FBI," he said. "And it would sure help if one of you gentlemen would call an ambulance." He glanced at Dex. "Maybe a couple of them."

John looked at me and I quickly recounted what had happened. He stared at me as I explained it all, shaking his head from time to time while the other two men with him just stood there with their eyes wide and their mouths wider until one of them had the presence of mind to call 911.

Finally I finished, but then I made a decision. "I need

you gentlemen to do something for me," I said. "I need to get those kids out of here, but without them seeing the bodies. Will you help me?"

John looked at me, and while I knew the man was shaken, I saw him pull himself together. "What do you want us to do?"

They followed me back up the stairs and I carefully opened the door. Jody had been smart enough to keep them away from it, so they couldn't see Harold when it opened. John and one of the other men stepped in behind me, and Jody looked at me to explain.

"Things are—there are things outside this room that you don't need to see," I said. "I'm going to put blankets around you kids, and these gentlemen are going to carry you down and take you to the general store for now. I'll be down there in a bit, and I'll answer all your questions when I get there. Okay?"

Jody looked at me. "Is she dead?" she asked.

I nodded. "Yes, she is," I said. "She didn't give me any choice, Jody."

She just looked at me for a moment, then tears began to flow again. I expected her to start screaming at me, but all she said was, "Thank you."

Ryan was also looking at me, but he didn't say anything. I took blankets off the bed and put them over their heads, and then the two men picked them up. John carried Jody while the other man took Ryan, and they hurried past Harold's body and started down the stairs. Because we couldn't disturb the crime scene, it hadn't been possible to move Maggie's body out of the way, so they were forced to step over her the same way I had.

John had called the sheriff from his cell phone, and we heard the sound of a helicopter a few minutes later. It landed less than a hundred yards away from the clinic building, and then four paramedics came rushing inside. One of them checked Maggie, which took only a second, and then went upstairs to look at Harold, while the other three began working on Dex and McIver.

McIver's bullet had hit him in almost the exact same spot that Dex's bullet had hit Garibaldi, and he had managed to stem most of the bleeding by simply holding his arm tight against himself. The paramedics packed the wound and wrapped it, then put him on a stretcher and rushed him out to the helicopter.

Dex was one of the luckiest men alive, according to the paramedic working on him. The bullet had struck him in the chest, and probably would have blown out a lung if it hadn't hit something in his pocket. That gun Maggie was using had been a nine millimeter, and the little book of quotations that I had picked up back at the general store had slowed the bullet down quite a bit, and one of his ribs took the rest of its momentum. It had stopped just short of actually punching into his lung, so that little book probably saved his life.

Ironically, when I was putting pressure on the wound, I hadn't even noticed the book under my hand. I guess I was just too worried about Dex to pay attention to details. Whatever the reason, I was really glad it had caught my eye.

The sheriff showed up around then, in another helicopter. He came stomping into the clinic after speaking briefly with McIver at the air ambulance, looked at me and asked, "Are you McGraw?"

"Yes, sir," I said. "I am."

"Well, good," he said. "FBI fella outside says you're the one who can explain to me just what the hell happened here."

I took a deep breath. "I'll be happy to do that, sir," I said, "but you have to follow us to the hospital." I pointed at Dex. "That's my fiancé, and they are about to load him up in the chopper to go. I'm going with him."

"You can join him later, young lady," the sheriff said. "I'll even see to it personally, but first I have to get a report on what took place here. We've got two dead bodies, two people wounded and blood seems to be just about everywhere. I understand there's a couple of kids down at the general store who just became orphans, and I want to know what the hell I'm dealing with before you get out of my sight."

I started to protest, but Dex waved a hand and I looked at him. "Do what he says," he said. "This is part of your job, remember? I'll be all right till you get there, don't worry."

I bit off what I wanted to say and nodded. "Okay," I said. "I'll be there soon as I can."

They carried Dex out to the helicopter, and I turned back to the sheriff. For the next hour, we went back and forth over what had taken place, and just how Dex and McIver and I had ended up there. I could tell the sheriff wasn't too pleased about having something like this in his jurisdiction, but he also seemed to understand that the situation was bigger than just his county.

Finally he said I could go, and I walked out to the Jeep. Luckily, Dex had left the keys in the ignition and I climbed in, ignoring the fact that I was smearing blood on the seat and other parts of the car, and started it up. I started to head for the hospital, but I had no idea where to go. That's when I remembered that I had promised Jody I would come to the general store and explain what had happened.

I pulled in at the store and parked on the side of the building, then walked inside. Bernice saw me come in and looked at me harshly, then motioned for me to follow her. She took me into a back room, where John and the other two men were sitting with Jody and Ryan.

Jody saw me come through the door and jumped to her feet, throwing her arms around me. She was crying again, sobbing piteously, and all I could do was hold her for a few moments. Finally, she started to relax her grip and looked up at me. I took her hand and we walked back to the table where they had been sitting, and I took a seat beside her.

"They said our dad is dead," she said. "Mom shot him, didn't she?"

I nodded. "Yes, she did. He was trying to save you, doing the only thing he knew how to do by trying to talk her down. Unfortunately, she was just too far gone."

"She always has been," Jody said, her face twisted in her grief and anger. "She was the most cruel, evil woman who ever lived."

"Jody," I said, "I talked to your school, and to some of your friends. They all told me that you always said your mom was great. If she was this bad, why didn't you ever tell anyone?"

"Because we knew what would happen if we did," she said. "We knew better than to make her angry, so we never told anybody. If she ever found out, we'd be—we just couldn't do it."

I looked at her, then turned to Ryan. He was staring at me, but he wasn't talking. I turned back to Jody.

"When she was in the hallway, she said something about how you knew what she would do if you made her angry," I said. "What was it? What was it she was threatening you with?"

Jody looked at me for a couple of seconds, then licked her lips. Without a word, she reached down and took hold of the hem of her shirt. She lifted it slightly, then tugged downward on the waistband of her pants, in the back. She was turned so that no one else could see what she was trying to show me, and I leaned over so I could see.

There, just below her waistline, I saw half a dozen rounded scars. I recognized them instantly, and knew what they were. Jody had been burned with cigarettes, and all of the marks were on parts of her body that would be covered all the time. Even if she were in a bathing suit, they wouldn't show, and the sheer cruelty of it shook me to my soul.

I raised my eyes to her face and she put her clothes back together. "You have a lot of those?" I asked.

She nodded. "Ryan, too," she said. "Mom didn't even smoke, but she always kept a pack of cigarettes in her purse because she said it was 'the most effective kind of punishment there was.'" She made finger quotes around that phrase. "And the worst part was that she was always smiling and giggling while she did it, like she was getting some kind of jollies out of it."

"Your father knew?"

She sniffled and wiped her nose on her sleeve. "Yes, but before you ask me why he never told, let me explain it. You see, this only started a couple of years ago. Before that everything was okay, but then Mom started acting weird and using this whenever she got mad at us. She told us that, if we ever told Daddy about it, she'd end up having to kill him, so we never told him. I mean, all you had to do was look in her eyes when she said it and you knew she really would, you know what I mean? It was like she went crazy or something. He didn't know anything about it until later, one day when he walked in and caught her doing it to Ryan. He said he was going to call the cops, but—a couple months before that, Mom got my dad to do something. She—she talked him into stealing some drugs from the hospital, some kind of painkillers she said she needed to help someone, and that it was really important. When he threatened to tell what she was doing to us that day, I guess she showed him that she had some kind of proof about him stealing the drugs, and that she'd put him in prison. She even laughed, and she told him that if he went to prison, that would mean she could do whatever she wanted with us, so he kept his mouth shut. He just tried to make sure she didn't get angry enough to take it out on us, and for a while things started to get better."

"Is that when he started talking about taking you and leaving her?" I asked. "You told some of your friends that you were going to be a nurse for your dad, so I figure he was letting you in on his plans."

She nodded. "Yes," she said. "We were planning to go on vacation, and Daddy said he had a plan so we could get away from her. I guess he paid somebody where she worked to make her stay an extra couple days, and things were going so well that he was able to convince her that it would be okay, that she could just come and join us later. She let us drive away in the camper, and as soon as we were gone he called that friend of his, the one who helped us hide. He said his friend wasn't really a good guy, but he knew how to make it happen. That guy arranged for the motorhome to get burned up with some dead people in it, so everyone would think we were all dead."

I looked at her for a moment, wishing there was something I could say or do to make life better for her. "Jody, do you have any other family? Is there someone who can take you and Ryan in?"

She shook her head. "Our grandparents are all dead, and we didn't have anybody else. Do you have any idea what's going to happen to us?"

My heart went out to these kids, but I wasn't sure what to say. A sheriff's deputy had shown up a little earlier, and had told John and Bernice that arrangements were being made for temporary foster care. They were actually just waiting for the Family Services people to arrive when I got there.

"I don't know right now," I said, "but I promise you this. I will keep watching out for you until we do, okay? And you've got my number, so you can call me anytime. I don't care what time it is, even the middle of the night, if you need to call me, you can. Okay?"

She nodded and sniffled. "Okay," she said. "When— when you came and found us in Wyoming, even Daddy said you seemed like a really good lady, but he said he looked inside your car and knew that you were from back in Tulsa. He said he just couldn't take a chance that you might let Mom know where we were. That's why we had to leave, that's why we ran. We've only been here a couple of days."

"Jody, if I had known the truth," I said, "I never would

have helped her find you. I have another job where I help people get out of bad situations, and I just wish I had known what she was really like."

She looked at me then, and suddenly she jumped up and threw her arms around my neck. "I know you don't know us," she said, "but right now, I think you're the only one who even cares about us at all. Please, please help us."

I held her tight, and promised her that I would do everything I possibly could.

EIGHTEEN

I stayed with them until Family Services got there, then made sure I knew where they were going. I gave each of the kids one of my business cards to make sure they had my number and told them to call me anytime they needed to, and that they could call collect if necessary. They were both crying as they were loaded into an SUV and driven away.

"You really care about them, don't you?" Bernice asked me.

"I do," I said. "I barely know them, but they've been on my mind for more than a week now. The trouble was that I thought their father was the bad guy, not their mother." I shook my head. "Listen, I need directions to the hospital. My fiancé was shot, and they took him to the hospital in a helicopter. How do I get there?"

It turned out there was a hospital in White Sulphur Springs, just thirty minutes away. I punched it into my phone and hit the directions button, and followed them out of Harmony Valley and back out to the main road. I drove a little faster than I should have, but I wanted to get to Dex. I reached the hospital in just a little under thirty minutes, then rushed into the emergency room and asked where to find him.

"Mr. Tate?" The receptionist looked at her computer, then nodded. "He's been admitted, he's up on the second floor. Room two oh six."

I thanked her and hurried off to find the elevator, then followed the signs to room two oh six. When I stepped inside, I found both Dex and Agent McIver there. They were both sitting up in bed and talking, but Dex spotted me first.

"Hey, babe," he said. "Can you believe they stuck me with this guy for a roommate?"

I was so relieved to see him not only alive, but conscious and seemingly in a good mood that I dropped into a chair beside his bed and started bawling like a big baby. I tried to tell him how happy I was, how thrilled I was that he was okay, but what came out sounded more like the sort of thing you hear out of kids in Walmart when they aren't getting their way.

Finally I got myself under control. The three of us sat there and talked about everything that had taken place, and once again I had to tell the story of what had happened upstairs. Both of them had been a little fuzzy when they were sitting on the floor, bleeding, so I didn't mind going through the story again.

Then I told them about the kids, and how terrible I felt that they were orphaned, now.

"Some people," McIver said, "are such perfect

psychopaths that they know how to pretend to be normal. I've known a few in my time, and it's almost impossible to spot them until they allow you to see their true selves. That's what you saw today, when Mrs. Logan dropped all her pretenses. Frankly, if you hadn't held yourself together, she probably would've killed us all before it was over. And that includes those kids; the way she was acting, I don't think she intended to take them home and try to be their mommy again. I think she was headed toward a murder-suicide situation. You did good work today, Ms. McGraw."

"Well, I did what I had to do," I said. "In considering the fact that I almost got you killed, I guess we can drop the Ms. McGraw stuff and you can just call me Cassie."

He grinned. "Okay, Cassie," he said. "And I'm Ben. Good to meet you."

He closed his eyes and leaned back, and I took it to mean he was trying to give me and Dex a little bit of privacy. I looked at my fiancé and felt the tears about to start again, so I decided to make a wisecrack instead. "So," I began. "How would you feel if I decided that we need to adopt a couple of kids?"

His eyes got wide. "Kids? As in, these two kids? I mean, I met Ryan and he seemed like a great boy, but we don't really even know them, Cassie."

"Ha," I said. "Remember I said I was going to get you back? Gotcha!"

He stared at me for a moment, then grinned. "You were just kidding, right? Just getting me back for that gag earlier?"

"Yeah," I said innocently. "And it worked."

"Oh, crap," he said. "You're not fooling me. You're honestly thinking about taking those kids in, aren't you?"

"Oh, no," I said. "I was just trying to..."

"Bull," Dex said. "Don't forget, Cassie, I can tell when you're lying. Is this really something you want to consider?"

I bit back the fib I was about to tell, and then I nodded. "Dex, they don't have anybody," I said. "As weird as it sounds, right now Jody thinks I'm the only person in the world who really cares about them. How can I not consider it?"

He looked at me for a couple of seconds, then shook his head. "I suppose there are worse ways to get a family," he said. "The question is, could we actually arrange it? I mean, doesn't the state of Montana take jurisdiction over them or something?"

"You'd have to have some good character references," McIver said without even opening his eyes. "Do you have those?"

"Oh, I'm sure we do," Dex said, chuckling. "Probably more than enough."

"Well, you've got one more. If you decide to do this, I mean. Personally, I think it's crazy, but remember, I read your file. Crazy seems to be part of who you are, Cassie."

I couldn't exactly argue with that, now, could I?

Dex was going to be in the hospital for at least a couple of days, they said, and I wasn't allowed to stay there so I found a motel not far away and got a room. I had grabbed some chicken on the way to the motel and sat there on the bed and ate it all, then got a shower and changed into clean clothes. I also took off that blasted mask and put the glass eye away. After that I felt more like myself again, so I sat down on the bed again and really thought about what I wanted to do.

Dex and I were getting married in three weeks, and that was definitely something I wanted. After I had been burned and was finally released from the hospital, the thought of ever getting married or even having a decent relationship was something I figured was in the realm of fantasy, and nowhere else. The fact I'd actually found a man who could love me, even with my ugly half-sister Freda, was like a fairy tale come true for me, and I was looking forward to my happily ever after.

Having kids, though, that was something I had avoided thinking about. While I was terribly scarred on the outside, and even a little bit down in the nether regions, everything inside was still in working order. I very carefully took a birth control pill every day, just to make sure there weren't any surprises in that regard, and I hadn't really considered whether Dex and I would ever have children. I mean, it wasn't even a conversation we had touched on, so where did I get off trying to adopt kids who were already half grown?

On the other hand, Dex had said that if I was really serious about it, he would go along with me. I looked at the clock and decided that a phone call couldn't hurt anything.

First, I called Alfie.

"Little Sleazer's Pizza," he said. "What can I get ya?"

"Information," I said. "Alfie, suppose Dex and I wanted to adopt a couple of kids, from Montana. They've just become orphaned, and they don't have anybody. What would I have to go through to accomplish that?"

There was utter silence on the line for almost ten seconds. "You know, it's funny you called me just now. You see, I was just watching CNN and heard this news story about a tragic murder-suicide situation up in Montana earlier today, and funny enough, there was some lady there with the same name as you when it happened. Now, in that story, there were a couple of kids who suddenly became orphans. Would we be talking about those same kids?"

"Yep," I said. "And don't give me any static, Dex has already said he would agree to this."

"Static? Static? When have I ever given you static? Okay, don't answer that, I give you static all the time. To answer your question, though, I'd have to do a little research. Off the top of my head, I'd say you need to get a good endorsement from Family Services back here in Tulsa, and let's face it, they would sing your praises from the top of the Empire State Building, so that's covered. You would need an attorney, in fact you would need two of them, one here and one in Montana; and you would probably need—well, me. Whenever you get involved in red tape like an adoption involves, it never hurts to have somebody who can slip in the back door and cut through a lot of it."

"Okay," I said. "Just in case I decide to do this, can you find me the best lawyer in White Sulphur Springs, Montana?"

"I'll do better than that," he said. "I'll find you the best lawyer in the whole damn state. God knows you can afford it. As for back here, who was that buddy of Dex's? He'd probably be ideal."

"Good, because he's still a friend of ours. Anything else you can think of?"

"Not at the moment, but I'll do some digging and see. Hey, was Dex one of the people who got shot?"

"Yes, but thankfully he's going to be okay. They're going to keep him in the hospital for a couple of days, mostly just for observation, but then we'll be headed back home."

"Good," he said. Then the line went dead.

I took a deep breath and collected my thoughts, then called David LaBarre. He answered the phone and was once again surprised that I was calling on his cell, rather than waiting for office hours. I told him what was going through my head and asked him how things were looking for me financially.

"Pretty good, actually," he said. "I've been working on some new investment strategies and they've been paying off. Your principal is up to almost three million, six hundred thousand dollars right now, even with all the money you've been spending lately. I keep most of it in some safe and conservative investments, but whenever I find something I think is really good, I put some of my own money in and match it with some of yours. If you lose, so do I, so I'm really, really careful not to let you lose money."

I chuckled. "Good," I said. "Do me a favor, and keep your eye out for a bigger house. If I go through with this, I'm going to need at least four bedrooms."

"You got it," he said. "And, Cassie? Having gotten to know you over the last couple of years, I think you'll make a great mom."

"Thanks, David," I said. "I'll keep you posted."

I put the phone away and tried to relax, but then I picked it up again and called Dex. It was only about nine o'clock, so he and McIver were watching television. When he answered the phone, I asked him if he was serious when he said he would stick with me if I decided I wanted to adopt those kids.

"Cassie," he said, "if you're trying to get rid of me, you're going to have to come up with something a lot worse than bringing a couple of snotty-nosed, bratty kids into the house. They don't scare me, not a bit."

I laughed. "Have I mentioned that I love you lately?"

"You know, come to think of it, you haven't. But don't worry, you don't always say it in words, but you definitely let me know."

"Well, I do," I said. "With all my heart."

"Ditto, babe," he said. "And just so you know, they already gave me a shot that's supposed to help me sleep, and it's starting to work. If I suddenly stop talking, that's probably why."

I laughed again. "That's okay, baby," I said. "You go ahead and get some rest, and I'll see you in the morning. By then, I might have some idea of just how crazy this whole thing is."

I hung up and put the phone away again, then remembered to get my charger and plug it in. The last thing I needed was for it to go dead if Dex or one of those kids was trying to call me.

I curled up in the bed and grabbed the pillow that Dex would've been sleeping on if he was with me and hugged it close. There was a sadness inside me, but there was also a feeling of love and a sense of adventure. I drifted off to sleep wondering which of those feelings was going to be waiting for me in the morning.

"Adventure," I said when I woke up. "Definitely adventure."

I went and found some breakfast, then headed back to the hospital. Because I was his fiancée, I was allowed to spend more time with Dex than just during regular visiting hours, but they still didn't want me getting there before ten a.m. I waited until a quarter of ten before I got sick of waiting and rode the elevator up to the second floor.

There was a nurse in Dex's room when I walked in, and she actually squeaked when she got a look at me. Her eyes went wide, and she squeaked like a mouse, I swear. If it hadn't been so funny, I probably would've felt insulted, but I was in too good a mood to let it bother me. Dex introduced me as his fiancée, and she quickly found the smile that had disappeared a few seconds earlier.

Dex seemed relieved to see me, but he waited until the nurse was gone before he told me why. It seemed that breakfast in the hospital consisted of a very small bowl of cereal and a piece of toast. The poor guy was starving and nobody was listening, so I went down to the snack machines and grabbed about ten bucks' worth of candy and chips. When I got back to the room, I laid it all on his tray and he started ripping things open.

Then he glanced over at McIver, who was watching him jealously. He grinned, grabbed a bag of chips and a candy bar and tossed them over. McIver caught them both in one hand and ripped the bag open with his teeth.

"How's the arm?" I asked him. "Is it as bad as Garibaldi's?"

"They don't think so," he said. "The doctor says I'll be in physical therapy for a few months, but he thinks I'll regain full use of it eventually. Just got to retrain the muscles that didn't get damaged to take over for the ones that did."

"Then, you're going to be off work for a while?"

"Yep, but that's okay. I'll be on recuperation leave for as long as it takes to get back to normal, so I keep getting paid. If it turns out I can't get back to normal, then I'm looking at medical retirement, which will give me three quarters of my pay for the rest of my life, along with free medical care. As crazy as it sounds, this could end up being one of the best things that ever happened to me."

I stared at him. "McIver, how old are you?"

"I'm fifty-nine," he said. "Only a few more years until mandatory retirement anyway, and medical retirement would get me even more money. If they don't retire me, they'll just put me on a desk after this, so I actually have a chance to live long enough to collect my pension, now."

I looked at Dex. "Is he being serious, or is he a smartass?"

"Neither one," Dex said. "He's on some really good drugs, that's all."

I sat and visited with both of them for a while, and then my phone rang. I took it out to look at it, and saw that it was Alfie calling.

"Alfie," I said, "what did you find out?"

"I found out that the best lawyer I can get you is going to cost you fifteen grand for an adoption case," he said. "His name is Saul Greenberg, and he's from Bozeman. When I explained to him what the situation was, he told me that he had seen the news about it and thought you were something of a hero. Otherwise, he would've cost you thirty grand, but he's that good. If you want to go through with this, and you're willing to pay his fees, he says he'll get on it today."

"Then let's do it," I said. "I got a feeling this is going to be tricky, so I want the best."

"You're damn right," Alfie said. "Tricky doesn't even start to describe what you're going to go through, but Saul has enough clout to make sure it will happen. Now, you just have to decide if you really want to do this. Are you with Dex?"

"Yeah," I said. "You want to talk to him?"

"Damn right." I handed the phone to Dex, and he put it to his ear.

"Yeah, buddy," he said. "What's up?" He listened for about a minute and a half, a grin slowly spreading across his face. Finally, he got the chance to speak again. "Yes, I understand what she's up to, and yes, I told her I'm with her on it all the way." He listened again, but not for as long this time. "I appreciate it, buddy," he said. "We'll talk to you later."

He handed the phone back. "He's already gone."

I looked at Dex. "Did he tell you what he was telling me?"

"Yep, and then some. He says we need to go home, because DFS has to do a home visit to see if the house is suitable." He cocked his head and looked me in the eye. "Come on, babe. You know this is what you want to do, and I'm with you a hundred percent of the way. And by the way, Alfie said he was going to text you the number of the lawyer, so you need to go ahead and get it started."

A tear started down my right cheek. "I love you so much," I said.

"Oh, geez, are you guys going to start that mushy stuff?" McIver asked. "Can't you wait until they take me down for an X-ray or something?"

"Shut up," Dex said. "I like her mushy stuff." He winked

at me. "You know how many guys wish they could tell an FBI agent to shut up? I can cross that off my bucket list."

I laughed at both of them, then looked at my phone. Sure enough, a text message had come in without me even noticing it. I opened it and tapped the number that it displayed, and I was talking to Saul Greenberg just a minute later.

"Ms. McGraw," he said. "It's good to finally talk to you. I've been following the news about you since yesterday, and it's been pretty enlightening. Then, I got a call from a friend of yours named Alfie, and he says you are looking at adopting the two children who were orphaned?"

"Yes, sir," I said. "If we can get it done, that's what I want to do."

"Ms. McGraw, there are three kinds of attorneys. The first one is the one who will tell you what you can't do. The second is the one who will tell you what you can do. I happen to be the third kind, who will ignore both of those and figure out how to accomplish what it is that you want to do. Of course we can get this done, but there's going to be a lot of work involved. Are you sure you're up for it?"

"Just tell me what I've got to do," I said. "I'm ready."

"Well, the first thing you have to do is retain me. Because of the fact you ended up saving those kids, I've agreed to reduce my usual rate by fifty percent, but that still means fifteen grand. Can you afford that?"

"Can you take a credit card over the phone?" I asked. He said he could, and I rattled off the number from memory. A moment later he came back on the phone.

"Okay, we're all set from that standpoint. Now, let's talk about what has to be done. The first thing you're going to need to do is go back home and make arrangements for your local agencies to do a home visit. They're going to inspect your house, make sure you have room for the kids and all that. Do you?"

"Well," I said slowly, "I'm probably going to have to get another house in a hurry. Mine is only a two bedroom."

"Is there any kind of an extra room on it, something that could become a bedroom temporarily?" he asked. "Even the garage, if you can get it sealed up pretty quickly."

"Hold on a moment," I said. I hit the mute button and looked at Dex. "He says is it possible we can turn the garage into a bedroom really quickly?"

Dex nodded. "Soon as you get off the phone, we'll get Jimmy on it. He can take all the crap from the garage and store it at the shop, for now."

I unmuted the phone and put it back to my ear. "I think we can get the garage redone in a hurry," I said. "My fiancé's employee is really good at that kind of work."

"Very good," Saul said. "And that brings up the next problem. Since the two of you are not yet married, that could throw a monkey wrench into the works. Have you got a date set?"

I blinked. "Yes," I said. "As a matter of fact, it's in about three weeks."

"Well, I'm going to advise you to speed things up," he said. "You can have a second wedding for the family, but I need you to be married when I file this paperwork. Can you arrange that?"

I looked at Dex, and said, "Mr. Greenberg, if we have to we'll make a stop in Las Vegas and let Elvis tie the knot for us. Don't worry, we'll take care of that part as fast as possible. I don't want to delay this any more than necessary."

"All right, then," he said. "I'll start looking into the children and what's going to be involved in their situation, while you get me an endorsement from your local agency and a copy of your marriage license. As soon as I have both of those, I'll get the petition filed. You have to come back to Montana for the hearings, you understand that, right?"

"That's not going to be a problem," I said. "You just tell us when to be here, and we will."

"Very good, then. If there's nothing else, I'll…"

"Just a moment," I said, "I just had a thought. Will we be able to visit with the kids before we go home?"

"They are currently in emergency foster care, so I'll have to make some calls. Normally, in a situation like that, they aren't allowed any kind of visits but we do have some extenuating circumstances in this case, since you're the one who protected them while their parents died. I've got your number, so I'll call you as soon as I find out."

I thanked him, and we said goodbye. I relaxed as much as I could and told Dex everything he had said, and McIver suggested we go to Reno instead of Las Vegas. According to him, the wedding chapels were cheaper there.

"I don't care where we go," Dex said. "I don't even care if they have to carry me in on a stretcher, as long as I get you to say I do."

I laughed, but then my phone rang and I saw that it was Saul calling back.

"Hello?"

"Ms. McGraw," he said. "One of the reasons it pays to have an attorney like me on the case for you is because just about everybody in the state owes me one favor or another. I was able to get you visitation rights with the children, and it's very reasonable. You can visit them tomorrow from nine a.m. to four p.m., and then once a week until this case is settled. And if anybody asks you tomorrow, you're already married. Got that?"

I laughed. "I got it," I said. "Thank you, Mr. Greenberg."

NINETEEN

Dex threw a couple of major fits in the hospital and managed to convince the doctor to let him go early the next morning. I was there at exactly seven thirty a.m. to pick him up, and he was screaming and yelling because a nurse had told him he had to ride down in a wheelchair, but McIver told him to suck it up and do what he had to do. He did, and waited until they got to the front door before he jumped out of the chair and ran to the Jeep. He jumped in, slammed the door and grabbed the seat belt, then told me to go, quick before they could catch him.

I couldn't help it, I laughed. We drove away and headed toward the restaurant I had already checked out. The temporary foster home the kids were in was only a couple of miles from the hospital, and from what I could tell it was more like some kind of orphanage or asylum. I googled it and the pictures looked like some sort of old hospital, maybe even an old jail or something, so I figured we both needed a good breakfast before we got there. Being hungry makes both of us irritable, and I didn't want to end up making a scene and alienating the people we would have to deal with to visit the kids.

Forty-five minutes later, after each of us had wolfed down a stack of pancakes and some eggs and sausage, we were back in the car and headed toward them. We pulled up just a few minutes before nine, and had to wait until the doors were unlocked for us.

"Mr. and Mrs. McGraw?" asked a lady who opened the door.

"It's Tate, actually," I said. "This is my husband, Dexter. I'm Cassie."

The ruse worked, because she smiled and invited us in.

"It's good to meet you," she said. "I'm Mrs. Whitlow, I'm the social worker for the home. I understand you're considering adopting these children?"

"We are," I said. "They actually don't have anyone else, so we are hopeful."

"Yes, it's such a tragedy. Have you known the children long?"

It dawned on me that we were getting a little bit of the third degree. "No, we haven't," I said. "We became familiar with them when I was hired as a private investigator to find them, and yes, since you've undoubtedly seen it on the news, I'm the person who shot and killed their mother. If you saw the news, then you also know that their mother suffered from some severe mental problems, and was presenting an immediate danger to these children. I've been assured by the FBI, who was present at the time, that it was a justifiable homicide."

Mrs. Whitlow jerked back visibly. "Well," she said,

"don't you think that might present some problems for the children?"

"I honestly don't know," I said. "What I can tell you is that the first words Jody said to me when I admitted that I had killed her mother were, 'Thank you.' Believe me, they knew just how dangerous she was, and why it was necessary for me to do what I did."

She looked for a moment like she had something else to say, but thought better of it. We were escorted to an office area, where we had to sign in and promise that we would make sure both the kids were brought back on time, no later than four p.m.

Once those formalities were out of the way, we were led into a waiting room and told to have a seat. We were there about five minutes, and then Jody and Ryan were brought in.

It was a good thing I had eaten. Both of the kids were still wearing the same clothes they had been in when I saw them at the general store, and I had my doubts whether they'd even had a bath since I had seen them last.

I turned to Mrs. Whitlow. "Was there nothing else they could wear?" I asked. "They've had these clothes on for days."

She looked down her nose at me. "They were taken in on an emergency basis," she said. "We have not had a chance to arrange clothing or anything else for them just yet. What they need will be provided to, I can assure you."

"You're damn right it will," I said. "The first place I'm taking them is to buy some clothes and other things they might need. In the future, if you realize they don't have something that they should, please feel free to call me and I'll be happy to provide it."

Her mouth turned into a thin, straight line as we led the kids out of the building. Both of them had been delighted to see us, judging from their reactions, but I was still a little concerned about how they were going to handle it when we were alone with them.

We were all quiet until we got into the Jeep, and then Jody leaned up between the front seats.

"We didn't think you were really going to come," she said. "They told us last night you were going to come to see us today, but they acted like they didn't believe it, so we weren't sure if it was really going to happen."

"Then why didn't you call me?" I asked. "You both have my number."

Ryan frowned. "We're not allowed to use a phone," he said. "That lady said we didn't have anyone to call, so we couldn't use the phone at all."

"We'll fix that," Dex said. "For now, let's go get you guys some clean clothes to wear and then we can figure out what might be fun to do around here, okay?"

"Can't we just leave?" Jody asked. "Couldn't you just take us home with you or something?"

I shook my head as I started the car. "Unfortunately, we can't do that." I took a deep breath. "Listen, kids, there's something we need to talk to you about. I know you don't have any other family, so—well, Dex and I were thinking about maybe taking you to live with us. How would you guys feel about that?"

I could see Jody's face in the rearview mirror, but Ryan

was lower in the seat. Jody looked like she was nervous, but she was trying to smile.

"Yeah, that would be fine," she said, but Dex cut her off.

"Jody, we know this is a very rough time for you kids," he said. "You're both probably still in shock over the things that happened a couple days ago, and nobody can blame you for that. Your lives have been turned upside down so many times the last few months that I think it's kind of a miracle you can even think. We don't expect you to jump up and down and start calling us Mom and Dad, or anything like that. We just want you to know that you're not alone."

Jody licked her lips and looked at me in the mirror. "Well, okay, but isn't it going to be a big pain in the butt, if you take us in? I mean, we don't really know each other, you know? How do you know we won't turn out just as crazy as our mother?"

"Uh-uh," I said, "none of that kind of talk. We don't know right now what might have caused your mother's problems, but I seriously doubt it's anything genetic. And you're right, we don't really know each other, but I think you and I had some sort of bonding experience the first time we met. You remember that? You actually told me then that you had been burned before, but I didn't understand what you meant."

She nodded. "Yeah, and I wish I had told you then. Maybe things would've been different."

"Maybe they would have," I said, "but I'd say the chance your mother was ever going to give up looking for you was pretty slim. I think that, sooner or later, there would have been some kind of confrontation. Maybe it wouldn't have turned out quite so bad, maybe it would've been worse, we don't know. All we have is the reality that we have to deal with today, and in that reality, we want to take you into our family. But you guys have to decide whether you're okay with that."

"But you guys aren't even who you said you were," Ryan said, and I could hear the anger in his voice. "You don't really build custom cars, do you?"

Dex turned around in the seat and looked at him. "Yes," he said, "as a matter of fact, I do. I have my own shop, and my helper and I have built a few, and we have a bunch more to go. If you decide you can put up with this, you'll be able to come hang out at the shop with me a lot. That's the best way I know to learn about cars, just by being around them."

I glanced around so I could see Ryan's face, and his eyes and mouth were both round. "You mean it?" he asked. "I mean, like for real?"

"Absolutely for real," Dex said. "I'd enjoy teaching you all about them."

Ryan had leaned forward so I could see him in the mirror. He licked his lips and looked down at the floorboard for a moment, then looked up again. "I kinda like that idea," he said softly.

Jody touched me on the shoulder. "We'd be back in Tulsa if we came to live with you?" she asked.

"Yes," I said. "That's where we live."

She looked at me in the mirror. "Could we go back to Clear Skies?"

I shot her my biggest smile. "You bet you can," I said. "I got to visit them the other day, and I think that's a really great school. And I happen to know that your friends would love to see you come back there."

"Yeah," Dex said, "but remember that they thought you were dead. It's going to be a bit of a shock when you turn up again, so we probably ought to let the school know in advance before you go back. That way, they can tell the kids so nobody freaks out and thinks you're a ghost."

Ryan actually laughed at that, and the sound did my heart a lot of good.

We got to a shopping mall I had seen signs for, and I pulled in and parked. We all got out of the Jeep and walked in together, and I noticed that Ryan had taken hold of Dex's hand. I glanced over at Jody, who was walking right beside me, and held out my hand. She looked at it, then looked up at my face for a moment before grasping it. If she had squeezed any tighter, I would've been afraid of losing circulation.

I took Jody and went one way while Dex took Ryan another. I told Jody that she could choose her own clothes as long as I thought they were reasonable, and she picked a couple of pairs of jeans and some shirts and put them into the cart I was pushing.

"Come on," I said. "You can do better than that. It may be a while before they release the stuff in your house out at Harmony Valley, so I want you to have plenty of clothes to wear. Get more."

She grinned at me, then picked a few more pairs of jeans and a couple of nice pairs of slacks, before she went back to where the shirts were hanging. She grabbed a few more and then I caught her looking at a rack of dresses.

"Go ahead," I said. "Get yourself a couple, I don't mind."

"Are you sure?" she asked, her face screwed up a bit. "This is going to cost a lot of money."

"I don't care," I said. "Money isn't something I worry about a lot. And don't take that the wrong way, that doesn't mean I'm going to spoil you rotten all the time, it just means we won't go without things we need. If you want a couple of dresses, get them."

She found three that she liked and couldn't decide, so I told her to get them all. After that, we went to make sure she had plenty of underclothes, and followed that up with a trip to the shoe department.

By the time we finished there, Dex called me to say that he and Ryan were done. We met up near the health and beauty section, and I bought them shampoo, soap, toothbrushes and toothpaste and other such sundries.

At that point, Dex snapped his fingers. "Almost forgot," he said. "These kids need something to sleep in."

We headed back to the boys' section first and found a couple of sets of pajamas for Ryan, then went to the girls' and I let Jody choose a couple of nightgowns. They were long and modest, so I didn't have a problem with them. I asked if either of them could think of anything else they needed, and both of them shook their heads.

I started to say, "Great," but Dex touched my arm. "What is it?" he asked. I noticed he was looking at Ryan, who was keeping his eyes down on the floor.

"Ryan?" I asked. "Is there something else you need?"

"He likes to read," Jody said. "They only have a few books at the home, and they're all pretty well torn up."

I made a mental note to get Saul to have that place investigated, but not until we got the kids out of there. "Well, we can fix that," I said. "There's a big bookstore right across the hall."

We paid for our purchases there, then went to the Books Galore Store and both kids seemed to have fun picking out books to take back with them. I let them each get several, reasoning that they could always be passed around to other kids when they were done with them. That made me think about other things the home might be lacking, so we picked up a few board games, as well.

By the time we were done with our shopping, it was almost ten thirty. We took everything and loaded it all into the back end of the Jeep, then went looking for something to do for fun.

There were theaters and we thought about going to a movie, but none of them would start until one o'clock, so we ended up playing mini golf. I was little bit surprised to find mini golf so far north, but we all had a good time and it was nice to see these kids begin to loosen up a bit. Jody was still sticking close to me, while Ryan was doing a fair impression of a mini-Dex, and I thought both of them were absolutely adorable.

An hour later, we decided it was time to go find some lunch, and I told the kids they could choose where we went. Both of them asked for pizza, and I commented that Alfie was going to love them.

"Who's Alfie?" Jody asked, and it seemed to me that she was suddenly nervous.

"Alfie? Alfie is a good friend of mine, another private investigator who helps me out a lot. He's also a dwarf, just barely more than half as tall as Ryan. He absolutely loves pizza, so I'm pretty sure you guys will get along well with him."

Relief flooded her face. "Okay, that's cool," she said. "It's just that my mom knew a guy named Alfie, and he wasn't a very nice man. He used to come over sometimes when my dad was gone, and he always made nasty comments to me."

"Really?" I said very calmly. "Do you know his last name?"

"Yeah, it was Donnelly. He worked with my mom, and I actually think they had some kind of a thing going on between them. I mean, he only came over when my dad wasn't home, and sometimes he was there when we got home from school."

"Well, you won't have to worry about him anymore. I'll make sure of it."

She smiled at me, and I sent a text to Alfie—our Alfie—a few minutes later, suggesting he try to find Alfie Donnelly and see whether there might be any nasty skeletons in his closet. I wanted something I could use to make sure he never bothered these kids again.

We found a pizza place and had lunch, then went to see a movie. When it was over, we unanimously decided to play another round of mini golf before it was time for the kids to go back. While we were playing, we explained that we had to go home in order to start making arrangements for them to come and live with us.

"Do you have to go?" Jody asked. "I mean, what if you go home and then decide not to come back?"

I pulled her into a hug. "Jody, that's not going to

happen," I said. "I promise you, that will not happen. We just have to jump through some hoops to make sure we can make this happen."

"But they won't even let us call you," she said. "I'm sorry, I'm just scared. I know you don't really know us, but you're really all we've got right now." She sniffled, and I saw the tears on her cheeks.

"And we are not going anywhere, not as far as you're concerned. Yes, we have to go home for a few days, but we'll be back to see you next week. They said we can come visit one day a week like this, and we're going to be here every week like clockwork, I promise." I held out my right hand and crooked my pinky at her. "Pinky swear," I said, and she looked at me like I was speaking a foreign language.

"I don't think they do that anymore," Dex said.

"Then they need to start," I said with a grin. I took hold of Jody's hand and held it up, then hooked my pinky into hers. "When we do this, it's called a pinky swear. It means I can't back out, okay?"

She giggled, and squeezed her pinky around mine. "Okay," she said.

We headed toward the car and drove back to the home. When we got there, we helped them carry their bags in and were met by Mrs. Whitlow at the door.

"Oh my goodness," she said. "I don't know that we can bring that much stuff in. They only have a limited amount of space, you know."

"Too bad," I said. "They don't exactly have anywhere else to put it, so you're going to have to make do. And while we're on the subject, considering the trauma these children have been through, I want to make sure they can call me whenever they need to. They have my number and they know they can call collect, so you don't even have to worry about toll charges. Is there going to be a problem with that?"

Mrs. Whitlow's eyes narrowed. "Now, see here, young lady," she began. "I understand that you might be accustomed to getting your own way back home, but you are not there. You can't come in here and start telling us..."

"Let me put this another way," I said. "If I ever find out that these children have not been allowed to call me when they need to, I'm going to come to the conclusion that there is something going on here at this facility that needs to be investigated. Now, considering my connections with the FBI and the local news services, I would just about bet you I can raise enough of a stink to have somebody come here and start looking through everything. Do you really want that to happen?"

She drew herself up as tall as she could and glared at me. "I can assure you," he said, "that everything here is done properly. We have nothing to hide."

"Lady, everybody has something to hide. I can flat-out guarantee you that if the authorities come in here and start going through all your records, they are undoubtedly going to find things that could seriously ruin whatever good deal you've got going on for yourself here."

I thought for a moment the woman was going to have a heart attack, but Dex stepped in at that moment. "Mrs. Whitlow?" he said. "I think I can simplify this a bit. You see, as we all know, these kids have been through a traumatic experience, and right now my wife and I are the only ones they really trust. If you prevent them from being able to contact us when they need to, that could cause irreparable emotional harm, and I'm quite certain you wouldn't want that to happen. Now, is there going to be any problem with them being able to call whenever they need to? Or should I just go out and buy them each a cell phone?"

She opened her mouth three times, but no words came out. Finally she managed, "Cell phones are not allowed. However, under the circumstances, I will allow them to use the office phone when necessary. The only thing I'm going to insist on is that we put some limits on how often they call. I'm thinking perhaps once a week?"

"You see, that's called compromise," I said. "And it's very good, but I'm thinking like once a day. You can handle that, can't you? And, of course, if it's an emergency of some kind, I don't care what time of day or night it is. You and your people *will* let them call me. Do we understand each other?"

The woman glared at me, but she nodded curtly once. "I'll see to it," she hissed at me.

She called a couple of people to help the kids carry their bags, and then we got the chance to say goodbye to them. I warned Mrs. Whitlow that we would be back in a week, and she barely managed a tight smile.

Jody hugged me tight. "You'll really come back?" she asked.

I leaned over and whispered in her ear. "I'll be back," I said. "Did you see the look on Mrs. Whitlow's face? Trust me, she knows I'm coming back and it scares the heck out of her."

Jody giggled and squeezed my neck once more. It took a moment for her to let go, and then I saw that Ryan was giving Dex the same treatment. When both of them finally let go and went back inside, we walked slowly to the Jeep and got in.

"I hate leaving them here," Dex said.

"I know what you mean," I said. "Those kids need us, babe."

"Yep," he said. "Yep, they do."

I started the Jeep and we headed back to the hotel. I hadn't wanted to travel after spending the day with them, so we had arranged a flight for the following morning. The plan was to get a good night's sleep and then get up early, fly home and get the process started.

And that's exactly what we did. We landed at just a little before two o'clock in the afternoon, reclaimed the Cuda from long-term parking and drove home. Jimmy was there when we arrived, and I was absolutely blown away by how much he had accomplished on the garage in such a short time.

Where the overhead door had been, there was now a wall with a pair of windows, and he was already hanging drywall inside. There were two-by-fours lying across the concrete floor, and some of them already had plywood decking nailed down to them. By the time he was finished, he said, it was going to add not one but two rooms to my house.

"I got to looking at it," he said, "and this is too big for just one room. What I'm doing, I'm shooting a hallway along the wall that connects to the house, and that lets me make two rooms that will each be ten feet by sixteen feet."

"That sounds like a great idea," I said. "We can use one of them for like a home office or something."

"Really? I figured you'd just put the two kids out here, so you and Dex have some privacy."

I remembered what Maggie had said about Ryan and the early onset of puberty. "No, I think they each need their space. The other bedroom in the house is on the opposite side of the kitchen, so we'll have plenty of privacy."

Dex just looked at me, but didn't say a word. I'm pretty sure he figured out on his own what I was thinking.

TWENTY

The next week was pretty hectic, as both of us worked with Jimmy to finish the new rooms. When the guys got tired of me being in the way, I went to the shop and got the rollback truck and went looking for furniture. I bought a set of rustic-looking bunk beds for Ryan, so he could have friends stay over sometimes, and a beautiful canopy bed for Jody. Despite everything she had been through, she had a distinct feminine nature, and I wanted to nurture that. When they called each day, we talked about the rooms and how they might want them laid out, so they had a pretty good idea of what I was doing.

And they did call every day. By the third day, I stopped hearing the desperate fear in their voices, the way they sounded when they were afraid we were going to tell them we were backing out. I think they were beginning to believe that we really did care about them, and that they really were going to have a new life ahead of them. I even contacted Eric Hamilton out at the school to let him know that we had found the kids and were hoping to adopt them, and that he might want to let the rest of the students know that they were alive after all. He assured me that they would be more than welcome to return, and Doctor Ely called me a little later to express her own relief and happiness.

Three days later, everything was finished and set up. When we were ready, I called John Drew, our attorney friend, and asked him to make arrangements for DFS to come and do their home inspection.

They came the following morning, and I was lucky enough that it was a caseworker I had dealt with before in a professional capacity. When we explained everything, she said the house looked fine and that she would be honored to sign off on it.

That was the worst hurdle we had to jump back home, and it only left that one little detail: the wedding. Rather than just do a JP service and hold a second wedding later, we called everyone and told them that things were being rushed and why. My parents arrived the next day, and Dex's mom and sisters only lived over in Broken Arrow, not far away. Everyone else we had invited to the wedding was close by except for my old college roommate, Brenda Wickham. Unfortunately, she couldn't make it on such short notice, but she gave us her blessing and I had to pick a new maid of honor in a hurry.

I chose Angie, and she was absolutely thrilled. We ended up buying her a dress off the rack because there wasn't time to have one fitted, and then it was time for the wedding. The preacher that we had arranged had agreed to the change in timetable, and we all met at the church at four o'clock in the afternoon.

The service was beautiful, and everyone told me what a beautiful bride I made. Personally, I credited that to the veil, because it kept Freda hidden away, but everyone cried. I even cried, and I hate to cry, but I couldn't help it when I saw that Dex had not only got me a custom engagement ring, but he'd also ordered a custom wedding ring to go with it. When he slipped it onto my fused fingers, the whole place burst out in applause and my tears started flowing.

Of course, the big reception we had planned had to be canceled, so we ended up taking everyone to Cracker Barrel. I had called ahead to make sure they would have room for us, and they didn't disappoint. All twenty-two in my wedding party were seated around a bunch of tables shoved hurriedly together, and I'd have to say it was one of the nicer receptions I've ever attended.

When it was over, Dex and I went home and locked the doors. Our first night together as husband and wife was everything I could ever have hoped it would be.

Our honeymoon took place in Montana. We had already planned on flying back up so we could visit the kids again, and we decided we might as well just take a week to enjoy for ourselves while we were at it. Dex arranged for the honeymoon suite at the nicest hotel in White Sulfur Springs—okay, it wasn't that bad—and he actually carried me over the threshold when we got there.

The next morning, we showed up right on time at nine a.m. The kids were ready to go, dressed in some of the new clothes we had bought them the week before and showing signs of recovering from the shocks they had been through. Of course, I wasn't naïve enough to believe they were not going to need counseling, and I had already spoken to Nicole about it. She was only waiting for them to arrive to start working with them, and I was confident she was the best person for the job.

We had a wonderful day with them, and even took them along while we went to drop off the marriage license and endorsement to Saul, the attorney. I was looking forward to meeting him at last, but he was unfortunately tied up in court that day, so we left it with his secretary and figured we would try again the next week.

It really was a fantastic day. We went and saw another movie, took a long, scenic drive around the countryside and mostly just let the kids talk to us. There were a couple of moments when I thought things might get bad, when Ryan started crying about missing his dad, but Jody comforted him through it. The girl had a maturity that was far beyond her years, and I was hoping she would be able to regain some of her childhood before it was too late.

After we took them back, we went out for dinner and then went back to our hotel. We had let the kids know that we were going to be in town for the whole week, and we were surprised the next day when Jody called to say that Mrs. Whitlow wanted to invite us to a second visit while we were there. We scheduled it for that Saturday and rented a pair of four-wheelers, then spent the day riding trails in the hills outside of town. It was a lot of fun, and with Jody on behind me and Ryan clinging to Dex, we had more laughs and delights then I had ever hoped to see out of them so soon.

Our next visit, the regular weekly one, marked the end of our honeymoon. We spent the day with the kids and then flew home that evening, but I was confident that both of them now trusted us to come back. We had promised to see them in another week, but we both felt it was time for us to get back to work.

The next day, while I was in my office, I got a text message telling me to call Alfie. I hit the icon to dial, and a moment later I heard, "Hello?"

I started to laugh and make a wisecrack, but suddenly a chill went down my spine. I remembered that silly conversation about how, if he ever answered the phone by simply saying hello, I would come running with gun in hand.

"Hey, Alfie," I said. "What's up?"

"Oh, not much," he said nonchalantly. "I was getting a little hungry and thought you might want to come over for lunch. Maybe grab some of those burgers we both like so much on the way. I'll be happy to pay you back when you get here."

Now I knew something was wrong. First off, Alfie can't stand burgers, and second, Alfie never, ever offered to pay us back when we brought food. Combined with the way he had answered, I knew that he was in some kind of trouble, and I was determined to find out what it was.

"Sure, I'll be glad to," I said. "Dex is tied up all day, anyway, so I could stand the company. I'll be there in about an hour."

"Sounds good," Alfie said. "Bye-bye."

That was another thing. Alfie never, ever says goodbye.

I hit the icon to call Dex as I was rushing out the back door. He answered on the second ring and I told him there was something wrong at Alfie's and we had to go right then. By the time I got through the alley, he was in the Mustang with the engine running and I simply jumped into the passenger seat.

"What's going on?" he asked.

"I don't know," I said, and then I explained about how he had answered the phone and the conversation we had about it some weeks before. When I added in his offer to pay for burgers we knew he didn't like, and then how he actually said goodbye before he hung up, Dex shoved his foot to the floor. We parked around the block from Alfie's building and jumped out, then hurried through the grounds until we were just outside his windows.

Unfortunately, the living room is adjacent to the central hallway of the apartment building, so we couldn't see him from the windows at the back. I started to head around toward the entrance, but Dex grabbed hold of my arm. He waggled a finger and put it to his lips, then took a pocket knife out and used it to slip the lock on the window.

This particular window opened into Alfie's bedroom, a place I had never seen and probably didn't want to. Beggars can't be choosers, though, so as soon as Dex raised it high enough, we both climbed through as quietly as we could. Once we were inside, Dex pushed the window back down and we moved silently to the door. It was slightly ajar, and we crouched down beside it and listened.

For a moment there was nothing but silence, and then we heard Alfie's voice. "You know," he was saying, "you would make me a lot less nervous if you would sit down and stop pacing around. She'll be here, don't worry, and then you can talk to her about whatever it is you need to know."

"Just shut up," said a man's voice. "Don't forget, Shorty,

I've got the gun. You make the wrong move and you just might end up even shorter."

"Hey, there's no need to get nasty," Alfie said. "I mean, what did I ever do to you anyway?"

"You stuck your nose in where it don't belong," the guy said. "I don't know what your beef is with me, but I know it has something to do with that broad, because her name keeps coming up. I just found out she's trying to adopt those kids, and I don't really give a crap about that, but I want to know where my stuff is."

"Well, just relax," Alfie said. "Like I said, she'll be here before too long."

We still couldn't see anything because the bedrooms in the apartment were on a hallway that divided it in half. There were two bedrooms, with a bathroom right in the middle, and the living room was directly across from that.

Dex took hold of the door and pulled it gently open. Luckily the hinges didn't squeak, and then we were crawling down the hallway. When we got to where it opened into the living room, Dex poked his head out for a couple of seconds, then pulled back. He told me with hand motions that the guy with the gun was at the far side of the room, looking directly at Alfie.

Suddenly I was pissed. I motioned for Dex to wait where he was, quietly got to my feet and stepped out into the living room.

"Surprise," I said, my gun in my hand. It was aimed directly at the other man, and he spun instantly to point his own gun at me.

"It's you," he said. "What's with the gun?"

"Oh, I don't know," I said. "It just really irritates me

when somebody points a gun at my friends. Now, why don't you put yours down, and then I won't shoot you."

The guy burst out laughing. "You won't shoot me? What makes you think I won't shoot you? Ever since you've been mixed up in all this, all you've done is make my life miserable. I had it made, I really had it made, and then you had to screw it all up."

I narrowed my eye. "What? What in the world are you talking about?"

"Maggie," the guy said. "Maggie Logan. Ever since she came to you, things have just gone crazy, and then you up and killed her. We were going to be together, as soon as she got her kids back, but you had to screw that up, too."

I cocked my head to the side, staring at the ceiling in shock. "Just who the hell are you?" I asked.

"Maggie and me were going to get married," the guy said. "I'm Alf, Alf Donnelly. Didn't she ever mention me?"

"No," I said. "No, she didn't." Of course, I recognized the name from what Jody had said, and I couldn't help wondering how he'd ended up here.

Well, you all know me fairly well by now. When I want to know something, I ask.

"What are you doing here? Why are you bothering my buddy, here?"

He glanced at Alfie, then looked back at me. "You mean Shorty, here? One of my buddies on the police force told me he was asking questions about me, so I decided to come find out why. When I got here, he told me that he works for you, and it all started to come together. You're trying to get our stuff, right?"

I was starting to feel like I was in the *Twilight Zone*, and if you don't know what that is, Google it. Let's just say it means there is something seriously wrong with the world, and that's how I was feeling.

"What stuff?" I asked, and I think my voice squeaked in my confusion. "I don't have a clue what you're talking about, man."

He took a step toward me, waving the gun. "Yeah, bull," he said. "Maggie had that scumbag husband of hers bringing stuff home from the hospital every day, and we were stashing it back so we could make a big score. Ever since you killed her, the cops have had the house sealed up and I can't get close to it. Did you guys find it already?"

"Stuff," I repeated. "Are you talking about drugs?"

"We just call it the stuff," he said. "We don't use that other word, that makes it sound a lot worse than it is."

I shook my head. "Well, I don't know how to tell you this," I said, "but I don't know anything about your 'stuff.' On the other hand, I'm pretty sure the police or the FBI have probably found it if it was in the house. Now, why don't you put down your gun and just walk away. If you keep holding it, this is only going to end in a bad situation."

He stood there and stared at me for a moment, and I honestly thought the guy was going to start crying. Whatever drugs he and Maggie had been stashing, I figured they must've been worth a lot of money. He was beginning to realize that, not only was his woman gone, but so was the dream of whatever they were hoping to do.

And then suddenly he screamed, and I just about jumped out of my skin. He put one hand on his head and started waving the gun around with the other, and then he pulled the trigger. His shot went wild and hit one of Alfie's computer monitors, and I fired my own gun a second later.

My bullet hit him low on the side, and he dropped his gun as he fell. Dex came rushing out and landed on top of him, while Alfie started screaming about his monitor at the same time he was dialing the phone.

Thirty minutes later, with police and an ambulance on the scene, we learned that Alfred Donnelly was a convicted drug dealer who had a fondness for pharmaceuticals. He claimed that he had met Maggie through another dealer, and that they had become lovers more than three years earlier. He even bragged about how many nights he spent inside the house with her, while her husband slept like a log in their bedroom.

My guess about the police having found his drugs was wrong, but I knew there was about to be a dedicated search. Donnelly was carted off to the hospital under arrest, and his record was long enough that it was unlikely he was ever coming out of the prison system again.

When everything was over, we ordered pizza and sat down with Alfie as he told us how this lunatic had shown up at his apartment door and forced his way inside. "I remembered what you said about if I ever answered the phone in a normal way," he said. "I had my phone in my pocket, so I stuck my hand in there and texted you by touch. When you called, I was thrilled." He grinned at me. "And I see you remembered. Thanks for the rescue, princess."

The next day, I found out that a large supply of pharmaceutical-grade opioids had been found hidden in the basement of Maggie Logan's home. Donnelly was charged with conspiring to steal pharmaceuticals, conspiracy to distribute pharmaceuticals and a host of other crimes that all added up to a couple of life sentences. I would be able to tell Jody that she never needed to worry about him again.

And then life settled into a routine. We worked three days each week, then hopped a plane to Montana to visit the kids, and then flew home. I managed to get a half dozen more women with their children out of abusive situations, and then we got the call we'd been waiting for. Saul Greenberg had completed all the paperwork in Montana for the adoption, and it was just coming down to the final hearing. That would be scheduled for the following Monday, a few days before our next scheduled visit, so we rearranged things to let us take the whole week off.

At nine a.m. on Monday morning, after arriving on a red-eye flight that got us to Bozeman at three a.m., we walked into the courthouse.

We were actually about a half hour early, so we took our time looking for the right courtroom. There was a smartly dressed, heavyset man standing just outside the courtroom doors, and he seemed relieved as soon as he got a look at my face.

"Cassie?" he asked, and I nodded. "Saul Greenberg," he said, and I shook his hand as I introduced Dex. "Come on, they'll be calling this case any second now."

"Any second?" I asked. "I thought it was supposed to begin at nine thirty?"

"It was, but the case before it got postponed. I'm just glad you happened to show up early, because I wouldn't want them to put this off for another month or so."

"What do we have to do?" I asked. "I mean, if there was

anything I was supposed to bring along, I probably don't have it."

"The only thing I need is for you to be here," he said. "Judge Zelinski is a golfing buddy, and I sent him all the information about you a couple weeks ago and he made a few of his own inquiries. Your Family Services people back in Tulsa think you are one of the best things that ever happened to them, do you know that? If the Pope saw the things they said, you'd be a saint. We are asking for an order granting you temporary guardianship until the adoption is finalized. The whole process takes another six months, and you'll have to come back then for the final disposition. That's when the Logans legally become your children, and the birth certificates will be reissued in your names."

I swallowed hard and we followed him into the courtroom. He pointed out a place for us to sit and then he went through the little gate and took a seat on the wall. A few minutes later, the bailiff called my name and Dex's, and we met Saul at the table.

"This is a petition for adoption by Dexter Tate and Cassandra McGraw, husband and wife, who have filed to adopt Jody and Ryan Logan. Is everyone present?"

"My clients are here, Your Honor," Saul said. "I understand the children are just down the hall, with the guardian ad litem."

The judge turned to the bailiff and said something softly, and we were left standing there for about a minute. A moment later he returned, and then the door at the back of the courtroom opened. I glanced back and saw Jody and Ryan come into the room, escorted by a tall lady in a business suit. She walked them right up through the little gate and to the table on the other side of the courtroom.

"Your Honor," she said, smiling at the judge. "I apologize for being tardy. The children needed a few minutes to compose themselves."

"Compose themselves?" the judge asked. "Do they need a recess?"

The lady smiled. "No, Your Honor," she said. "I think this is just a very exciting day for both of them. They've been visiting with the petitioners regularly while in state care, and they're quite thrilled about the prospect of going home with them today."

I looked over at the kids and tried to smile, knowing they had a clear view of Freda from that angle. Jody saw me looking and gave me a little wave and a smile, bouncing a bit as she fought to contain herself, and Ryan kept shooting his eyes our way with the biggest grin on his face. I glanced back at Jody and it suddenly dawned on me that she no longer looked like the young woman I had seen when she was serving as nurse to her dad so many weeks ago; she had allowed herself to relax and let go of the forced maturity. Now, at last, she looked like exactly what she was: a fifteen-year-old girl.

"Then let's get back to work, here, folks," said the judge. "All the paperwork on this petition is in order, but I'm a little concerned about how quickly it's happening. My understanding is that Mr. Tate and Ms. McGraw are requesting a temporary guardianship be ordered, so that they can take the children back to Oklahoma with them while the adoption is pending. Is that correct, Mr. Greenberg?"

"Yes, Your Honor, that's correct."

"Now, I have to say that Mr. Greenberg has done a very exhaustive background investigation on this couple, and frankly, I have never seen people so profoundly endorsed by officials of the state, particularly the director of the Department of Family Services in Tulsa. According to their reports, Ms. McGraw has been responsible for saving many, many lives of women and children in abusive situations." He looked up at me. "Is any of that actually true?"

I blinked. "Well, all of it, Your Honor," I said. "That's what I do for a living—I work with abused women and children. I run my own private abuse counseling clinic, and I work closely with the local police and prosecutors when necessary. I also work with DFS pretty regularly."

"So I've been told. I understand you are also a licensed private investigator?"

"Yes, Your Honor, I am."

"I think we all know a little bit about your recent exploits in that line—you were all over the news a few weeks ago. Okay, you seem all right. As for Mr. Tate, he also has some glowing reports on his character, not the least of which comes from the FBI." He looked up at Dex. "Special Agent McIver made a point of calling my office a couple of weeks ago to make sure I'd gotten his recommendation. I'm supposed to tell both of you that he's taking medical retirement and hopes you won't be strangers."

He turned back to the lady with Jody and Ryan. "Ms. Jorgensen, you were appointed guardian ad litem for these children when the petition was filed. Have you had sufficient opportunity to interview them regarding this petition?"

"I have, Your Honor," she said.

"And can you make a report to this court regarding your opinion on placing these children with this couple?"

"I can, Your Honor." She handed a sheet of paper to the bailiff, who passed it up to the judge. The judge glanced over it, then looked up at her again. I suppose that was a signal for her to give the report verbally, because that's what she did. "Your Honor, I find that it would undoubtedly be in the best interest of these children to be placed with this couple. While they have not known her for very long, it was Ms. McGraw who put her own life at risk to protect them a few weeks ago, when their mother was threatening their lives. Considering the things they've told me and a counselor about the suffering they endured at their mother's hand, it isn't difficult for me to understand why they regard Ms. McGraw as their hero, and why they would like to be under her protection and that of her husband on a regular basis. For these reasons, I do officially recommend granting this petition, including the order for temporary guardianship."

My heart was racing, and from the way Dex was clinging to my hand, I think his was probably pounding pretty hard, as well. When Ms. Jorgensen had finished speaking, I saw Jody smiling and bouncing up and down without even trying to hold it in, and Ryan finally turned and looked directly at us. I waved at him, but that was when I realized he was really looking at Dex. I guess my guy had made quite an impression on him during our visits, and I could certainly understand that.

"All right," the judge said. "Now I'd like to hear from the children themselves. Jody LeeAnn Logan, do you wish to be placed with this couple?"

"Yes, Your Honor," Jody said. I had the feeling that Ms.

Jorgensen had coached them in what to say, but that was understandable under the circumstances.

"And do you understand that they are petitioning to adopt you, and that if that petition is granted, you would then become their child and they would become your parents, from now on? You would no longer have the last name of Logan, but of Tate, do you understand that?"

"Yes, Your Honor," Jody said, and it was obvious that it was all she could do to contain her delight.

The judge looked at her for a second, and then he winked. He turned his attention to Ryan.

"Ryan Michael Logan, do you wish to be placed with this couple?"

"Yeah," Ryan said emphatically, and almost everyone in the courtroom began to chuckle. Ms. Jorgensen leaned down and whispered to him, and then he said, "I'm sorry, yes, Your Honor."

"And you also understand that they wish to adopt you, and that if that petition is granted, you would be their child and they would be your parents from now on? You would no longer have the last name of Logan, but of Tate, and do you understand that?"

Ryan nodded. "Yes, Your Honor," he said solemnly.

"Well, I can't find any reason not to go along with this," the judge said. "The order for temporary guardianship is granted effective immediately, and the petition for adoption will be placed on the docket for six months from now. Assuming there have been no problems during that time, I think we can safely say the adoption will be granted and made permanent. In the meantime, the temporary guardianship gives you, Mr. Tate and Ms. McGraw, complete and total authority over these children. It also conveys to you complete responsibility for their health and welfare. I've been assured that you are aware of those facts and completely willing to accept them, so that means we are all done for today." He smiled, and this time he winked at me and Dex. "I'll see you all in about six months. The clerk will notify you as to when the hearing will take place."

My head was spinning. I looked at Saul, and he was smiling as he urged us to turn around and look at the children. Ms. Jorgensen was walking toward us, holding each of them by the hand, but then they broke free and ran the last few feet. Ryan ran straight to Dex, who didn't surprise me at all when he dropped to his knees and threw his arms around the boy, but Jody came to me. She stood in front of me for a moment, then threw out her arms and rushed forward. I wrapped my arms around her and pulled her close, and we both began to cry.

We stood there like that for about a minute, and then the judge cleared his throat. "I don't mean to be rude, folks, but we do have some other cases we have to deal with here today." I glanced at him and saw that he was smiling.

I pulled back and looked into Jody's face. "You guys ready to go home?" I asked.

She wiped her eyes and smiled at me. "Yeah," she said. "We're ready. We are so ready."

Thanks so much for reading the Cassie McGraw series. If you enjoyed it, you'll probably also enjoy the Sam Prichard series. Here's a quick sneak peek of THE GRAVE MAN to give it a try!

Scan the QR code below to purchase THE GRAVE MAN.

Or go to: righthouse.com/the-grave-man

NOTE: flip to the very end to read an exclusive sneak peak...

DON'T MISS ANYTHING!

If you want to stay up to date on all new releases in this series, with this author, or with any of our new deals, you can do so by joining our newsletters below.

In addition, you will immediately gain access to our entire *Right House VIP Library,* which includes many riveting Mystery and Thriller novels for your enjoyment.

righthouse.com/email

(Easy to unsubscribe. No spam. Ever.)

ALSO BY DAVID ARCHER

Up to date books can be found at:
www.righthouse.com/david-archer

ROGUE THRILLERS
Gates of Hell (Book 1)
Hell's Fury (Book 2)

JACOB HUNTER THRILLERS
The Kyiv File (Book 1)
The Bogota File (Book 2)

PETER BLACK THRILLERS
Burden of the Assassin (Book 1)
The Man Without A Face (Book 2)
Unpunished Deeds (Book 3)
Hunter Killer (Book 4)
Silent Shadows (Book 5)
The Last Run (Book 6)
Dark Corners (Book 7)
Ghost Operative (Book 8)
A Fire Burning (Book9)

ALEX MASON THRILLERS
Odin (Book 1)
Ice Cold Spy (Book 2)
Mason's Law (Book 3)
Assets and Liabilities (Book 4)

Russian Roulette (Book 5)
Executive Order (Book 6)
Dead Man Talking (Book 7)
All The King's Men (Book 8)
Flashpoint (Book 9)
Brotherhood of the Goat (Book 10)
Dead Hot (Book 11)
Blood on Megiddo (Book 12)
Son of Hell (Book 13)

NOAH WOLF THRILLERS
Code Name Camelot (Book 1)
Lone Wolf (Book 2)
In Sheep's Clothing (Book 3)
Hit for Hire (Book 4)
The Wolf's Bite (Book 5)
Black Sheep (Book 6)
Balance of Power (Book 7)
Time to Hunt (Book 8)
Red Square (Book 9)
Highest Order (Book 10)
Edge of Anarchy (Book 11)
Unknown Evil (Book 12)
Black Harvest (Book 13)
World Order (Book 14)
Caged Animal (Book 15)
Deep Allegiance (Book 16)
Pack Leader (Book 17)
High Treason (Book 18)
A Wolf Among Men (Book 19)
Rogue Intelligence (Book 20)

Alpha (Book 21)
Rogue Wolf (Book 22)
Shadows of Allegiance (Book 23)
In the Grip of Darkness (Book 24)

SAM PRICHARD MYSTERIES
The Grave Man (Book 1)
Death Sung Softly (Book 2)
Love and War (Book 3)
Framed (Book 4)
The Kill List (Book 5)
Drifter: Part One (Book 6)
Drifter: Part Two (Book 7)
Drifter: Part Three (Book 8)
The Last Song (Book 9)
Ghost (Book 10)
Hidden Agenda (Book 11)

SAM AND INDIE MYSTERIES
Aces and Eights (Book 1)
Fact or Fiction (Book 2)
Close to Home (Book 3)
Brave New World (Book 4)
Innocent Conspiracy (Book 5)
Unfinished Business (Book 6)
Live Bait (Book 7)
Alter Ego (Book 8)
More Than It Seems (Book 9)
Moving On (Book 10)
Worst Nightmare (Book 11)
Chasing Ghosts (Book 12)

Serial Superstition (Book 13)

CHANCE REDDICK THRILLERS
Innocent Injustice (Book 1)
Angel of Justice (Book 2)
High Stakes Hunting (Book 3)
Personal Asset (Book 4)

CASSIE MCGRAW MYSTERIES
What Lies Beneath (Book 1)
Can't Fight Fate (Book 2)
One Last Game (Book 3)
Never Really Gone (Book 4)

ABOUT US

Right House is an independent publisher created by authors for readers. We specialize in Action, Thriller, Mystery, and Crime novels.

If you enjoyed this novel, then there is a good chance you will like what else we have to offer! Please stay up to date by using any of the links below.

Join our mailing lists to stay up to date -->
righthouse.com/email
Visit our website --> righthouse.com
Contact us --> contact@righthouse.com

 facebook.com/righthousebooks

 x.com/righthousebooks

 instagram.com/righthousebooks

EXCLUSIVE SNEAK PEAK OF...

THE GRAVE MAN

CHAPTER 1

GOING TO THE OFFICE WASN'T AS PLEASANT lately, Sam thought, as he made his way through the back entry to the detectives' division. There weren't so many people there that day, and it seemed like a lot of them were avoiding the place, just staying away as much as they could. He could understand that.

After almost ten years as a Denver cop, Sam was sick of seeing what humanity was really capable of. He had grown up reading cop stories, always seeing how the cops would save the day, watching them rescue the innocent and punish the guilty every week on TV, until he finally knew that he had to be one himself. After a short stint in the Army that never even got him out of the country, he'd come home and applied for the academy. He'd been accepted, and that was the start of an illustrious career.

Now, it was all he could do to drag himself out of bed in the mornings, make himself come in and see what new horrors he'd have to deal with. The past four months he'd been on loan to the DEA, and they'd made some big drug busts, shut down some of the most evil purveyors of sin and death that ever lived, but they were like the mythical hydra— as soon as you cut off one of its heads, three more grew back to take its place.

Sam wanted to stop cutting off heads and find the creature's heart, but there was almost no evidence as to where that heart might be. They knew there was something big behind the drug operations in the city, but it was so well organized and so carefully designed that no one seemed to have any idea where or how to find it.

His cell rang as he sat down at his desk, and he saw his partner's number. Dan Jacobs was already out on his station, watching one of the dealers they'd identified the day before.

"Yo," Sam answered.

"Sam, it's Dan. I been thinkin', and it seems to me that we might be lookin' in the wrong direction, y'know?"

Sam blinked a couple of times. "Danny, I've been awake for about fifteen minutes, and haven't even opened my Starbuck's yet. What the heck are you talkin' about?"

"I'm sayin', maybe we're goin' about this all the wrong way, tryin' to find dealers and trail 'em, follow the tracks up the ladder. There's something about this whole setup that smacks of serious organization, something big enough to hide in plain sight, know what I mean? If it's that well laid out, we can follow minions all day long, we're never gonna find the top guy, because they don't ever see the top guys."

Sam nodded. "Yeah, you're probably right," he said, "but unless you got a crystal ball lead on where else to go, I don't know what good it's doin' us. Where else we gonna find any leads at all? Got a clue, there?"

"Maybe," Dan said. "We've been tailing a lot of these clowns the past few weeks, right? Have you noticed one thing they all do the same?"

Sam thought about it, but nothing jumped out at him. He looked at it from a couple of different angles, then shook his head. Into the phone, he said, "Nope. So, what is it?"

"Facebook. No matter what else they're doin', these bastards never miss checking in on Facebook every day, several times a day. They go on, look at what people are sayin' on their pages, sometimes they answer and sometimes they don't, and then they go back to their drug dealin' ways."

Sam rubbed his temple. "Dan, everyone does that. Everyone on freakin' earth is on Facebook, and always checkin' it out. That's just part of modern livin', old buddy!"

"I know, I know, but hear me out. The only time they ever go make a drop or get money is right after they're on Facebook. I think maybe the stuff that's being said on there is some sort of code or somethin', a way to let 'em know when and where, y'know?"

Sam's phone beeped. It was their boss, Agent Carlson. "Dan, I got Carlson beepin' in, lemme call you back." He hit the button to switch calls before his partner could answer. "Prichard," he said.

"Sam, we got a hit on the north side crew; they got a big load in, overnight, and they're cuttin' it out today. I'm pulling everyone in, we're gonna take 'em down. Where's Dan at?"

"He's on a stakeout, watchin' Pink Dog and his crew. Want me to bring him along?"

"Yeah, get him. Meet us at the back of the AT&T

building downtown, by their freight entrance. We're staging there. Can you make it in twenty?"

Sam checked his phone, thinking about how no one bothered to use watches, anymore. "Yeah, we'll be there. Later."

He hung up and dialed Dan back, told him where to go, and hung up again, grabbing his coffee and rushing back out to his car. The AT&T Building was downtown, which meant the raid was going to be in a high-traffic area. That was never good, and Sam got that nagging feeling in the pit of his stomach that he often got when things were likely to go wrong. He'd never come to the point of thinking of it as a predictor, but he'd felt it before, when things went way out of control, so it made him nervous and cautious. If something bad was going to happen, he wanted to do everything in his power to make sure it didn't happen to him or his partner!

He made his way across town quickly, but without turning on his Christmas lights. Whoever they were about to hit would certainly be listening to scanners and checking traffic reports, so any mention of a police car moving toward them with lights on would spook them. The idea in these cases was to avoid notice, catch them completely off guard, so that no one had any chance to destroy or tamper with evidence.

That was the big problem with drug raids, he thought. You never knew who on the inside of any gang might have connections on the force, and it wasn't uncommon for a cop to accidentally let slip something that gave them a tip-off. Even worse were the times when the perp was a cop's kin, and got a quick warning by cell phone minutes before a bust.

That happened far more often than anyone wanted to admit; it's not that the cop involved was actually dirty, it was just a last-ditch attempt to get a nephew or cousin to walk away from the criminal life before it was too late.

Problem was, those phone calls and tips sometimes got officers killed. How could any cop live with that? Geez, how could any person live with it? Knowing you got a cop killed just to save someone from what would probably be nothing more than a slap on the wrist would be an awfully heavy load of guilt to bear.

Sam didn't have any nephews or cousins, and wouldn't tip one off anyway. His attitude was that if you made your bed, you had to lie in it, so if someone close to him got jammed up, that was their problem. Sure, if it was someone who might have a chance of coming out and going straight, he might stand up for them at sentencing, or something like that, but he'd never risk letting a perp know what was going down. He'd let his own mother get busted before he'd do that.

Good thing Mom wasn't into drugs, wasn't it?

Sam didn't have anyone he was that close to. His dad had died when he was a teenager, leaving a lot of weight on some young shoulders, but Sam had done his best to hold the rest of the family together. His mom was managing, working as a real estate agent for one of the better companies, but the market was slow, so she was lucky she was even earning a living. Now and then she'd get a little behind on some bills, and Sam would help out.

His sister Carrie was out in California somewhere, trying to become an actress. He didn't hear from her except maybe at Christmastime, and once in a blue moon when she also needed to borrow a few bucks. He always sent it, because that's what big brothers do, and what else did he have to spend any money on?

He'd been married, once, back when he was young and new on the force and thought a cop could have a family life. Jeanie was beautiful and sexy, and thought that the young cop who had pulled her over for a broken taillight was the hottest thing she'd ever seen, so she'd scribbled her phone number on the back of the warning ticket he gave her and handed it back to him. He'd called her the next day and they'd dated for four months, then married in a surprise elopement and bought a house through his mom two weeks later.

The house was awesome, with a big yard, a two-car garage and a decent-sized pool in the back. There were four bedrooms, for all the kids they planned to have, with one downstairs and three upstairs, and three bathrooms so no one would ever have to dance outside a bathroom door for too long. It was a wonderful house, and he looked forward to the day it would have kids running through it.

He was doing a lot of double shifts back then, saving up money so they could pay for the house they'd bought, and Jeanie said she understood and was proud of him. She lasted less than ten months before the long hours finally got to her, and he came home to find her packed and gone to her mother's house in Tampa, with a note explaining that she'd "sort of met someone." She filed for divorce, and since they hadn't had any kids yet and she didn't want anything from him, he didn't fight it. He kept the house, even though it was way too big for him all by himself, so he just lived on the first floor.

His only hobby was in his garage; during one case, a drug dealer was busted hauling a quarter-million bucks worth of meth and coke in a 1969 Corvette Stingray, and his vehicle was seized. The car was damaged during the bust, so Sam watched, and when it came up for auction, he bid on it and won, and was gradually rebuilding it. It was actually close to being finished, but Sam was always looking for one more thing to fix, afraid of not having even the car to occupy his lonely days when there was nothing left to do to it.

Okay, he told himself, *enough Memory Lane crap. Let's get back to reality!*

The AT&T Building was looming ahead, and he wheeled the big Dodge Charger squad car into the service and delivery driveway. He saw the staging ahead, with six DEA blackouts—the big black SUVs the agency used—and a SWAT van from the Denver PD. Parking out of the way, he got out and grabbed his vest and gear from the trunk before walking over to where Carlson stood.

"So what have we got?" he asked, and Carlson frowned up at him. His DEA boss stood about five foot eight, and was a classic case of "little man syndrome" if Sam had ever seen one.

"We've got about forty perps in a small warehouse, with somewhere between fifteen and twenty mil in pot and cocaine they're divvying up. Word is this is a new deal between some of the street gangs, that they're splitting up the city into territories and working together to run all the dope."

Sam shrugged. "Okay, so we take 'em down today, they'll be back with another load somewhere else tomorrow. Hell, half the assholes we arrest today will be back out before then, and workin' with the next new batch by morning."

Carlson leaned back and looked at him, as Dan Jacobs walked up from his own car. "So you think we should just leave 'em alone and let 'em keep pushing this crap on the streets? The more we take away from them, the more they gotta spend to get it back. If we can hurt them economically, then we got a chance of slowing this stuff down, getting it off the streets and away from our kids."

"Hey, I'm not arguin', boss, you're preachin' to the choir! I just wish the courts would work with us, instead of against us! If we could keep some of these creeps locked up, that would slow the operations down, too."

Dan laughed. "Save it for the next election and run for office, why don't you? That's the only way you'll ever get that song and dance out there."

Sam glared at him. "Excuse me, sir, I ain't no politician! I prefer to be honest and work for my livin'!"

Carlson growled, "Okay, knock off the funnies. Let's group up. You guys will be with Matheny's group, going in the front door. The others will be crashing the back and side doors, and SWAT's here to back us up if needed." He led the way to where the rest of the agents and officers were standing around, already geared up. "All right, we're about to go. Remember, we don't want any grandstanding. This is a sweep, plain and simple; we're going in to round 'em up and take their goodies, and that's it. No heroics, and hopefully they won't be trying any, either! Everyone ready?"

There was an answering chorus of "*Hoo-Rah!*" and Sam fought back the urge to laugh; not one of these guys had ever been a Marine, he was sure, but they did love to play tough. He nudged Dan, beside him.

"I'm so glad I've got you on my flank," he said softly. "I wouldn't trust one of those yahoos with my dog's life, and I ain't even got a dog."

"Yeah, well, you just remember that while I've got your back, you're the yahoo who's got mine! Let's get both of us in there and out alive, deal?"

"Deal!" Sam said, and they bumped elbows as they got into the back of one of the blackouts.

The trucks bounced them around as they pulled out of the lot, and Sam thought of the way they showed scenes like this in movies, with special vehicles where cops who looked more like soldiers were lined along the wall of something like a Hummer, with special armor and helmets protecting them, and weapons that looked like something from the future bristling everywhere. He stifled a laugh, fighting it down from that nervousness in his gut. Last thing he needed at that moment was someone thinking he was losing it.

When the action began, it was all at once. The trucks slid to a stop, each at its pre-designated spot, and the men and women inside poured out. They ran to position at the door, four on each side, as the ram slammed into the doorknob and bashed it open, and then all of them were inside, weapons ready, screaming, "Federal Agents, get on the ground!"

The building was an open warehouse design, with only a few pillars holding up the ceiling, and they could all see the activity going on out on the floor. There were several tables set up, and multiple piles of bricks of marijuana and bags of white powder. Each table held a mix of the two, and the mixes were being plastic wrapped together into big bundles. The people working looked up as the cops and agents entered, but not one of them made a move to duck until more cops came pouring in through other doors, all screaming the same things.

Suddenly, all hell broke loose, as half a dozen of the workers reached for handguns and began firing wildly around at any of the cops they could see. There was the staccato rattle of automatic weapons fire, and instantly, everything seemed to go into slow motion for Sam. He saw one of the officers he'd worked with go down with a bullet to his head, and the shooter who got him took a dozen rounds that turned him into hamburger. Another shooter fired off several shots, and another cop went down, a woman, the left side of her face apparently gone, and Sam thought about the three kids she was so proud of, but there wasn't any time for that, so he turned to the shooter and blew him away.

Dan let out a strangled scream and Sam spun to see why; his partner was down, holding his side. The shooter had come from behind them, and Sam fired without even thinking as the guy aimed at Dan again and readied another squeeze on the trigger. The shooter went down in a spray of blood and brains, and Sam started toward Dan, but then a semi-truck slammed into him and he was thrown down onto the concrete floor, his head hitting it hard. He was stunned, and the noises around him seemed muffled, suddenly, like he had ducked underwater.

He knew it hadn't been a truck that got him; he knew it was bullets, and probably several of them. He was hit, and while all he could feel was a dull ache at the moment, he knew it was probably bad, and so he decided to take as many of these assholes with him as he could, just to even out the score. He rolled over to find a target, but everything was already over, and all the remaining perps were down with their hands on their heads. There were four of them over to the side, obviously dead, and he saw people working on his comrades who'd gone down.

Johnson, that was the name of the woman, and he saw enough to know that she wasn't dead. She was holding something against her own face, so maybe the wound was only bloody, and not as deadly as it had looked. One of the male officers who went down had been covered by a jacket, his face no longer visible at all, so Sam knew he was gone. He wasn't sure who it was, and that made him wonder if anyone knew he and Dan had been hit.

Dan—he rolled back to find his partner, and saw him lying there not five feet away. He was alive, and even threw a smile at Sam, but it took a second to register what he was saying.

"...we got 'em, Sam, we got 'em, we got the bastards who got us! I shot yours, and you got mine, ain't that cool?"

Sam managed a smile and gave a thumbs up, but he couldn't get his head to work well enough to speak. He tried to raise it and look around, but something big and dark fell over him, and everything was gone.

———

WHEN THE LIGHTS came up again, Sam thought he must have died, because this much white must be Heaven. He'd always known he was good with the Lord, ever since that church camp when he was twelve, and even though he'd made a few mistakes along the way, he was still sure of his ticket to the Pearly Gates. He was glad he'd never let himself get like so many others who tossed it off, pretended they cared about God but didn't really even believe in him. Sam believed. He'd held on to that faith, and now that he'd bought the farm, here he was, in what had to be Heaven, because no place on earth could ever look so clean!

A nurse walked in and saw that he was awake, and the whole fantasy of Heaven popped like a bubble. "Aw, crap," he said, and the nurse raised her eyebrows.

"Excuse me?" she asked.

Sam shook his head. "Sorry about that," he said, "it had nothing to do with you. It was just I thought for a minute I'd got killed and gone to Heaven, and I was kinda enjoying the idea. Then you came in and I realized I was still alive and stuck in this mess."

The nurse scowled. "Well, forgive me for ruining your day, Mr. Prichard, but it's good to see you awake, anyhow. The doctor wanted to know as soon as you woke up, so I'll go call him now." She turned and flounced out the door.

"Bout damn time you woke up," he heard from over to his left, and he looked over to see Dan there in another bed. "I been layin' here a day and a half waitin' for you to decide if you was gonna live or not. Glad you decided to stick it out!"

Sam smiled at his partner, and felt a sharp pain in his right hip as he rolled his head to look closer at him. "Ow," he said, and then again, "Ow! How bad you get hit, Danny?"

"Not terrible, just took one in the side that didn't even manage to hit anything important. Hurts like hell, though."

Sam looked at the bracelet on his right wrist, but it said nothing about what might be wrong with him. He felt his hip, and realized that there was an awful lot of gauze there, and it was terribly numb. "What happened to me?" he asked, but Dan shrugged his shoulders.

"I dunno," he said. "Docs won't tell me squat, on account of you never makin' an honest woman outta me."

Sam's eyes narrowed. "What?"

"Because we ain't married, or otherwise related, the docs say I got no right to know how bad you got hit, and wouldn't tell me zilch. I tried to explain that your partner is closer than a wife, but they didn't buy it."

"Good," Sam said, "I don't buy that crap either. If you were closer than a wife, you'd be over doin' my dishes."

"Well, well, Mr. Prichard," came another voice, and Sam turned to see a doctor walk in. "How are you feeling today?"

"I ain't worth a crap!" Sam answered. "I'm tryin' to find out how bad a shape I'm in, so if you're not the guy who can tell me, go find him, okay?"

The doctor smiled. "I'm Doctor Schmidt, and I'm definitely the guy," he said, "so relax and stop picking on my nurses." He picked up a clipboard that was hanging on the foot of the bed and glanced through the top couple of pages.

Sam shifted his position, and said, "Ow!" The doctor looked up and smiled.

"Well, that tells me that you know where you got shot, anyway. Your right hip was hit three times, all of them deflected down into it from your bulletproof vest. The right acetabulum, the socket that your thighbone's ball end fits into, was shattered, and we had to go in and basically put it all back together with several tubes of superglue and a handful of screws. You're going to be in a wheelchair for a while, because the glue and screws we put in won't stand up to a lot of walking around, and we don't want to put a cast on you at this point."

Sam was stunned. "A wheelchair? A *wheelchair*? What kinda cop you know goes around in a wheelchair? How long will I be outta work, Doc?" The doctor suddenly looked uncomfortable, and Sam sensed what was coming. "What?" he demanded. "What is it you ain't told me yet?"

"Mr. Prichard," Doctor Schmidt began, "what you need to understand is that this is something that is beyond any degree of medical skill to repair…"

Sam held up a hand to stop him. "Just hold it," he said, "just hold it. I get the feeling you're about to say something I don't wanna hear, and I want to take a minute and get myself ready, okay? You here with me, Danny?"

"Right here, Sam, I'm right here."

Sam closed his eyes tightly for a couple of seconds, and then forced himself to take a deep breath and relax. He opened his eyes again and looked at Doctor Schmidt.

"Okay, go ahead, then," he said.

Doctor Schmidt looked at him for a long moment, then sighed. "Mr. Prichard, the degree of damage to your acetabulum means that you will never walk normally again. Your right hip will have very limited range of motion, and simple things like normal running and jogging will be impossible to you. You will have difficulty with stairs, and will find ramps easier to handle. You will almost certainly need a cane a good part of the time, and that's even after physical therapy that will probably take a year or more. I'm afraid there is no possibility that you'll ever be able to return to active police work."

Sam lay there for a long moment without saying a word,

then turned to look at Dan Jacobs. "You hear this crap?" he asked, and Dan nodded.

"I heard it, Sammy."

The two old friends looked at one another for a long time, and then Sam closed his eyes. The doctor left the room after a few moments more, and Dan lay there in silence, wondering how his friend was going to get through this one.

When morning came, Sam woke to find a whole new world being thrown at him. No sooner than breakfast was over, he was suddenly invaded by four people from HR, who had all kinds of forms for him to sign.

"What we're doing," said the guy in the fanciest suit, "is giving you full medical retirement, in accordance with the union's policies and procedures. That means that you'll get seventy-five percent of your current income for life, with bi-annual cost-of-living raises, and full medical coverage from now on, as well. We need you to understand that this is not disability income, and you may apply for state or federal disability income if you wish, but you would probably be denied because of your medical retirement income, so there isn't a lot of point."

The lone woman in the group shoved the suit aside and got right in Sam's face, which wouldn't have been such a bad thing under other circumstances, since she was cute. "Now, we also need you to understand that you have to comply with the instructions of your physician, and that any failure to comply, such as refusal of medications or treatments, refusal of surgery or physical therapy, and similar issues, can result in the loss of your medical retirement certification and income, including your medical insurance coverage and..."

The four of them droned on for quite a while, but Sam

caught the gist of it. As long as he cooperated and did what the nice doctors wanted him to do, he'd get paid to stay home and take it easy. Since he couldn't be a cop anymore, that was fine with him; maybe he could finally get the Corvette out and drive it. It would be months before he was out of the wheelchair anyway.

The suits also told him that they were paying for a nice new powered wheelchair, and would have someone build a ramp at his house, leading up to his front porch. The doors and such were already wide enough, and since he only lived on the bottom floor, it was no big deal. He'd manage, and when he was inside and no one could see him, he and that wheelchair wouldn't need to be such buddies all the time, anyway; what the docs didn't know wouldn't hurt Sam, he figured.

The only bad part of all of this was that he could no longer be a cop, which was all he'd ever wanted to be. He'd given most of his life to it in one way or another, even down to losing his wife over the job; if the truth were to be told, he didn't work the double shifts as much for the money as for the love of the job, so he could only blame himself for Jeanie finding another set of arms to roll around in.

Without being a cop, Sam Prichard wasn't really all that sure who he was. He was told that he'd have to go to a therapy group once a week, some deal about how to cope when you're no longer on the force, so he figured he could let his feelings out there, some. He knew some guys didn't like to talk at those shindigs, but he wasn't gonna be one of them. He was losing a big part of his identity, and he needed help to cope with that, so he would take advantage of what-ever was offered.

He was released from the hospital a little more than a week after being admitted and rushed into surgery, and he was surprised when Dan Jacobs and Agent Carlson were the ones to show up and drive him home. Dan would be on desk duty for another week or so, but Carlson had not been hurt; Sam was actually glad to see the little butthole.

"You ready to stop pretending to be hurt and get off your lazy rear end?" Carlson asked.

"Ready as I'm gonna be, I guess. Good of you guys to come help the hospital toss me out on my ear!"

Dan grinned. "Yeah, isn't it? But then, what are friends for?"

They helped him into the car, and drove him to his house. The new powered chair had been delivered there, and was waiting to be assembled in his garage, courtesy of his mom, who had met the truck there and opened the garage door so they could put it inside.

They opened the garage to get it out, but there was a hang-up. "The dang thing's still in the box, Ben," Dan said. "What good is that gonna do you?"

Carlson, surprising Sam once again, pointed to the big toolboxes that stood over by the Vette. "I bet there's instructions," he said. Sam and Dan looked at him like he'd grown a third ear. "What?" he shot back. "Look, maybe we're not Santa's elves, but we're not stupid, either! We can put it together, don't you think? What do you say, Jacobs, you in?"

Sam laughed at the look on Dan's face. "I'll tell you what," he said. "If you guys'll stick around and help me get Franken Wheelie all put together, I'll order in pizza and a twelve pack o' beer. Deal?"

The guys accepted his offer, and the beast was together

and working an hour later. That prompted a goofy session in which they each took turns driving it around the garage and the yard. That ran down the not-yet-fully charged battery, so by the time they were ready to take it inside the house, they had to push it, and then Sam had to plug it into the wall and let it charge overnight. Luckily, there was an outlet right next to his couch, which is where he ended up sleeping.

He could walk short distances with a cane, but the docs insisted he do so as little as possible. They didn't have to say it too often, because it hurt like hell every time he tried, and since he'd be doing a lot of it during physical therapy, he thought he'd save that pain for those days. Still, it meant he could get to the bathroom without "the Monster," as he called the powered chair, and that was a good thing. Big mother wouldn't even fit through the bathroom door!

Once he was home, things began to settle in for him. He had some money put back, so he bought himself a used minivan, an old Chevy Astro, and had a ramp built into the back end of it so he could put right inside and then get into the driver's seat and go wherever he needed to go. The ramp would fold down to let him get in and out, and fold up so he could close the doors and drive, so it was a pretty good setup. Of course, the only places he ever went were to physical therapy and group sessions, the grocery store, the parts store, and out to eat now and then.

After three months, the docs said he could give up the wheelchair and start walking around with the cane. It still hurt, but like they said, the pain was a sign that he was getting stronger and making improvement, so he parked the electric scooter in the garage and went to walking, He still liked the van, though; for some reason, sitting up higher in it was easier than getting in and out of a car would be, so he didn't trade it off like he'd planned.

At six months, he was starting to walk around a bit without the cane, and that's when he broke down and bought himself a motorcycle. His legs were strong enough to hold him up at stoplights, and it was something he'd always enjoyed but never felt he had time for, so this was his chance. It felt good, and he noticed that he was even being checked out by some girls now and then.

His bike wasn't a Harley, but that didn't seem to matter to the girls. His old Honda Shadow, a sort of "Harley wannabe," got some attention as he rode it around town, and now and then, he'd even get to talk to a girl at a stop light. Once, a girl pulled up beside him and said absolutely nothing, but hurriedly dug out a piece of paper and scribbled a number on it. She handed it to him, held her hand to her face as if it were a phone and mouthed the words, "Call me!" as she drove away.

You sure don't get that on a powered wheelchair, he said to himself. *Should have bought a motorcycle sooner!*

He tucked the number into his shirt pocket, and found it later that evening when he was getting ready to shower. He looked at the name, Judy, thinking about how long it had been since he'd even been on a date, then grabbed his phone and called.

"Hi," he said when a feminine voice answered. "Is this Judy? You gave me your number today, and this is the first chance I've had to give you a—yes, on the motorcycle, that was me, yeah. Well, I would have called sooner, but I've been pretty busy today. What do I do? Well, I, um, I'm a retired cop, but I'm still called in sometimes as a, as a consultant!

When they have a big case, y'know, sometimes I get called in to give my opinion about certain parts of it. Why am I retired? Oh, that's because I got shot a while back, and they gave me a medical retirement. I've got a bad leg, so I can't run like you have to when you take the police physical and such. Yeah, it's rough, but I'm a survivor. Well, I was thinking that if you wanted to, we could maybe go for a ride this Saturday? I love to ride up into the mountains, just get some clear mountain air, y'know? You would? That'd be great, Judy! Sure, I can pick you up there! Ten AM, that's perfect! I'll see you then!"

Saturday morning saw Sam out on the bike a little before ten, spare helmet strapped onto the sissy bar and ready to go out with a woman for the first time in more than three years. He climbed on and rode to Judy's house, over on the west end of Aurora. She saw him ride up and came running out, wearing a nice light leather jacket and some of the tightest jeans he'd ever seen spray painted onto a woman!

"Hi, Judy," he said, and she rushed up and kissed him full on the mouth. "Oh," she said, "I have been going nuts waiting for you to get here! Do you know how long it's been since I was on a motorcycle? Oh, god, I think it's been at least five years, and that is just too long! I've been dying to get back on one for so long!"

She climbed on, and they took off, riding up 225 until it hit I-70, then following the Interstate west into the foothills of the Rockies. They rode for about four hours, and stopped at Aspen for lunch, visiting the historic Woody Creek Tavern for their famous tilapia tacos. Sam was ready to sit and rest a bit, his hip giving him fits for spending so much time on the bike—he hadn't really ridden into the mountains before—but Judy was ready to go again as soon as lunch was over.

Sam stalled as long as he could, then forced himself to smile as he got the bike fired up again. When he got her back home and dropped her off, Judy invited him to come in and stay a while, but he begged off and said he'd call her the next day.

He never called her again.

Another woman he met on the bike was Kathy, a short blonde who said she was a little afraid of motorcycles, but that she did like to have a thrill, now and then. He made a date with her for one evening that weekend, and she nervously climbed on and clung to him for half an hour as he cruised her around the city. She laughed in his ear at how much fun it was, and when he offered to buy her dinner, she asked if they could just go to one of the outdoor eateries, so he chose the Appaloosa Grill, one of the more refined patio dining experiences in Denver. She sat and talked with him for a couple of hours, and Sam was actually beginning to think he might want to date her again. He said so, and that was when she told him that she really enjoyed the ride, but she just didn't feel a connection to him, that going out with him felt more like hanging out with a brother than going on a date. He smiled and told her he understood, and took her home as soon as he got the chance.

He came to the conclusion that motorcycle dates weren't all they were cracked up to be, and stopped paying a lot of attention to the girls who flirted when he was on two wheels.

Sam was settled into the life of the medically retired cop. He tinkered with his car, tinkered with his bike, watched a lot of TV and Netflix, and tried not to think too much or too often about what Dan was doing, or his old team. Dan had come by a few times, but nobody wants to hang out with the guy who has cancer, and being forced into retirement was like having the big C to cops who were still on active duty. Sam couldn't blame him for not coming by anymore. He'd even stopped calling, finally, and Sam was sort of glad. It was too hard to find things to talk about that weren't connected to the old days.

He'd given up on all of those past hopes and dreams. That was why it was such a shock when he got dragged back into cop work once again.

Scan the QR code below to purchase THE GRAVE MAN. Or go to: righthouse.com/the-grave-man